BULLSEYE

BULLSEYE

International Bestselling Author
MONICA JAMES

BULLSEYE
(The Monsters Within Duet, Book One)

Cover Design: Perfect Pear Creative Covers
Cover Model: Andrew England
Photographer: James Rupapara
Editing: Editing 4 Indies
Formatting: E.M. Tippetts Book Designs

Follow me on:
authormonicajames.com

OTHER BOOKS BY
MONICA JAMES

THE I SURRENDER SERIES

I Surrender

Surrender to Me

Surrendered

White

SOMETHING LIKE NORMAL SERIES

Something like Normal

Something like Redemption

Something like Love

A HARD LOVE ROMANCE

Dirty Dix

Wicked Dix

The Hunt

MEMORIES FROM YESTERDAY DUET

Forgetting You, Forgetting Me

Forgetting You, Remembering Me

DEDICATION

Elle Kennedy, I loaf you. Let's never take a boat ride again.
P.S. I hope our dogs never get kidnapped.
And baby carrots make me bloated.

AUTHOR'S NOTE

CHAPTER ONE

Bull

"**A** pair of motorcycle boots, size thirteen. A Harley-Davidson T-shirt. A pair of blue jeans ripped in both knees. A black hoodie. A leather wallet containing eighty-five dollars. And a silver necklace with a St. Christopher medallion.

"Here is two hundred and fifty dollars, a map, and three condoms. You got someone picking you up?"

Shaking my head, I reach for my belongings spread out on the long wooden counter before me.

"The nearest bus stop is half a mile that way." He points over his shoulder.

"I'll walk," I reply bluntly, kicking off my white sneakers and shedding myself of this uniform that has been my second skin for twelve long years. I don't care that someone's grandma gasps from just feet away when she sees my tighty-whities. I need to get it the fuck...*off* me.

"Walk to where? Things have changed since you've been locked up. Folk ain't like they used to be."

"I'll figure it out." My jeans are a little loose around the middle, which is no surprise. You wouldn't even feed your dog the shit I've been eating in here. However, the T-shirt is tight across my chest and upper arms. Boots and hoodie still fit. The chain is the last thing I put on.

Pederson cocks a disbelieving brow and shrugs. "Don't say I didn't warn you. Good luck, Bull. You're gonna need it."

I nod in gratitude. He was the only guard in this hellhole who actually gave a rat's ass if I lived or died.

I don't bother taking one last look at the place that has been my home for over a decade because every corner, every crevice of this shithole will be burned into my memory for as long as I live. You don't forget Kinkora Correctional Facility, and it sure as shit doesn't forget you. Half the crims are locked back up within six months of release because it's easier to deal with the politics *inside* the walls, than on the outside.

The rules on the inside are easy:

1. *Don't trust anyone.*
2. *Don't show emotion.*
3. *Don't snitch.*

Follow these three simple rules, and you'll do just fine.

What's completely foreign to me and my brothers before me are the rules on the outside. I've almost forgotten society's rules, because when doing time, you abide by an entirely different law. Inside, it's survival of the fittest, and unlike real life, the difference will cost you your life.

Pederson presses a button behind the counter, granting me my freedom. I shoulder open the glass door and stroll toward the steel gates that swing open slowly. The guards watch me closely. I can smell their fear. They weren't so attentive when they turned a blind eye the night I got shivved in my cell, thanks to some white supremacist assholes who didn't appreciate me calling Hitler a mama's boy.

But that's in the past because unlike my predecessors, I refuse to become a statistic. I'd rather end my own life than be trapped in a six-by-eight cell ever again.

Once the gate is open, I take my first steps as a free man.

Looking from left to right, I see that Detroit hasn't changed an iota. It's still a piece of shit wasteland where dreams go to die.

I toss the map and condoms into the dirt and decide to head north. If I remember correctly, there's a cheap motel a couple of miles away. The deserted road has represented my freedom for so long, so I can't help but think I should feel something, anything, to be walking along it. But I'm dead inside, and I don't feel a thing.

Refer to prison rule number two.

The farther away I walk, the more isolated things become. I'm thirty years old, and I have no idea where I'm headed. Not just literally, but figuratively as well. I have no skills, no trade, and no special talents. I was just a punk ass kid who should have studied harder in school.

If I was more like my older brother, Damian, I could have

been a fucking astronaut by now. I don't blame my parents for the way I ended up because it wasn't their fault. It was mine. I had idle hands and used them time and time again as the devil's plaything.

Blood.

So much blood.

I swallow down the memory that plagues me every time I close my fucking eyes. If I'm going to survive this, then I need to learn how to survive with my eyes opened *and* closed. It's the only way I won't end up back inside.

The cool breeze has me drawing the hood over my shaved head 'cause the dark storm clouds ahead look angry as shit. Moments later, the heavens open and dump angel piss all over me. I pick up the pace to a steady run when I see the red flashing neon sign of Hudson's Motel a few blocks ahead.

Even though the name has changed, it's still the same run-down dump it was twelve years ago. No amount of paint can polish this shithole. But this shithole will be my home until I can put my plan into motion.

So home sweet fucking home.

The bell above the door sounds sick as I shove open the woodgrain, happy to get inside and out of this biblical weather. Behind the white reception desk sits a middle-aged woman flicking through a magazine while smoking a thin cigar.

Her blue eyes flick up and meet mine. "Hey, sugar. You're all wet. Did you walk here in the rain?"

Nodding, I slip the hood off my head and wipe a hand over the short dark bristles on my skull.

Reaching into my back pocket, I pull out a hundred-dollar bill. The skull tattoo on the back of my hand catches her attention. "How many nights can I stay here with this?"

Her red fingernails are like talons as she draws the tattered money toward her. She fingers the note and looks at me carefully. "You just get out?"

I nod once again.

She must be able to smell the felon all over me. "For you, sugar, this will buy you a week."

"Thanks."

"No problem." She reaches into her low-cut neckline and produces a creased white business card. "If you're needing anything, give me a call."

She leans across the counter, holding the card between two fingers. I accept it and read the name.

Venus Bisset—Manager.

"I appreciate it," I say, holding up the card.

"Oh, sugar," she purrs. "With pretty eyes like yours, don't hesitate to call me. Day or night." She winks her ridiculously long fake eyelashes, which look like caterpillars have mutated on her eyelids.

"Thanks, Venus."

"Thank *you*. I've never seen someone with two different eye colors before. It's as if heaven and hell are fighting their own personal battle, wanting to conquer the other side," she reveals, appearing in awe of my genetic anomaly.

Her gaze darts from my left eye, which is a bright blue, to my right, which on any given day can appear green or amber. Her attention swings back to my left—the blue always seems to win.

"Which side is winning out?" she asks as I slip my hood back over my head.

"Ask me that next week."

She smirks, licking her red painted lips before shuffling through her drawer, which holds a stack of white key cards. "I'll sign you in. What's your name?"

Shuffling my boots, I give her the name I've been known by since *that night*. But this name can also be comparable to who I've become. "Bullseye. But call me Bull."

"Don't say much, do you?"

I nod curtly because she's right: I don't fill the void with nonsense. I speak only when necessary.

"I'll make sure you'll have no problems. I don't want problems." She slides the key across the surface, not asking about my nickname.

"Neither do I." I reach for the key card, but Venus slaps her hand over mine. My hand instantly curls into a fist, and my entire body goes into fight mode, but I take a small breath, reining in my need to inflict pain.

"Ice machine is just around the corner, and all rooms are nonsmoking." One wouldn't dare pollute this upstanding establishment.

She lets me go and smiles. "Enjoy your stay. You're in room fourteen. You need me, you've got my number."

Instantly, I draw my hand back and unclench it slowly. Venus seems unmoved by my weird behavior.

With the key card in hand, I thank Venus, before walking out the door. The moment I'm outside, I take two deep breaths to subdue the roaring demons within. Being touched is my hard limit. Don't touch me, and we won't have a problem.

I don't like people being all up in my grill. After being inside for so long, you forget the touch of another human, and you learn to live with it. And, after a while, I began to like it. I liked the solitude because touch connects you with another, and that's something I'm not interested in.

Getting my shit together, I stroll down the covered concrete walkway. My room is the second to last door on the left. I swipe the card over the sensor and wait for it to beep, permitting me entry. When I open the door, the four in my room number creaks and suddenly falls, swinging from side to side and hanging upside down. Its derelict condition reveals what I'm in for once I step inside.

Without further delay, I enter my room, and it's exactly what I expected—a small, simply furnished room with a private bathroom.

Closing and locking the door behind me, I kick off my boots and turn on the wall heater. The red carpet is filthy, and the cigarette burns hint that those before me didn't give a shit about the no smoking rule.

I walk across the room and into the bathroom. Flicking on the dim light, I see I have a shower/bath combo, a sink, a mirror, and a toilet. Some cheap toiletries are neatly arranged on the cracked marbled counter. Looking at the small shower, I realize I'll enjoy this the most. Being able to take a warm shower without having to look over your shoulder, worried you'll get knifed or fucked for your bar of soap, will be nice.

Stripping, I hang up my clothes on the silver hook and turn

the water to hot. The bathroom instantly fills with steam. Not caring that the temperature burns my skin, I step under the spray, the constant chill from my bones slowly disappearing as I turn my body from side to side.

Being robbed of the simple pleasures in life may seem unfair, but I deserve it. I deserve it all.

When I think about how I robbed someone of simple, everyday luxuries, I suddenly feel underserving of this small piece of happiness. I don't deserve happiness. I gave up that right when I made the biggest mistake of my life.

Squeezing my eyes shut, I breathe through the memories as I turn the faucet to cold. Bracing my palms on the tiled wall, I drop my head between my splayed arms. The silver chain dangles like a pendulum around my neck. I pray the cold water will wash away my sins, but it never does. It just highlights that no matter whether I'm free or behind bars, I'll forever be enslaved to the past and what I have to do to feed the demons inside me.

I'll forever be imprisoned to the day I picked up a gun and shot a man in cold blood. However, the only regret I have… is that I got caught.

Thanks to my trip down misery lane, I'm left restless and not in a good headspace. Maybe I could score some pussy to help take the edge off. But I haven't been with a woman in so long, I'd probably embarrass myself the moment she undresses. I'm not here for that though. I have a job to do.

Wallowing in my self-pity isn't doing me any good, so I grab my key card and slip it into the back pocket of my still damp jeans. I noticed a Goodwill store a few blocks up. I'll walk off the heaviness and hope like hell this feeling of despair goes away.

Not that it ever does. But maybe today is different.

It's dark out, and the heavy rain has turned to a light drizzle. Keeping my head down, I walk to the store, not interested in bumping into any trouble. I plan on staying hidden in the shadows because there is no way I'm going back inside.

They say prison changes a man, and they're right. I learned that quickly when my eighteen-year-old ass got thrown into a cesspool of the depraved and was expected to fend for myself.

I thought I was a gangster, and my smart mouth would get me through, but all it got me was three busted ribs, two black eyes, and a different use for my smart mouth. From that day forward, ties to my past were brutalized, and I was no longer Cody Bishop. I was Bullseye. A nickname I earned from the vicious men I called my roomies when they learned my story.

After that, the naïve wannabe gangster became the unfeeling asshole I am today. Prison taught me how to lie, cheat, and steal. I wasn't interested in being anyone's bitch, so I transformed from the gangly teenager to a six-foot-four, two-hundred-pound fighting machine. I worked out when we had yard time, and when we were herded back into our cells, I did what I could in my six-by-eight space.

Training kept me sane. And it was the only thing that kept

me safe. But no matter how big you are, someone is always bigger and badder. And my big bad came in the form of a neo-Nazi by the name of Snow White. He got his name thanks to the drugs he dealt before he got caught.

I subconsciously rub over the six-inch scar that runs from my right kidney up to my spleen. I was told that getting stabbed seventeen times and surviving was a miracle, but I don't agree. Dying would have been the easy way out. But surviving alongside Snow and thugs just like him trained me to become who I am today. And that's someone you don't fuck with.

I push open the glass door of the small, overcrowded Goodwill store and head over to the men's apparel section. I don't need much, so I grab the essentials. After the bored teenager rings up my haul, I pay and then shove all my belongings into the duffel I also bought.

"Have a nice day," she robotically says even though it's pitch black outside. Detroit does that to people. Before long, all days blend together, becoming one long, tiresome, monotonous day.

The store clerk's interest is suddenly piqued, however, when I take off my thin hoodie and slip into the black leather jacket I just bought.

She couldn't be much older than eighteen, and I revisit the idea that maybe I could burn off some steam by scoring some pussy. But the idea falls flat on its ass when an older man comes into the store, his arms filled with goods. He stops in his tracks when he sees me.

"Brandy, everything okay?" His gaze darts back and forth

between us.

"Yes, Dad, everything is fine," she replies, clearing her throat, appearing embarrassed to be caught staring.

"Okay then." He walks past me and nods. "You got everything you need?"

He's doing a poor job at disguising his disgust that I'm anywhere near his beloved Brandy. But I don't blame him. I need to get used to these side glances and being treated like the inked-up criminal that I am.

Quickly shouldering the duffel, I nod once and exit the store, feeling even worse than when I walked in.

A flickering pink light up ahead catches my eye. If I believed in God, I would take this as a sign. When I reach the black painted building, I look up and see the dancing light indicates there are *Girls, Girls, Girls* inside. There's no need to guess what this business is with a name like The Pink Oyster.

The derelict appearance gives me hope that maybe I'll find who I'm looking for inside. It seems my plan is to be set in motion sooner than I had intended. Pushing open the heavy black door, I step inside.

Flashes of red and yellow and the harsh intermittent strobe lighting cut through the misted fog. The mirrored disco ball above the stage throws flashes of light across the black walls. The half-naked blonde twirling around the silver pole on the stage confirms what I thought to be true.

I walk past a crowd of men who are wolf-whistling in front of the stage, throwing dollar bills at the now naked girl. She's too skinny for my taste, so I make my way over to the bar.

"Budweiser," I shout at the bartender to be heard over the

rock song blasting through the speakers.

She nods, and I don't fail to notice her watch me with interest as she opens my bottle of beer. "Two dollars." She places my bottle on the bar, and I give her a five. "You new 'round here?"

I nod and reach for my beer.

Searching my surroundings, I hope to see a familiar face. I don't.

"What's your name?" she asks, handing me my change.

"Bull," I reply, placing the bills in the clam-shaped tip jar.

"Well, Bull, welcome to The Pink Oyster. I'm Lotus. If you need anything, you come see me, okay? I own this fine establishment, and we like gentlemen like yourself to be regular customers."

"Thanks. I'll keep that in mind." Lotus is a pretty, forty-something blonde. I can see nothing but kindness behind her green eyes. It's a look I haven't seen in a long time.

"You looking for any company?"

"Company?" I arch a brow as I take a long pull of my beer. Fuck, it tastes good. Even though I wasn't the legal drinking age when I got locked up, that didn't stop me from getting wasted almost every night since…

I shove down the memories and focus on Lotus because I need to keep a clear head to do this.

"Yes. Not only are my girls brilliant dancers, they are brilliant companions, too."

Lotus sees my confusion and smiles. "Don't worry. This is a legal business. We offer a little extra something out back in our VIP rooms. Nothing illegal, though. Just some extra one-on-one time with the girls."

"Thanks, but I'm sure pretty girls like yours are way out of my price range."

"No problem. If you change your mind, let me know."

Before I have a chance to reply, the already dim lights darken, and the crowd goes wild.

"You know what time it is?" the cowboy dressed emcee says. The mob hollers eagerly in response. "It's the one, the only, Detroit's crème de le crème…Tigerlily!" He hurries off backstage while most men rush to the tip rail—the seats closest to the stage.

I wonder why they're slobbering all over themselves.

Spinning on my shaky stool, I lean against the bar and cross my arms, watching with interest as "Closer" by Nine Inch Nails begins to play over the speakers.

Music has changed a lot since I've been inside, but this song is one I know. It's one I grew up with.

The stage is cloaked in black, and the choice of music adds to the mystery. But when I see the red curtain at the back of the stage part and a slender brunette prowl out, I edge forward. The strobe lights distort her form, but from what I can see, I'm interested.

She moves her body like a true dancer, instead of just using the pole to give her patrons a gimmicky show. This girl has training because she can dance. She's in sync with the rhythm, making every lithe movement an accent of the song.

Her skimpy thong and bikini top allow me to see her toned and strong body.

When the song kicks to the chorus, she latches onto the

pole, revealing her strength, as she twirls around it, using only her legs to keep herself upright. She scales that pole with the strength and speed of an Olympic gymnast, and when she dismounts, she lands on her feet at the front of the stage, crouched low.

When she flicks back her long hair and focuses her eyes on the crowd, I swear to god, every guy's dick stands to attention. A wicked grin slashes at her full lips. She's aware of the effect she has on these walking hard-ons. Seductively rolling her hips, she comes to a slow stand.

Even though I'm hidden in a dark corner in the back of the room, I feel as if she's staring right at me. But a good performer does that—makes you feel like they're performing just for you.

Sliding off the red glittery bikini top, she covers her full, natural tits, only removing her hands at the end of the song. Before the stage goes dark, I get a glimpse of her perky pink nipples. Holy…shit.

Green bills litter the stage, and Tigerlily discreetly bends forward and collects her earnings. I see her subtly avoiding the leering hands of the perverts in the front. She smiles and plays off their crude remarks, but it obviously bothers her that she's viewed as just a piece of ass.

"Change your mind?" Lotus asks, as I throw back my beer, watching Tigerlily.

"Maybe. How much?" I wipe my lips with the back of my hand.

"She's too much, handsome," says a voice to my left. "So am I. But I'd make an exception for you."

The blonde who was dancing on the stage before Tigerlily steps in front of me. She's wearing a short blue dress that drops into a very low V in the front, showing off her fake tits. She's not unattractive, by any means, but I'm not here for pussy, contrary to my surroundings.

"Hi, I'm Tawny. I'm Lotus's number one girl, aren't I?" she says, looking over my shoulder at Lotus.

Lotus playfully scoffs in response, while continuing to serve thirsty patrons.

Tawny smiles at me, making no secret that she's sizing me up. "So, handsome, whaddya say?"

"Thank you, but—" I don't have time to finish my sentence, however, because before I know it, Tigerlily re-enters the room, wearing a red dress that clings to her shapely body like a second skin. Now that the lights are a little brighter, I can see her better. Her brown hair is long and wavy. Her monster heels give her some height, but without them, she's short.

Tawny turns to see what's captured my attention and rolls her eyes. "Forget it. She doesn't do new customers. And besides, I think she'll have her hands full with Thumper."

When I look at who she's referring to, I wonder if Thumper lost his way to his fraternity. He's in a varsity jacket and looks like some rich college kid whose mom still calls him Sweetie.

Thumper is about five seconds from losing a finger because Tigerlily is trying to get up from his lap. His group of dipshit minions are laughing as he manhandles her, thinking her apparent discomfort is funny. When he slips a hand underneath her dress, she pushes back appalled and slaps him—hard. Good for her. The meathead reddens and tightens his hold around her.

Even though she can hold her own, I jump up before I can question what the fuck I'm doing. Shoving past Tawny, I charge over to the asshole. I've seen his kind one too many times before. But I've never seen anyone like Tigerlily.

The moment I reach the table, I grip her bicep and yank her up before Thumper has a chance to say jackshit. She yelps in protest, but has no choice as I shove her behind me. Thumper glares up at me. This dog isn't happy I've taken away his toy.

"Excuse me. Me and Tigerlily were talking." His friends are silent, watching for any sign to intervene.

"Well, you're done talking," I reply calmly.

He tongues his cheek, furious. "We're done when I say we're done," he spits, standing abruptly and kicking back his chair.

He's a few inches shorter than I am but tries to make up for it by puffing out his chest. I can't help but snicker.

"You have anything else you want to say to him?" I ask Tigerlily, my eyes never wavering from Thumper.

"No," she says with bitter conviction.

I like how she doesn't cower in fear. She had no qualms about slapping Thumper, even though I'm pretty sure she'll get into shit for scaring off clients. Her name takes on another meaning, and I decide Tiger is a better suited moniker for her.

"You heard the lady," I taunt. "You're done."

"Who the fuck do you think you are?" he snarls, rounding the table and getting into my face.

As long as he doesn't touch me, this doesn't have to

end badly...for him. "I'm someone who doesn't manhandle women. Now, you have two options." I raise a finger. "One, you can sit the fuck back down and enjoy the show." I then raise another finger. "Or two, you can enjoy a ride in the back of an ambulance. The choice is yours."

His nostrils flare as he exhales angrily while clenching his jaw. He assesses whether he can take me, but I stand my ground, not at all intimidated by his smoke and mirrors.

"Fuck this place!" he finally says, childishly sweeping his hand across the table and hurling all the glasses and pitchers of beer to the floor.

One glass is left standing, and as he goes to smack it off the table, I seize his forearm and squeeze hard. He peers down at my left hand, appearing to read over the word tattooed across my knuckles. It says wolf. The right hand says lone.

"You touch that glass, and I'll break it over your head." My threat isn't empty.

When he senses I'm not playing, he rips his arm from my grip and glares. "C'mon, boys. Let's go. This place is a dump anyway. And their beer tastes like piss."

Thumper and his friends brush past me, but I stand solid, protecting Tiger until the last of them is gone.

I take a deep breath, then drop to a squat to pick up the broken glass. I have no idea what came over me. So much for staying hidden in the shadows. The need to protect Tiger was instinctive, and I don't know why. What I do know is that she's dangerous, and I need to stay away.

Twelve long years of planning won't be thrown away for a nice ass.

However, the moment she squats down beside me, all thoughts of staying away get shot to shit. "Hi." Her voice is sweet like cotton candy.

I meet her big green eyes and nod.

"Thanks for what you did. Thumper is a jerk, but he's one of my clients who's into the girlfriend experience." When I arch a brow, she clarifies, "I pretend to flirt with him, and he tips me generously. I can handle myself but thank you. Things were getting a little out of hand." She licks her glossy red lips, and I instantly have the urge to wipe my thumb across her mouth, smudging her perfect lipstick and leaving her a beautiful mess.

I nod again, not interested in small talk.

"I'm Tigerlily. Lily," she amends quickly, extending her small hand.

Glancing down at it, I don't shake it. "Bull."

She appears embarrassed and quickly jerks her hand back.

"Get up from there," Lotus demands, hands on her hips as she stands by the table. She has every right to be pissed at me for throwing out her customers. I obviously misread the situation. Thumper wanted the girlfriend experience, meaning he wanted Tiger to beat his ass? There is so much wrong with that picture.

With hands filled with broken glass, I stand and place the pieces on the table. Tiger also stands.

"Sorry. I'll split," I say to Lotus, as she watches me closely.

She raises a thin eyebrow. "You got someplace to be?"

"No, but I figured you'd want me gone. I just lost you paying customers," I explain bluntly.

When she shakes her head, I wonder what's going on. "You just did what my main bouncer, Andre, should have done."

"Oh?" I reply, running a hand over my head. "I didn't realize you had any bouncers working here."

"Exactly my point," she counters, drumming her fingers against her waist. "Andre was too busy chatting up some barfly to notice that one of the girls he is paid to protect was getting manhandled." She looks over at the giant who is standing sheepishly by her side.

I instantly don't like Andre. Apart from the fact he looks like a slimy greaseball with his thinning ponytail and black handlebar moustache, he dropped the ball when it came to protecting someone who was relying on him to keep them safe.

"You want a job?" Lotus asks unexpectedly. Both Andre's and my eyes widen.

"A job?" I question, in case I've misheard her.

She nods, her blonde ponytail bopping with the sharp movement. "Yes. It appears Andre needs help."

Andre looks moments away from ripping off my arms. "I don't want to step on anyone's toes." But tough fucking luck. "But I can start tomorrow."

"Great. Come in around five p.m."

Fucking A. Seems my plan of blending into society has come about sooner than I thought. I planned to be a chameleon and appear to be on the right path. Although a more "respectable" job would probably be better suited, this will get my PO off my ass. It's a perfect ruse.

My revenge starts now.

As Lotus brushes the glass into a trash can, I say, "You know, I can fix this table for you." I place my palm on the top and rock it, showing her how unsteady it is. I couldn't help but notice this place is in desperate need of some maintenance. I almost fell on my ass thanks to the shaky barstool.

She stops mid sweep, her lips shaping into a slanted grin. "Good with your hands, are you?"

Her comment drips with innuendo, and I can't help but smirk. "You have no idea."

She fans her cheeks dramatically. "Come in at twelve."

With nothing further to say, I turn and am about to head back to the bar to finish my beer, until I notice both Tiger and Tawny are watching me. I suddenly feel very uncomfortable.

Lotus picks up on my discomfort immediately. "You want to be a Bird Dog here; you've got to be comfortable around the girls. Tawny?" She looks at the attentive blonde. "You happy to take Bull out back?"

Bird Dog must be slang for a bouncer who takes care of whatever happens "out back."

"Yes, Lotus," she replies, grinning wickedly.

"What happens out back?" I ask, not interested in surprises.

When Tawny gradually bends forward and whispers into my ear, "You'll see," I hold my breath because she's too close.

Before I can say thanks but no thanks, as I'm not going anywhere with Tawny, Tiger steps forward. "Lotus, let me."

Both Lotus and Tawny swivel toward her, visibly stunned. "What?"

The pink to her cheeks hints she's either embarrassed or maybe she's hot. Shit if I know how to read a woman. "Seeing as Bull came to my aid, I figure I owe him."

"You owe me nothing," I bark, not interested in being anyone's charity case.

Her eyes soften, and I instantly feel like a dick for snapping. "I'd still like to say thanks."

"You can buy me a beer." I attempt to turn, but she quickly latches onto my forearm. The leather of my jacket creaks under her grip while I clench my jaw.

Tiger reads my discomfort about being touched and instantly retreats. When she does, I exhale.

"Fine. If you want to go with Bull, then go," Lotus says, waving us away. The club is starting to get busy, and I know Lotus needs to get back to the bar.

Tawny folds her arms over her chest. "That doesn't seem fair. It was my gig two minutes ago."

Lotus clucks her tongue. "Go take a break."

Tawny's not happy but, eventually, stomps off.

Tiger smiles shyly, brushing a piece of dark hair behind her ear. When she gestures with her head that I'm to follow, I eye her suspiciously. "It's okay, Bull. I won't bite."

The humor in her voice has me finally nodding.

She takes that as her cue to lead the way. I follow her firm ass as she guides me through the club.

We walk down a corridor lit only by dim fluorescents. The plain scenery doesn't give much away. Tiger opens the last door on the left and walks inside. As soon as I enter, I see a chair in the middle of the room that is lit up a bright red by a spotlight.

This must be the VIP room. So a Bird Dog is someone who monitors the private dance rooms.

Tiger notices me taking in my surroundings and smiles. "See, it's not that scary, right?"

The jury is still out on that one.

"Take a seat," she directs, pointing at the steel chair.

I look at her suspiciously. "Why?"

"Just trust me." She attempts to push me down, but my arm snaps out, and I grip her wrist before she can make contact with me. She flinches, but her gaze never wavers from mine. "I won't hurt you. I promise."

But that's the problem…I can't promise I won't hurt her.

Her eyes are filled with nothing but resolve, so I slowly release her.

We both stand still, holding our own, and I like her even more because she doesn't appear afraid or even intimidated that I tower over her.

Eventually, I take a seat, then watch as she walks to the corner of the room and loads up some device. I'm pretty sure it's an iPod, but I've never seen one in the flesh, so I can't really tell.

She presses a few buttons and the lights dim. I can barely see my hand in front of my face, but as the room flicks over to a deep pink, Tiger glows like a Christmas tree.

Marilyn Manson's cover of "Tainted Love" fills the room. A song I recognize. I watch with interest as she moves in time to the music, closing her eyes and appearing to get lost in the beat.

Just as when I first saw her dance, I am hooked on how she uses her body as a conduit. She turns her back and unfastens the low zipper on her dress. Once it's down, she shimmies out of it and tosses it aside. She spins around and brushes her hair over her shoulders, revealing a gold bra that barely covers her full, round tits.

She breathlessly stalks over to me while I lean back in my seat, unsure of what comes next.

With no hesitation, she climbs onto my lap, but she suspends herself over me, using her muscles to balance her weight. She mimics the motion of wrapping her arms around my neck but still doesn't touch me.

I don't like this intimacy, but she doesn't force me to move closer. She simply turns around so her back is facing my front. My arms are rigid by my side, my hands curling into fists. When she begins circling her hips and shaking her ass, I almost lose my shit and give in.

I interlace my hands behind my neck, watching her give me a lap dance that isn't really a lap dance at all because she isn't touching me. Surely, this song will end soon. I don't know how long I'll be able to sit here and not let the demons win.

Bloodlust and revenge drive my demons, and all they want to do is cause pain because misery loves company. I want to watch the world burn with me. But the monster inside me has always lingered. It was just waiting for the right moment to slither out of hell.

As the tempo increases, so do her movements, and no matter how hard I try, I can't deny the fact that her beauty fucking turns me on. I haven't been this close to a woman's body in so long, and I've forgotten how soft and supple their curves are. And how good they smell. Tiger smells like cherry blossoms.

I continue breathing slowly, attempting to control my craving. But as she spins around and hovers over me, I grunt low, unable to hide my longing. Her chest is inches from my face, and suddenly, I turn my cheek to the side.

But with a hesitant finger, she deliberately places it under my chin, coaxing me to look at her with an arrogant smirk. She sweeps her pointer across the small tattoo under my right eye, admiring the cross with interest, as I sure as shit don't look like a religious man.

I don't know what she's doing, so when she reaches for my hands and draws them to her chest, I almost rocket off my chair in surprise.

The moment I feel her soft tits, my hard-on presses against her, but I jerk my hips away, feeling suffocated. She surprises me when she gasps and begins rocking her hips over my cock. She is still suspended over me, using her impressive core strength, so she is merely going through the motions.

Her hands are secured over mine, encouraging me to fondle her tits. As I feel her nipples swell underneath my hands, we both hiss at the sensation. I remember what they looked like on stage. But regardless of how good she feels— and she feels fan-*fucking*-tastic—I need to end this. Now.

But before I know what she's doing, she swoops forward and fucking kisses me.

I'm stunned at the unfamiliar feel of someone's lips on mine, and when she softly coaxes my sealed mouth open with her warm tongue, it brings home the fact that I haven't kissed a woman since I was seventeen years old.

I don't know what I thought I'd feel, but for once in my life, the shadow of anger and pain lessens for a split moment in time. But it doesn't last. It never does.

She tastes of bubblegum, but underneath her sweetness is a goodness I want to corrupt. I want to thread my hands through her long hair and pull—hard—until she's squirming, begging me to stop. I want to bite her, bind her, mark her because her purity is contagious, and I wonder if I can steal it to erase the tarnish burdening my soul.

I want to see her beg. I want to make her bleed.

I'm an undeserving, vile monster. Tiger knows I don't like to be touched, so she keeps her distance. Most would acknowledge her kindness, but I'm not most. I want to exploit her weakness because I thrive on pain.

I don't even realize the music has ended because I'm torn between right and wrong. But this is done. Over. There isn't a hero in me. And that's what someone like Tiger deserves.

Like a butterfly, she is so beautiful, but all I want to do is tear off her wings.

With that as my driving force, I turn my cheek, severing our connection. Tiger reads my retreat loud and clear, even though she's confused. But that's not my problem. I go to stand, forcing her to do the same.

"Thanks for the dance." Unable to help myself, I slowly rub my thumb across her supple lips, smudging her lipstick across her mouth—the mouth I just fucking owned. Seeing her disheveled is a shot of heroin to a fiend like me.

The tremble to her lips reveals her nerves, which just confirms what I need to do.

"I'll catch ya round, darlin.'"

She appears to want to say something, but soon changes her mind. She simply nods and nervously walks over to where she dropped her dress, turning her back so she can slip it on.

There is no room for small talk because I don't engage in pretenses. This is me. A coldhearted bastard. A depraved animal. My story doesn't end with Prince Charming saving the princess and living happily ever after with her because...I killed the fucking prince.

CHAPTER TWO

Bull

"**M**orning, bright eyes. You sleep okay?"

"I did. Thanks, Venus," I reply, looking over from the tattered town map taped to the wall.

Venus is dressed in a pink jumpsuit with a matching pink wig. The silk scarf she wears does a poor job to hide her Adam's apple. I don't know why she bothers with it. She needs to own her shit. But I suppose Detroit is unforgiving to misfits like us.

"Do you know if the bus still drives past Oakland Road?" I ask, tracing my finger down a blue line that runs through the middle of town.

"If I recall correctly, yes, it does. You going to take the bus?"

"Yeah. I was thinking about it."

"You don't have a car?"

I shake my head and meet her eyes. "I don't have a license."

She pulls back, shocked. "How old were you when you got locked up?"

I rub the back of my neck. "Just turned eighteen."

Pity flashes over her. "Oh, I'm real sorry to hear that."

She has nothing to be sorry for. And she better stop looking at me with pity in her eyes. "Don't be. Jail was probably the best place for me."

She leans on the counter, listening intently. "Whatcha get done for?"

And there it is. The dreaded question.

I have to get used to saying it, so I may as well start now. "Murder," I reveal frankly, watching her face drop.

I also better start getting used to that look.

She clears her throat after a few uncomfortable seconds. "Well, if anyone deserves a second chance, it's you."

She catches me off guard with that unexpected reply. But she doesn't know me. And if she knew my story, and what I'm planning to do, she wouldn't be so quick with the touchy-feely crap.

"I'll be back later." I zip up my leather jacket. "I got a job."

"Oh, yeah? Where?"

"The Pink Oyster."

She grins, rocking back on her stool. "The ladies just can't keep away from you, can they?"

My lips twitch in a resemblance of a smile.

It's another cold as fuck morning, so I slip the gray beanie over my head and walk the mile to the bus stop. Thankfully, I don't have to wait long. It's funny because although I haven't been on a bus in a very long time, the sights, sounds, and smells are exactly the same.

I close my eyes, recalling the last time. It was with my brother, Damian, on the night of the big game. He could have driven with friends, but he wanted to ride with me.

"C'mon, squirt. It'll be fun."

"I don't even like football."

Damian laughed. "You will when you see the cheerleaders."

Scrunching up my face, I replied, "Gross. Girls are weird."

"That's 'cause you just turned fifteen. Give it a couple of years, and they'll be anything but gross." He messed up my hair as we pulled up at our school for the big game.

"I doubt it."

"Trust me, squirt. You'll change your mind."

He picked up his gym bag and helmet. My brother, the quarterback.

My eyes snap open when the bus comes to a slow stop. Rubbing the sleep away, I see that I'm a block away from where I want to be. Nothing has changed. It's just as I remember it and still as depressing as the day I was last here.

A light layer of frost covers the foliage, and even the flowers are wilting in the harsh autumn. It appears every living thing wants to forget it exists in here.

The grass crunches underneath my shoes as a light drizzle begins to fall. But I don't let the weather deter me from doing something I've wanted to do for years. My memory serves me well, and I walk on autopilot to the last grave in a row that replicates the ones before and after it. But this row is special.

It's special because it holds the grave of my brother.

"Hey, Damian." I drop to a squat.

Dried flowers sit by his headstone, and I instantly kick myself for not bringing him fresh ones. "I'm out. Twelve years pale in comparison to a lifetime of hell you've endured because of me.

"I haven't heard from Mom and Dad in over nine years. Not that I can blame them, though, because I told them to stay away. If only it was me and not you, things would have been better for everyone. If only I'd gone straight home after the game, things would have been so different. For starters, you'd be alive."

Sighing, I cast my eyes downward, ashamed. "I'm sorry, bro. I'm the reason you're…dead. I'll never forgive myself for what I did.

"You saved me—literally, and in turn, you died because you're a fucking hero. You sacrificed your life to save me. But my life wasn't worth the sacrifice. It never was.

"But I won't let your death be in vain. I promise," I vow, clutching the pendant around my neck. It once belonged to Damian. His good luck charm.

This is the only place I'll allow myself to grieve. Allow myself the penance I don't deserve.

"I'm sorry it was you. If I could trade places, I would in

a heartbeat. You were always the good one, and I…" I pause, peering down at the pocket watch tattooed on the back of my hand. "I was always waiting for something better to come along. I wish I realized that something better was you."

Kissing my middle and pointer fingers, I place them on Damian's marble headstone, before coming to a slow stand. "They will pay. Every one of them. And when they do…we'll meet again. Rest in peace, brother. I love you."

Damian is the only person who I ever told I loved. I didn't even say it to my parents. But with him, we weren't just brothers; we were best friends. I looked up to him— fuck, everyone did. Everyone wanted to be friends with him. There was something special about him, something everyone wanted to be a part of.

That something special was taken away the night he was murdered…thanks to me.

With nothing further to say, I turn around and leave my brother to rot in the grave where he's been for the past fourteen years. In my mind, he is forever young. A seventeen-year-old kid who had his whole life ahead of him before it was cruelly stolen.

My fists clench as I think about the reason that is, the reason both Damian's and my life changed forever. One simple fucking decision destroyed the lives of so many, but I can't take it back. What's done can never be undone, and I have to live with that guilt for the rest of my lousy existence.

But I've thrived on that guilt since I buried my brother. Only one thing kept me going on the inside, and that was revenge. And now that I'm out…burn, motherfuckers, burn.

Done with the reminiscing, I wait at the bus stop, not sure when or if I'll ever return. My parents haven't visited in a while; my brother's unadorned grave is a sure sign of this, which is a change from when he first got buried six feet under. My mom would visit every day, and my dad had to pry her away to come home.

But then she was back the next day, crying and cursing the universe that it took the wrong son.

As the bus pulls up, I amble up the steps, sinking into a seat toward the back. Peering out the window, I wonder where my parents are. The last I heard, they were finally getting a divorce. Dad found solace in a woman half his age, and my mom found her happily ever after in her prescription pill bottles.

But I don't judge. Fuck, I'm the reason their life turned to shit. Before this happened, we were one big happy family. Damian was the golden boy, but I wasn't jealous. I could only ever wish to be half the man he was.

He was the type of person who helped elderly people across the road or tended to a bird with a broken wing. Me, I preferred to put the bird out of its misery and laugh at the old farts who shuffled along. We were so different, but Damian never judged me. He loved me regardless of my flaws.

My reflection stares back at me from the dirty bus window, and as I peer into my mismatched eyes, I wonder if my brother would love me now. Scoffing, I shove such sentiments aside because I don't deserve love. I deserve to be alone, just as Damian is.

When the bus pulls up at a stop a few blocks away from

The Pink Oyster, I get off and walk the rest of the way, thankful Lotus saw something in me that I don't. I'll do my job without a fuss and keep my nose clean because I'm here for a reason. However, when I push open the back door and see Andre talking to one of the girls, I know that keeping my nose clean with this asshole on my ass will be fucking hard.

Nodding a curt hello, I make my way through the club, hoping to find Lotus, so I can keep interaction with Andre to a minimum. She's in a small room down the hallway that serves as her office. The door is open, but I knock, nonetheless.

"Hi, Bull," she says, peering up at me briefly, before returning to the mountain of paperwork in front of her.

"Hey. You got any tools I can use?"

Lotus sweeps her hand to the corner of the room where I see a metal toolbox and a first-aid kit close by. It seems her office has many uses. Not wanting to disturb her, I enter quickly and grab what I need.

Just as I'm about to leave, Lotus huffs and throws her pen onto the messy desk. "I give up," she grumbles, rubbing her tired eyes. "Why isn't this adding up?"

I don't know if she's speaking to me or not, so I assume she isn't and continue toward the door.

"I don't suppose you're any good with numbers?"

I stop in my tracks and turn over my shoulder to look at the scribbled piece of paper in front of her. She appears half hopeful since I didn't blow her off. Doing a quick calculation in my head, I see where she's gone wrong.

"You didn't carry the one," I say, looking at the figures on the page.

I'm guessing these are the takings of the club. Or maybe she's doing her taxes. Fucked if I know. Whatever it is, she quickly peers down at the sums in front of her and hums in realization. "Holy shit, you're right."

"Of course, I'm right," I counter while she smirks. "A lot has changed since I've been locked up, but math isn't one of them."

I instantly regret my overshare as I've just revealed I've been inside. But Lotus doesn't flinch or look at me with judgment. She merely nods with a smile.

"A jack-of-all-trades. If you're not careful, I'll have you doing my books as well."

"I'll be out there if you need me." I don't linger and make my way into the club.

Andre is helping himself to the top shelf vodka, which is a total dick move because I doubt he has any intention of paying for it. I don't like freeloaders or cheapskates. Life isn't free. But I ignore him and go to work testing the stability of the barstools.

They're all unsteady, so I open the toolbox and hunt for what I need. Seconds later, a huge shadow casts over me, hinting I have an audience. I don't take the bait because I know exactly who is lurking.

If this assclown is looking for a fight, he is shit out of luck. No matter how badly I want to kick his ass, I won't, because I refuse to disrespect Lotus in that way. Just as I'm about to lift the stool and lay it on the bar, Andre slams his paw onto the counter and blocks me. I don't flinch as I lift my eyes slowly. We lock gazes, and it's evident he is intent on making my life hell.

Isn't he lucky that I don't give a shit?

Chewing on a toothpick, he tries to intimidate me as he stares me down. His attempt is laughable. Lifting the stool, I place it on the bar, regardless of the location of his hand.

He swiftly draws it back. "Looks like Lotus has found herself a little bitch," he taunts, removing the toothpick from between his rubbery lips.

Ignoring him, I drop eye level with the stool and examine the legs.

"Are you deaf and stupid? I'm talking to you." He yanks the top of the stool, sending it crashing to the floor.

Taking two deep breaths, I rise calmly, refusing to buckle. Andre clenches his fists with a sneer, awaiting my retaliation.

He'll be waiting a long time.

Reaching for another stool, I repeat the same action I did with the first. The uneven leg is more evident on this stool, so I hunt through the toolbox for a small saw. Andre doesn't like to be ignored.

"Listen, freak," he spits, thankfully keeping his hands to himself. "Stay out of my way, and we won't have a problem."

It's evident he's not going anywhere unless I reply, so I give him a brisk nod. "Suits me fine."

Andre must feel as if I'm challenging his top dog position, which is ironic, considering I don't want any part of it. I'm not interested in being alpha over this dipshit, because there is no competition. "You're one weird motherfucker."

"Thank you," I counter, returning to my search inside the toolbox. He's gone a few seconds later but not before swiping a bottle of vodka.

Exhaling slowly, I rein in my anger and focus on fixing the barstools. The cheap wooden legs are easy to cut through, and it doesn't take me too long to even them up. As I'm sanding the legs down before I replace the caps so they're stable, a waft of something sweet catches the air.

Wiping the sweat from my brow with the back of my hand, I turn over my shoulder to see I'm no longer alone.

"Hey, handsome," Tawny says with a smile. She makes no secret that she's eye fucking me as her blue eyes study me from head to toe.

I'm in black ripped jeans and a white V-neck T-shirt, which exposes the tattoo sleeves on both my arms and also the ink on my neck. Tawny tilts her head to get a better look, but she'll be looking for a while. My tattoos are private. I didn't get them for people to fawn over or ask questions. I got them as a permanent reminder of what I've done. And what I must do to avenge my brother.

Clearing my throat seems to snap her from her gawking.

"Are you done out here?" she asks, gesturing with her chin to the stools.

"Almost. Why?"

"A couple of lights have blown in the dressing room. I would change them myself, but I just got my nails done." To confirm her claims, she wiggles her long Barbie pink nails at me.

This is clearly a ploy to get me alone, but I have a job to do. The sooner Tawny knows I'm not here for anything but that, the better it'll be for us both. So I nod. "Sure."

Tawny's face lights up. "Thanks so much."

I gesture for her to lead the way.

She ensures the way is led by her wiggling her ass in the cutoffs she's wearing. Her long legs seem amplified thanks to the cowboy boots she's sporting. As I observed last night, she isn't unattractive in the slightest, but she just doesn't do it for me. It has nothing to do with her looks, and everything to do with the fact that I wouldn't have to work for it.

She's basically serving her tits to me on a silver platter, but I'm not interested. Nothing in my life has been easy, and I don't expect women to be either.

The dressing room is bigger than I thought. It has four different shaped mirrors attached to the walls, and each mirror is bordered with lights. The tables are littered with lotions and makeup. The backs of chairs have colored feather boas twirled around them.

In the corner of the room are lockers. But as far as change rooms are concerned, there are none. There is nowhere private for the girls to change from their costumes once their dance number is up. It's a communal room where protecting one's modesty is nonexistent.

Kind of like the showers in prison.

"It's these lights," Tawny says, interrupting my thoughts. When she passes me a box of bulbs, I see where a few of the lights on the mirrors have blown.

Ensuring our fingers don't touch, I reach for the box and walk over to the first mirror. I can see Tawny's reflection as I turn off the switch and unscrew the bulb. She is anything but shy as she openly stares at me.

"So your name is Bull?" she asks, as that's what Lotus

referred to me as.

I nod in response.

"Were you born here, *Bull*?" My name trickles off her tongue like honey.

"Yes, sadly," I reply, replacing one bulb. Only five more to go.

"Me too. I always thought I was destined for bigger and better things, but here I am." She spreads her arms out wide. "I tried going to college, but it wasn't for me. Stripping was supposed to be a temporary thing; yet, three years later, I'm still here."

"Nothing wrong with being a stripper," I state, peering at her briefly in the mirror. "The douchebags think they're in control, but you're not the one throwing cash at them."

"I never thought about it that way," she muses.

"Well, now you can." I move to the next mirror and unscrew the bulb. Just as I reach for a replacement, I feel and smell Tawny behind me. I spin around and grip her wrist, stopping her in midair from touching me.

Her lips pull into a sassy smirk. She thinks this is a game, but it's not. "Wow, you have like superhero reflexes. Is there something you're not telling me?" she teases, batting her eyelashes. "With all that muscle, you could easily be Superman."

She leans in close, too close, but I stand my ground. "I'm not the hero in this story, Tawny."

"You don't want to be my white knight?" she asks, her tone filled with sarcasm. I have no idea what that means until she clarifies. "Someone who thinks they can save a dancer from a life of stripping."

"Definitely not me." I snicker.

"Then what are you?" she challenges, pushing out her chest. Her tits are mere inches away from me, which means they're mere inches too close.

Tightening my hold on her wrist, I lower my face to hers. She inhales sharply as her straight white teeth tug deliberately on her bottom lip. "I'm the bad guy," I reply dangerously low.

I'm not trying to be melodramatic. It's the truth. Yet my words only seem to excite her all the more.

Her pupils dilate, and her cheeks flourish a wicked red. "I like bad boys," she hums, breathing deeply.

My demons roar to the surface, demanding I show her just how bad I can really be. But I shove them down deep. I don't shit where I sleep. "Do yourself a favor then…don't like me."

She wets her lips, ready to speak, but when I hear a familiar voice, my attention drifts to the door. When I see who enters, memories of when I saw her last slam into me, and I squeeze Tawny's wrist unintentionally.

Tiger has her cell pressed to her ear, talking happily to whoever is on the other end. "I'll see you later. I love you, baby." When she sees us, though, she stops dead in her tracks, replacing her smile with a stiff upper lip. She's clearly confused as to what she just walked into.

Instantly, I let Tawny go, as the exchange looked rather heated, and it was, just not in the way Tiger thinks. When she finds her footing, she shakes her head, as if clearing the haze. "Oh, sorry. I didn't think anyone was in here. I just need to grab my purse. I forgot it last night. I'll be out of your hair in a second," she says in a rushed breath.

Tawny remains close to me, appearing to gloat. I immediately take three steps away.

Tiger marches past us and heads straight for the lockers. She turns the dial, which is an amateur move, as I now know what the combination to her lock is.

1021.

I wonder what the significance is? Maybe her birthday? Or maybe it's the birthday of the person, or rather, the *baby* she just told she loved?

What does it matter? I need to stop fixating on her.

I quickly turn around and finish replacing the bulbs on the mirrors while Tawny takes a seat and lights up a cigarette. The girls don't make small talk, which makes me think they don't like one another. When the locker door slams shut, I look in the mirror, wondering what's going on.

Tiger has her back turned, so I take this opportunity to watch her unguarded. She's in yoga pants, a baggy tee, and well-loved Chucks. Her long hair is twisted into a high knot on her head. When she turns, I see that her face barely has any makeup on, which I like.

Last night, I had the inexplicable urge to wipe the red lipstick from her mouth. However, I had no issues devouring her mouth with it on. My cock twitches at the memory. But that memory is soon replaced with pain and blood, and how I wanted to corrupt her, to taint her, so I'm not the only one marred with this blemish on my soul.

She meets my eyes in the mirror, but it's only for a split

second before I swiftly busy myself with changing the bulbs. I need to be more careful. She is toxic, which will only lead to trouble...for her.

"Well, see ya," she calls out. It's evident she's hoping for a response.

Tawny blows a ring of smoke in reply while I simply ignore her. A sigh leaves her before she walks out the door.

After a few moments of silence, Tawny smugly says, "You weren't kidding. You really are the bad guy."

Hell to the fuck yes I am.

I just did Tiger a favor. She just doesn't know it yet. Now, she can go home to her *baby*, safe as safe can be, because me, I would only send her castle crumbling to the ground.

CHAPTER THREE

Lily

"**O**ne, two, three. One, two, three. Heels should be touching with your toes turned out. Good, Jennifer. Now move your feet apart. Very good, Roberta. One, two, three. Open your arms wide but don't stretch them back."

The music wafts softly from the speakers as I walk around the small ballet studio, teaching my students the basics of ballet.

It's here where I usually feel at peace, at home, but today, my five-year-old pupils have more coordination than I do. I leap into a jeté, determined to escape the memories that have plagued me since I got sucked into heaven and hell.

The music ends, alerting me the hour-long class has come to an end already. I spaced, which has *never* happened before.

Regardless of the shit that's happened in my life—and believe me, there has been some major *shit*—I have always been able to focus the moment I stepped into this room. This is my happy place.

But clearly, today is different, and that's thanks to...*him*. Ugh, fuck...*him*.

"All right, class. You all did so well. I'll see you next week."

"Yes, Ms. Hope." My students run to their gym bags, chatting animatedly amongst each other, while I open the door. Parents rush in, eager to see their children. Melanie Arnolds, a soccer mom with too much time and money on her hands, makes a beeline for me, which is no surprise, as she does this every week. Although, I much prefer her to her sleazeball husband, Derrick.

She's a parent who hovers, but she's a parent who also pays my bills, so I await the inquisition with a smile. "Lillian," she calls out with a wave of her hand, jingling her Tiffany bracelets. "Can I speak to you for a second?"

I have no idea why she's phrased it as a question since I have no say in the matter. But I only broaden my smile. "Of course, Melanie. And please, call me Lily." I've only told her this for the past three months because only one person gets to call me that name. Maybe one day it'll sink in. However, today is not that day.

She gestures with her eyes that she wants to speak in private, so I humor her, and we walk to the back of the room. When we're huddled in the corner, she tugs at her pearl earring. "I know I sound like a nag, but I really think Brenda would excel in a different class."

I open my mouth, but soon close it when Melanie reveals she's not done.

"She knows all the routines by heart. She practices every day. I know you aren't allowed to play favorites, but she is clearly your best student." She winks mischievously as if we're in some secret club.

We're not.

And this is the reason I have a closed-door policy. No parent is permitted inside my studio because of the Melanie Arnolds of this world. They believe their child is a ballet prodigy when, in reality, they're as graceful as a one-legged fish.

But putting my professional face on, I smile gently. "Brenda is exceptional, and I can see she is practicing, but I can't move her to the next level until she sits her exams. I know it may seem unfair, but I don't make the rules."

"But this is your class," she presses, pursing her Botox-infused lips.

"I realize that, but Ms. Everland is the director of this academy, and if I were to bend the rules, then I would get into serious trouble. Not to mention the fact that Brenda isn't ready."

Melanie flinches, her face stuck on resting bitch mode. "She is better than kids twice her age. I don't understand why you're hesitating."

"I only want what's best for Brenda. Please trust me. I will talk to Ms. Everland, but—" I don't have a chance to finish my sentence—which would have been "but it won't make a difference"—before I'm interrupted.

Melanie claps her hands together, her bright yellow nails resembling talons, as she clearly thinks she's won me over. "Oh, Lillian! You won't regret it."

I already do.

When she peers around the room and turns her back, I arch a brow, wondering what in the hell she's doing. I watch in confusion as she reaches into her Chanel clutch and produces a bundle of crisp hundred-dollar bills. That confusion soon transforms into utter offense.

"Here, take this. Spoil yourself." Is she really trying to... bribe me? Bribe me so her five-year-old daughter can move up a grade? This would be comical if she wasn't serious.

I step back two feet, shaking my head discreetly. "No, I couldn't."

"I insist." She attempts to shove it into my hand, but I clench it tight, seconds away from slapping the filler from her cheeks.

"Thank you, Melanie, but no." She looks at me as though I've just spoken a foreign word, which, in her world, I probably have, and that word is no.

"Are you sure? This is pocket money for me," she states flippantly, insulting me further.

Her "pocket money" would pay my rent for a month, but I'll be damned if I tell her that. But I don't need to. She knows. All these moms and dads know what I am. It's what draws a distinct line between us.

The rich and the poor.

And the fact I'm being persuaded to take this large wad of cash from a mom whose designer pantsuit costs more than my truck hints to where I sit on the social ladder. I teach this class, dealing with pretentious parents, and at night, I take off my clothes because I do what I have to in order to survive.

If this were a fairy tale, I would have graduated high school and gone to Juilliard or SAB, living out my dream of becoming a world-renowned ballerina. But life very rarely goes as planned. I was a naïve kid with adolescent dreams. And something big made me grow the fuck up and left me with this…this life of a stranger.

Blinking back my tears, I sigh in relief when Brenda attempts to dance over. She ends up bumping into a barre.

"Hi, Brenda," I say exceptionally loud, alerting Melanie that her daughter is about to witness her mother bribing her teacher. Melanie thankfully gets the hint and shoves the money back into her clutch.

Before Melanie has a chance to corner me any further, I step to the side and pat Brenda on the head. "You did so good today. I'm really proud of you. I'll see you next week." She smiles her toothless grin while I excuse myself and say farewell to the remaining parents and students.

When they're all gone, I lock the door, walk over to the iPod, and select "Smells like Teen Spirit" by Nirvana. The thrashy guitars cut through the once tranquil ballet studio, bringing me alive. I move my body to the upbeat tempo, and when the chorus kicks in, I let loose.

All my frustrations seep from me as I sweat away my pain. My body aches as I leap high, landing on my toes. I turn and turn, around and around, until the room spins away before me. But that doesn't stop me. It only encourages me to continue.

The dizzier I become, the further away those different colored eyes fade—a sea green-amber kiss from hell.

An anger blisters throughout, and I take it out on my body as I continue to dance a ballet fit for the devil. My body is and has always been a channel, and even though I have the perfect poker face, when I dance, every emotion explodes out of me.

I dance with my heart; that's what my teacher and the closest thing I have to a mom, Avery Everland, told me. She first saw me dance in my trailer park home when I was six years old. I had no training and no clue what I was doing, but that didn't stop me.

Dancing was my escape. It was here I could chase the demons plaguing my soul.

Avery saved me from becoming a statistic. I didn't have two pennies to rub together, thanks to my father leaving before I was born, and my mom being too caught up in finding herself a Prince Charming instead of saving herself.

I have an older brother, but just like my father, he left me too.

Memories of abandonment flash before me, and I scream in fury, punishing my body because it's the only way to feel. My heart threatens to rip apart my rib cage, but would that be so bad? Twenty-eight years of hell can all end right here, right now.

As I spin faster and faster, my blistered toes beseech me to finish, but I can't. It's only when I dance that I feel free, free from this life that turned out nothing like I thought. The song comes to a close, and I end with a sequence of fast pique turns. Around and around, always running away, and when the last note fades, I face reality, breathless and spent.

My winded pants fill the small room as I take a moment to catch my breath. I always feel most alive when I take my last step, gratified that I've overcome the past. But today, the weight returns, and that's thanks to someone I most definitely need to stay away from.

He reeks of trouble, trouble with a capital T, so why am I drawn to him? Something about him calls to me, a deep, carnal yearning, which has me forgetting my number one rule—your heart can only be broken if you let it.

I haven't had a boyfriend for years because men only hurt me and then they leave. All but one, and that's the reason I'm single and working at The Pink Oyster.

Sighing, I stop with the moping and grab my bag. I slip out of my ballet slippers and put on my Chucks, ready for the drive home. The drive from Cleveland to Detroit is long, but I wouldn't have it any other way.

Here, no one knows who I am, not even Avery. I wouldn't jeopardize her that way.

I can't risk anyone knowing what I do at night because a prestige academy like Everland's would never survive such a scandal. It doesn't matter that I'm the best damn teacher this school has or that I work my ass off. None of that matters when you take your clothes off for a living.

You're seen as a slut, a lower-class citizen, but I dare any of these pretentious moms to live a day in my shoes. I do what's necessary to survive—I always have—and I make no apologies. I couldn't give a fuck what anyone thinks of me, but working in a different state does make things easier for...my son—the love of my life.

Avery's brother lived in the same trailer park as I did, and from the first time we met, she took me under her wing and made me into the woman I am today. She taught me everything I know, all because she saw something special in me.

When she dropped by the trailer, she would take me to her studio. Those visits were the only thing that helped me through my childhood. I would sweep the floors and clean the toilets—whatever I could do to help—and in return, she paid me in ballet lessons.

She never asked me to do the chores, but I wanted to because I didn't want to be a freeloader. She saved me from a lifetime of pain. She allowed me to be someone other than me for a few hours, away from my mom, and away from a life that caused me nothing but pain.

Eventually, Avery moved her studio from Detroit to Cleveland, which is why I am here. No one would ever hire me, considering my past and lack of experience, but as I said, I owed Avery everything. She never married and didn't have any children, so I'm all she has.

Shouldering my bag, I switch off the lights and lock up the studio. My truck is parked in the parking lot out back, a short walk around the building. But nonetheless, I ensure my mace and cell are in my jacket pocket.

Lately, I can't shake the feeling that I'm being watched. I'm probably just being paranoid, but too much shit has happened in my life for me to be careless, which is why I have no idea why the new guy at work is getting under my skin.

Even thinking about him has my skin breaking into goose bumps, but they soon scatter when heat washes over me. He had no issues getting up close and personal with Tawny today, but with me, it seems he can't get away fast enough.

Last night was a perfect example of this.

I let my guard down—the one and only time—and look what happened. He did what every other jerk has done—tossed me aside. Groaning at my stupidity, I remember how his soft lips felt against mine. They were cautious, timid almost, the tremble to them revealing he was nervous, which most certainly did not match the way he looked.

I have never seen someone so…imposing before. He scares but intrigues me all in the same breath. Could it be because I see a prisoner trapped within, desperate to break free, just like me? He looks at me as though I'll break, but I won't. I can hold my own.

His hair is short, but I can see it's dark in color. His eyes are so unusual, but in a good way, a way which sucks you into the abyss of sin. His upturned nose only adds to his arrogance, his lips are wicked and full, and his slightly longer canine teeth play into his animalistic vibe.

He is tall, mysterious, and smells like a juniper dream. He's covered in so many tattoos, and I have the urge to study each one, hoping they will shed light on just who this man is. His hands and fingers are inked, and so are his arms, which I saw today as that tight white T-shirt clung to his muscled body like a second skin.

The intricate tattoo on his neck consists of two skeleton hands clutching either side of his neck. They appear to be squeezing his throat tight. It has me wondering if it's somehow connected to the Roman numeral number four on the back of his neck.

So much about him fascinates me, which is why I need to stay away.

Regardless of how good it felt, I shouldn't have kissed him. It was a mistake, but it was like I fell under his spell, a spell I'm certain he doesn't even know he cast. He has no idea the effect he has on others. There's a magnetism about him that has everyone turning their head the moment he enters a room.

I don't feel threatened by him. God knows I should, but when he jumped to my defense without a second thought, it showed me that underneath his hard exterior, there is something special, something different.

Something I want.

His darkness dances with mine. I can feel it. This darkness inside me has been festering since everyone I loved left me. Everyone has a cross to bear, but mine seems to become heavier and heavier with each step I take.

So when I saw him today touching that vulture, Tawny, I realized I need to stay away from Bull. I can't afford any distractions.

I have a plan, and that plan is to save enough money to get Jordy and me the fuck out of Detroit. I want him to have a normal childhood and not have to mourn the death of a friend. I want him to be able to walk to school without being jumped for his lunch money.

The money Avery pays me barely covers my rent, which is why I dance. The money is good, the hours work around the ballet classes and babysitters, and I can dance. I'm not cut out to work nine to five as a slave to some chauvinist boss because I don't obey the rules. I never have.

Dancing is my way to be free. And I was until Bull walked into my life and tilted it upside down.

"Stop being such an idiot," I whisper to myself, as I walk to my truck. It's an old pickup, but she does the job.

The daylight has already given way to night. I quicken my step, keys in hand, but when I hear a bottle roll along the ground, the hair on the back of my neck stands on end. With mace in the other hand, I run to my truck and unlock it quickly, before diving into the driver's seat. Then I slam the door and press the lock down.

After three attempts, my truck finally roars to life. When I turn the headlights on, I'm half expecting the boogeyman to appear in front of me. Putting the truck into drive, I pull out of the lot and focus on the road and not on the fact that the boogeyman destroyed me long ago.

The long drive back home had me thinking about my brother, Christopher. He left a few months after Jordy was born. Although he never told me, I knew my pregnancy broke his heart.

When Jordy was born, I promised myself that I would protect him with my life. I was sixteen, and Christopher was twenty when I gave birth to Jordy. I was a single parent, but even if Jordy's dad was in the picture, I wouldn't tell Christopher who he was because Christopher would have killed him.

Jordy's dad, Michael, was Christopher's best friend. I was young and stupid, but I never regretted getting pregnant or falling in love. Jordy is the best thing that's ever happened to me. And so was his father, until he left town.

Michael is the only man I've ever loved, and when he left, I promised never to be vulnerable to that kind of heartache again.

Shuddering at the memories, I quickly make a beeline for the dressing room since my shift started fifteen minutes ago. I hate being late, but I had to drop by and see Jordy first. My neighbor, Erika, is looking after him.

Christopher made sure I was fed, went to school, and was well looked after when our mom remarried and moved to Vegas. She left us the trailer, which cleared her conscience of abandoning her kids, but I had to move out of the trailer after Christopher left. There were too many memories there. So I moved into a small two-bedroom apartment. The place isn't flashy, but it's close to Jordy's school.

Every day I wake up promising myself this life isn't forever. Before working at The Pink Oyster, I worked any job that I could to bring home an income. But it was never enough, which is why I've danced for the past nine months.

The money is good because, unlike at most clubs, Lotus

pays a wage. It's small, but it's an incentive to stay because it's a steady paycheck. Her house fee is half of what the other clubs charge, and she doesn't charge an off-stage fee. If we don't want to work onstage and just want to do lap dances in the VIP room to earn more money, then we can. Tip-outs aren't mandatory either, which is why Lotus doesn't have a DJ.

We keep what we make and aren't expected to tip the staff because there isn't anyone to tip.

Basically, Lotus is the best boss I could ever ask for, and as for the clientele, I can treat them like dirt, and they keep coming back for more. *Win-win.*

"You're late." Bae smiles at me as she shimmies out of a gold dress. "I covered for you, so don't worry."

"Oh, thank you." I press my lips to her forehead before rushing to my locker. "What's it like out there?"

Bae slips into sweats and a baggy T-shirt as her shift is over. "The usual," she replies with a shrug. "Dogs in heat, but full of Georges. One guy actually asked me to squash his balls with my heels."

We both shudder in disgust.

The world is full of sick perverts, but we deal because most are Georges—generous tippers. Bae and I have given them what most of our clients want—the girlfriend experience. We've spun hurl stories, tricking them into thinking they're our white knights.

We give them this, and they chum the waters—tipping big, so we pay more attention to them for the rest of the night.

Stripping isn't about taking off your clothes—it's about strategy. Men mistake Bae to be a delicate little flower because she's barely five feet and weighs next to nothing. But she's lithe like a tiger. And as for me, I dance my ass off, sticking to my motto of less is more, and they tip me big.

It's all about the hustle. They think they're in control, but they're not. We're the ones hustling them.

Tossing my bag onto the floor, I strip out of my jeans and sweater. I showered before coming here, but I still feel dirty the moment I take off my bra and thong. When I put on my uniform—because that's what every outfit I wear in this place is—I become Tigerlily.

Tonight, I'm dancing to "Rock You Like A Hurricane" by Scorpions. I don't ever refer to what I do as stripping. Yes, I take off my clothes, but I'm not a stripper. I'm a dancer, who just happens to take off her clothes.

I very rarely dance to pop music because it doesn't have the same feel as a rock song. Rock songs are filled with angst, passion, and sex. And seeing as I haven't had sex for many, *many* years, at least I can feel sexy when on stage.

"Have you met the new muscle?" Bae asks, fanning her cheeks as I slip into my baby blue netted crop top and matching thong.

This is a little risqué for me, as I usually don't wear anything completely see-through, but just the mention of Bull, as I know that's who Bae is referring to, has me wanting to rub everything I have—not literally—in his face. I still don't understand what about him gets under my skin, but on that stage, I will show him who's boss.

Last night when he disregarded me like nothing, and even today in this dressing room, he really pissed me off. It's evident he doesn't like to be touched, which is why I gave him an air dance. I thought I was being nice and respecting his boundaries, but then he goes and throws it into my *face* by being all up in Tawny's *face*.

Fuck him.

"Earth to Lily," Bae teases, snapping her fingers in front of me.

"Yes, I've seen him. He looks like another tattooed asshole with a chip on his shoulder."

"A chip on his very muscled, very broad shoulder," she amends, giggling when I roll my eyes.

Hunting through my makeup bag, I quickly slick myself up with oil. I then apply my booty dust, so my body shimmers. My makeup consists of silver glitter eye shadow, fake lashes, flawless foundation, and shiny red lips.

Smacking my lips together, I remove the elastic band from my hair and shake it out. As I look in the mirror, a devilish smile tugs at my mouth. I look wild and feral. I look in control.

The men out there may think they own me, but they don't. I own them…all of them except one.

Tossing my things into my locker, I begin to stretch and warm up because I never get on stage unprepared. I can't afford any injuries. Once my muscles are limbered up, I slip into my six-inch blue glitter heels and smile at Bae.

"How do I look?"

"God help every man out there," she replies, grinning. "Although I'm pretty sure only one man out there needs all the help he can get."

I arch a brow, confused.

Her grin grows wider. "I heard the new muscle asking if you were coming in tonight."

"Oh?" I reply, surprised.

"Yeah, which is why I asked if you had met him. I wondered if maybe he was the one to end your drought," she playfully teases. Bae knows of my "drought" because she's the closest thing I have to a friend.

"Ugh." I screw up my face, tossing a wand of lip gloss at her while she ducks and laughs. "I'd rather stay celibate for the rest of my life. Thank you very much."

"Ah-ha," she replies, so not believing me. "He's so fucking...big. I wonder if his co—"

Thankfully, Ricky, the emcee, announces my name, ending a conversation I have no intention of ever finishing.

"We will continue this conversation later." Bae giggles when I smack her ass on the way out the door.

The walk toward the curtain is an adrenaline rush for me. I get off on performing because losing myself in the music, to dancing, is when I feel most alive. As the music commences, I crack my neck from side to side and shake out my arms.

The anticipation is the best part. I don't come out right away. I let these animals wait. This is my show, so I come when I'm ready...which is now.

Splitting the curtain, I emerge into the bright lights, fucking victorious as I strut my shit on stage. The catcalls from the men in the tip rail have me smirking. Show them a little tit and ass, and they are ready to throw down their life savings. Bills instantly litter the stage, only cementing my point.

I move in time with the music, using every part of my body as a weapon. The pole is an essential prop to my show because its shape is the perfect analogy for what all those morons down there wish I would do to *their* pole.

In their fucking dreams.

I climb it with ease, before twirling around it and flipping upside down. Hooking my ankle around the pole, I hold it with one hand and thrust my pelvis a couple of times in sync with the music, causing the catcalls to sound loudly around me.

I still can't believe these douchebags eat this shit up.

I continue my routine, pointing my toes as I extend my body outward using my core. If anyone in this audience had any clue, they'd be able to see my ballet background, but they don't care. All they care about is seeing me naked.

Anger courses through me, and I spin quickly. Every one of them is just like all the other men in my life— looking at me like I'm nothing but a toy. Dismounting fiercely, I land on the edge of the stage, crouched low.

When a hand extends forward, attempting to touch me, I instantly recoil and dance out of reach. This isn't a petting zoo. The strobe lights begin to flicker, and I move like I'm possessed. The crowd goes wild as I tear at the thin fabric of my top and toss the garment into the audience.

I'm about to cover my breasts, but when a flash of bright blue with a kiss of amber green flicker before me, I suddenly stop, baring myself to him. I have no idea where he was, but he's now just feet away from the stage. The men are out of their seats, hollering loudly as they watch me fervently, which is the reason he's so close. He's only doing his job.

But when those mismatched eyes eat me alive as he rubs two tattooed fingers across his supple lips, I want to believe he's here because he feels this electrical pulse between us too. My skin is set alight by the feral scowl spread across his bowed lips because he looks dangerously pissed off.

The look only incites me to dance faster, shaking my body with confidence. Bull soon turns around, facing the audience, which has me celebrating in triumph. His submission is my victory, and I end the set, breathless, slathered in sweat and grinning a winner's smirk.

The stage is drowned in black before the room erupts into pandemonium.

"Hollllyyyyy shit!" Ricky hollers, walking onto the stage as the lights and background music come back on. "Give my girl Tigerlily another round of applause!"

The salivating men do as they're asked as I bend forward, arm wrapped around my breasts to collect my cash. There is so much green scattered everywhere that Ricky bends down to help me gather it all up. Just as I reach for a twenty, a sweaty, unwanted hand seizes my forearm.

I don't even have a chance to move because a black shadow coolly glides forward and bends back the wrist of my manhandler. The man yelps and instantly lets me go. I peer into the eyes of Bull, and every fiber of my body is aware of his presence.

"Thanks," I curtly say.

He merely nods in response, standing guard over me as I collect my earnings. Once I'm done, I quickly scamper through the curtain, where I can finally breathe again.

CHAPTER FOUR

Cody

"**A**re you sure we should be here?" My best friend Gary Buchanan asks, as we crouch low, remaining hidden by the trees.

"Yes, now stop being such a pussy and let's go."

Gary is right; we shouldn't be here. It's way past curfew, but what my parents don't know won't hurt them.

We creep toward the scorching bonfire, making sure to stay low because this place is off-limits to two snotty-nosed kids like us.

The Titans, my brother's football team, won the finals, thanks to Damian scoring a touchdown with three seconds left on the clock. My brother, the hometown hero, saved the game, which is really no surprise, and to celebrate, they've all gone to Pinnacle Point, a local hangout in the woods for the seniors.

The party is in full swing. The beer flows freely, and endless girls flock around Damian. He isn't interested in them, however, because he's been dating his girlfriend, Lyndsay, for two years. They really are disgusting with how they look at one another with gaga eyes. But what would I know about love? I've never even kissed a girl.

Gary and I were too interested in riding our dirt bikes to pay attention to any girls. But that changed the moment Damian dragged me to his stupid football game tonight, and I saw a brunette cheerleader with a beautiful smile.

I don't know her name, which is why I'm here. I want to find out. Damian warned me about the cheerleaders, and he was right. I could always ask him who she is, but I want to do this on my own. I've always lived in my brother's shadow, which has never bothered me before, but finding out who the mystery girl is on my own feels like a step toward manhood.

I know that's fucking lame, but it would be even lamer if my brother introduced his younger brother to the woman of his dreams.

With that as my mindset, we creep closer, eyeing the unfolding scene. People are kissing around the fire, while others are dancing and laughing and having a good time. I scan the area, hoping to see my cheerleader. I do.

"There she is!" I hiss, elbowing Gary in the ribs.

He yelps, jumping away from me. "Yeah, so what? What are you going to do? You can't talk to her. Your parents will ground you for a week if they find out you're here. We're supposed to be having a sleepover at my house."

He's right.

My parents are a little heavy handed with me because I'm not the golden boy like Damian. I don't do what I'm told. I suppose you can call me the black sheep or the rebel in the family, but I don't mind. Damian wouldn't rat me out, but I know he would make me feel guilty for disobeying my parents. His honesty would rub off on me, and then I would eventually cave, telling them what I did.

So it goes without saying, he can't see me.

The cheerleader is still in her uniform, talking to a group of girls. Finding my balls, I walk toward her. Gary stays behind me, being my lookout. Damian is across the field, so I think I'm safe for now.

I don't know how this is done, but I decide to take a page out of my brother's book and use one of his lines. When I stop feet away from them, she turns and looks at me with big blue eyes.

"Hello, gorgeous," I say with confidence, smirking.

Her friends grin, muffling their laughter behind their hands.

"Hi," she finally replies, sipping her drink from a blue cup.

"I saw you cheerleading tonight. At the game," I stupidly add, because where else would she be cheering?

But I keep my cool.

"Oh, awesome." I need to take the hint, but I can't. I want to be the one this time; the one who shines.

"So, can I have your number?"

Her friends all cackle loudly while Gary groans, hinting

this is going down as the worst pickup attempt in history.

I should abort, but I can't. "My name is Cody. Cody Bishop."

They suddenly stop giggling, their mouths dropping open for another reason this time. "Is your brother Damian Bishop?" one of the girls asks.

Goddammit.

This is not what I wanted. I wanted to do this on my own merit and not because of who my brother is. But I nod, nonetheless.

The cheerleader, whose name I don't even know, smirks, looking over my shoulder. "Give me your phone."

"Sonya!" one of her friend's scolds with a giggle. "He's too young."

A name. Finally. Sonya, my queen.

I hunt through my jeans for my cell and hand it over to her. She accepts with a lopsided smirk. When she punches in her number, I can't believe my luck. Her friend's stare on with wide eyes while I fucking feel like Hercules.

That is, until Sonya gives me back my phone and says, "Can you give my number to your brother?"

Gasping like a fish out of water, I suddenly feel like she's kicked me in the nuts. I don't know what to say, so I nod like a pussy. "Sure."

"Thanks, Cody." Sonya bends forward and kisses my cheek. The kiss is chaste, as it's evident she feels sorry for me because living in Damian Bishop's shadow is like being eclipsed by the sun.

She quickly shrinks back, yelping, and I have no idea why

that is until someone yanks my bicep and spins me around. He towers over me and lifts me with ease, so we're eye to eye.

"Let me go, motherfucker!" I curse, attempting to break free.

He snickers in response. "Whatcha doing out here, kid? Isn't it past your bedtime?"

"Fuck you." I spit in his face, which has the desired effect when he drops me to my feet. Instantly, I knee him in the balls. When he wheezes and folds in half, I punch him in the face. I am suddenly so angry.

I may be scrawny, but I'm scrappy and know how to fight. Damian would talk it through, but I'm not fucking Damian— I'm not perfect like him.

The guy's deadbeat friends come running over, fists raised and ready to battle. Gary is no help as he runs and hides behind the girls. I'm outnumbered, four to one, but I suddenly feel alive. This is my fight, *mine*, not Damian's.

And that fact spurs me forward as I clothesline one meathead. He drops to the ground with a thud. Before I know it, it's a flurry of fists, and I attack anything that stands in my way. I'm working on pure adrenaline and ignore the screams around me. It's sheer mayhem.

Just as I knee some asshole in the face, I hear a bottle smash, then see its serrated edge come toward me. I jump back, arms raised. The guy who I kneed in the balls is out for revenge. I never take my eyes off him as he circles me.

"Punching above your weight, don't you think? Going for the prettiest girl here." This dickhead is definitely the ringleader. He has soulless black eyes, eyes I will never forget.

He also has a small blue shark tattoo on the side of his neck.

"Leave him alone!" someone who I'm guessing is Sonya screams.

These assholes don't go to our school. I would recognize them if they did. I realize I've gotten myself in some serious shit, and now that the adrenaline has worn off, I'm suddenly afraid. Just as the bastard lunges for me, he is thrown to the side with brutal force.

I turn my chin to see Damian hulked out, ready to take anyone on. "Pick on someone your own size, you white trash assholes!" he roars, arms spread out wide like a fucking superhero.

The guys rush forward, getting in a few punches, before Damian flings them aside like ants. Watching on with wide eyes, I can't believe my brother is taking them on and winning. I did help, but he makes my attempt laughable.

"Eat shit, asshole!" I scream from the sidelines, cheering my brother on.

When the four chumps realize they've lost, they scamper away with their tails between their legs like the cowards that they are. I won my first fight. Well, sort of.

Damian turns to me with that big brother look in his eyes. "Home, now."

"Aww, c'mon, bro. Let's celebrate your ass whooping with a beer."

Sonya giggles, which makes me think I might have half a shot. But when Damian wipes the blood from his lip with the back of his hand, struggling to stand, I realize I better get both our asses home. "Fine. But you're coming with me."

I'm expecting him to argue, but he nods, cringing. He's definitely going to have a shiner in the morning.

Lyndsay offers to come with us, but Damian shakes his head. "You stay, babe. All your friends are here. Call me when you get home."

"Are you sure?" she asks, chewing on her bottom lip.

This is so Damian. Thinking of others.

"Yes. Besides, I need to get Squirt home." He looks at me pointedly while I give him wide eyes. He's just ruined my chances with Sonya. No one wants to hook up with a "Squirt."

Damian and Lyndsay kiss while I pretend to gag.

Sonya smiles at me before mouthing, "Call me." Well, maybe I was wrong. Looks like this night just turned into the best one of my life.

Damian messes up my hair before we commence a slow climb up the hill to where he parked his truck. He's unsteady on his feet, revealing he's hurting, but he doesn't say a word.

"Want me to drive?" I offer. It's the least I can do, seeing as he saved my ass from being cut into Swiss cheese.

Damian digs into his varsity jacket pocket, producing his keys. "Don't tell Mom," he teases, while I grin.

The terrain is thick with trees, and although this is the shortcut, it would probably have been easier if we took the path. We walk slow as Damian tries to catch his breath.

"So, sweet on Sonya Teller, hey?"

When I don't reply, he nudges me in the ribs playfully. "I told ya, cheerleaders—"

But I'll never know what he was going to say because one second he is standing beside me and the next, I'm suspended in midair.

Instantly, I kick out, but it's useless. Some asshole has his arms around my middle, holding me prisoner as three of his friends emerge from the darkness and attack Damian.

"No!" I scream, attempting to break free, but it's pointless. The guy has a strong hold on me. I smell beer and weed on his rank breath. "Let me go."

"Sorry, no can do. It's time you became a man."

I soon recognize these bastards as the four who attacked us earlier. But unlike before, they've caught an injured Damian unaware. They pounce on him, kicking him in the ribs, the face, the stomach—wherever they can. He tries to fight them off, but they knee him so hard in the nose that it shatters under the force.

He falls onto his back, gasping for air. He's hurt really bad.

I watch helplessly, unable to do anything, as they beat my brother senselessly, unable to do anything but squirm with all my might.

The ringleader laughs when Damian reaches for him, trying in vain to fight him off. "Not so tough now, are you, quarterback?"

"Leave him alone!" I yell, flailing wildly against the man who is holding me to his chest. He is one big ass, strong motherfucker who has about a hundred pounds on me.

Damian groans, clawing at the dirt as he commences a slow crawl away from his three attackers. The sight kills me because he looks so weak. But they won't show him the same mercy he showed them. The ringleader stands in front of him, unzips his black jeans, and begins pissing on Damian's head.

"You fucking asshole! Stop it!" I thrash about, intent on murder.

One of them plants his boot in the small of Damian's back to stop him from moving while another drops to his knees, bends Damian's wrist back with a crack, and yanks his championship ring from his finger. It isn't enough that they're degrading and breaking him; they have to steal from him too.

They laugh hysterically at my brother's expense. Three against one is hardly fair, but there is no fair in this situation.

"Thanks for my ring," the guy who took it from Damian mocks, slipping the ring onto his middle finger. "I like your jacket. I always wanted to be quarterback. But they said I was too small. Not so small now, am I, asshole?"

"Hold him up," the leader orders the guy who is holding him down. He does as he's told. He yanks on Damian's hair, forcing him back at a sickening angle. Damian groans, covered in blood and piss.

Once his zipper is done back up, the ringleader comes up behind him and rips the jacket off him. He then throws it to the asshole who took Damian's ring.

Now that they've stolen from him and beaten him, surely, they'll leave us alone. But they don't. The ringleader punches Damian so hard in the jaw, I see one of his teeth soar through the air and land in the dirt.

"No!" I scream over and over, frantically trying to break free. The asshole holding me just clutches me tighter, laughing as he watches his friends viciously beat my brother.

The thief and the leader of the pack take turns punching him until his chin sags to his chest. A trickle of blood seeps from his mouth, staining the dirt red. The moonlight catches something shiny—Damian's St. Christopher medallion.

He never takes it off. He calls it his good luck charm. But now it's nothing but something else they can steal. The ringleader yanks it off his limp neck, breaking the chain. He nods to his friend holding him, who shoves Damian back into the dirt.

He collapses into a heap, wheezing.

The sight is my undoing. Damian is being hurt because of me...and I refuse to accept that reality.

Something so fierce overwhelms me, and I strike my head backward, connecting with the meathead's face. A pained oof leaves him, and I drop to the dirt. I scramble to stand, my useless legs turning to Jell-O, but I finally find my footing and run toward Damian.

"No...Squirt, don't," he breathlessly warns, thrusting out his broken hand, but I don't listen. It's time I saved him. I'm so engrossed in getting to him that I don't see it happening before it's too late.

Out of nowhere, someone comes charging toward me, a rock in hand, ready to end my miserable existence once and for all. I don't have time to move. I'm cornered, trapped. I brace for death, but I don't feel anything. Maybe I'm already dead.

When nothing happens, I slowly peel open my eyes and find myself in the same position I was in, but I don't understand what I'm witnessing. The leader stands motionless before me, rock in hand, blood dripping from his fingers. A sinister smirk twists his lips as he stares down at the ground.

I follow his line of sight and see…no, please God no.

There is a calm before the storm, a calm that allows me to observe a sight my brain refuses to process because there is no fucking way. Laying before me is my brother, but something is very wrong. A bloodcurdling scream rips from my chest and is the wake-up call I needed. It kick-starts the beginning of the end.

"Damian?" I say, unsure if what I'm seeing is true. But when bright red stains the earth beneath him, I know that this is really happening.

"Oh my god." The soil kicks up as I run over to him, shoving the four assholes out of the way. Dropping to my knees, I cradle him against my chest, and my stomach drops when his body is limp. "Damian, can you hear me?"

He blinks his eyes rapidly, but he doesn't speak. He looks to be in shock.

"Someone call 911!" I yell so loudly it tears at my vocal cords. "Please!" I've lost my cell in the ruckus.

I brush the blond hair from his brow, and my hand comes away a bright red. I don't understand why. I embrace him close to me, but my white T-shirt is suddenly tainted a bright crimson. Lifting him gently, I feel vomit rising when I see a gaping hole in the back of his head—a hole which was made by the motherfucker who still holds the weapon in his hand.

I meet his dead eyes and make a promise, here and now, that I will find him and deliver him the same fate. "Still think you're better than me, pretty boy?" he snarls, spitting on me and my brother. The final insult before he hurls the rock at one of his friends.

The motherfucker who held my brother down like a dog holds the rock, eyes wide. He seems to be caught in a fog. "Please," I beg. "Call an ambulance. My brother is dying. Please help him."

Now that the severity of what they've done has sunk in, he seems to be in shock. "Jaws?" he finally says.

But Jaws, the ringleader, shakes his head. His tattoo now makes perfect sense. "You want to go to prison? Is that it? Be my guest and call the fucking police. Tell them what you did." Jaws digs into his pocket and offers him his cell. "Your life will be over…just like his." There is nothing but hatred as he glares down at Damian.

I look back and forth between them, pleading for them to show mercy, but in the end, fear will always win.

Like the coward he is, he takes off into the night, leaving the scene of an accident, leaving my brother to die. They soon all follow suit with Jaws the last to leave.

His parting words will change me forever because he's right. "This is on you, kid." He slips into the darkness free, even though he's guilty of murder.

I can't chase him. I'm helpless or, rather, useless because this *is* my fault.

"Come back here! I will find you, you motherfuckers! I will kill you! I promise you! You're all fucking dead!" Spittle coats my chin as I rock my brother, cradling him to my chest. "Damian, I'm so s-sorry. Please don't die."

My tears trickle onto Damian's cheeks as I hug him tight. Looking into the starless sky, I shout at the universe, begging for someone to show mercy to my brother because he doesn't deserve to die. If anyone deserves to die, it's me.

If only I didn't follow him. If only I stayed at Gary's, none of this would have happened.

"I'm sorry," I repeat over and over, rocking my gasping brother. I'm covered in his blood: it's sticky and hot and makes me want to puke.

I attempt to stop the bleeding from the back of his head by placing my hand over the gaping wound, but all I feel is mush. I realize that mush is his brain. That bastard cracked open his skull.

"I promise you I'll be good. Just please, don't die," I plead with Damian, looking into his eyes. "I love you, bro. Don't leave me. Please, please don't leave m-me."

His silver chain sits a few feet away, dropped in the dirt as the cowards fled into the night. With one arm, I stretch and reach for it, needing all the good luck I can find.

My brother isn't going to die. He's strong. A fucking superhero. Look at what he did. Somehow, beaten and broken, he found the strength to rise to protect me. If it wasn't for him intervening, standing in front of me and taking the blow meant for me, I would be the one lying on this cold ground, bleeding out. Someone like Damian doesn't die, not at seventeen, not with his whole life ahead of him. Life isn't that cruel. Is it?

However, when I hear Lyndsay bellow a hysterical wail, I realize that yes, life *is* that fucking cruel. It took away my brother. It took away the one person who didn't deserve to die.

Peering down slowly, I look into the lifeless eyes of my brother because he's fucking dead...dead... because of me.

Bull

I jolt upright, covered in sweat.

Frantically reaching for the bedside lamp, I flick it on, breathing a sigh of relief when I realize where I am. It was just a dream or, more accurately, the nightmare that has plagued me for the past fourteen years.

Running a hand over the short bristles of my hair, I kick off the blankets and sit on the edge of the bed. Cradling my face, I lower my head and inhale deeply, feeling Damian's medallion burn against my skin.

Damian's death kick-started the demise of my family.

Once the paramedics arrived, they confirmed what I knew to be true. Damian's cause of death was blunt force trauma to the head—aka a fucking rock split his skull open like a melon. The police came soon after, taking everyone's statements, but no one would help as they didn't see the actual murder. And besides, they were running scared.

The guys who gatecrashed the party were known to some, but no one was willing to point the finger. The murder weapon could have been any of the hundred rocks lying around. So, with no evidence or reliable eyewitness accounts, and a crime like my brothers happening almost every day in Detroit, the case remained unsolved.

No one was charged, meaning no one was punished for killing my brother. Where was the justice in that? I told the police over and over what they looked like, but without a name—as the nickname Jaws wasn't enough—and no solid leads, Damian was just another statistic.

The cops saw me as just another punk ass kid.

My mom had a mental breakdown while my dad closed himself off to any emotion. They told me it was okay and that it wasn't my fault, but when they lowered my brother into his grave, his white casket holding his broken body, it was clear that they'd wished it was my corpse they were burying and not my brother's.

My mom and dad were never the same after that. They seemed to hate one another, blaming the other for Damian's death when, in reality, they should have blamed me. But they didn't. They did something worse. They forgot I existed.

But that spurred me on to do what the police didn't. I would find those assholes and make them pay.

From the scraps of information I had, they belonged to a gang. So I took to the streets, looking for them. But I was an outsider, a privileged rich kid who was trespassing where I didn't belong. For months, I searched for them, but no one would talk. It was like they had disappeared into thin air.

Desperate and so fucking riddled with guilt, I got messed up with drugs, alcohol, girls—anything to numb the pain. I dropped out of school and ran with the wrong crowd of people who were just as fucked up as I was. I covered my body in tattoos and piercings as the pain made me feel something, but I was still dead inside.

I wanted to expose the sins on my skin, so everyone could see what I had done.

I moved out, squatting anywhere, not really caring if I lived or died. I was so fucking alone, but I deserved it. Damian would always be alone, so I vowed to be as well.

For two fucking years, I was barely alive, floating in and out of life as a stranger in my own skin. I hadn't seen my parents in months, and although they pretended to miss me, it was clear I only served as a reminder of everything they'd lost. When I left, they never asked if I'd be back.

One night, I went to score some weed when the hair on the back of my neck stood on end. I didn't know why, but when I turned and looked over my shoulder, it was like I came alive for the first time in two years.

I saw him. The spineless asshole who had a part in taking my brother's life. I would never forget him—his face was burned onto my very soul. I'd asked him for help, and in return, he ran. He had a chance to redeem himself, but now, he was shit out of luck. He may not have struck my brother, but they all played a part in his death.

Remembering my promise to kill him and remembering the paramedics prying away my brother's dead body from my arms, I was animated with a fire I hadn't felt in so long. I was seventeen, two days shy of becoming an official adult, but I was an adult long before my eighteenth birthday.

I didn't know how to make the constant grief go away. I didn't know how to make it right until I saw him.

At that moment, I knew what I had to do.

In my mind, I believed an eye for an eye would make

everything better. I'd save my parents' marriage, and I would avenge my brother's death. By killing this asshole, I believed that things would go back to the way they were.

I became obsessed, and I made it my business to know the comings and goings of one of the men who'd killed my brother.

He worked the night shift at a 7-Eleven, which was perfect. I could carry out my surveillance in the shadows, where I belonged. For two weeks, I stalked him, and when I was ready, I bought a gun off the street, so no one could trace it back to me.

I wasn't high or drunk when I lingered in the alleyway behind the store. I was calm. I waited for him to take out the trash as he did every night before 2 a.m. When the back door opened and he walked out carrying the black trash bag over his shoulder, I realized this was my moment, my moment to avenge Damian.

I stepped from the shadows, pulled the gun from my jacket, and aimed. His nametag read Lachlan. At first, he was confused, but when he saw me, he knew...he knew his day had come.

The trash bag fell to the ground as he begged for his life. He dropped to his knees, pleading I forgive him for what he did. He said it was an accident, that he didn't mean to hurt my brother, but it was too late: his apologies meant nothing to me.

He lived two years that Damian didn't, and that was two years too long. It was time.

I asked him where Jaws was, but he denied knowing his

whereabouts. That just sped up the inevitable because I knew he was lying. I cocked the gun and placed my finger on the trigger, but when he began to sob and pissed his pants, a voice I hadn't heard in so long pleaded for me not to do this. It wouldn't bring him back; it would only make things worse. But what was worse than living this life without my brother?

But that voice belonged to my brother, and it was like seeing his killer somehow brought him back to life.

The voice told me to forgive Lachlan because Damian had. He accepted his death, and now it was my turn to do the same.

Every inch of my body retaliated, desperate for bloodshed and vengeance. But when I looked into Lachlan's eyes, I realized that I was no better than him if I took his life. I was so fucking lost, but I knew I wasn't a killer.

If I did this, there would be no turning back and no tomorrow. Once again, Damian's words of wisdom saved me.

Just as I eased my finger off the trigger, Lachlan put his hand into his pocket with a grin. Instantly, visions of blood, Damian's warm, thick blood swarmed me, and my paranoid mind saw myself in a grave right next to my brother's. I wouldn't hesitate again.

Aiming the gun, I fired once with no emotion. It was the first time I shot a gun, a perfect bull's-eye straight through the middle of his chest. Lachlan blinked once before falling forward with a thud. His outstretched hand held a black velvet box, a box which I later discovered held an engagement ring.

I shot him because I thought he was reaching for a gun, but in reality, he wanted to thank me for sparing his life because he had a whole life planned with someone special. But I ruined that the moment I shot him in cold blood.

That night was the first and only time I heard Damian's voice, a sure sign he no longer called me brother. So, on that night, Cody Bishop also died, and Bullseye was born.

CHAPTER FIVE

Bull

I hadn't slept, and after reliving a nightmare I wish I could forget, I got up in the middle of the night and ran five miles. I felt remotely better, but no matter how tired I was, I knew insomnia had her grip on me and wouldn't let go.

I didn't sleep much in prison, and when I did, it was always with one eye open. Seems not much has changed. But I can't let Franca Brown be aware of this fact because if she doesn't see a change, or smells a hint of depravity on me, she'll have no issues throwing my ass back into prison. And I can't let that happen because I have work to do.

Fourteen years ago, I promised to kill those fuckers. And they're already dead. They just don't know it yet.

The only intel I got in prison was that Jaws was the kingpin of this town and a feared motherfucker. The other two were just his lackeys, meaning they're the weakest links. I will find them, and they will lead me to him.

Jaws's specialty was guns and drugs, and he had a thing for strippers, which is why I couldn't believe my luck when I stumbled across The Pink Oyster and was offered a job. I have eyes on the inside now. If his itch needs to be scratched, I'll happily scratch it with a sawed-off shotgun.

For twelve years, I lived and breathed only one thing, and that was revenge, and now it's coming to fruition. The plan is simple—find those fuckers and don't get caught. Like I said, there is no way I'm going back inside. Once it's done, and I've avenged my brother, I'll lay beside him where I belong.

However, Franca, my parole officer, cannot know of this plan, so I put on my game face as I have a date with destiny in fifteen minutes.

Once I showered, shaved, and looked like a Boy Scout in a cheap white shirt, black trousers, and suspenders, I caught the bus downtown. Franca wanted to meet at some diner. The thought of mingling with civilians is as painful as it sounds, but I don't want to hint that anything is amiss.

I need to convince Franca that I'm embracing my freedom by hugging grandmas and petting puppies and other shit like that. I don't want her to know that I'm plotting ways to kill and kill slowly. Although I don't have much of a clue on where to start, I do know that I need money to change that.

It's amazing the shit people will do for some green. I have nothing to lose and everything to gain, and I intend on digging deep until I find a lead. But in this town, money talks, which is why The Pink Oyster has been my saving grace—the perfect cover to earn some bank and get the ball rolling.

Even though Andre is a fucking tool, and Tawny can't take a hint, working there is tolerable. Lotus and the other girls are cool, but as for Tiger...my cheeks billow as I exhale in frustration. I'm still undecided about her. She confuses me. Two nights ago, when I saw her dance, I almost lost my shit. She pushes all my buttons, and the dirty fucker inside me wants to push hers...so fucking hard.

A frustrated grunt leaves me as I rub both hands over my skull, wanting to punch my own sorry ass. This needs to stop. The last time I obsessed over a girl, things didn't end well for anyone. And I have a feeling now would be no different.

Shoving open the door to the diner, I groan because Franca is already here. She's early. Sitting in a red booth in the back, she looks over the menu, pursing her pink lips from side to side. The guys in the booth across from her make it no secret that they're checking her out. If they only knew they were eye fucking the devil incarnate.

Franca is in her thirties. She's busty, blonde, and gave the guys at Kinkora some spank bank material, guards included. But her good looks haven't duped me. She is a wiseass with no filter and doesn't have time to fuck around.

Beneath that black blazer, I know she's packing heat, and she will have no issues beating me to death if I don't answer her questions adequately. She may look soft and cuddly, but she's the fucking ice queen, which is why she's been assigned to me.

Taking a seat across the table from her, I eye the guys near me, suggesting it's time they roll their tongues back into their mouths. They must be able to smell the felon on me because they soon return to whatever bullshit they were discussing over their coffee and OJ. Such trivial nonsense will never make sense to me. Who has time for chitchat?

Franca clearly does not. She doesn't even look up to greet me, though she knows I'm here.

I sit tall, waiting for her to speak because this is all a power play to her. Even though I'm no longer inside, she wants to ensure I still know who's boss. Like I could ever forget. I may be out, but I'll never be a free man.

After two minutes, she lowers her menu and smiles. It's not a welcoming sight.

"Hello, Cody."

"Sup," I reply. She knows I don't go by that name anymore, which is why she used it. That person died the night my brother did. Cody would never have the balls to do what I've done or what I intend to do. Cody was young and weak, but Bull, he's filled with bloodlust and hate.

If this were an Oprah moment, I'm sure she'd say Cody Bishop was still locked deep inside. But this is real life, and all I am is Bull—the cold-blooded murderer out for revenge.

"Staying out of trouble?"

"Sure."

Franca pushes her black-rimmed glasses up her nose, thoroughly enjoying this game. "You got a place to live?"

"Not yet. I'm staying at Hudson's Motel." Before she has a chance to ask if someone can vouch for me, I reach into my pocket and slide Venus's card across the table. "Call her and check."

She takes the business card and slides it in the inner pocket of her blazer. While doing so, I see her shoulder holster. "What about work?"

I nod, coolly folding my fingers over my stomach as I lean back into the booth. "Working at The Pink Oyster."

She cocks a brow. "The strip club?"

"Oh, you know of it?" I smirk.

She licks her top lip. "I do. I just didn't think you'd be shaking your ass so soon after prison. I thought you'd be happy to give it a rest."

Inhaling, I don't let her comment get to me. I think of the bigger picture. "I'm working as a bouncer," I clarify. "And I'm helping to fix the place up."

"No surprise, that place is a shithole," she states, reaching for her peppermint tea.

A waitress comes by the table and fills my cup with coffee and then disappears as quickly as she came. I envy her as I wish I could do the same.

Once Franca is done sipping her tea, she reaches for the brown paper bag near her and slides it toward me.

I eye it suspiciously.

"I need a piss sample," she explains flippantly. "Got to make sure you aren't getting into any trouble, and that you're clean. Being around pussy, alcohol, and drugs is not ideal, but you're working, so I'll cut you some slack."

If she's expecting me to thank her, she'll be waiting until her home, hell, freezes over.

When I grasp the top of the bag, she places her fingers over mine. Every part of me tenses. Franca merely grins, humored by my discomfort. "Don't fuck this up, Bull. You got a lighter sentence because of your circumstances and age. And the fact you took the plea deal. I mean, the first time you fired a gun, you killed someone," she bluntly reminds me.

I don't need a reminder. I got caught because an off-duty cop was inside the 7-Eleven, buying his dollar pepperoni pizza and Pepsi. When he heard the shot, he came running into the alley and caught me standing there startled with the smoking gun in my hand. I stupidly shared with him the fact I popped my gun cherry by killing a guy, which is the reason I got a lighter sentence. Whether a blessing or curse, I've yet to decide.

"But don't for one second," Franca continues, interrupting my reminiscing, "think I'll be going easy on you. Never forget who holds your balls."

All the terms of my parole are about to be forgotten if she doesn't take her fucking hands off me.

"You don't follow the rules, I will fuck you up. We clear?" The stare she levels me with reveals she is serious.

"Oh, we're clear," I reply, not intimated by her. "Now, would you so kindly... *fucking* remove your hand from mine. Please?"

I'm not asking. I'm warning her. She may be in charge, but I'll be damned if I cower in fear like a chump. She won't stand in my way.

It's the ultimate stare off, but she eventually concedes.

Without wasting a second, I stand, taking the bag with me. Making my way to the bathroom, I realize that I have a problem—a big problem—and that problem is Franca Brown.

Thankfully, Franca didn't linger once I gave her my word and piss. She said she'd be seeing me soon. I don't like the sound of that, but as long as I keep her in the dark, she has nothing on me.

Frustrated and feeling the need to break something, I decided to get pierced. Before I got locked up, I was pierced all over. Deciding to start small, I got a hoop in my left nostril. I don't do things in halves, which is why I got my tragus, forward helix, outer conch, and rook pierced on both ears.

I ran out of time because I was due in at work, but I promised the piercer I'd be back for both nipples, my tongue, and of course, my cock. That pain was unlike anything I'd felt before, which is why I want to do it again.

Seeing Franca today has left me fucking restless. Holy shit, I need to blow off some fucking steam before I explode. When I open the door and walk straight into Tiger, my feelings of exploding are amplified tenfold.

Instantly, I reach out, holding her upper arms so she doesn't fall on her ass. I don't fail to notice the goose bumps prickling her soft skin. She peers up at me from under her long lashes.

"Th-thanks," she stutters, eyes locked on mine.

"No problem," I reply, still holding her tightly.

This should be the moment I let her go, but I physically can't. I would rather cut off my hands than stop touching her, which I don't fail to understand the importance of. "What are you doing in today? You're not supposed to be working."

When her mouth parts, displaying her surprise that I'm aware of her hours, I quickly let her go. I feel like a fucking stalker, so I go to turn, but she stops me when she rockets forward and grips my wrist.

Clenching my jaw, I suppress the voices in my head to hurt her. "I like your piercings," she says on a rushed breath. "And your suspenders."

I open, but soon close my mouth because I have no idea what to say. Is she trying to make small talk? Or worse yet—chitchat?

In response, I grunt and nod, subtly moving my wrist out from under her hand. She appears angered all of a sudden, her cheeks flashing a deep red. Her eyes transform from green to pissed off in a nanosecond.

Lotus walks over to us, interrupting an exchange that probably would have ended badly for…me. Tiger tests me with those pursed lips as she stares a hole straight through me. My cock instantly twitches because hot damn, she isn't afraid of me…but she should be.

"Oh, good, you're here. I wanted to call your cell, but then realized I don't have your number," Lotus says, either oblivious or ignoring the weird vibe between Tiger and me.

"I don't have one," I reply, keeping my eyes trained on Tiger. In response, she puffs out her chest and plants her hands on her small hips, challenging me.

Sweet fuck, why is she baiting me?

"You don't have a cell or number?" Lotus asks in case she's

had a lapse in hearing.

Her question has me quickly putting an end to this stare off because I don't want Tiger knowing the reason I don't have a cell. Lotus knows I was locked up, but I don't want everyone knowing my business. The less people know about me, the better.

"Both," I coolly reply with a shrug, focusing on Lotus. I can feel Tiger's eyes all over me.

She is walking a very dangerous line.

"Not a slave to technology. I like that. But I need my staff, especially my muscle, to be accessible. I have an old cell in my office you can have."

Although that's awfully generous, I shake my head. I don't like taking things because strings are almost always attached. And I don't want any strings. "Thank you, but no. If that's the case, then I will buy one with my next paycheck."

"Oh, speaking of…come with me." Before I have a chance to get a word in edgewise, Lotus is walking in the direction of her office.

That's a hint to follow, and it's also an excuse to get the fuck away from Tiger, who looks seconds away from ripping off my balls. I don't know what I did to piss her off, but the look suits her. I knew she could hold her own, but holy fuck, she's a spitfire. Another reason I need to stay away.

I don't back down from a challenge, and if Tiger isn't careful, sooner or later, I will take the bait. And if that happens, I will break her—piece by piece.

I quickly follow Lotus, pushing past Tiger without a word. She doesn't budge when our bodies touch, which just inflames this hunger within.

Lotus waits for me in her office as I enter, and she gestures for me to close the door. I do.

"The other day, I wasn't kidding when I said I'd have you doing my books," she says, going straight in for the kill. "I have enough on my plate, and you'd be doing me a huge favor. I'll pay you, of course, for all the extra stuff you're doing around here."

I rock back on my heels, mulling over her proposal. "You barely know me." I'm not doing myself any favors, but I need to know why she'd trust me with her books after such a short amount of time.

"I know enough," she counters, opening her desk drawer and lighting a cigarette. "So whatcha say?"

I have no idea why she's putting her faith in me, but I eventually nod. "Okay."

She grins, blowing a ring of smoke. "Great. I don't suppose you'd want to start now?"

Arching a brow, I wonder why she's in such a rush. Alarm bells sound, but for some reason, I don't see Lotus as a threat. "Just tell me what you need."

She pushes back from her desk, the wheels of her chair whining across the floor. "I want it all," she replies, sealing this partnership with four simple words.

I've been stuck at this desk for hours, checking over everything twice. Lotus left me alone because the reason Tiger was in today is because the club is closed for a private event—Lotus's fortieth birthday.

She's invited everyone and anyone, which is another reason she wanted to call me before I came in. She wanted to give me the heads-up that I wouldn't be working tonight per se. But it seems that even though I'm not needed as a bouncer, Lotus has put me to work doing her books. And after looking over them, I can see why she needs another set of eyes to tell her what she knows to be true.

Things weren't adding up because she didn't want them to. But there is no sugarcoating the truth—Lotus is broke.

The money she makes barely covers her bills. The girls pay her a lousy house fee to dance there, and she doesn't bother with an offstage fee. The girls can pretty much do what they want. She also pays them an hourly rate, which is unheard of in this industry, unless you're a porn star or well-known dancer.

To make a profit, she will have to cut back on everything.

The music blares in the club along with the lively voices of the patrons. There is way too much pep for my liking, hence the reason Lotus wanted to call me. People, socializing, and pop music are so not my scene. I'm glad to be hidden away from the festivities and plan on leaving soon.

I'm hunched over the desk, writing everything down when the door opens and in sways Lotus with a bottle of vodka hanging from her fingers. After two attempts, she finally gets the door closed. Leaning back in my seat, I wait for her to speak.

She hiccups before slumping into the chair in front of me. "How bad is it?"

Sighing, I toss the pen onto the desk and shrug. "It's bad, but I have a feeling you already knew that."

She touches her nose, pointing her finger my way. "You got me."

"If you knew how bad things were, why would you bother asking me to look over your books?" I'm curious about her motives.

She takes a long sip of vodka, wiping her lips with the back of her hand. When the bottle is empty, she rolls it across the floor. "Because I wanted to make sure I wasn't missing anything, and when I saw how good you were with figures, I thought you'd be able to see something I didn't. But it seems I wasn't missing anything at all. I'm broke, right?"

"Yes," I reply without pause. If she wanted me to soften the blow, she chose the wrong man.

A small laugh leaves her, but it's filled with sadness. "Oh, Bull, what am I going to do?" She places her face in her hands.

If I had a heart, this would be the moment when I say some bullshit line to make her feel better. But I merely stare into thin air.

"I can't sell this place. No one would buy it. It's barely standing. You've seen the condition it's in. How can I compete with Blue Bloods? They've got a ping pong show, for Christ's sake!" She sits upright, shaking her head in defeat.

"What's so special about Blue Bloods?" I ask, making a mental note to scope the place out.

"For starters, the place isn't falling apart. However, Carlos has so many girls working for him, they will do anything, and I mean *anything*, for tips. The competition is tough. They gaslight as a gentlemen's club, but it's no secret if you wanted your dick sucked or wanted to rough one of the girls up, the management would happily turn a blind eye."

I grip the arms of the chair beneath me. Sounds like a place where Jaws would thrive. "Why the fuck would anyone want to work there?"

"Because they're too afraid to leave," Lotus explains. "This business is filled with sick, dangerous perverts, in case you haven't noticed. But I wanted my club to be different. I wanted my girls to be empowered while working here, not enslaved to the sexist bullshit we have to endure because we have a pussy and tits."

Amen.

"But I don't think I have a choice. If I don't come up with—" She looks at me, waiting for me to fill in the blanks.

Peering down at the scribbled notes beside me, I say, "Twenty-one thousand three hundred and seventy-two dollars and six cents."

She sighs. "If I don't come up with twenty-one thousand three hundred and seventy-two dollars and six cents, then I can kiss my dreams goodbye. Not to mention, my girls will be unemployed. That asshole Carlos is circling this place like a shark. He can smell blood, or more specifically, he can smell Tigerlily."

My spine stiffens like a rod. "What's that supposed to mean?"

Lotus tilts her head slightly, clearly stunned by my sudden need to punch something. I can't help it. Everything about this fuckstick Carlos leaves me itching for a fight.

"He wants Lily to work for him and has for a while now. He's promised to pay her a ridiculously high fee for dancing there, and he won't touch her tips. He won't charge her a house fee or an offstage fee. And doesn't expect her to tip-out. She'll have her own dressing room. Anything to sweeten the deal. Essentially, he's offering to pay her a shitload of money to work there.

"She won't go because she's loyal. But if I'm forced to sell or close this place down, she won't have a choice. Finding work in this town that pays enough to survive is close to impossible."

"You could change your liquor supplier. Increase the house fee. Stop paying the girls an hourly rate and just let them survive off their tips, which is what most strip clubs do. Take a profit from their tips," I offer, flicking through the notepad. "I've written out a list of things you could do to help lessen the debt."

"I can't do that to my girls. Besides, if I do all that, will I be able to keep this place afloat?"

With the money that's currently coming in and what's going out to expenses, it may help pay back some of what she owes, but in regard to profit, she won't be seeing that anytime soon.

"Thought so," Lotus says, reading my expression. "I either sell or—"

"Or?" I question, my interest piqued.

She pops her lips, as if weighing how much she should share. "Or I could use the place for something other than stripping."

"Like?" I coax, not liking the sound of this.

"A customer who I've come to know well is looking for a place to run his…business out of. He needs it to be discreet because well—" Her pause gives her away, but I don't adlib. I merely wait for her to spit it out.

"Because…it's an underground fighting ring."

Well, fuck me, I was not expecting her to say that. Underground fighting may introduce me to some shady characters. Perfect.

"He wouldn't need to use the club often. He said maybe twice a month because he moves around to remain undetected. But the money he's offered to pay me, Bull, it would dig me out of debt in a few months. I said no. It's too risky. But now, I might not have a choice.

"Tonight was a trial," she reveals, tonguing her upper lip. "I wanted to see what would happen if I closed the club for a 'private event.' I decided to test drive it and see what happened when we turned patrons away. It went better than expected. They all wanted to know what was so important inside. You know what happens when you tell someone not to touch something?"

I lean back in my seat. "They want to touch it," I reply, realizing she hasn't made this decision on a whim. Lotus has thought this through.

"Exactly," she says animatedly. "I could offer the club to him, closing it a couple of times a month. The mystery would excite the customers. Maybe it'll breathe new life into the place. I don't know. I need to do something."

I understand her rationale, but this isn't Hollywood. A local fight club here in Detroit is asking for trouble. She said it's underground, and the fact her friend moves from place to place is smart on their behalf, but if they get caught here in Lotus's club, it's her ass on the line.

She'll get shut down.

"I don't need to tell you this is a fucking stupid idea," I say bluntly. "But if you're doing this, I can't be here. My PO will have my balls, and I'll go back to prison."

Lotus frowns, as if just remembering the reality that I'm neutered to the state. "Shit, I'm sorry. I didn't think."

But I wave her off. "It's fine. I just need you to know that I'm out." And I will be. But that doesn't mean I can't observe from afar.

"Nothing is set in stone, but if I go ahead, I will let you know," she says quickly. "I don't want you getting into trouble."

I nod in gratitude but am pissed off it's come to this. The corporate, greedy shitheads of America strike again. The rich are getting richer, and the poor are getting poorer. Where's the justice in that?

"Go out there and have a drink for me. I only turn forty once," she says, attempting to lighten the mood.

Standing, I don't see the point in dragging this out, so I decide to leave. "I'll be in tomorrow."

Lotus quickly leaps from her chair and opens the desk drawer. She pushes aside some papers and retrieves a black phone. "Here, take it."

I eye it, shaking my head.

Before I have a chance to refuse again, she grips my hand and places it into my palm. "I insist."

This place is on the brink of foreclosure, and this woman is giving me a phone. Her kindness confuses me because it's been a long time since I've experienced anything like it.

Suddenly leery of this "warm" feeling in the pit of my stomach, I nod and shove the phone into my pocket. "Thanks."

I don't wait around for any other sentimental crap as I head to the door and open it. But then I stop in my tracks when Lotus says, "Carlos is out there. You can't miss him."

Her comment has me casually asking, "You don't know if some dude by the name of Jaws has come in here, do you?"

She seems to ponder the question, before replying, "Doesn't ring any bells."

Not wanting to rouse any suspicion, I nod. Just because she doesn't know him doesn't mean he doesn't come here. I have to stick it out. It's the best chance I have.

When I walk out into the hallway, I push past the masses loitering in the corridor, desperate to get the fuck out of here before I suffocate. The club is filled to the brim as partygoers use the stage as their dance floor. The strobe lights flash in time with the dance music blaring over the speakers, making it hard to see.

Just as I'm about to push past a couple making out in front of me because they're blocking my exit, something from the corner of the room catches my eye. Every part of my body is telling me to ignore it, but I can't because that *something* is Tiger and some slimeball who is way too close to her.

They're sitting in a booth, which is harmless enough, but when he leans in even closer to whisper into her ear, I have the urge to rip out his tongue. I watch with interest as she pulls back, mouth parted, stunned.

Her beau grins a shit-eating smile, while I clench my fists. The urge to hit something overcomes me.

Tiger suddenly bursts into laughter, reaching for her drink, but the straw misses her mouth. After three attempts, she finally maneuvers it. Taking a closer look at her clumsy demeanor, there is no doubt that she's drunk, drunk with some asshole who looks like the date rape king.

Eyeing his posse, he has two men flanking his front while another man stands behind the booth. They are definitely packing heat under their jackets. When the date rapist places his arm across the back of the leather, lounging like he's royalty, I take a stab that this is Carlos.

Lotus did say I can't miss him. Besides the fact he looks like an utter tool in his unbuttoned white shirt, revealing his gold chains and black nest on his chest, and the band of merry men surrounding him, how he is basically drooling all over Tiger confirms my thoughts.

He's looking at her like she's his next meal, and what Lotus said about him being a shark seems to sum this asshole up perfectly. He's not interested in her merely working for him. He's interested in her period, which just put him on my shit list.

I don't know why this bothers me, but it does. And before I know what I'm doing, I'm strolling toward the duo with my eyes on the prize. Tiger is too busy slurping down her drink to notice my arrival, but Carlos's monkeys instantly jump to attention.

One of them stops me from advancing any farther when he slaps his palm against my chest. With zero fucks given, I peer down at his fingers then back up at him. It seems a look can convey a thousand words as he slowly removes himself from my personal space.

Carlos is aware of my presence, but like any predator, he watches and learns.

"You got any business being here?" one trained lap dog asks me.

In response, I smile. However, it's anything but welcoming. "I should be the one asking you that. You're not welcome here. Get out."

The moron looks at his lackey, clearly confused by my bluntness. So I decide to clarify any misunderstanding. "You can walk out the door on your own accord," I calmly explain, leveling them both with a look as I point over my shoulder toward the exit, "or I can break both your legs."

A mixture of emotion passes between them, but at the forefront is anger that I would speak to them this way. "Who the fuck do you think you are?" says the bald dude who is five seconds away from losing a finger if he touches me again.

"Can you keep a secret?" I reply lightly, giving them a false sense of security. I soon shatter their refuge as I'm so done talking. Cupping my mouth, I lean in close and drop my voice an octave. "I'm Batman."

They are taken aback by my response, but their egos won't allow me to have the last word, especially when I'm making a fool of them and their pathetic attempts to intimidate me. They both reach into their jackets for their guns but are stopped swiftly when Carlos puts his hands on their shoulders.

He stands above them as the booth is on a higher level and locks his eyes with mine.

It's instant mutual hatred as Carlos sizes me up. My hackles stand on end, daring him to stop hiding behind his men like a little bitch and fight me. But men like Carlos don't get their hands dirty. They have enough money and power to bribe others to do the dirty work for them.

He coaxes the men to the side, allowing him to come face to face with me. His astute brown eyes examine me closely, looking for a weakness he can exploit. But he's looking in the wrong direction.

"What's going on?" Tiger says with a slur. When she stands to see what the commotion is, our gazes lock, and her mouth parts. "Oh, it's *you*."

I want to reprimand her for the company she keeps, but I don't show any emotion. It will end badly for us both if I do.

"Come on, I'm taking you home," I state, as this isn't up for discussion.

She's giving me seasickness from the way she sways on her feet, hinting she is way drunker than I thought. Carlos watches our exchange with interest because he still has no idea who I am.

When Tiger continues staring at me as though she's witnessing the second coming of Christ, I attempt to reach for her arm, but she recoils, knocking her off balance. She stabilizes herself by gripping the top of the booth.

"I said I'm taking you home," I repeat dangerously slow.

"And I say fuck you," she counters quickly, folding her arms across her chest in defiance.

I blink once because I'm caught off guard by her sassiness. Carlos's lips twitch.

Strike one, motherfucker.

"If this is your pickup line, may I suggest you try a different tactic."

Both my face and Tiger's screw up at his suggestion. "The only thing he knows how to pick up is cooties off Tawny. And whoever else is throwing themselves at him," Tiger spits with fire, before giggling hysterically. "I said cooties."

What in the ever-living fuck? Tawny? Cooties? I am so fucking confused.

"All right, that's enough." She is clearly intoxicated and needs to get away from fuckers like Carlos.

I march forward, ready to take her kicking and screaming if I must, but when one of the men attempts to grab me, I swiftly elbow him in the nose. It squishes under impact, and he lets out a howl. In my defense, I did warn him.

The move was so quick that his partner is left dick in hand and appears to be in disbelief that it happened. But when his friend cups his face, bright red blood slipping through his fingers, there is no mistaking that I broke his fucking nose.

Tiger gasps, eyes wide, while Carlos stands, unbending. If I didn't know any better, I'd say he was impressed. I shove past him, marching up the two stairs and into the booth.

Tiger is still motionless, but when I lunge for her, she shrinks back, wagging her finger at me. "Who do you think you are?" It seems to be the question on everyone's lips tonight. "You barely speak to me, and when you finally do, it's to scold me for having fun. Screw you."

"If you're having fun with this dipshit, then you really need to get out more. I won't tell you again," I warn, giving her one last chance to comply.

But I should have known nothing is ever easy when it comes to this woman.

"*Tell me?* No, nuh-uh." She reaches out and flicks one of my suspenders with her pointer finger. It snaps against my chest with a sharp crack. "You don't get to boss me around, buddy." She staggers forward and shoves me. Well, I think that's what she was attempting to do because I peer down at her palms, which are still firmly planted on my chest.

My body reacts just how I anticipated—I want to eat her alive.

It's a knee-jerk reaction as I grip her wrist, but instead of squeezing, I am suddenly mesmerized by the beating of her pulse and unconsciously rub my thumb over her soft skin. The touch only seems to provoke her further.

She wets her pink lips, reminding me of how they felt when she pressed them against mine. When her green eyes spark, she rouses my demons who whisper sweet nothings into my ear, begging I maim her for having such a smart mouth.

Images of Tiger on her knees before me as I punish her flood my brain. I want to do despicable, deplorable things to her, but that's not even the most fucked-up part. I want to defile her in the most depraved ways, and I think...she wants me to.

She isn't afraid of me, but I want her to be. Her rebellion sets me on fire, and it does something I never thought was possible again—it makes me feel alive.

Unable to help myself, I openly look at her, giving her a glimpse inside my blackened world. I will corrupt and pollute any purity because that's what I do. I destroy. But I can promise I will do so while making it feel good.

"Oh, god," she whimpers, fisting my shirt between her fingers.

Internally, I'm beating my chest like a fucking caveman because her pleas are music to my corrupt soul.

She blushes a sweet pink, only stroking my ego all the more. That lasts for roughly three seconds before her sweet pink turns white and then a sickly green. I know what's happening, but it's too late.

Tiger's whimpers weren't because she had fallen under my spell. No, it was because she was asking for divine intervention to stop from throwing up all over me. But God can't help either one of us because once she's done puking her guts out, she wipes her mouth with the back of hand, peers up at me sheepishly, and promptly passes out.

CHAPTER SIX

Lily

The first thing I notice is that I'm wrapped in a delicious smelling bubble of sin. The second thing is that I have no idea where I am. Groaning, I attempt to pry open my eyes, but they feel like they're weighed down with lead.

My brain is absolute mush, and I can't recall what the last thing I remember is. The only thing I'm certain of is that I'm lying against something soft that smells of juniper and a punch of spice. I want to roll in it because it smells so fucking good.

I don't remember using a new laundry detergent, so I wonder what this fragrance is. Churning through the fog, I attempt to recount the last time I smelled it. A warmth spreads over me before it turns to dread.

Oh, shit.

Ignoring every protesting muscle in my body, I jolt upright, brushing the matted hair from my face. My heart is in my throat as I frantically scan my unfamiliar surroundings. Where the fuck am I?

Another thought smashes into me.

Jordy.

Kicking off the blankets, I'm about to leap from this bed, but I notice two things—I'm not alone, and I'm not wearing any clothes. A lamp flicks on, which has me yelping.

I clutch the blanket to my chest, ready to fight for my life, but when I see who is before me, I don't know whether to be relieved or terrified. Bull is sitting in a ratty armchair in the corner of the room, playing the part of creeper perfectly.

Sitting casually with his ankle crossed over his knee, he watches me with those fucking devilish eyes. His fingers are steepled in front of his lips. I don't know why I'm here, but when I realize *where* I am, my stomach drops. I'm in a motel room, a cheap one at that, with Bull sitting feet away.

The last thing I remember is…*fuck.*

I'm still in my bra and underwear, but where are my clothes? More importantly, why am I in a motel room with a man who is nothing but trouble?

However, all of that can wait.

"Wh-where's my phone?" I sound like I gargled glass shards, but he's heard me loud and clear. He gestures with his head toward the nightstand.

I pounce on it, unlocking it with unsteady fingers. I'm about to call Erika, but when I see a thread of messages, I cock my head in confusion. Rubbing the sleep from my eyes to ensure I'm not seeing things, I read over an exchange of texts from my cell to Erika's.

> Where are you?
> Did you want me to feed Jordy?
> Are you okay?

When that text wasn't answered, Erika sent another string of messages, asking if Jordy should stay at her house, until finally, someone replied.

> Tiger is working late. Yes, to all your questions. She's fine.

Short and sweet—no guessing who replied on my behalf because I was too busy getting wasted instead of being a good mom.

Slumping back against the headboard, I run a hand over my face, beyond disappointed in my behavior last night. I was supposed to only have one drink, but that turned into ten when the man of the hour made me feel like shit once again.

I quickly send a text to Erika, thanking her for looking after Jordy and also letting her know I'll be home soon. I leave out how I have to find my clothes first. Tossing my cell onto the nightstand, I gather the courage to look at Bull, whose poker face is still set in stone.

"Where are my clothes?"

He points at the bathroom but doesn't speak. His silence

only provokes my ire.

"Why am I here? In this cheap motel with you?" The moment the question leaves me, I pale before I begin burning up.

It doesn't take a genius to put two and two together. I'm almost naked in a motel room with the man I've had this weird sexual chemistry with since the moment we met. I don't particularly like him, and he most certainly doesn't like me, which is the perfect recipe for hot, angry sex.

"Oh, god," I groan, covering my face with my palms, uncaring that I'm no longer covered. What does it matter? He saw it all last night.

"Did we...?" I don't even have the balls to ask him if we slept together. "I can't believe after practically being a nun for years, I finally get lucky in a shithole, and I can't even remember it. Please tell me we were careful?"

I omit my next question, which would have been, 'Was I any good?'

"I may be a fucked-up, sadistic bastard who is into some weird ass shit..." Has his voice always been this smooth? "But necrophilia isn't one of them."

"What?" I finally uncover my face, arching a brow.

When he pushes off the chair and stands, I hold my breath. He ambles over, coming to stop at the foot of the bed. "You're not wearing any clothes because you vomited all over them. And me. You're here because I have no idea where you live, and I wasn't going to rummage through your shit. This *shithole* is where I'm staying at the moment."

He licks his upper lip, folding his muscled arms across his

broad chest. "And no, we did not have sex."

Well, holy shit. He answered all my questions, but I still have a thousand more. This is the most he's ever spoken to me, though, so I don't push my luck. I suddenly feel like the world's biggest idiot for so many reasons.

"I'm sorry I called this place a shithole." I apologize because I just insulted his home. "Thank you for taking care of me. I was a mess last night. I'm so embarrassed."

"You shouldn't have drunk that much, especially around assholes like Carlos."

He's right. On both accounts.

I want to tell him the reason I did so was because of the way he treated me. The way he disregards me provokes me in ways I can't explain. And whenever we touch, he makes it evident he'd rather take a swim in a tankful of piranhas.

I don't know why he gets under my skin: he just does.

Thoughts of skin have me remembering how much skin I'm currently flaunting. I had no issues with my nakedness before because I thought he'd seen it all last night. But now that I know the truth, I realize what he did was actually really chivalrous, and in return, I've accused him of defiling my unconscious state and revealed the fact that I'm a born-again virgin.

This cannot get any worse.

"Is Jordy your...cat?" he asks, bringing home the fact that I'm a terrible mom.

Of course, he'd think I had a cat. What kind of mom leaves her son alone while she gets drunk with strange men?

I suddenly remember his reply to Erika. He called me

Tiger. I suppose it's short for my stage name, but Tiger and Bull—this can only lead to disaster.

Nodding quickly, I wrap the blanket tightly around me, before carefully getting out of bed. "Yes, he's my cat." I don't know why I just lied. I suppose I'm not ready to share that I have a son with someone I just met—regardless of this strange connection we have.

"And I'm a shitty mom for leaving him with my friend. I better get home." However, the issue of not having any clothes may hinder my departure.

Bull sighs before sauntering over to the dresser. He doesn't even know he's *sauntering*. This man radiates swagger. He produces a pair of sweats and a well-loved AC/DC T-shirt. "Here."

With no other choice, I shuffle over, ensuring I don't fall onto my ass, and reach for his clothes. Our fingers brush, but I muffle my whimper. "Thank you again." I desperately want to ask why he came to my rescue last night, but I don't.

I feel dwarfed in his presence as he holds me prisoner with an intense stare. "Can I ask you a question?"

"Two minutes ago, I thought we got busy, so you don't have to ask permission," I tease lightly.

But when Bull cocks a brow, appearing confused by my taunt, I clarify, "Of course you can."

"What did Carlos whisper in your ear?"

I screw up my nose as I have no idea what he said to me because I'm sure it was the usual shit. But when Bull seems to hang onto my reply, I dig deep and remember. "He asked what it would take for me to come work for him."

Bull clenches his jaw.

"I've told him I'm not leaving Lotus. She's been good to me, and I would never do that to her. When I told him no, he offered to buy me a car. My reply was something along the lines of I'm not a whore. And his response was my girl could never be a whore." I roll my eyes because his cheesy line still makes me want to hurl.

Carlos has made it no secret that he wants me to dance at his club, and he's also been very forthright about how that's not the only thing he wants. Lotus can't kick him out because he's a paying customer when he comes in to watch me dance. I only humor him because he leaves me ridiculous tips.

He sees me as a pawn, so I play the game.

But I would never fall for his bullshit. He promises me cars, money, and my own private dressing room at his club Blue Bloods. But men like Carlos are collectors, and I'm just a trophy he wants to add to his collection.

He could promise me the world, and it still wouldn't make a difference. He doesn't stir a longing deep within me where I find it impossible to breathe when he's near. Even though I haven't dated in a very long time, I know when I'm attracted to someone, and I'm definitely not attracted to Carlos.

However, the man standing in front of me, watching me closely, stirs something I've not felt before. I don't understand my response to him. I know nothing about him, but that intrigues me all the more. I'm so used to men being all up in my face all the time, but with Bull, it's different.

I wonder why he's living here. What happened to his home? I can't shake the feeling he's hiding something monumental, something which has shaped him into this sometimes shy, always brutal creature.

So much is going on behind those mismatched eyes, eyes I can't stop looking into because it seems as though he's battling both good and bad. Light and dark. I wonder which side will eventually win.

Taking a small step forward, he peers down at me, studying my body language with what seems to be inexperience. Sometimes, he comes across as so…naïve to the happenings of the world. I know he felt something when I kissed him. His erection was a sure sign of it.

But most of the time, my presence seems to repulse him.

I'm so confused, and his eyes are the perfect analogy to how I feel. I like and hate him all in the same breath; both sides fighting for domination over the other. The jury is still out on which side will win.

"Your eyes are really something," I stupidly say aloud, caught under their spell. When I realize what I just said, I open my mouth, ready to backtrack, but then decide not to.

I can acknowledge this weird, tangible tension between us. And I want him to also.

His chest rises and falls steadily, the tempo almost lulling me into a contented slumber. What is it about him that sucks me into this blackened abyss?

"Something what?" he asks, his breathing even while I'm moments away from gasping for air.

Even though I'm wrapped up tight, I suddenly feel naked. I've never felt more exposed than I do right now, which is saying a lot, seeing as I take off my clothes most nights. But the way Bull studies me, awaiting my answer, leaves me stripped bare before him.

And at that moment, I realize I am in so much fucking trouble.

With nothing to lose, I lick my lips before replying, "Something...special."

He sighs deeply, giving nothing away. But I don't expect him to.

With nothing further to say, I turn around and make my way into the bathroom. When I close the door, I press my back against it and let out what feels like the breath I've been holding since we first locked eyes. I don't know what's going on between us, but I do know I like it. I like it a lot.

I knock on Erika's door, feeling like the world's shittiest mother. It opens, and when I see my neighbor, I sheepishly offer the bunch of flowers I bought for her. They're wilted, but it was all I could find at the local corner store.

She accepts them with a slanted smile. "Come in."

I commence my walk of shame, feeling even worse when I round the corner and see Jordy sitting cross-legged on the couch, eating a bowl of cereal with Erika's son, Patrick, who is the same age. They're watching TV and don't notice I'm here. "Hi, baby," I say, hoping my guilt doesn't show. It does.

"Hey, Mom," Jordy replies, looking at me briefly before returning to whatever show is on the TV. This is how our conversations usually go lately. He's so angry with me, and I don't know why.

Erika is at my side, peering down at my baggy clothes with a confused grin. "Do you want a coffee? I just made a pot."

Erika has been a life saver. She's looked after Jordy when my babysitters have been late or haven't turned up at all. Patrick and Jordy have become best friends, and Erika makes it no secret she wishes we followed in their footsteps.

But I barely have enough time to be friends with myself and my son, let alone my neighbor. And besides, if we happened to become friends, I'd have to tell her the truth. She doesn't know I strip. No one does. She thinks I work the night shift at a Walmart downtown between my ballet classes.

This is how I live my life—a lie. I distance myself from everyone, even Avery, because it's just easier this way.

"I wish I could, but I have so much to do today. It's my only day off." This isn't a lie.

Once I've showered, I thought Jordy and I could go to the movies. We haven't had enough mother and son time, and although he'll think it's lame when I bribe him with the latest *Avengers* film and whatever snacks he wants, I know he'll cave.

Erika nods with a smile, which has me feeling beyond shitty for not wanting to spend time with her. "Come on, Jordy. Let's go home."

He grumbles under his breath but eventually stands and goes to grab his things.

I wait for him to stop dawdling, but I suppose as a preteen, he has no concept of time. When he finally emerges,

I thank Erika and say goodbye to Patrick. When Jordy and Pat do some weird gangster handshake, I pale because this is the reason I want to get the hell out of Detroit.

Jordy is about to leave, but I clear my throat, giving him "the look." He reads it loud and clear. "Thanks, Ms. Howard, for letting me stay the night."

"Of course, honey, you're welcome anytime."

Placing my hand on Jordy's shoulder, I give Erika a thank-you smile, and we leave her apartment. My apartment is just down the hall from hers. Once I open the door, I instantly want to curl under my blankets and sleep the day away.

But I had enough me time last night when I got drunk and then woke up in a motel room.

Shaking those thoughts aside, I walk into the kitchen, desperate for some coffee. As I put the kettle on, I call out to Jordy who went to his bedroom. "How about we go see the new *Avengers* movie today? It'll be fun."

"Sure," he replies, a lot less enthused than I am. But that's okay. At least he agreed.

Being a single mom has been tough. I've tried my hardest to be there for him, but with no family or friends, he had to grow up fast. When I look at him, I can't help but feel guilty for robbing him of his childhood; on the many nights I was forced to work late, he had to fend for himself.

I always had neighbors and Avery who helped me out, but it wasn't the same for Jordy. I know, in a way, he despises me, blaming me for his father leaving. His father was the love of my life, a good man who I could only love in secret.

I was head over heels for my brother's best friend, but they were opposites. I never understood how they were friends, but I suppose growing up poor creates a bond like no other. I was barely sixteen when I found out I was pregnant. But for the first time in my life, I was happy because Michael wanted to have the baby.

He said he'd tell Christopher about us because he didn't want us to be a secret anymore. But he soon proved to be another disappointment in life because I wasn't even six weeks pregnant when he left us.

He left without a word, and to this day, I have no idea where he is.

I was heartbroken, but I couldn't share that with Christopher. No matter that I would now be a single mom, I would never betray Michael like he did to me. When I began to show, Christopher's big brother protective mode went into overdrive, demanding I tell him who the father was.

But I never told. And after a while, Christopher stopped asking.

I only met a few of his friends because he was very protective of me. He rarely let me out of his sight, but the times he did was when I could be alone with Michael.

I didn't know what he did late at night, but I imagined it wasn't good, especially when I was cleaning blood and god knows whatever else from his clothes. But I didn't judge. We all had our flaws. And that's how I remember my brother.

He wasn't perfect, but he was all I had in this world. So when he also left me, a small part of me went with him. Getting pregnant changed our relationship. I was his little sister, the person he protected, but having a baby changed that. It wasn't just us anymore. I hurt him. I also betrayed him by going behind his back. All he did was try to better my life, and in return, I fell in love with his best friend when I knew it would wound him. I live with that guilt every day of my life.

Although I don't know where he is, I continue to hope he'll come back into my life and let me make it up to him.

I know Jordy is missing a male figure in his life, which is the reason he's acting out. His psychologists have confirmed it. He's been kicked out of five different schools for fighting, bullying, and vandalism, among other things.

His psychologist diagnosed him with ADHD. And the reason he hates school so much is because he's dyslexic. I can't blame him for being frustrated because kids can be cruel. I work so much because even though the private school he's currently enrolled in is smaller and better catered for his needs, it's not cheap.

Neither are his therapy sessions as well as his tutoring.

I can't afford all of this waiting tables. And I have no other qualifications other than my love for dance. Everything I do, I do for Jordy because when I look into his blue eyes, all I see staring back at me is his smart, funny, and gentle father who wouldn't hurt a soul. He was perfect.

But me, I am anything but perfect, and I can't help but blame myself for the way Jordy turned out. My genes polluted the gene pool, not Michael's. And I will spend the rest of my life making it up to my son. I won't allow him to live the same childhood I did.

When Jordy walks into the kitchen, I quickly wipe away the lone tear with the back of my hand. I don't want him to see me cry.

"What time is the movie?" he asks, slumping into a kitchen chair. He's wearing clothes about two sizes too big for him and has a red bandana wrapped around his head. He looks like his uncle used to.

Switching off the kettle, I reach for the instant coffee. "About two hours," I reply. "But we're not going anywhere with you dressed like that."

"Like what?" he rebukes, poking out his bottom lip.

"Like a wannabe gangster."

"I am a gangster," he says proudly while the spoon trembles in my hand.

"In this house, you're Jordan Hope. Now go change."

"Mom!" he whines, but this isn't up for discussion.

When he sees I'm serious, he stomps off to his room, mumbling under his breath. If only my mom did that to Christopher, our lives would have turned out so differently. But you live and you learn, and I won't make the same mistakes she did.

The movie was great, and mother son day was a complete success. When we bumped into one of Jordy's friends at the mall, he begged to go to his house to play the latest video game and have a sleepover. I only agreed because his friend's mom was there and said it was okay.

Parenting is about balance, and I don't want to give my

son too much freedom like my mom did with Christopher and me, but I don't want to be a helicopter parent either.

Once I got home, I crashed, absolutely exhausted. The only thing that wakes me is a knock on the door. Groaning, I fumble for the clock on my bedside table and see that it's after ten. Who the hell is knocking on my door at this time of night?

Kicking off the blankets, I tiptoe through the apartment. When I get to the front door, I look through the peephole but don't see anyone outside. I'm wondering if I dreamed it but decide to open the door a fraction to make sure.

Unlocking the door, I open it slowly, but keep the chain in place. As I peer through the crack, I see a small gift box with a pink ribbon sitting in front of my door. Getting on my knees, I reach through the gap and drag the box inside.

Once the door is shut and relocked, I turn the box over, but there is no card or sender's address. Curiosity gets the better of me, and I pad back into my bedroom. Sitting on the end of the bed, I carefully unwrap the meticulously wrapped box.

The blue velvet box feels expensive, and when I open it, the diamond earrings only confirm my thoughts. There is a small card inside, and although what's written on there isn't much, it's enough.

Only the best for my girl.
~C

There is only one person whose name just happens to

start with a C who thinks I'm his girl. Fucking Carlos.

The earrings are beautiful, and their sparkle practically reflects rainbows all over the room, but I would rather be eclipsed in darkness than be bought this way. This is just a chance to flash his wealth, hoping I finally cave.

But I'm not a whore. This expensive gift and his promises to take care of me only seem to deepen the line in the sand between us. He thinks he can buy me because I'm poor and he's, well, he's an asshole who needs to be put in his place.

I have no idea how he knows where I live, and if he thinks leaving gifts at my doorstep is cute, he's shit out of luck.

Springing into action, I rip off my pajamas and step into my jeans. I'm about to put on a sweater, but Bull's AC/DC T-shirt catches my eye. I regretfully took it off when I showered earlier today, but now, I lunge for it, and the moment I slip it over my head, I inhale deeply because all I can smell is him.

It's way too big, so I tie a knot in it and wear it Daisy Duke style.

I remember the way he looked last night in his suspenders, black pants, and white button-down with the sleeves rolled up, exposing his taut, tattooed forearms. He looked like he ate a hipster for breakfast and stole his clothes.

Once I'm in my Chucks and black hoodie, I grab my keys, only to realize my truck is still at work. Bull must have caught an Uber or cab back to the motel with me in tow. My plan to rip Carlos a new one is put on pause, but when I look at my reflection in the mirror, or more accurately, when I look at Bull's T-shirt, I'm suddenly zapped with a surge of adrenaline.

He's never backed down from a fight before and neither

will I.

As I'm charging out my front door, I organize an Uber, who thankfully arrives only seconds after I catch the elevator downstairs. The driver isn't one to socialize, which suits me just fine. I send a text to Jordy's friend's mom, who confirms the boys are having a fun time.

It's a rainy night in Detroit, but give it a month or so, and the snow will commence. Once the Uber drops me off at work, thankfully not asking any questions, I slip on my hood and lower my face, wanting to remain incognito.

My truck is parked out back, so I quicken my steps as one of the dim streetlights has blown. The area isn't normally well lit, so now, it's almost impossible to see in front of you. The wind howls around me.

Just as I round the brick wall and see my truck, I sigh in relief, but that is short lived because by the time I realize what's happening, it's too late. I don't have a chance to fight or scream. I'm lifted off the ground, and a hand clamps over my mouth as an unknown assailant drags me toward the alley.

I wriggle madly, kicking and flailing with muffled screams, but my assailant, who I'm certain is a man, snickers at my attempts to flee. His humor surpasses my sudden fear, and I bite down so hard, I taste blood. He grunts in pain, taking his hand off my mouth for a split second, and that is all the time I need. I scream so loudly it hurts my own ears, but the sound is my ticket to freedom.

He fumbles, attempting to silence me, but his panic allows me to strike my foot backward and connect with his shin. His knee buckles, and he loosens his hold around me. Instantly, I scramble free, finding my footing on the wet ground.

I make it only two feet before the asshole grips my hair and thrusts my head back at a painful angle. I fight like a wild cat, attempting to turn around and connect with any part of his body I can reach, but I drop to my knees in agony when he punches me in the kidney.

Gasping for breath, I clutch my back, my body aching. I want to curl into a ball because it hurts so badly. But I won't surrender. With a roar, I swivel on my knees, primed on punching him in the balls, but he wraps his hand around my throat, forcing me to stand.

I slap at his hand because his grip is so tight that I can't breathe. But when he tightens his hold, it appears that's what he wants. He's fucking choking me.

He's wearing a ski mask, so his identity is concealed, which has me wondering what the fuck I ever did to him. His eyes look...familiar. But I don't know where I've seen them before. Was I right? *Was* someone watching me all along?

I'm being choked to death in a parking lot by an unknown assailant. I refuse to accept this as my fate.

I swing out, hoping to connect with him, but the harder I fight, the more air I need. And seeing as I'm being choked, air is something I don't have. I begin to panic; my eyes widen as I frantically claw at the hand around my throat.

In response, he lifts me off the ground.

I'm certain my neck is about to snap, and tears begin to fall. I'm not sad; I'm so angry it has come to this. Another statistic, the news will say, because I got what I deserved. That's how fucked up this world is.

"Please…don't," I beg, coughing and spluttering as I gasp for air. "I have…a s-son."

But he only presses down on my windpipe harder.

Jordy will be alone. If I die, he will have no one. This can't end this way. Hell to the fuck no.

My legs are strong, thanks to all the dancing, so I steady my breathing and kick out. I connect with something solid, and the air suddenly returns to my lungs. On my hands and knees, I inhale rapidly, desperate to fill my oxygen-deprived lungs.

I give myself a moment of reprieve and am about to fight for my life, but when I peer up, I see something that makes no sense. My assailant is no longer the hunter—he is now the hunted.

Time moves in slow motion as I watch a feral force comparable to a hurricane rain down fury like no other on my assailant. He staggers back, attempting to stay upright, but my hurricane doesn't let him.

In quick succession, he punches my attacker in the ribs and stomach, then repeats on both sides. It's a flurry of fists, and blinking prevents me from witnessing the attack because it's so fast. However, when my rescuer turns to face me, the air is siphoned from my lungs for another reason.

I can't breathe because my savior is Bull.

Coming to a shaky stand, I watch on the sidelines as Bull beats the living shit out of my assailant. The guy tries to connect with him, but Bull is too fast. He ducks and weaves, his lips twisting into a mocking grin. It's the first time I've seen him smile.

He's baiting the guy to fight him. It's like he is getting off on the altercation.

Something shiny catches the moonlight before Bull brings his foot down on the guy's knee, shattering his kneecap. He drops to the ground with a thud, shrieking in pain. He begs for mercy, but Bull shows him none as he pins the guy to the asphalt by holding down his shoulder and connecting with his face over and over again.

The ski mask isn't a suit of armor, and before long, the man stops moving. But that doesn't deter Bull. He continues to hit him, the sounds a hollow emptiness, which turn my stomach. He is brutal, frenzied, a vision of destruction and pain.

"Bu—" I try to speak, but I feel like my vocal cords have been grated raw. But even if I could speak, I don't think I'd be able to stop Bull. He won't be satisfied until this man is dead.

As much as he deserves it, I can't live with that on my conscience, so with a stagger, I hobble toward Bull. The man's head lolls from side to side from the fierce punches. He no longer puts up a fight because I think he's out cold.

Just as Bull is about to bring down his fist, I snare it midair. He snarls, swiveling to look at who dares to stop him, but when he sees it's me, he blinks once.

"He's had enough," I croak in a whisper.

Bull's lip curls, ready to fight me like a dog protecting his bone, but not overthinking it, I slide my hand toward his and interlock our fingers. The warm blood seeps between my fingers, but I only squeeze harder.

"He's had enough when he's stopped breathing," he spits

with venom. He tightens our connection, fire burning behind his glare.

"Please, don't do this. Let the police take care of him."

From the corner of my eye, I see a small group of people huddled off to the side. No doubt, the police have already been called.

Bull examines me closely as if he's witnessing something he's not seen before. I don't know what it is, but it makes me tremble all over.

With our fingers still locked, he nods once. "I can't be here when they do."

I don't know why that is, but I don't care. "My truck is here."

Bull clenches his jaw as though he is once again battling heaven and hell. He looks down at the non-moving man as if transfixed by the sight. When his shoulders shudder on a deep exhale, I know I've won.

Severing our connection, he rises slowly. "Let's go."

I desperately want to see who this masked coward is, but when the street is lit up with approaching blue and red lights, that's our cue to leave.

Bull turns quickly but stumbles to the left. We both are puzzled by the movement because he wasn't the one who got beaten unconscious until I scan down his body and yelp. "Oh my god! You've b-been st-stabbed!"

With a shaky finger, I point at his torso.

Bull's attention focuses on the silver knife protruding from his side. "It's just a scratch," he states with a shrug.

"A scratch?" I cry, bile rising when he touches the wound

and his fingers come away red.

"Yes, I'm good. Where's your truck?"

My eyes are glued to the knife impaling his side. "You ne-need to go to the hospital." Hysteria begins to rise. I was running on adrenaline, but now that that's worn off, I am seconds away from losing it.

"I'm so s-sorry. This is my fault."

My knees buckle, and I'm about to hit the pavement. But that doesn't happen because with a poised move, Bull wraps one large hand around the back of my neck while the other grips my waist. This is the first time he's touched me without flinching.

Our faces are inches apart, and this close to him, I take him in. He is rugged, wild, dominant, but I don't feel afraid. "Never apologize for something that isn't your fault."

My mouth opens and closes uselessly because I can't construct a coherent sentence.

"Now, give me your keys. I'm driving."

The wailing of the police sirens gets louder, and that's all the wake-up call I need. Licking my lips nervously, I state with newfound confidence, "No one drives my truck. And you've been stabbed, just in case you've forgotten."

Bull's lips tilt into a semblance of a smile, and the sight stirs deeply within me. "Then let's haul ass...Tiger."

My head bobbles a nod, and we commence a quick walk toward my truck. Both our faces are downturned, disguising who we are, but when Bull walks past the man on the ground, he clenches his jaw. I know it's killing him not to take off the ski mask, and if his fury wasn't clouding his judgment, he probably would have done so before rendering him unconscious. But now, to do so, Bull would have to reveal his identity to the nosy bystanders. And he clearly doesn't want to do that.

After fumbling with the zipper on my backpack, I finally get out my keys. Unlocking my door, I get into the driver's side before whimpering in absolute pain as I reach across the middle console to open Bull's door. He jumps in, appearing untroubled by the knife sticking out of his side.

My truck is slow to start, but once the engine turns over, I tear out of the parking lot, the realization of what just happened hitting hard. My hands are shaking so badly, I grip the steering wheel tighter to maintain control.

Bull leans back in the chair, breathing deeply through his nose. He must be in pain. And when I hit the curb because my eyes are on him and not the road, he grunts loudly.

"Oh god, I'm sorry."

"Stop apologizing," he barks through a winded breath. "Where you going?"

"To the hospital," I hoarsely reply, thankful the traffic is light.

"No, no hospital. Take me back to the motel," he argues.

"Are you mad?" I exclaim with a winded wheeze, flicking my attention back and forth between him and the road. "Your name suits you perfectly. You're stubborn like a bull!"

He groans in frustration, arching his head backward to lean on the headrest. "I'm stubborn?" he argues. "Why are *you* so fucking stubborn, woman?"

"Um, firstly, do not call me woman. This isn't the Stone Age."

"Duly noted," he replies, appearing, god forbid, humored by my response.

"And I'm taking you to the hospital because you've been stabbed!"

"Yes, I know. I can feel it." His lips twitch. "There is no need to keep reminding me."

Is he making jokes?

This night just keeps getting crazier by the minute.

"No hospital."

When he refuses to budge about the hospital, I take a left and head to the motel. "Once you drop me off, you need to go to the hospital, though. You're hurt."

My entire body chooses this moment to spasm in pain, but I ignore it, and his bossiness, and shake my head firmly. "No, I'm not leaving you. You've been sta—" I bite my lip as he knows what he's been.

"Nice T-shirt," he says, while I keep my eyes ahead, embarrassed. We ride the rest of the short trip to the motel in silence.

When I pull into the parking lot, I park in front of his room. I kill the engine and quickly open my door to help him out. But he's already hobbling to his room. I chase after him, winded and in agony, but I mask it because I'm not the one with a knife in my torso.

When Bull opens the door, he limps to the bathroom while I close and lock the door behind me. I don't know what the right protocol is here. Should I call someone?

I lean against the door, biting my thumbnail nervously. When Bull emerges from the bathroom with supplies in hand, I pale.

"Can you get whatever alcohol there is out of the minibar?" When I merely stare at him wide-eyed, he adds, "Please."

Working on autopilot, I quickly do as he asks. There are two bottles of scotch and one bottle of vodka. I grab all three.

He slumps onto the end of the bed, tossing the towels and sewing kit onto the mattress. When I see the complimentary kit, I cover my mouth to hold back the vomit.

"Let me drive you to the hospital," I plead, as there is no way he will be able to sew himself back up with the flimsy needle and thread.

He ignores me and instead gestures with his head for the alcohol.

My legs are trembling as I walk over to the bed and pass them to him. He accepts and throws them onto the mattress. "If you're queasy or going to faint, it's best you leave now."

"Why?" I squeak, suddenly feeling unsteady on my feet.

"Because I'm going to take this knife out," he replies as though we're discussing the weather.

"Oh, sweet baby Jesus!" I begin to pace the room, interlocking my hands behind my neck.

Bull allows me the time to process the inevitable, but I shake my head animatedly and woman the fuck up. "It'll be fine," I say aloud, more for myself than for Bull. I've had a baby, for fuck's sake. What can be worse than that?

Taking three deep breaths, I nod quickly. "Okay, do it."

Bull exhales sharply, one hand supporting his flesh beneath the wound while the other grips the handle of the knife. Those eyes focus on mine, and somehow, they tell me it'll be all right. He's about to pull a knife out of his body, and he's the one comforting me.

My infatuation for this man just grows.

"One." He inhales, thoughtfully giving me a countdown.

"Two," I squeak, unable to look away from his bloody fingers gripping the handle. My mouth is parted, in the midst of saying three, but Bull doesn't give me a chance because he swiftly yanks out the knife and drops it to the floor with a thud.

"And th-three," I stammer, needing to talk before I pass out.

Bull swiftly reaches for the towel and places it over the wound while I sway on my feet. There is so much…blood. The white towel is soon soaked a bright red. Bull casually peers down, patiently waiting for the bleeding to stop.

He breathes evenly through his nose, but when he shifts and finches slightly, the sight of him in pain has me forgetting my queasiness, and I rush over to the bed. Sitting near him, I slowly reach out to remove his hand.

His body tenses, but he allows me to touch him. "Stop worrying about me. I'm fine."

Ignoring him, I gently remove the towel from his wound, but I can't see anything because his T-shirt is in the way. "Take off your shirt," I demand, not even thinking twice about my request.

He hesitates. The tangible tension filling the room is bound to suffocate me. Needing to say something, my lips turn up into a small grin. "You've seen me with no clothes on. Now it's my turn."

The gap between us suddenly crackles with an electrical charge I feel all the way to my toes.

His hesitation has me wetting my lips because I'm suddenly parched, but water won't satisfy the thirst I feel. With eyes pinned to me, he reaches behind his head and grips the back of his collar as he unhurriedly exposes inch after glorious inch of inked skin.

It's too much, too fast, but I can't look away. I am transfixed by his strong, muscled chest, and defined abs that ripple as he twists and tosses his shirt to the floor. He is covered in tattoos, and when I say covered, I mean there isn't much skin left to ink.

The artwork seems to emphasize his tapered waist and well-defined V muscle. It's a visual feast as I examine every hardened inch of him, wanting nothing more than to study each tattoo. But when a trickle of red pours from a small hole in his side, I stop gawking and quickly reach for the clean towel. Pressing it over his wound, I don't have the guts to look at him as I don't trust the look in my eyes.

The room falls silent, our heavy breathing the only sounds filling the small room. I don't know how much pressure to apply. "Am I hurting you?" I ask softly. Using my hair as a shield, I'm unable to look at him just yet.

"No," he replies in a tone similar to mine.

Nodding, I continue pressing the towel to his wound, wishing I knew what to say. The towel isn't as soaked as the first, which has me hoping the bleeding has slowed. I glance at the sewing kit on the bed, my stomach roiling.

When Bull shifts slightly, I can't help the gasp which

escapes me. "What happened?" I ask before I can stop myself. Even beneath his tattoos, the large scar on his side is clearly visible. When I take a closer look, however, that isn't the only scar he has. He has many. The one down his left eyebrow has always left me curious.

When he doesn't reply, I peer up at him from under my lashes, holding my breath. "Life," he finally replies, setting me alight with one word and the weight of a thousand pounds.

My skin breaks out into goose bumps when he wraps his fingers around my wrist. I don't know what he's doing until he gently coaxes my hand away from his wound. Snapping to attention, I notice the bleeding has stopped, but the red, angry slash is still very much open.

Swallowing, I dare not breathe as he reaches for the mini bottle of scotch and unscrews the lid. He takes a swig, then offers me one. I shake my head. He pours the remaining alcohol over his wound, closing his eyes briefly.

This would probably be easier in the bathroom, but I have a feeling we both need to be sitting for what's about to happen next. Bull opens the sewing kit, and with bloody fingers, he begins to thread the cotton through the eye of the needle.

His fingers are steady while I have to sit on mine to stop the trembling.

He opens another bottle of scotch, and this time, he throws back the entire bottle. Once he's done, he inhales and gathers the flesh around the wound. As he is about to pierce his skin with the needle, I lunge forward, cupping my hand over his.

"Let me," I offer. I feel like this is something I need to do.

Bull seems almost…fascinated by us touching, and I don't know why that is. His blood stains us both, and while most would be repulsed by the sight, it seems to excite him. But I established long ago that Bull isn't like most.

With a sharp nod, he allows me to take the needle from his hand. Rising from the bed, I gradually drop to my knees before him. Something dark overtakes him, but that darkness enlivens me. It has every fiber of my body standing to command.

Focusing, I gently pinch his skin and look up at him. "Tell me if you need me to stop."

"I won't need to." There is nothing arrogant about his reply. His candor is sincere. With a firm nod, I will my shaky fingers to still and pierce his skin.

The gasp leaves me and not him, as he is unmoving, like he didn't just get stabbed once again. Thinking this is similar to a Band-Aid, I pull the thread through and then pierce his flesh once again. I stitch him up carefully, ensuring the gap is small between each one.

Each time the needle penetrates his flesh, my nausea rises, but I stamp it down. His body is hot to the touch, and it thaws the chill from my bones. Before long, I'm burning up for so many different reasons. His signature fragrance is amplified tenfold. I chew the inside of my cheek to suppress my whimper.

I'm almost done, proud of my efforts not to pass out or throw up, but when Bull's hard abs undulate as he appears uncertain for a second before he leans forward, I realize I might pass out for an entirely different reason. If not for my heightened state, I would have missed it, but it feels like a lover's caress when Bull cautiously takes a strand of my hair between his fingers.

He gently slides his fingertips over my locks, as if feeling something for the first time. I pause, unsure what's going on. "Your hair…it smells like cherry blossoms," he finally declares in what sounds like awe, breaking the silence.

"It's my sh-shampoo," I stutter, unable to meet his eyes. When he doesn't say anything else, I continue to stitch him up. He doesn't let go of my hair.

I have no idea how I was able to keep my hand steady, but once the wound is closed, I tie a knot in the cotton and snip it with the scissors. Leaning back on my heels to examine my handiwork, my hair slips from Bull's fingers.

"All done," I state, finally finding the nerve to look up at him. "I still think you need to see a doctor."

"I'll be fine," he rebukes, reaching for the vodka and offering it to me. This time, I accept. I drink half and then hand him the rest.

He takes his time savoring it, his predominant Adam's apple bobbing as the liquor slides down his throat. I can't help myself and give in to temptation, tilting my head to examine his tattoos. His entire chest is inked with a detailed piece of what looks to be the four horsemen of the apocalypse riding into a barren forest with twisted, bare trees. Down his ribs and stomach is a scene straight from hell.

There are half skeletal, half living men riding horses with swords raised, prepared for battle. Throughout the intricate piece lay broken men, dead or begging for mercy. But nothing is merciful about this tattoo. He has what appears to be the all-seeing eye in a triangle in the middle of his chest. The eye follows me. So do the owl's eyes he has inked on his right forearm. Always alert, always watching.

His right bicep has an hourglass. The pocket watch he has tattooed on the back of his hand has me wondering what his fascination with time is. And on his left bicep, he has a spread of four aces. However, on his tattoo, the traditional playing card suits are replaced with images that must mean something to him.

There is what appears to be a lion, a green diamond, a blindfolded woman, and a blue shark. The lion has a cross tattooed in the corner where the image of the suit should be. I have no idea what it means, but the closer I look and uncover the hidden images beneath the artwork, the more curious I become.

I can't see his back, but from the small glimpse I saw, it too is covered. He has all the pieces to this complex puzzle inked on his skin, and all I want to do is study each one. The silver medallion of St. Christopher he wears around his neck is just another riddle. Bull doesn't strike me as a religious person, so I wonder what its significance is to him.

"I don't think tonight was a random attack," Bull says, snapping me from my gawking. "He would have stolen something. Or tried to rape you."

I gulp at his candidness because he's right. At no time during the assault did I think he wanted to steal my bag or virtue. He was out for blood.

I'm still on my knees and lost in thought when, with a

hesitant touch, Bull reaches down and cups my throat gently. With his fingertips, he caresses my neck slowly where I have bruises forming from the hands that tried to squeeze the life from me. "He was trying to kill you," he states, dangerously low.

I remain perfectly still, not daring to breathe as I am utterly intoxicated by this moment, by him.

Bull can feel the steady beat of my pulse, which begins to pound faster and faster as he examines me more closely. "Is there someone who wants you dead?"

"I don't think so," I reply, my reddening cheeks betraying my response to him.

"Thinking so isn't going to cut it. It's the difference between life and death." His grip on me tightens, emphasizing his warning.

The line between pleasure and pain begins to blur, but I don't move. The way he touches me is hypnotic, and I forget everything but this sensation, which makes no sense. "I have no idea. But lately, I've felt like someone has been watching me," I explain on a rushed breath.

"For how long?"

"Not long," I reply, hating how flippant I sound, but it's the truth. I don't know how long because ever since Christopher left, I've always been looking over my shoulder.

"Any clients or ex-boyfriends you pissed off who would want to settle a score?"

He strokes his thumb over my pulse, his gaze never wavering from mine as he awaits my reply. But being this way with him has me forgetting my own name. I haven't felt *this* in so very long, and I don't know what to think or how to react to the way my body, my entire being responds to him.

It doesn't make a lick of sense because I barely know him. But I've felt this undeniable pull from the first moment I saw him in the club. He guards secrets—deep, dark ones—yet that only lures me in deeper.

"No. I don't have issues with anyone that would warrant my attack," I finally reply. I decide to omit the fact his eyes looked familiar because I can't even remember what they looked like.

Bull nods sharply before removing his hand. I instantly miss his touch. "You need to be careful. I'll keep an eye out at the club. You should tell Lotus."

Reality kicks in, and I realize I'm still kneeling between Bull's legs. Unable to help myself, my gaze drifts to the front of his black jeans. Memories of his arousal pressed against me have me rising quickly because, unlike Bull, I can't hide my emotions.

"Thank you for coming to my rescue yet again. If it wasn't for you..." I rub my arms, a sudden chill coming over me.

"There's no need to thank me," he rebukes, coming to a stand as something changes inside him. I don't know why thanking him has pissed him off, but it has.

For a split moment, his walls were lowered, and what I saw took my breath away, but they're erected again, and the hard-hearted, aloof bastard is back. I don't like this version.

I don't know what's supposed to happen because now that he's stitched up and I'm as okay as I can be, considering what happened, it's time for me to go home. That awkward tension lingers in the air because if Bull asked me to stay the night, I don't know what I would say.

Most men would try to take advantage of this situation, but not Bull. I respect him for that, but on the flipside, I also feel like the ugly duckling.

Men usually throw themselves at my feet, but I still don't even know if Bull likes me. And when he stands in the middle of the room, basically showing me the door, I take that as confirmation that whatever I feel is one-sided. He is just another asshole. One I need to forget about.

"I'll see you at work." I try to keep the emotion from my voice.

Suddenly, the walls close in on me, and I grab my bag, marching for the door. However, Bull steps to the left, blocking my exit.

My chest rises and falls rapidly as I'm provoked for so many different reasons. Pissed off, annoyed, infuriated, confused…aroused. I need to get out of here. But I'm not going anywhere, thanks to the giant standing in front of me.

He casually folds his arms across his still bare chest, watching me. Always watching. "You seem"—he pauses, searching for the right word before he settles on—"angry. Are you?"

Scoffing, I can't believe he's asking me this. How clueless can he be? "I'm fine." I am so far from being fine, but I'll be damned if I tell him that.

I attempt to push past him, but he moves with me, foiling my escape. "I can call Venus and ask if there are any rooms available if you want to stay here?"

I blink once, stunned. Is he really proposing for me to stay in another room? Is the thought of staying in the same room as me that repulsive? And who the hell is Venus? "That's not necessary. Your virtue is safe with me. I'm going home."

"You *are* angry with me," he says, as though he's just solved the world's greatest mystery.

"No shit. Move." I once again try to shove past him, but he is built like a brick shithouse and won't move.

"Why are you angry? You can't stay here, so I thought—"

Oh, the nerve.

"Do me a favor and don't *think* whenever I'm involved. Thank you, or not, seeing as when I thanked you, you looked like I just told you to go fuck yourself, which is what I probably should have said because—"

I'm cut off mid rant as one second, I'm fuming, and the next, my back is shoved up against the door with Bull holding me prisoner. His hands are on either side of my head. I push off the door, only to be jostled back down.

"What's wrong?" he has the gall to ask, inches from my face. But I don't allow this closeness to distract me.

Standing on tippy toes, I glare at him with nothing but spite. "Are you seriously asking me this?" When he doesn't reply, it's apparent that he is. "I don't know what your problem is. You've been nothing but an asshole to me since we met. I don't know what I did to piss you off, but I don't appreciate being treated this way."

"Treated what way? Are you angry because you want to spend the night with me?" He appears genuinely confused, but I don't care. It's time he gets unconfused.

"Oh, get over yourself!" I exclaim, my temper mounting. "I don't want to spend the night with you."

"Good," he replies firmly, insulting me further.

"Yes, good. Great. Fucking perfect. Now get out of my way so I don't take up any more of your precious time."

"Tiger—"

"My name is Lily," I bark, cutting him off. "I know you probably only see me as some whore, shaking my ass for cash, but I'm a lot more than that."

"I don't think that," he chides. Clearly offended, he's flaring his nostrils, but screw him.

"I don't care what a sorry sack of shit like you thinks of me." He clenches his jaw, but I continue. "We're not friends, and we never will be. I've never even seen you smile. You have permanent resting bitch face, but in your case, you *are* a bitch."

He purses those sinful lips, mulling over my outburst that has come out of left field. I wait for him to prove me wrong and show me that what I feel isn't imagined and runs both ways. I want him to acknowledge me as someone special because just once in my life, I want to be someone's destination and not merely a layover.

But he doesn't. He is just another asshole I need to forget.

"Resting bitch what?" he questions, making me feel like a fool.

Charring whatever obsession I feel for him, I promise myself here and now never to allow this man to get the better of me again.

Standing tall, I disregard his distaste for intimacy and press my chest to his. When he flinches, I rejoice. "It doesn't matter. *You* don't matter. Now move."

Bull's heavy breathing blows wisps of my hair from my cheeks. He's barely holding back. I don't know whether he wants to fight or fuck me, but I don't stick around to find out. I shove against his chest, not looking back as I turn the door handle and leave his brand of trouble behind.

Bull just did me a favor. So why do I feel so hollow inside?

CHAPTER SEVEN

Bull

Reading over the description for resting bitch face on Google for the third time, I don't know whether to be insulted or amused that Tiger thinks this of me.

Last night was strange, to say the least. For one, why the fuck was she wearing my T-shirt?

Once she left in a huff, I took a shower—a cold one. Her smart mouth and constant need to defy me had me barely holding on. She is playing with fire, and she knows it. But that doesn't stop her. If anything, it spurs her on.

I don't frighten her. I infuriate her, which is something I have fucking zero experience with. Around her, I feel like a blind man whose sight is slowly returning. I didn't mean to reach out and touch her hair, but everything about this woman leaves me curious. It's as if I'm experiencing everything for the first time. And I suppose in some ways, I am.

When locked up, you adjust to the dismal sights and sounds. You become institutionalized, and the violence, the screams at night become your norm. I still remember the squeak of the guards' shoes as they walked the halls. And the buzzing of the light that never switched off. I remember everything, but what I don't remember is how to be normal.

So when I offered to call Venus, it wasn't because I didn't want Tiger to stay with me. It was because that was *exactly* what I wanted. And that cannot happen.

Tiger is a distraction; one I can't afford. I'm here to get my vengeance, not fuck around. Someone is out to get her, and if I hadn't heard her scream last night, that fucker would have killed her. And that infuriates me more than it should.

I can't get involved with her problems. I have enough of my own. But staying away from her is proving to be harder than I thought. Her touch both subdues and provokes my demons all in the same breath. I've never had that happen before.

Her small body pressed to mine shouldn't have felt so good, but it did. The fact our exchange was heated, and she was mouthing off, only had me wanting to punish her all the more. Pain is what I get off on, and each time Tiger proves to me that she can hold her own, the need to discipline her only grows stronger.

I'm not the good guy, I know this, and being around Tiger only wants me to prove just how bad I can truly be. Prove it to her, and me, because I can never lose sight of what I am.

"Remind me why I bother."

Shaking my head, I look up from my cell to see Lotus standing in the bathroom doorway, holding two bottles of beer. She looks like shit.

I've been in here fixing the leaky taps and toilets. Pocketing my phone, I wash my hands and accept the beer she's holding. "Bother with what?" I ask, throwing back my Budweiser.

"With all of this." She gestures with her hands to the club. "Andre is off sick for the week, so are you okay to work his shifts?"

"No problem." Here's to hoping he never comes back.

"And Lily won't be in for a few days," she goes on to add. "I know about last night. I told her to take all the time she needs. That leaves me short my best girl, but this place is already up shit creek without a paddle. So what's another drama?"

She doesn't mention my involvement, which has me guessing Tiger didn't reveal I was there.

Something lingers on her tongue, and when she closes the door, hinting she wants privacy, I guess it has something to do with what we discussed the other night. "I wanted you know that I've made the call to my friend. Nothing is set in stone," she says quickly, "but I have to think of this place."

"You don't owe me an explanation, Lotus. This is your club. You do what you want," I state bluntly. "I appreciate the heads-up, though."

She sips her beer, gauging what to say. "I know you can't be here because of your parole conditions. You're straight-up, no bullshit, and I like that. I'm glad I went with my gut."

I arch a brow, confused.

She clarifies a moment later. "My gut told me to take a chance on you because beneath all this…" She uses her finger to gesture up and down my body. "There is a good man."

Before I have a chance to argue that she's very, very wrong, she smiles. "You may not see it, but I do. Maybe one day you will too. Come see me when you're done. It's payday." She turns the way she came, leaving me speechless.

Although I appreciate what she said, she's wrong. So fucking wrong. She has no idea of the extent I will go to find those motherfuckers and end this once and for all. I will sacrifice anything, anyone to get what I want.

Something itches beneath the surface, but I don't know what it is. Whatever it is, I squash it down deep, just as I do with this obsession I have with Tiger. The knuckle tattoos are a reminder of what I am.

A lone wolf, ready to tear apart anything that stands in my way.

The bathrooms are fixed, but they are in desperate need of some paint. The scribble on the walls dates back to the 80s. I know Lotus can't afford to do that. She can't afford to do anything. This place will go bust in a couple of months if things don't change.

As I'm walking toward Lotus's office, I hear some voices inside the club. One of them is Lotus, so I'm about to turn the corner, but what I hear has me stopping dead in my tracks.

She seems to be talking business.

"I can't get caught, Stevie. If I do this, you have to promise me that won't happen."

"Lotus, we both lose if that happens." A man who I'm presuming is Stevie says.

Lotus hesitates before she replies, "I suppose you're right."

"See, it'll be easy. Let's help one another. You need money, and I need a club. I promise you; it'll be fine. I have been doing this for years, and not once have I been caught. I'm smart. The location is never the same. We move around to keep the cops off our asses."

Deciding to sneak a peek at who Stevie is, I quietly peer around the doorway and see Lotus talking to a man in a flashy suit. He looks like a soulless businessman in the midst of a transaction.

However, the other man, whose back is turned to me, evokes something dark, something feral in me. My palms begin to itch, and I suddenly have déjà vu. Everything is heightened. My breathing is amplified. The blood thunders through my veins.

As a huge motherfucker, there is no doubt he's the muscle for Stevie. I don't believe in God, ghosts, or anything I can't see, but I see this asshole. When you're locked up, you immediately got a sense of who you liked, and who you didn't, and there is something about this fucker that I do not like.

I can't go out there because I have the element of surprise on my side, but I need to see his face. I've only felt this way one other time, so I need to be sure I'm just tripping balls, and he isn't one of *them*.

"Kong," Tawny says with a smirk as she enters the bar.

The muscle has a name, but he still doesn't have a face. He turns in her direction, but I can't see jack shit, thanks to the angle. When he speaks, however, I don't need a face because that voice…is burned onto my soul.

"Hey, sweetness. Lookin' good."

Tawny says something in response, but I don't hear anything. It's like my brain is shut off to any other stimuli because all it can process is that standing a few feet away is the man who's haunted me for the past fourteen years.

The man who held me back and forced me to watch as my brother was beat to a pulp is here, and he has a name…Kong. He was the muscle who restrained me when I was kid, and he's muscle now. But the difference is, I'm no longer a kid, and I have muscles of my own.

The urge to kill him where he stands is almost unbearable, but I breathe deeply through my nose to calm myself. To ensure I don't end up back inside, I have to watch and learn. I have to be smart.

Bunching my fists by my side, I watch as Tawny flirts with this motherfucker, and he reciprocates. When she walks past him and squeezes his bicep, I am struck with an idea that will not fail. I never believed in fate or destiny, but maybe Tawny can change that.

I will do what I must to get what I want. If Tawny knows who Kong is, then I have to use her in any way that I can. Jaws and Kong both have a thing for strip clubs, it seems. I wonder if they both have a thing for Tawny?

Lotus wraps the meeting up, not wanting Tawny to know

why Stevie and Kong are here. "You staying for the show?" Tawny asks Kong, which confirms she knows him because he's a customer.

"Not tonight, sweetness. Another time, though." He bends forward to whisper something into her ear, and when he does...I finally see it.

Him.

"Sorry, no can do. It's time you became a man."

His words have played on a loop in my mind for fourteen years. How can a single sentence have the power to ruin one's life? But it has, and now it's time to return the favor.

It takes every ounce of my strength to keep from going out there and stabbing Kong in the jugular. But all in due time. He's already dead. While me...I've never felt more alive.

Letting Kong leave was one of the hardest things I've ever had to do in my life. I wanted nothing more than to end him where he stood. But my vengeance will come, and when it does, it will be painful and slow. For that to happen, however, I need Tawny.

She seems awfully friendly with him, which means she can fill in the blanks. I need to know any and all information she has on him. From the sounds of it, Lotus has agreed to work with Stevie, which means I will be seeing Kong very soon.

But I need the upper hand before that happens. So when

I hear Tawny's heels clicking down the corridor, I put my plan into action. Grabbing the bottle of beer I stole from some creeper asshole in the club, I deliberately spill it all over the front of my T-shirt. When Tawny approaches, I quickly roll the bottle under the lockers and slip the tee off over my head, so when she enters the dressing room, I'm shirtless.

I have my back turned to her as I busy myself looking for a towel on the shelf. The moment her heels stop clacking, I inhale in victory.

"Oh, hi," she says in a low voice.

Turning over my shoulder, I nod curtly, not wanting her to sense something is amiss. "Hey. Sorry, I'll be gone in a second. Some asshole spilled beer all over me. I was looking for a towel."

Grabbing a towel, I begin wiping down my chest. My T-shirt is tossed over the back of a chair. Tawny saunters into the dressing room, eyes watching my every move. Before I was locked up, I was told by many that I was good-looking. I took their word for it.

From the way Tiger ate me up last night, which fucking threw me, and now Tawny, it looks like I haven't lost my appeal. But none of that matters to me. It's just a means to an end. I will use whatever I can to get what I want. And nothing will stand in my way.

Once I'm "clean," I meet Tawny's heated stare. "How's it going out there?"

Making small talk isn't my thing, but I can't go in guns blazing, even though I would very much like to—literally.

Tawny must have just come from a private dance because

she's in a dress, which means she's going on a break soon.

"It's going all right. The crowd is slow tonight, meaning the tips are too," she replies, fingering over my T-shirt. "Your shirt is soaked."

"I know," I respond, running a hand through my hair.

"You could always wear no shirt," she suggests with a slanted grin as she admires my biceps. "I wouldn't mind."

Hook, line, and sinker.

"The dude you were talking to earlier today might not agree."

Tawny should never play poker because she has zero ability to mask her emotions. "Who? *Kong?*" she asks with a playful scoff. She's pretending to play dumb, but she is thrilled I noticed.

Shrugging casually, I fold my arms across my chest. "Is that his name?"

"Yes, Kong, although his real name is Ethan Da Silva. But don't tell him I told you that. He has an image to uphold."

And the bastard has a name.

"How do you know him?"

Tawny wets her lips. "He's been coming in here for a while now. He tips real well. Most married men do," she adds with a wink. "They think if they tip big, it'll somehow excuse the fact their cock is hard for someone other than their wife."

"How do you know all this stuff about him?"

She strides toward me while I stand rigid. "I know a lot of stuff," she replies flirtatiously, running a fingernail over my bicep.

This is getting off track. I need to redirect her. "I bet you don't know where he works. Where he trains. Who he runs with," I add for good measure.

This is a test, and Tawny has passed with flying colors. "I bet you I do. Why are you so interested in him anyway?"

Deflecting her comment, I grip her wrist, but instead of pushing her away, I drag her toward me. Her pupils dilate as her cheeks flush. "I wanted to know if he's competition or not. That's all."

A gasp escapes her. "Oh, really? I didn't think you were interested in playing the game."

Oh, I am so interested in playing. Just not the way she thinks.

"What gave you that impression?" I ask coolly.

"I thought you were interested in Lily," she explains. The moment Tawny says Tiger's name, it's like I'm doused with a bucket of ice-cold water.

What I'm doing or, more accurately, what I'm prepared to do, suddenly feels like a dick move. It doesn't take a genius to see Tawny's interest in me. If she propositions me and, in exchange, she gives me everything she has on Kong, I will gladly fuck her into next week.

She doesn't seem like the type of girl who's into relationships, but even if she were, she'd be shit out of luck. I'm no one's happily ever after. No strings is fine with me, but something niggles in the back of my mind, and that thing is Tiger.

I don't have a conscience. I will happily fuck up Kong's family, dog and cat included, but the thought of Tiger finding out about Tawny and me has me feeling…guilt? Is that what this feeling is? I honestly don't know because I haven't felt it before.

As the product of a justice system that taught me how to switch off my emotions in order to survive, this is new territory for me. Tawny wants to fuck me, but Tiger...what does she want? I don't know.

Is she just being nice to me...stitched me up because she's a good person? Or does she have an ulterior motive? But more importantly, why the fuck do I care? I haven't *cared* about anything or anyone in so long. This feeling is foreign, and I feel like I'm about to freak the fuck out.

Shaking my head, I need to snap the hell out of this, which is why I walk Tawny toward the wall and smash her up against it. Her panic soon transforms before my eyes.

"I'm only interested in having a good time," I reply to her comment. But by good time, I mean cutting Kong up into tiny pieces while he's still alive.

Tawny is oblivious to my perversion, however. "He works as personal security. He trains at Gumbo's Gym." She smirks. "Let's just say he's at the gym more than he's at home."

I have no idea how she knows this, nor do I care, but she's just given me my golden ticket. And when she leans in close, peering up at me from under her fake lashes, it's evident she wants payment.

"See, I told you I know stuff," she purrs, her gaze dropping to my mouth. "How about I show you what else I know?"

This was the price I knew I had to pay, but when she balances on tippy toes and presses her lips to mine, I freeze up. Every muscle in my body tenses and not in a good way.

Her lips are like tentacles, and she's everywhere, forcing me to open up to her in every possible way.

There is absolutely zero effort on my side, but Tawny is oblivious as she moans into my mouth, her tongue burrowing deeper and deeper. She presses her chest to mine, attempting to coax me into reciprocating.

But there is no way that is happening.

She's the one who's imprisoned with her back pressed to the wall, but I suddenly feel trapped. When she drapes her arms around my neck, I grunt, but it's not in arousal. It's from needing to get the fuck away from her.

She is too much—too clingy, too warm, too desperate, kissing me wildly, but I feel nothing, nada unlike when I... holy shit. The only other kiss I can compare this to is the one I shared with Tiger. Thinking of her plump lips, supple body, and delicious smell, I respond in a way that surprises me.

I kiss Tawny back.

Although it's not her lips I want, my body remembers the way Tiger felt and craves for a release. Threading my fingers through Tawny's hair, Tiger's last words spoken to me spark to life, and my desire turns to fury.

"It doesn't matter. You don't matter."

Even though she's right, I can't stop this hollow void inside me from growing bigger and bigger. And I act out the only way I know, the only way I've conditioned myself to behave.

My grip on Tawny's hair tightens, dealing with this dead weight festering inside me. I pull, yanking her head back at an awkward angle but continue to kiss her. She nibbles on my lip and tongue, so I bite hers back—hard.

She whimpers, surrendering way too easily, which bores

me. I want a challenge. She allows me to kiss her without remorse, dominating her lips and body any way I please. Her tongue darts in and out of my mouth, trying to duel with mine, but she's no competition. Her taste, her mouth, *her...* she isn't what, *who* I want. She is like watered down vodka, and when I realize why that is, I growl in anger, pinning her even harder to the wall.

She doesn't stir a carnal hunger within, nor does she do what I thought impossible...she doesn't make me feel. Tiger, however...does. I don't know *what* she makes me feel, but at least it's something. I'm dead inside; let's not mistake me for anything other than a man living with one sole purpose in life. But since I met her, Tiger has made me feel something other than this emptiness that has plagued me for fourteen fucking years.

Goddammit. I want bubblegum kisses, not this lackluster embrace.

"Oh, fuck, sorry! I didn't realize—" A stunned voice snaps me to the now, and I sever my kiss with Tawny.

She whimpers, attempting to nuzzle her nose against mine. But I don't nuzzle or cuddle. I don't even kiss. But Bae's wide eyes and gaping mouth reveal what a liar I am.

I instantly let Tawny go, feeling nothing but disgust at myself. She, on the other hand, looks victorious. When I see her red, puffy lips, the lips I just defiled, the need to flee just about suffocates me. I don't bother saying goodbye to either woman as I make my way toward the door. I may appear aloof, but as I exit, I hang my head in...shame.

Shame.

Another feeling I haven't felt in a very long time.

CHAPTER EIGHT

Bull

For three fucking days, I've tailed this motherfucker. And for three fucking days, I've had to stop myself from running him over with the truck I borrowed from Lotus. I still don't have my license, but I'll rectify that soon.

Lotus has been very generous and paid me more than she should have. I think it might be hush money, but she has nothing to worry about. I don't snitch. Besides, my hands are full with plotting ways to kill Kong. I have dreamed of this moment for so many years, and now that the reality is within reach, I feel like a kid in a candy store.

Stabbing. Shooting. Hanging. Drowning. Dissection… while still alive. The possibilities are endless. Lachlan's death was merciful. He didn't suffer enough. But I've learned. He was a trial run. And now, I am a master of all things torturous and bloody.

Between my shifts at work, I've come down here to Gumbo's Gym or followed Kong to work. Stevie wasn't kidding when he said he moves around. He doesn't even appear to have a fixed location for his office. But he's smart. A moving operation is hard for the cops to find, which has me thinking.

I need a kill site.

I can't exactly take Kong back to the motel. Venus is anal about smoking in the rooms. I imagine she wouldn't be too impressed with severed limbs in the bathtub and blood splatter on the walls. But abandoned buildings are common in Detroit. I just need to find the right one.

So much planning is needed, which is why I have my notepad rested against the steering wheel as I detail everything that needs to be done. With Elvis's "Don't Be Cruel" sounding softly over the radio, I jot down possible locations and dates for this to all go down.

Gumbo's has wide windows, which allows me to look in and keep an eye on Kong. I don't want him to see me, so I maintain the upper hand. The element of surprise is the key ingredient to ensure this goes off without a hitch.

Keeping busy, doing what I do best, has been a welcomed distraction. After the incident with Tawny, I've been laying low. Tiger isn't back yet. I'd be a liar if I didn't admit I wanted to know where she is or how she's doing. And if she's still angry with me.

This is still so foreign to me. Planning murder is easier than dealing with whatever this...feeling is in my stomach whenever I think about Tiger.

As for Tawny, she thinks I'm playing hard to get. But I ain't playing. When she tried to kiss me again, I made it clear it wasn't happening. If she couldn't take the hint when I told her this, then that was not my problem.

Staring down at the page in front of me, I groan when I see I've unintentionally written Tiger's name instead of Kong's. This needs to stop. I need to be on my A game, and when I see Kong walk to his huge pickup, this is a perfect example of why.

I didn't even notice him leave.

Quickly writing down the time in my log, I sink low in my seat, not wanting him to see me. I'm parked across the road, but I can't be too careful. He throws his gym bag into the tailgate and is about to walk to the driver's side, but then he stops.

He tilts his head to look under his back tire. Shuffling up so I can see better, I watch as he bends down and picks up something small, black, and fluffy. A kitten. His white teeth glow in the dark as he lifts the kitten high in the air.

The image sends a shiver through me as I was once that kitten.

At first, I think maybe Kong has a thing for cats, but when he places the kitten back behind his tire and grabs some kind of protein bar out of his gym bag, it's clear what he intends to do.

He breaks off a piece of the bar and places it near the kitten. The scrawny thing happily eats the offering, not realizing this is his last meal as there is no doubt Kong plans to run it over with his truck. I grip the steering wheel, breathing deeply through my nose.

The thing is fucking tiny, helpless, and at the mercy of this motherfucker. I'm assaulted by images of that night, of when I too was tiny, helpless, and at the mercy of this motherfucker just like this kitten. But I'm no longer helpless.

"No," I snarl, closing my eyes and telling myself that saving that kitten is not my problem. But it wasn't Lachlan's problem either when he could have helped my brother but didn't. He ran. Like a fucking gutless chump.

And I will be the same if I don't help the fluffball.

"Motherfucker," I curse under my breath as I open the truck door and jog across the road. When Kong's pickup roars to life, I quicken my pace, and before he has a chance to reverse, I snatch the kitten out from under the back tire.

Kong's brake lights blister red, just like his rage as he slams the truck in park and jumps out. "What the fuck, asshole? You got a death wish?" he exclaims, arms spread out wide.

Yes, I wished you were dead.

He approaches me while I freeze. I can't even breathe. After all these years, I'm face to face with one of my brother's killers, and I'm holding a fucking kitten…which is the perfect ruse. This just may work in my favor.

"Sorry, man, this fluffball is my meal ticket, and when I say meal, I mean pussy," I crudely say, holding out the cat. He purrs in support.

Say the magical word—pussy—to any dickhead, and you're instantly best friends. Kong eyes me, folding his arms across his chest. He's weighing me up. Am I friend or foe? Or more importantly, has he seen me before?

He examines me closely, looking into my eyes, the only thing that would have given me away. But thanks to the blue contact I wear, I am just like everyone else now. I must pass his test.

"Your bitch busting your balls too?" he says as though we're friends in some secret club.

"Don't they all?" I snicker with an eye roll.

Tawny said Kong spends more time at the gym than at home, and I figure she knows this because he's taken her here to work out in a different way. He clearly has no respect for women, which is why I've decided to use this angle.

"Fucking oath, brother. I'm Kong." He extends his hand. Every muscle in my body is demanding I break his wrist, just as his friend did to Damian.

But it's because of that, that I shake his hand. His handshake is firm, throwing down the testosterone vibes. He wants to establish himself as alpha. He can establish whatever he wants because when this is done, I will be the alpha when I end his fucking life.

"Tommy," I reply, giving him the most generic name I can think of.

"You new 'round here? I haven't seen you before."

"Yeah. I just moved from Seattle. My kid's mom lived there, so ya know, I split."

Kong cackles because, apparently, abandoning your family is a cause for laughter. The need to end him is too tempting. I don't trust myself. But now isn't the time. "I better go. Pussy is waiting," I say.

Just as I go to turn, he stops me. "If you ever need work, call me. My boss is always looking for…talent like you."

Talent. He means fighters. And just like that, a plan is hatched.

"Sounds like your boss is a smart man."

Kong walks to the tailgate and reaches into his bag. I stand perfectly still. When he produces a white card, I accept it. Looking at it, I find just a number printed on it. "That's where you can reach me…for now."

Not only do they change locations often, it's apparent they change phone numbers as well.

"Done. Thanks, Kong. I'll see you around." And I mean every single word.

Without lingering, I turn and walk down the street. I can't get into my truck because this kitten is supposed to be for a girl who lives around here. And I also don't want him to know what I drive. I turn the corner, listening for the obnoxious roar of his engine.

When it fades into the night, I sigh in relief and lean against a brick wall. Adrenaline courses through my body, and I don't ever remember feeling this alive, which is ironic, considering what I plan to do to Kong.

He's given me my in. If I fight, I gain his trust. And gaining his trust allows me to find the whereabouts of the other two assholes. Lotus will only be a problem if she finds out, but she won't. Only when I earn his trust will I attack. The poetic justice behind it is just too tempting to pass up.

The kitten squawks, reminding me that he's still here. I don't need him anymore, so I lower him to the ground.

"Thanks for helping me out back there."

But he looks up at me, before rubbing his small head around my ankle. "What the fuck are you doing? I don't have any food. Shoo. Go, be free."

But he doesn't move.

I don't know what he wants, but it's not my problem. "Survival of the fittest, Fluffball."

I take off down the street, but when I hear another squawk, I look over my shoulder to see the kitten following me. "What the hell, man? Are you lost?"

He merely walks toward me and sits beside my feet. I don't even like cats. I mean, what do they do other than sleep, shit, eat, and demand attention on their terms? My cell chirps, and when I see it's Lotus, I arch a brow.

I'm not due in to work for another couple of hours as I'm working the graveyard shift. "Sup?" I answer, wondering what's wrong.

I instantly hear catcalls and rowdy assholes in the background. "Sorry to call, Bull. I know you don't start for another couple of hours."

"What's up?"

Her pause is all the answer I need. "It's Lily—"

"Be there in ten." I hang up before she even has a chance to finish her sentence.

Peering down at the fluffball at my feet, I groan before picking him up by the scruff of his neck. "This is a one-night only deal."

With cat in tow, I sprint to my truck, ready to save someone else.

Having no clue what cats eat, I leave Fluffball in the truck with some jerky and water. I take out my contact as I don't want to give anything away. The club is packed, which is a good thing for Lotus. As for me, it makes it fucking impossible to push through the drunk dickheads who are hollering over Bae up on stage.

I shove them aside and make a beeline straight for Lotus who is behind the bar. When she sees me, she gestures with her head toward the dressing rooms as she continues pouring beer. I have no idea what I'll find, so I quicken my pace and charge down the corridor.

I practically barge into the room, ready for any scenario. However, when I see Tiger sitting on the sofa with her knees drawn to her chest and her mascara running black tears down her cheeks, I realize I am ready for anything *but* this.

I jar to a stop, unsure what the hell is going on.

Tiger lifts her eyes, and when she sees me, she quickly wipes away her tears with the back of her hand. I stare at her, dick in hand, because what the fuck am I supposed to say? Maybe I jumped the gun when Lotus called. I just didn't think, which again—a rookie move. The need to get here overrode good sense, which was my bad because now I look like a fucking chump.

"Did your cat die?" I blurt out, before cursing my sorry ass.

Tiger purses her puffy lips in confusion, which is a reasonable response because why the hell did I just ask her that? I don't know what's upset her. Her cat dying seems like a probable cause.

Wiping her eyes again, she shakes her head. "No, my cat didn't die."

"Oh. Want another one?" I ask, the words flowing from me like verbal diarrhea.

She continues looking at me as though I've gone mad. But been there, done that. Still there.

Finding my balls, I walk toward her slowly, my feet giving me the finger as I have no control over my movements. "I was"—I pause, deciding to leave out the fact I was planning a man's murder—"out for a run and found a cat. I don't really know what you're supposed to do with one, so you know, I thought if yours was dead, you could have this one."

She blinks once while I wonder if I sound as stupid as I feel.

Something overwhelming weighs heavy in the air. In prison, this was a sure sign a fight was about to break out. But in the real world, with Tiger, I don't know what it means.

"You're not supposed to do anything with them," she replies, sniffing. "They're cats. They'll tell you when they want something."

"Good to know," I say, rocking back on my heels.

Her red-rimmed eyes fucking stab at me. She looks so… helpless. So sad. I am so confused by all of this.

"You're so socially awkward," she declares, and I merely shrug in response. "It's like you've been living on a different planet."

If only she knew the half of it.

"A normal person would ask why I'm crying."

"I never claimed to be normal," I reply without hesitation.

She huffs, blowing the hair from her cheeks. "And what I would answer," she says, ignoring me, "is that my life is fucking ruined."

When she buries her face into her hands and her shoulders begin to shudder, I look at the exit, desperate to flee. I don't do emotion. I don't know how. I'm broken. So I stand in the middle of the room, watching her cry, and when she slowly lifts her chin, all I want to do is taste her tears.

"Did you hear what I said?" she furiously asks. "My life is ruined!"

"Stop being so melodramatic," I state because I can work with her anger. I can't comfort her like a normal human being, but I can provoke her because when she jumps up and storms over to me, something beautiful is born before my eyes.

"Melodramatic!" she yells, shoving me in the chest. "You asshole! If only you knew the half of it, you wouldn't be so quick to judge. But you probably don't care, seeing as you're too busy with Tawny!"

She's in her heels, which puts her under my chin, but she doesn't let the height difference intimidate her. Her green eyes narrow. Her chest puffs outward with her breathless rage. I stand tall and indifferent, waiting for her next move.

"Are you seriously going to stand there and not say a word?"

"You seem to be doing enough talking for the both of us."

"Ugh!" she groans, her hatred for me making me rock

hard. "How can you be such a coldhearted bastard to me, but to her…"

Her pause has me stepping forward, pressing us front to front. "To her what?" The heat from her body burns through my clothes.

"But to her, you…you fucking *kiss* her! Don't try to deny it. Bae told me she walked in on you and Tawny kissing."

"I wasn't going to deny it," I counter coolly, putting an end to her rant.

Tiger's mouth opens, then soon shuts. "It doesn't matter anyway," she confesses, running a hand down her exhausted face. "Some asshole is out there who can ruin everything for me. After the attack and now this, I'm starting to think it's time I take Carlos up on his offer."

Hell to the fucking *no*. That ain't happening. Here, I can watch her.

Her admission has me gritting my teeth together. "Who?"

She purses her lips in confusion. "What?"

I don't have time for this. "Who is here?"

"Some guy," she replies with a small shrug.

"Which guy?" I ask, my nostrils flaring. Her evasiveness isn't helping my sudden need to kill something.

She must be able to read my impatience because she gives me what I want. "I-I teach ballet to kids." She waits for me to process her news. I nod once. "One of my pupils' father is here for a bachelor party. He's always flirted with me, but I've made it clear it'll never happen."

She swallows, the subtle pink to her cheeks turning a bright red as she averts her gaze. "He saw me dancing, and when I was done, he asked for a private dance. I refused. Lotus was fine with me saying no. But he threatened to tell everyone at the ballet school what I do if I don't—"

Gripping her chin, I tip her face toward mine. "If you don't what?" I question, savoring the tremble to her lips.

"Fuck him," she finally replies, appearing belittled by this jerkoff. And she has every right to.

"What does he look like?" My voice is smooth, but inside, a rage is beginning to fester.

"I—" She falters, shaking her head.

"Tell me," I press, gripping her chin harder.

"Bull, no," she pleads. But it's too fucking late.

Inhaling a heavy breath through my nose, I cup her cheek and lock eyes with her. "So help me god"—I take a moment to compose myself—"if you don't tell me who he is, I will kill every last motherfucker in this place until I find him."

A small gasp escapes her parted lips when she realizes my threat isn't empty. "He's wearing a white shirt. Red vest. And black p-pants."

Her stutter reveals she's scared of me. Good. "See, that wasn't so hard now, was it?"

I may not understand emotion, but I understand violence.

"What are you going to do?" she asks, her skin as cold as ice beneath my hand. I'm suddenly mesmerized by the strands of her hair as they brush the tips of my fingers. "Bull?"

"Take care of your problem," I reply, tilting my head when her green eyes begin to water.

"Why? Why do you even care?" She sniffs back her tears, but it's too late. I've seen them, and I want to claim each one.

With a cautious touch, I wipe away a stray tear with my thumb. "Because…no one makes you cry—" Her mouth parts. She seems…touched. That is, until I sever our connection, only to put my thumb into my mouth. Her salty sadness is a potent drug to a fiend like me.

"Except me," I conclude, meaning every single word. She stands speechless as I walk from the dressing room and into the club.

It doesn't take me long to find the asshole in question. He's sitting with a group of dipshits who are tossing dollar bills onto the stage. Tawny is dancing, and when she sees me, her eyes light up. I wish they wouldn't.

Ignoring her, I march over to the dickhead, tap him on the shoulder, and yell into his ear, "Tigerlily owes you a dance. Come with me."

His head bobs up and down, and he stands quickly, throwing back the remainder of his beer. He high-fives one of his friends, who makes a crude and immature gesture of his finger going through a circle he's made with his thumb and finger on the other hand.

The urge to beat him senseless only rises.

He follows me as I lead him through the club, disregarding Tawny who has stopped dancing to watch where I'm going. As we walk down the corridor and into one of the private dance rooms, I decide that I won't kill him; I'll only hurt him a little.

"Where's that cock tease?" he asks, looking around the room for her. "She's gotten my dick so hard all these months parading around in that tutu. It's time she pays up."

Okay. I take it back. I'm going to hurt him a lot.

I close the door and lock it, sealing his fate. When he

turns over his shoulder to say something, I put an end to his talking when I punch him straight in the nose. He staggers back two steps, hollering as he cups his bleeding nose.

"What the fuck, man?" he cries through his fingers.

"I was going to ask you the same question," I mock, sauntering toward him. "The fuck you doing threatening one of my girls?"

I ignore the fact I just referred to Tiger as mine and focus on why the dipshit is still breathing.

"I-I'm sorry," he splutters, his hands coated in his blood.

The sight gives me so much pleasure, and I draw the violence deep into my lungs. "Too late."

I advance, laughing when he uses the flimsy chair as a barricade between us. "I have money. Lots of it!" he cries, only making things worse for himself.

He rummages through his pants pocket with one hand as the other nurses his bloody nose, so I take this opportunity to show him what I think of his offer. Placing my boot against the edge of the seat, I push the chair forward, and the top metal rail connects with his balls.

He wheezes, dropping to the floor on his knees.

I kick the chair away, needing an open battleground. He scampers away on his knees, but I kick him in the lower back. He falls flat onto his stomach. "Please," he begs, but his pleas mean jack shit to me.

When he attempts to rise, I place my boot in the middle of his spine, intent on squashing him like the cockroach he is. "You're going to forget you ever saw Lily here tonight. We clear?"

"Yes!" he screams, squirming.

"I don't believe you." I press down harder on his back, leaving a dusty boot print on his pristine vest.

"I swear it! I won't tell a soul. Just please let me go."

He's begging. What a wimp.

However, I'm suddenly fixated on a smell that awakens this darkness within—cherry blossoms. "You think you're better than me, is that it?"

Dipshit's head faces the door, the locked door where Tiger just walked through thanks to the key she holds. He lifts his neck, and when he sees her, he thrashes about angrily.

"I don't think...I am," he snarls, finding his balls at the wrong fucking time.

I chuckle, shaking my head at his stupidity.

Tiger locks the door behind her as she strolls into the room, standing in front of the dipshit. She meets my eyes, and I am left utterly speechless by her savage beauty. She is going to make him pay. "You wanted me to suck it? Wasn't that what you said in my ear?"

In response, I press down onto his spine. "Answer her."

"All right! Fuck!" he cries, panicking as he extends his hands out in surrender. "Yes, but I was joking."

Tiger snickers, folding her arms across her chest. "I'll make you a deal. I'll *suck it* once you do."

My heart fucking explodes into a billion macabre pieces as she lifts his chin with the tip of her stiletto only to shove it into his mouth. She isn't gentle and forces her shoe down his throat. He gags, tapping out, but she merely curls her lip in disgust.

"What's wrong, Derrick? Don't like it when the shoe is on the other foot?" Oh, my fuck. Beautiful and funny—I am fucking done for.

She continues feeding him her shoe while he gags, his muffled pleas only making this disturbed scene all the more perfect. I watch her openly, unable to look away from this fierce, ruthless woman. She meets my eyes, and something passes between us.

It's a dark, twisted mess—and I want to choke it with my bare hands.

Tiger removes her foot while Derrick coughs madly. "Apologize to the lady," I snarl, feeling his vertebrae crunch under my boot. "Tell her you won't bother her again."

"I'm sorry! I won't tell anyone I saw you here."

"I don't believe you. What do you think, Tiger?"

Her nickname spills from me, but instead of regretting the oversight, something unexpected happens—I fucking smile. My cheeks actually hurt as the sensation feels strange on me. I can't remember the last time I smiled.

But that doesn't matter because I will never forget this moment.

She taps her chin as if deep in thought. "Nope, Bull, I don't."

"Jesus Christ!" Derrick screeches. "You're both fucked up."

Tiger looks at me and smiles, shrugging nonchalantly. "I suppose we are."

Something sluggish inside me begins to slither and wrap its way around my deadened heart. It squeezes tightly, leaving me breathless, but when Tiger drops to a squat and grips Derrick by the hair, forcing his head back at a painful angle, I realize I'm left gasping for air because of her.

I knew she had a temper, but seeing it flourish before me is something else.

"You will tell Melanie to back off and let me teach my class. And you will forget you ever saw me here, understand? 'Cause if you don't…" She trails off, reaching into her pocket for a pair of lace underwear. She twirls them around her finger. "I will have some incriminating words of my own."

The asshole just got played.

"Fine, okay. I won't tell anyone!" he exclaims, wriggling madly.

Only when she sighs in victory do I lessen the pressure on his back. But when he rears up and spits in her face, I decide to clear up any confusion on his behalf. Without hesitating, I yank him up and punch him in the ribs, the stomach, and lastly, break his nose for a second time.

When he howls in pain, attempting to punch me, I deliver an upper cut that knocks him out cold.

Both Tiger and I watch emotionless as he twitches, blood spilling from his nose. Sadly, he is still breathing.

The adrenaline of the fight thrums through me, and it takes every ounce of willpower not to grab Tiger and throw her up against the wall. Her chest rises and falls quickly, betraying her excitement. With a bleeding, unconscious body between us, I've never felt more connected with another human than I do right now.

She peers up at me from under her lashes, the pink to her

cheeks hinting at her arousal over what we just did. I never mistook her for anything but fierce, but holy shit, tonight... her need for vengeance sang to mine.

Tiger is savage. And her darkness dances with mine.

"What happens now?" she asks softly, but nothing is tender about her appearance. She is sparking to life in front of me.

I want so badly to touch her, but I don't trust myself. I will fucking rip her in two. So I inhale, subduing the devil for now. "You go out there and don't allow anyone to make you feel worthless ever again. Underneath this fancy façade,"—I toe Derrick's limp body—"is a weak, pathetic coward. But you, you're real. Never forget that. Never lose sight of who you are. And what you want."

She licks her lips nervously, rousing this hunger.

"Someone can only make you feel like shit if you let them." She appears to hold her breath when I deliver a final yet powerful word. "Don't."

The static crackling between us constricts every part of me. But eventually, with a nod, she turns. I step forward, giving in to the demons, and catch her unaware as I press my chest to her back.

Her hitched breath and trembling body betray her. And it's fucking beautiful.

Extending my hand, I whisper into her ear, "Leave the underwear."

She does as I say before she rushes out the door, leaving me with this foreign sensation of...feeling.

CHAPTER NINE

Lily

I know I promised myself I would never let him get the better of me again, but I can't stay away.

I've tried. I've really tried. But after last night, it seems this just may be a losing battle. I know I shouldn't want him, but that doesn't stop me from seeking him out.

Watching Bull reprimand Derrick that way triggered something inside me. Mostly, I've kept my temper under control, but when I let loose last night, instead of holding back as I have in the past, it was the most liberating feeling I've had in years.

Society's rules scold us from acting on our deepest, darkest emotions. But those rules don't apply to Bull. He calls it how he sees it, and I admire his no bullshit attitude. I don't know anything about him, but I can't help but feel that this world we live in is something foreign to him.

He's so naïve at times—as though he's an alien, assessing our planet for the first time.

When Bae told me she walked in on him and Tawny kissing, I was furious. I didn't understand why he would do that. Tawny doesn't seem to be his "type" because someone like Bull doesn't have a "type." His tattoo of *Lone Wolf* describes him perfectly, which had me guessing that he was using Tawny.

I don't know what for, but I refuse to believe it's anything more than a strategic move. He just appeared out of nowhere. I want to know his backstory, which is why I'm standing on his doorstep, holding two coffee cups.

I dropped Jordy off at school before coming here. I have no game plan. I just know that I'm in the right place. I'm about to knock but am caught unawares when the door opens, and I'm confronted with a sight that should be illegal so early in the morning.

Bull stands before me shirtless.

Thankfully, he's in black sweats, even though they sit low on his tapered waist. The silver chain he wears hangs low between his muscled pecs. I guess he doesn't take it off. When I roll my tongue back into my mouth, I offer him a cup of coffee before pushing past him.

His unmade bed is thankfully empty of Tawny or anyone else, bar a black fluffy kitten curled in a contented ball on his pillow. Sitting at the foot of the bed, I sip my coffee, watching him close the door. Before he has a chance to speak, I beat him to the punch.

"What did you do with Derrick?" The thought of him going back to Melanie Arnolds battered and bruised has me smiling, but I hide my delight behind the rim of the coffee cup.

"I took care of it," he finally replies, looking at me closely. His hair has grown a little longer, and I wonder what he'd look like with it long.

Rolling my eyes, I question, "What does that mean?"

His sigh of frustration amuses me beyond words. It's good to know I can get under his skin because he sure as hell is under mine.

As I'm sipping my coffee, he asks, "What's your number?" which results in third-degree burns on my tongue.

"What do you want my number for?" I lisp, due to the scalding coffee that I inhaled, thanks to his question.

Folding his arms across his broad, tattooed chest, he arches a dark brow. "Do you always question everything?"

"Yes," I reply, deadpanning him. "Especially when some strange man asks for my number."

Bull nods, tonguing his cheek in thought. "Good. You should," he finally says. "You asked what I did with Derrick. So I was going to show you."

I gulp.

"Where's your phone?"

He gestures with his head to the nightstand.

Leaning across the twisted sheets and blankets, I ignore how good they smell as I reach for the cell. I'm about to pass it to him, but stop when he says, "Put in your number. There's no passcode."

I blink once, stunned by his trust in me. He doesn't seem like the type of person who trusts easily, so this is a big deal. But not wanting to make a fuss, I go to his contacts. I'm expecting to see a list of numbers belonging to family and friends, but I am surprised and also saddened to see that I am, in fact, his first contact.

With fumbling fingers, I put in my name, number, and address before tossing him the cell. He catches it in one hand with his catlike reflexes. He scrolls through his phone, giving nothing away, before my cell pings, alerting me to a text message.

Placing the coffee between my legs, I hunt through my bag, and when I see what's on my screen, I gasp, before bursting into laughter. The lace underwear, which stare at me from my cell now sit beside me, thanks to Bull flinging them my way.

"I think lace suits him," Bull teases, referring to the picture he sent me of Derrick wearing nothing but the underwear. He's on all fours with one of the girls behind him, mid flogging. For good measure, he's wearing a ball gag.

"There's some collateral in case he gets lippy. He won't, though. I know guys like him. They care more about themselves and their precious reputations. You'll be fine."

My hand trembles because this is the nicest thing anyone has ever done for me, and I know how messed up that is, considering the context. But Bull has constantly saved my ass when he didn't have to. I want to thank him, but the last time I did that, things went south. And when Lotus offered him this phone, he was clearly uncomfortable. He doesn't like to owe people. Besides his pride, I sense there is another reason for it.

So I nod instead, placing my cell back into my bag. I'm suddenly struck with an idea.

"Will you take a drive with me?"

He arches a brow, suspicion clouding his expression. "To where?"

Deciding to use his words back at him, I ask, "Do you always question everything?"

And in response, he does the same. "Yes. Especially when some strange woman asks me to take a drive with her."

I can't help but smile as I air quote. "You've seen me naked, Bull. I'm hardly some 'strange woman.'"

However, when he tongues his upper lip while eating me up from head to toe, I drop my hands into my lap, suddenly wishing I had used another phrase.

He walks toward me slowly, bending forward and whispering into my ear, "I haven't seen you completely naked."

Swallowing past the lump in my throat, I counter, "Not many people have." And it's true. I never take off all my clothes. The outfits I wear don't leave much to the imagination, but the scrap of material covering my dignity makes all the difference. As for another man seeing me naked, the last time I had sex, I was drunk, and it was dark. Not my finest moment.

A heavy exhale leaves Bull, his hot breath burning me alive.

He pulls back, stopping inches from my face. His lips are so close to mine, all it would take is for me to shift slightly, and I could experience that sinful mouth again. But I don't. I grip the sheets beneath me, and I measure my breaths as best

I can.

"Okay."

"Okay?" I question hoarsely.

Bull nods, examining my face so closely, I dare not breathe. "I'll go for a drive with you," he clarifies, while my head bobbles uselessly.

I watch as he hunts through the dresser for a white T-shirt and slips it over his head. Covering all that inked skin should be a crime. Without thought, he takes off his sweats, giving me a glorious view of what he's packing beneath his black boxer briefs.

Both his legs are also heavily tattooed, but he doesn't give me a chance to admire them for too long because he's stepping into ripped black jeans seconds later. I don't conceal the fact I was checking him out because what would be the point?

Bull has this ability to read people. He may not know it, but I can see it when he looks at others and at me. He sizes everyone up, cataloguing everything he can about them, about their environment—just as any predator does.

He puts on socks and laces his motorcycle boots, then grabs a black hoodie.

I can't help but notice he has zero belongings. Wherever he moved from, he didn't bring much with him. His lack of possessions, as well as no contacts in his phone, leaves me with so many questions. I don't have a budding social life, but I at least have a few numbers in my cell.

"Ready?" Bull asks, putting a hold on my conspiracy theories for now.

Grabbing my coffee, I give the black kitten a pat on the

head. He barely moves, way too comfortable in his new home.

"Bye, Fluffball."

I look at Bull and smile. "Fluffball? Is that his name?"

Bull raises his shoulders. "I guess so. I've given him plenty of opportunities to leave, but he won't go."

"I think he likes you," I state, coming to a stand.

Bull appears surprised but also disgusted by my suggestion as he curls his lip. "Then I feel sorry for him."

He's not looking for any sympathy. He means it. He clearly doesn't see what I do when I look at him. I don't have a chance to correct him before he continues.

"Let's bounce," he says, putting on his hoodie. Nodding, I follow him out the door. We get into my truck and hit the road.

The music from the radio fills the silence as Bull seems content to look out the windshield. I keep my eyes on the road, which is harder than it sounds. I am drawn to Bull in ways I don't understand. He hasn't shared anything about himself with me, but I'm hoping that will change very soon.

"Does it hurt?" Bull asks after a long stretch of silence.

"Does what hurt?" I question, keeping my eyes forward.

"Your neck. You still have bruises from when…" He trails off, leaving his sentence unfinished.

Instantly, I touch the side of my throat where that bastard's hands almost squeezed the life from me. If not for Bull, I would hate to think where I would be. "Not anymore."

"Did you report it to the police?"

Shaking my head, I return my focus to the road.

"Why not?"

Clenching the wheel, I shrug. "They'll ask too many questions, and besides, a stripper getting attacked isn't high on their priority list." Although I don't see myself as a stripper, no matter what I say, the police will just think it's some client I pissed off because I didn't give him a hand job under the table.

I also didn't want to report it because of the way Bull responded when I told him the cops were coming.

He was involved, so if I report it, they'll ask him questions, and I don't want to involve him in any more of my shit after everything he's done for me.

"You're not worried he'll come back?"

"Of course, I am, which is why I was thinking of talking to Carlos."

A grinding fills the truck. I don't read into it.

"I don't want to leave Lotus, but you're right when you said he was out for blood. He knew me, but the question is, why would he want me dead?"

Needing a change in pace, I ask, "Do you have any siblings? I have a brother, but he left years ago. So it's just me and, um, Jordy." *My son, not cat,* I silently add.

Something shifts in the air.

Bull doesn't reply, and just when I think he won't answer, he says, "No. I do not."

That is definitely a touchy topic for him, so I don't press. "What about your parents?"

"What about them? I haven't spoken to them in years. Mom found comfort in prescription pills. While my dad found his happily ever after in a woman half his age. But I don't blame them."

"Oh?" I question because they don't sound like very supportive parents. I should know.

"Everyone has their reasons, Tiger. We all deal with life differently."

That doesn't really answer my question, but I decide to let it go because when I turn left onto a deserted gravel road, I need a moment to compose myself. I haven't been here in so very long, but the feelings this place evoke in me are just the same.

The trailers are decayed and barely standing, but the homey ornaments like gnomes, potted plants, and wind chimes all hint that regardless of their run-down condition, they are someone's home—just as they once were mine.

I continue driving until I get to the last trailer on the right. It's obvious no one lives here anymore. The open door, attached by only one hinge, flaps in the wind, and all but one window is smashed. I park the truck and kill the engine, unable to make eye contact with Bull.

Opening the door, I walk to the front of my truck and stand in front of my once home. This trailer was where I was raised and where my dreams went to die. The only fond memories I associate with this place are the ones involving Jordy.

When I think of my mom and the deadbeat losers she brought here, I clench my fists by my side. After a few minutes, Bull stands by me. He doesn't say a word, but that's okay because I came here to exorcise my demons as well as his.

"It's funny how when I was younger, this place was my

whole world. It looked so big, but now, I see it for what it is—nothing."

He still doesn't speak.

"Not what you were expecting?" I ask, unable to keep the mockery from my tone. I want Bull to see that whatever secrets he guards, I can handle it. I'm not a princess who needs protecting, contrary of him coming to my aid time and time again.

"I'm the last person to judge," he finally says.

Swallowing down my nerves, I confess, "I brought you here because I wanted to share a part of myself with you. And I hope one day, you'll do the same."

I'm not expecting anything in return, but I should know by now that I should expect the unexpected whenever Bull is involved. "What if you don't like what you see?" he asks honestly.

Turning my head, I look at him, really look at him, and see that beneath his hard exterior lies a broken man. "I've liked what I've seen so far."

He meets my eyes with nothing but sheer confusion in his. "Why?"

"Why do I like you?" I question, shocked and saddened by his uncertainty.

He nods once, jaw clenched tight.

Sighing, I direct my attention back to the trailer. "Because you're the first person who has treated me like a human being and not a thing. I don't know anything about you, but I want to. I know you want me to be afraid of you...but I'm not."

"You should be," he says with grave sincerity. "I'm not a

good person." But his warning falls on deaf ears.

I decide to share something with him that I haven't with a lot of people. "We're the same, Bull." Before he has a chance to argue or scoff, I continue. "Both guarded and afraid of letting anyone in. I don't know what your reason is or what secrets you keep, but mine is…Jordy isn't my cat."

Filling my lungs with air, I confess, "Jordy is my son."

I have zero regrets for sharing this with Bull. After seeing his contact list, I think Bull needs a friend. And friends share stuff like their kids with each other. I'm not expecting anything in return, but it feels good to share this with him.

"Which is why I have been thinking about Carlos's offer. Not only would the extra money help, but I'm all Jordy has. I have no idea who my dad is. My mom and brother may as well be lost to me. If something were to happen to me, Jordy would be all alone." I rub my arms, chilled by the bitter wind as well as the thought of my son being an orphan.

"He's my whole life, and everything I do is for him. I work two jobs because his school isn't cheap. I hate not being able to spend more time with him, but I want to provide for him in a way my mother didn't for me."

Now that I've opened up, I can't seem to stop sharing.

"Jordy is a…difficult kid. When my brother left, it took a toll on us both. Christopher was never a saint, but he was good to me. Jordy never knew his dad, Michael, so Christopher was the only male in his life. I know Jordy idolizes his father, even though he doesn't know him. It's hard to compete with a ghost."

"What happened to Jordy's dad?" Bull asks when I finally

take a breath.

Swallowing down my sadness, I reply, "He left. I have no idea where he is. When I told him I was pregnant, he was so happy, but it was all bullshit. A week later, Christopher told me he left town."

Clenching my fists, I chase the tears away. "He didn't even have the balls to say goodbye. I was sixteen, pregnant by my brother's best friend, and all alone. Jordy wants to know who his dad is, but how do you tell your son his father was a deadbeat loser who wasn't man enough to stick around?"

I leave crescent moons in my palms from clenching my hands so tight. This is the first time I've told anyone this. Bae knows the basics, but I haven't gone into detail because I was never comfortable sharing this with anyone…until now.

"But I suppose I wasn't worth sticking around for," I whisper with regret. "I'm a loner by choice. The less people I let into my life, the less chance there is for me to get hurt. I have a couple of friends, but even then, I missed out on college and doing all the things teenagers do because I was raising a kid. If Jordy's dad hadn't left, I can't help but think how different my life would have been. Would I have followed my dreams of studying dance and going to some fancy school? My teacher, and now boss, seems to think I had the potential to get that far. But all of that had to be put on hold because I chose to have my child instead."

The tears I've tried so hard to keep at bay push past the floodgates. "You think you're a bad person, but deep down, we're all bad. Late at night, when I'm lying in bed, I can't help but wonder if I made the right decision," I whisper, ashamed.

"I love Jordy so much. But the person I am now compared to who I thought I would be are so different. Sometimes, I feel as if there are two versions of me. And I don't know who I like more. What sort of person, what sort of *mother* does that make me?

"What sort of sister does it make me for going behind my brother's back when I knew it would hurt him? He did everything for me, and I thank him by sleeping with his best friend."

Casting my eyes downward, I hide behind my hair because I'm embarrassed for confessing such truths. I wouldn't blame Bull if he never spoke to me again. But what he does next has my heart—my untouched, mutilated heart—beating a little quicker.

Gently prying my fingers open, he places a rock in my palm. "It makes you human. Take back your life. It's yours and no one else's."

Peering down at our union, with his hand overlapping mine, I fall deeper under his spell. How can someone shake everything I worked so hard for beyond repair?

Squeezing my hand, he severs our connection while I clench the rock. This trailer imprisons my memories within its rusty walls. It's time I set them free.

With a guttural cry, I throw the rock, breaking the only remaining window. The sound unleashes something dark and sinister within me, and I scream. Frantically scanning the ground, I pick up another rock, not content until I smash out the rest of the window.

Once it's shattered, an unstoppable force has me gathering

rock after rock and hurling them one by one at the trailer. Each time I hear the dull thud of metal, a small part of me stitches itself back to my soul.

I'm covered in sweat, adrenaline coursing through me, but I can't stop. Each strike has me screaming in victory, and Bull's words make perfect sense. This *is* my life. No one else's but mine. Wishing for a better life doesn't make me a shitty person. It makes me human.

With one final launch, I tear a hole through the flimsy metal wall. The blood gushes in my veins, and I'm currently a live wire as I breathlessly turn to look at Bull. He stands on the sidelines without an ounce of judgment reflected in those amazing eyes.

He accepts me for me and, unlike most, doesn't expect anything in return.

I am possessed as I march over to him and fist his T-shirt in my hands. He doesn't waver. He stands tall, allowing me to take what I want. "Why did you kiss Tawny?" I cry, grasping him harder.

His lips tip into a lopsided smirk. "She is merely a means to an end."

"So what am I?" I am clearly a masochist and want to know it all. "You kissed me. Am I merely a means to an end, too?"

Bull licks his upper lip, smoldering before me and fiercely confessing, "I don't know what you are."

"Do you like her? Tawny?" I add, suddenly needing to do something with my mouth other than kiss Bull.

"No," he replies bluntly.

"And me? Do you...like me?"

The air sizzles between us, but I welcome the burn.

"I like the thought of seeing you beg...seeing you bound... seeing you bleed," he concludes, while I swallow past the lump in my throat.

"And do you feel that way about Tawny?"

"No. I do not."

I don't understand it, but Bull dances with violence the way most do with love. But if this is the price I have to pay to get close to him, to continue this feeling of being...alive, then I'll do it. I want it all.

"And what if I want that?" I ask, skating closer and closer to the gates of hell as I get lost in his eyes.

"Be careful what you wish for. I'm not the Prince Charming in your story."

"I don't want Prince Charming. In case you haven't noticed, I'm not the princess who needs rescuing." I dare him to fight me.

"I will break you," he warns, and there is nothing melodramatic about his claim. It's a promise.

"I don't believe you," I challenge, standing on tippy toes to bring us eye to eye.

Bull's arms are rigid by his side. He is allowing me to manhandle him, to take my frustrations out on him, and that empowers me beyond words. If I were to do this to any other man, they would have lost control the moment I played rough. But not Bull.

He is coolly composed, showing no emotion, while me, I am a bundle of nerves. Being this close to him has every fiber of my body throbbing in want, need, desire. I have never felt this carnal…hunger before. It's addictive, and like an addict, I want more, more, more.

When he lays his cards on the table, I'm certain I will buckle with his promises.

"If you're looking for a good time, then I can do that. If you want someone to"— he pauses, before smirking—"fuck you and lick your pussy until you're screaming for more, then I can be that man. I can rough you up if you want, make you beg." My pounding heart almost spills onto the floor. "I can be whatever you want me to be. I just can't be your forever. I do what I want, when I want. I don't do romance. This is who I am. Don't try to fix me because I was broken long ago."

My cheeks blister because if that was supposed to scare me, it's done the complete opposite. There are no empty promises, no confusion as to what this, to what *he* is. Any sane woman would leave with her dignity intact, but not me. His warning only provokes me.

I don't have a chance to speak, however, because his cell chimes, severing the dangerous current between us. Instantly, I let him go, allowing him to reach for his phone in his back pocket. When he answers, I notice he keeps the exchange short, disconnecting the call within a few moments.

"I have to go."

"Oh?" I reply, hiding my disappointment. I was hoping we'd continue where we left off. But the call just ruined the mood.

I want to ask who it was, but I don't. "Okay. I'll drive you back."

He nods and heads for the truck. His urgency has me wondering where he's going. And more importantly, who called. I want to ask but decide not to push my luck.

Bull is a complex man, and like a moth to a flame, I am drawn to his darkness. Before I met him, I didn't even realize those depravities were inside me. But they are. They excite me. They make me feel alive.

There is no turning back now.

CHAPTER TEN

Bull

Kong called me with an address. It was that easy.

I messaged him early this morning to tell him I was interested in whatever his boss was offering. I knew what the terms were but played dumb when he told me the ins and outs of what I was to do.

There's a fight tonight in some deserted neighborhood about an hour away. The rules were simple—fight and win. For my trouble, I would get paid a thousand dollars. If I won, I would get double that. Kong told me this was just a base rate. With each fight and win, the amount would increase. But the money isn't my motivator—seeing him dead is.

So I agreed.

I called Lotus and told her I wouldn't be in tonight. I said

I was sick. I hated lying, but this is my chance to put my plan into motion. Losing isn't an option. The more wins, the closer I get to earning Kong's trust.

I need to know who the other two assholes he ran with are. The thing about a successful predator is that they study their surroundings and familiarize themselves with every variable to ensure that when they strike, they do so with efficiency and skill.

There is no room for errors. Or distractions.

Gripping the steering wheel, I follow the GPS, refusing to think about her—again.

Tiger is a distraction, a dangerous one. Today, it took every shred of control I had not to give in to temptation and deliver on the things I promised. It was supposed to scare her, give her insight into who I am and what I would do to her.

I expected her to run. She didn't.

Taking me to her childhood home and telling me about her life and her son were her way of trying to connect with me. For some unknown reason, she likes me. I don't know why. She sees something in me that I don't.

I'm trying my hardest to keep her from my shit, but it seems she doesn't want to stay away. I can never tell her what I have planned, so it doesn't seem fair to start anything with her because she is bound to get hurt. But I'm finding it harder and harder to fight these urges inside me.

When the GPS spits out that the destination is a couple of blocks away, I'm thankful I'm able to act on these urges in a different way. I'm looking forward to making someone bleed.

Parking my truck, I look at the derelict warehouse in

front of me. There is no one around. Locking my door, I slip my hood over my head and keep my chin downturned as I make my way to the steel fence. It has a small hole cut out of it. Ducking low, I step through it and scope out my surroundings.

The warehouse is dark, hinting no one is inside. But the deserted exterior is just a front for what's really going on inside or, more specifically, what's going on inside the soundproof basement. I shoulder open the unlocked door, ensuring to close it behind me.

Kong was a little vague in his instructions—enter through the door in the main office. Peering from left to right and up over the three floors, I wish he'd been a little more specific because I see about thirty doors that could be classified as the main office.

But I know this was done with intent. He isn't going to spoon-feed me, so this is a test—one that I don't plan on failing. I'm not going to play lucky dip, hoping I stumble across the right door. I'll use my senses.

Closing my eyes, I listen carefully for vibrations, the ones responsible for giving us the sense we're being watched. I inhale deeply, sifting through the smell of musty garbage to chase any sign of life.

Late at night, when you're trapped behind bars, using every skill at your disposal will help save your life. I learned this the hard way. But I learned, and I use that knowledge to feel for the pulse of energy...

Gotcha.

Opening my eyes, I zero in on a door on the second floor.

I have no idea how a room from the second floor can lead to the basement, but I'm about to find out as I climb the rusty staircase. When I get to the door in question, I open it with caution but am surprised when I see there is no door inside. It's just an empty room with a blacked-out window.

Removing my hood, I scan my surroundings, refusing to believe I'm wrong. I'm rarely wrong, especially when it comes to stuff like this.

Walking vigilantly inside, I tilt my head, examining the wooden floor. The surface is even with no raised edges to hint at a trapdoor, so that just leaves the window. It's stiff as I try to jimmy it open, but it eventually gives.

When I open it, I find scaffolding that allows access to a small building behind the main warehouse. The only way to get to it is through the warehouse, which is a smart move. Stepping out of the window, I climb down the scaffolding and jump to the ground.

There still isn't any noise, but when I enter the building and find two beefy men guarding a metal door, I know things are about to get real. They stop talking and look at me closely.

"I'm Tommy," I state bluntly. "If there is some secret handshake, I don't know it. So don't waste my time and let me in."

I'm not in the mood for twenty questions.

One of the guys speaks into a walkie-talkie before nodding. "Kong is waiting for you."

He unlocks the door, granting me entry. Rookie move on their part as they haven't searched me. But I shove past them. The boisterous roars of what awaits me downstairs has me putting on my game face as I unhurriedly walk down the stairs.

When I descend the final step, I see a space that is a lot bigger than I thought. About three hundred men and women stand around two fighters who are covered in sweat and blood. They are both of average size, and I wonder if Kong recruited them, too.

There isn't a ring. Just a circle of fervent bystanders surrounding the men, eager for bloodshed. The crowd is mixed with people from all walks of life, as it seems there is no discrimination when it comes to seeing someone bleed for money.

Kong is leaning against the back wall, watching on intently. I don't see Stevie, which leads me to believe he's more of a behind-the-scenes man. Jaws isn't here either. I can't hide my anger over that fact. Brushing past the screaming mob, I make my way toward Kong. It still takes all my willpower not to stab him where he stands. But I rein in my wrath by reminding myself of the greater good.

"Yo," I say with a nod.

Kong smiles, unfolding his arms. "Holy shit. You found the place. I'm impressed. Most don't make it this far."

"I'm not most," I reply smartly.

"I can see that. You're up in a few. You can change in there." He gestures with his chin toward the bathrooms.

I don't waste a second and walk toward them because being near him for too long fuels the raging inferno within.

I keep my eyes ahead, but suddenly, the hair at the back of my neck stands on end. Turning over my shoulder, I scan my surroundings but don't recognize any faces, so I continue my walk toward the bathrooms. When I enter, I see a small changing room off to the left. I wouldn't usually bother, but there is no way I'm fighting with my face exposed. It's too risky. If Franca gets a sniff of anything illegal, she'll fry my ass.

Kicking off my boots and socks, I drop my duffel onto the bench and hunt for my things. Stripping out of my jeans, I put on the gym shorts and a long-sleeved top with hood. My face isn't the only thing recognizable. I need to cover as much of my body as I can.

Walking over to the sink, I turn the faucets to cold and cup the water. Splashing it onto my face and over my head, I look at myself in the cracked mirror. This moment will define everything and kick-start my vengeance.

Bracing the sink, I give myself a pep talk. "Don't fuck this up." The medal around my neck catches the dim lighting.

It's time.

Placing the necklace under my top, I reach for the skull design face shield and position it over my face, ensuring it sits under my eyes. Once it's in position, I slip on my hood. I tape up my hands, clenching them into fists to ensure I have enough slack. Taking a moment, I admire my new uniform, liking this one a lot better than the one I was stuck with for twelve years.

The elongated teeth on my mask look fucking feral, as though I'm seconds away from eating my opponent alive. And I suppose in some ways, I am. Cracking my neck from side to side, I bounce on the spot to warm up. My entire body is itching for a fight because each breath Kong takes is like spitting on my brother's grave.

The thought has me clenching my jaw.

A loud roar sounds from outside, hinting the fight is over. It's my time to shine.

"Tommy?" Kong shouts when he opens the bathroom door. He rounds the corner, and when he sees me in my full getup, he grins. "Fucking hell. You're going to annihilate Jacko."

I don't argue because he's right. My body is vibrating with violent energy.

I follow Kong out the door, shutting out all outside stimuli to focus on the bald guy who is built like a brick shithouse. He stands in the middle of the room, delivering a quick succession of punches in the air. He's fast but heavy on his feet.

The crowd parts, allowing us through. So much green is being exchanged left and right. I don't know who's the favorite, but I don't care. When I get within a few feet of Jacko, I shove past Kong, and it's game on.

Jacko is ready and gets into defense, but I won't fight fair. There is no fair in what I have to do. I charge forward, slamming my fist into his jaw. He staggers back, shaking his head to clear the fog, but I don't give him a reprieve.

I'm on him like a pit bull, delivering a combo of punches to his ribs, stomach, and then his face. I connect with whatever part of him I can. He tries to defend himself, but I'm a feral force and won't stop. Each time I hit him, the crowd erupts in cheers, exposing their love for bloodshed.

The pandemonium is a drug to me, and I continue circling him, jabbing out and connecting with whatever I can as he tries to hit me. He's bleeding from a cut above his eye and mouth, but that doesn't deter him.

Kudos to him.

I duck low when he tries to hit me, but the bastard catches me unaware and kicks me in the ribs. I'm still sore from being stabbed, so I stumble back, winded, which is my bad because Jacko launches forward and punches me in the face. The asshole can pack a punch, and my vision blurs.

"Come on, you fairy. Are you going to fight or suck my dick?"

His repulsive slur incites me, and I soon recover, circling him with fists raised.

We're dancing a deadly tango as the element of surprise for me is now gone as Jacko learns my moves. Our eyes are locked, watching the other closely, because one wrong move will cost us. Jacko steps forward, attempting to punch me, but I duck low and strike his flank quickly.

A pained *oof* leaves him, but he soon recovers, and he kicks me once again, this time, in the stomach. I'm propelled backward, only to be pushed back into the "ring" by eager bystanders who won't be satisfied until one of us is dead.

Jacko punches me in the temple, the nose, and then the chin. He tries to connect with my ribs, but I jump back with a smirk. Blood splashes onto the concrete from my nose, but the crowd can't see me bleed, thanks to the bandana over my face.

He spits, a splatter of red staining the floor. He's hurt. The sight is truly beautiful to a fiend like me. I make quick eye contact with Kong who is watching on behind the crowd.

He is a tall motherfucker, so he stands out, but when I see his victorious smirk, thinking he's won because of me...I am possessed with a fury that wants to kill anyone who stands in my way.

Jacko comes at me with a roar, but I use my anger to deliver a combination of punches that sends Jacko staggering backward. I charge forward, hitting any part of his body I can, because with each strike, it takes me closer and closer to seeing Kong dead.

I punch Jacko in the face, knocking out two teeth, and when he sags forward, I deliver an uppercut that sends him soaring through the air. He lands on his back with a thud, and before he can get back up, I dive on top of him, pinning him to the floor as I punch him in the face over and over again.

His head lolls, but I don't stop. The soft flesh feels like heaven beneath my fists. He stops struggling, hinting he's out cold, but I still don't stop. All I can think about is Damian. How he was humiliated, beaten, and bruised for no reason. He died because four motherfuckers decided to play God.

I don't care who I have to use and abuse to get what I want, and when I lock eyes with Kong, all I want is to see him pay.

With one final blow, I connect with Jacko's face before coming to a breathless, slow stand. My body is trembling as adrenaline courses through me. Jacko is not getting up anytime soon, which sends the crowd wild. Someone pats me on the back, but I nudge them away, ready to break their fucking hand.

I look down at my clenched, unsteady fists, and the once

white tape is now stained a bright red. This is all I know to survive—blood and pain.

"Fuck!" Kong screams to be heard over the manic crowd as he rushes toward me. "You're one scary ass motherfucker."

He doesn't know the half of it.

"Here." He digs into his pocket and discreetly shoves a wad of cash into my palm. "There's more where that came from. I'll call you. The bookies are going to love you."

I don't bother sticking around because this first step is enough for now. Kong merely sees me as dollar signs. He bets on the right horse, and I make him rich. Little does he know he's betting on the wrong horse.

Pocketing the cash, I push my way through the crowd, on the lookout for Jaws, but then a young woman in fancy jewels steps in my path, blocking me. Her red lips tip into a slanted grin, and she whispers into my ear, "Let's fuck."

Her candidness catches me by surprise, and I can't deny the win has left me pumped and ready to blow off some steam. She looks like a rich daddy's girl who lost her way home, so I toy with the idea. There are no empty promises. We both know what this is.

But I'm not her puppet or a blow-up toy for her to get her rocks off with. And besides, she does nothing to appease this throbbing in my cock because it craves someone else.

Just as I'm about to decline, a flash of pink catches my eye.

Focusing ahead, I see the back of a woman as she shoves her way through the crowd. She has on a cotton candy-colored wig cut in a bob. I don't know why, but her urgency has alarm bells ringing, and without thought, I chase after her—the predator in me relishes the chase.

When the masses see me coming, they part quickly. They've seen me fight. They don't fancy getting caught in the crossfire. For her, however, no one moves, which allows me to catch up to her quickly. She is almost at the staircase, causing me to hasten my steps. She can't get away.

But when some asshole tries to congratulate me, blocking my path, he allows the scared little lamb to slip away. I push him aside, continuing the chase, before this woman slips through my fingers. She takes two steps at a time, and all I can see is that she's wearing sunglasses too big for her face.

She's clearly trying to disguise her appearance, and the fact she's running from me has me wondering why. The mystery has the adrenaline surging through me, and it doesn't take long until I'm following closely behind her.

She fumbles with the handle but, eventually, bursts through the door, almost knocking into the two dickheads manning the entrance to the floor. They try to grab her but fumble because she's lithe and graceful like a...dancer.

Holy mother of fuck.

I'm hot on her heels, every part of me throbbing in need. She takes a left, which is the wrong fucking way. The hunter in me savors her mishap, and when she sees the corridor is a dead end, she yanks open the closest door and dives for the safety of a room.

She frantically tries to close the door, but I'm too fucking fast and grip the edge, pushing it open. She stumbles back with the force, almost falling onto her ass. I slam the door shut, trapping us both. When she realizes she's ambushed, she spins, turning her back to me.

Her small shoulders rise and fall quickly as she gulps in lungsful of air. We're both in disguise, both hiding who we really are. I need to see her to ensure she's real. With three quickened strides, I'm across the room, gripping her upper arm.

She violently shakes me off, refusing to turn around.

"Why are you here?" I snarl, but my question remains unanswered. Her silence enrages me all the more. "Answer me!"

"Fuck you!" she replies fiercely.

She doesn't want to play. Well, too bad, because I do—if only she knew just how badly I want to play with her.

She refuses to face me, so with no choice, I tug off her wig. When a cascade of soft brown hair tumbles down her back and the smell of cherry blossoms assaults me, I curse the day our paths crossed.

Her hands frantically attempt to cover her hair, but it's too late. I know who she is, so now the question is, what will I do?

"Did you follow me?" I ask to her back, which pisses me off as she still refuses to face me. "This will not end well for you if you keep ignoring me. Answer my question."

Silence.

I am splattered in blood, my face shielded by a menacing skeleton bandana, and she is still not afraid of me. Her courage is so fucking potent, I can't breathe.

"Turn around," I demand, and the tremble to her shoulders gives me a shot of the most intoxicating drug. "What do you want from me?"

Even though she won't answer, it doesn't deter me from asking her questions.

"Do you want me to hurt you? Is that it? Make me understand what you want because I can only offer you pain!" I exclaim, my bloody fists a confirmation of this.

This silent treatment is feeding my demons; they demand I make her pay.

"Fine, have it your way then. Maybe I'll go find someone who *does* want to talk to me."

It's a trigger for her and works like a fucking charm.

She swivels around so forcefully, a breath catches in my throat. I watch as she rips off her sunglasses, exposing those savage green eyes. She gives me one fucking second to process what I see before she storms over to me and rips off my face shield.

I can only imagine what she sees because the sticky blood coating my skin is my warpaint. But she doesn't recoil. Oh no, Tiger doesn't cower in the face of fear. She doesn't recoil—period.

She stands on tippy toes and smashes her lips to mine.

My mouth hinges open, needing a second to get up to speed, but that's all it needs before I'm kissing the ever-living fuck out of her. Every part of me aches because nothing is gentle about her kisses, but the pain only heightens this depravity within me.

She bites me, clawing at my shirt, while I fist her long hair. Our tongues duel, refusing to surrender to the other because we both want to be alpha. I walk her toward the wall, slamming her against it as I press my chest to hers.

She moans into my mouth, sucking my tongue and biting my bottom lip, and all I taste is bubblegum. The kiss is frenzied and wild, and I can't stop. I want to fucking eat her alive. Her long hair feels like silk beneath my fingers, which has me remembering I'm touching her with filthy hands.

Breaking the kiss, I stare her in the eye. "Why are you here?"

My blood paints her face, which strokes the caveman within. I've fucking marked her, but it's not enough. With three fingers, I slowly smear my blood across her mouth and cheeks. Now she looks like the fucking warrior that she is.

Tiger licks her lips, no doubt tasting the metallic sting I left behind. "I don't know," she finally speaks.

"So you followed me?"

She nods slowly.

"Why? I don't understand. Help me understand." I don't know why she would waste her time on someone like me.

She simply cups my cheek and shrugs. "I don't have the answers."

"Then what do you want?"

Her chest pushes against mine as she gasps for breath. And with one simple word, she steals mine. "You."

I don't know what to say. Or do. Or...feel.

"Every time I see you with another woman, this...monster comes out of me. And I don't know why."

"You're not the monster. I am. I'm the one covered in another man's blood." To prove my point, I raise a bloody fist. "You saw me beat him within an inch of his life. I only stopped because he isn't why I'm here. I have an end game, and everyone is disposable. Even you," I add, watching her slender throat dip as she swallows.

This is when she's supposed to leave the room and never look back. I've just given her a get out of jail free card. I don't expect her to stick around, who would? I have nothing, *nothing* to offer her. A world full of pain is all I can promise.

I wait calmly for her to leave. But she doesn't.

With a sigh, she begins to unwrap the tape from around my hands. She won't meet my eyes, but instead busies herself with ridding the bloody reminder from my skin. Once she's undone the tape, she hesitantly grips my chin and turns my cheek to look at my injuries.

"Does it hurt?" she asks. I shake my head, unsure what the fuck is going on.

She brushes her thumb over my lips, nursing me softly. She appears to be in thought. Here's to hoping she realizes what a big fucking mistake this is. "What's your end game?" she softly asks, her fingers drifting too close to my throat.

Gripping her wrist, I stop her from touching me because this has gone too far. "That's none of your concern," I snarl because she can never know—ever.

"Why were you fighting tonight? Why did you cover your face? Your eyes? What are you hiding?" she asks, cementing what I have to do. "What are you running from?"

"Just because you shared something with me doesn't mean we're going to have a heart to heart over coffee. And the reason for that is…I don't have a heart."

She licks her lips quickly. She's nervous. Good. "I don't believe y-you."

"Well, you should," I state, inches from her face. "You want to see something in me that's not there."

Before she has a chance to reply, I turn her fiercely, so her back is pressed to my front. Our reflections are echoed in the dirty mirror in front of us. She is trembling all over.

"See that?" I snarl, peering at our bloody image in the mirror. "Nothing but an empty shell."

"What happened to y-you?"

"You don't want to know," I counter in warning.

"You're not bad. I can see it behind your eyes."

But I cut her off. This has gone too far. The only way to stop this is to hurt her. She is nosy and smart, and sooner or later, she will uncover what I did and what I plan to do. "I *am* bad, Tiger." She doesn't seem to believe me. So it's time I showed her just how bad I can be.

Fisting her hair, I tilt her head to the side and bite the column of her neck, feeding the devil within me. She cries but doesn't retreat. While I'm sucking at her soft, delicious flesh, I reach around to the front of her jeans and unsnap the top button.

The sight is almost too much.

A heavy intake of breath fills her lungs, and on her exhale, I slip my fingers into her underwear. Her sex is hot and bare and…wet. With nothing but pure possession, I sink two fingers into her slick pussy. Her mouth parts with the intrusion, and her body seizes around me. She isn't ready for me, but her pained hiss fuels my darkness. She feels incredible.

"Don't mistake me for anything but that." I begin to finger her—in and out, in and out. She wriggles, whimpering, but I suckle on her neck, only burying my fingers deeper.

"Oh, god." She squeezes her eyes shut.

"I will use you because I can. Because you let me."

To prove my point, I stretch her wide, ignoring how fucking tight she is. I know I'm hurting her, but this is the only way I can get her to listen.

She moves with me, gently arching into my touch as she pants softly. If I didn't know any better, I'd say she was enjoying this. But I shove that sick thought aside.

Licking down her throat sluggishly, I pump my fingers, picking up speed. Tiger moans, attempting to move her hips, coaxing me to give her clit some attention, but I'm holding her prisoner in every way possible. My cock is hard, so fucking hard, but this isn't about gratification. This is about punishment. This is about showing Tiger who I am.

"Are you trying to fill the hole in your little family, is that it?"

Her eyes snap open, the fire consuming the green. Good, she's angry. I can work with that. "How d-dare you."

"Maybe Michael didn't want to be stuck with a needy woman? You don't have the best track record with people sticking around."

Finally succumbing to her demands, I rub over her clit, giving her a taste because that's all she'll ever get. "You... make...me...sick," she pants, a sheen of goose bumps covering her skin.

"Good," I praise, continuing the unforgiving tempo of my fingers. I may not have done this in a very long time, but her body is made for me. Another reason I need this to stop.

She wants to tell me to go to hell, but she can't. She locks eyes with me and we watch the strangers who wear our faces, staring back at us as I work her pussy passionately.

"Your entire family left. If your own family can't love you, then what does that say about you?"

Her lower lip quivers, punching a hole straight through me, but I persevere. If I don't, I will just drag her down with me. And I won't do that to her. This is for her own good.

Adding to the insults, I grin. "But this is what you've wanted, isn't it? I mean, you've practically begged for it since we met."

Her beautiful green eyes fill with tears, tears which I instigated because I'm a cruel bastard who destroys everything I touch.

"Fuck you." She thrashes against me in a half desperate attempt to flee. In response, I rub circles over her clit fervently.

She doesn't want to feel this way about me, but she does. It takes all my willpower for my face and body not to betray my response to her. She is getting under my skin, and I need it to stop. She makes me want things I don't deserve.

So I begin fingering her at a punishing speed, deeper and deeper as I work her clit as well. I get lost in the small whimpers slipping past her parted lips. The vision of us reflected in the mirror pleases me more than I care to admit. I am punishing myself as well as her.

"That's exactly what I'm doing, darlin'," I smugly counter, my aloofness having the desired effect. "Isn't that what you've wanted me to do this entire time?"

"I hate you." Her words are empty.

My body dwarfs hers, her supple body bending to my touch. She should be repulsed, and I know for the most part, she is, but a small, depraved part of her likes it. She likes me, regardless of what she says.

"You may hate me..." I whisper into her ear, "but your pussy certainly doesn't."

A tear trickles down her cheek, which is what I wanted, regardless of this heavy weight within my chest. "Why are you so m-mean?"

"It's all I know how to be," I confess with bitterness. "This is who I am."

Angered at what I must do, I'm ruthless as I work her body fiercely, and with a feral hunger, I suck and bite at her soft skin. She shudders, and a sob tumbles from her mouth as she comes violently around my fingers.

I am transfixed by the mirror image—her cheeks are flushed, her hair wild, and her body contorts against me, milking everything I give because when she comes down from her high, she knows what this is. She knows what I've just done.

Even though the tremors still wrack her body, I slip my fingers from her pussy, instantly missing the warmth. She slumps forward with a whimper but never takes her eyes off me as I place my fingers, the same ones that were inside her seconds ago, into my mouth. Her taste is like a punch to my solar plexus—the most potent drug.

Rubbing her scent over my lips, I suckle my fingers, almost buckling. But I don't let it show. I'm not done.

"No wonder he didn't stick around...your apple pie looks

a lot better than it tastes." The words rattle in my cheeks when she spins, slapping me hard.

"Don't you ever speak to me again." Her chest heaves, and the flush to her body is because of me. But so are her tears.

She shoves past me, collecting her wig and glasses from the floor. She runs for the door, her feet skidding along the floor. When she opens the door and leaves me standing in the room alone, I realize this is the first time in a long time that I don't want to be.

CHAPTER ELEVEN

Lily

"Can we talk?"

Lost in my head, a place I've been in for the past few days, I look up from my desk and see Avery standing in the doorway. "Of course. You never have to ask me that."

When she enters and shuts the door behind her, I know that whatever she wants to discuss can't be good. This week can go to hell.

"Lily, I'm selling."

"Selling what?" I ask, watching as she takes a seat in front of me.

"The studio," she clarifies, while I almost choke.

"What? Why?" I manage to wheeze.

She nervously adjusts her crystal ballerina brooch. "It's time to retire. I can't keep up anymore—"

"Let me help," I interrupt, unable to accept her words as truth. "I'll work more. I'll do whatever it takes."

She smiles, but I've known Avery for the majority of my life. I know when her mind is made up. "It's not that simple. No one wants to learn ballet anymore. Kids can become a ballerina by watching YouTube. I'm barely keeping this place afloat."

What a sad, sad world we live in. "I didn't know. Is there anything I can do?"

She shakes her head sadly. "I've spoken to a realtor. She thinks I can get a good price on the building. It's in an up-and-coming neighborhood. They'll probably tear it down and make apartments."

My heart sinks at the prospect. "So you wouldn't sell the studio as is? I mean, maybe someone else could take it over?" A small part of me hopes that maybe this doesn't have to be so bad. Maybe someone can just buy her out. I'll have a new boss, but that's okay. I can live with that over the prospect of seeing a place I call my second home be torn down for another fucking high-rise.

But Avery sighs, putting an end to that fantasy. "Finding a buyer is going to take time. And"—her pause has me arching a brow—"that's something I don't have much of."

"What do you mean?" I ask, my heart constricting. I don't understand.

When tears fill her eyes, everything comes crumbling to the ground. "Turns out that cough that wouldn't go away was actually more serious than I thought."

When I continue staring at her, eyes wide, she clarifies, "I have lung cancer, Lily. The doctors say I have one, two years if I'm lucky."

"*What?*" Although I can hear her loud and clear, my brain refuses to process what she says. "No. That's not p-possible."

Avery is the healthiest person I know. She's never smoked a day in her life. There has to be some mistake.

"I didn't want to say anything until I was sure. But I saw my doctor last week. I'm sorry I didn't tell you sooner." She wrings her wrinkled hands in front of her, while I suddenly feel like I can't breathe. "I was just trying to find the right time."

"Please don't apologize. I'm the one who's sorry. I should have gone with you." If I wasn't so lost in my head, I would have seen that something was wrong. "So you're selling because you have to? Not because you want to?"

She nods sadly. "This place is my home. I have loved working here, working with you. I just can't—" When her lower lip trembles, I jump up from my seat and throw my arms around her.

"Oh, god. I'm so sorry, Avery." She sobs into my shoulder, clutching onto me with all her might. "I'm here for you. I promise. We will do this together."

I'm trying to be strong for her because that's what she's been for me. When my own mother left me, she took on the role without a second thought. It's now my turn to support her. "Leave everything to me, all right?"

She holds on tight, nodding quickly. "You're not alone in

this. You saved me once. And now it's time I do the same."

She doesn't reply but, instead, allows me to comfort her because we're family. And I will do *anything* to protect my family. Sometimes, life presents you with unseen opportunities, and although scary, you have to take a leap of faith.

Now is one of those times.

Lotus leans back in her seat, listening to me detail my current predicament. When I'm done, I exhale because I didn't want to stop in the middle of my story. I was afraid of what she'd say because when her usual rosy complexion paled, I knew I was ripping out her heart.

She takes a minute to digest everything. "I'm so sorry to hear about Avery. I know she's like a mother to you."

I nod in gratitude, but brace for what's to come.

"I can't match what Carlos is offering you, Lily. I'm sorry. This place is barely surviving as it is. If I were to play favorites, it wouldn't be fair to the other girls. Is there anything I can say to make you stay? I have a plan," she reveals. "I just need a little time."

"And that's something I don't have," I sadly state. "I wouldn't even consider this if I wasn't desperate. You've been so good to me, but I have to think of my family."

"Did what happen in the parking lot affect your decision also?"

Nodding, I shudder, thinking of my attacker's hands around my throat. "It did. I just feel like it's time to move on. It kills me to do this, but all these factors have helped make my decision."

Lotus frowns, looking beyond exhausted.

I feel like an ungrateful bitch, but with everything that's happened—the attack, Derrick knowing where I work, Avery's health, and the son of a bitch whose name I refuse to use, it just feels like now is the time for a change.

I don't want to work in a strip club forever, and if I can make enough money to buy the studio from Avery, then I won't have to. She's selling because she has to, but if I can afford to buy it, then she can stay there for as long as she wants.

She explained that the doctors suggested she try some trial treatments, but they're not cheap. Even with her savings, it wouldn't cover half the cost, which is why she needs to sell. I just need enough for a down payment and hopefully, the bank will lend me the rest.

I have a good savings account, but I want more, and I want it fast.

Avery is tired. I was too caught up in my own drama to see it. But now that I know what's wrong, I will do everything in my power to make her life as easy as I can. Being an employee is a lot simpler than being an owner. And it's time I help make Avery's life simpler.

"When are you leaving?"

"Effective immediately," I say, hating that my decision has hurt Lotus.

"Fuck." She sighs, reaching for the bottle of vodka in front of her. "I assume you've called Carlos already?"

I nod.

Before I came here, I made the call to ensure Carlos and I were on the same page. I didn't need the fancy shit he promised me. I just needed more money and wanted to make sure I didn't have to pay him anything for dancing there— no tip-outs, offstage fees, or house fees. I told him what my conditions were and that I was going to ask Lotus first. If she couldn't match what he was offering, then I would work for him.

He was cocky because he knew she couldn't. I hate doing this, but my hands are tied.

"It must be me. Andre resigned this morning. And now you," Lotus says, pouring herself a large glass of vodka.

"He resigned?" I can't hide my surprise.

She nods while sipping her drink. "Yup. Said his talent wasn't being appreciated, whatever the fuck that means because he has no talent."

Now I feel like an even bigger asshole. "I'm sorry, Lotus. I really am. For what it's worth, it's me, not you." The cliched line actually explains this situation perfectly.

Not wanting to draw out the inevitable, I stand and head to clear out my locker. I don't want to make a fuss. Before I turn to leave, Lotus leaves me with some words of wisdom. "Don't be fooled by him, Lily. There is a reason apart from your talent that he wants you. The Pink Oyster is always your home."

This is why I respect and love Lotus so much. I'm the one leaving her, and here she is, offering me advice and a second chance in case things with Carlos don't work out. "Thanks, and I won't," I reply, giving her a small smile before walking out the door.

I hide my tears as I'm not leaving because I hate my job— I'm leaving because I want to better the lives of the people I love. No one is in the dressing room, which is a relief. I want to slip away without any goodbyes.

It doesn't take me long to pack everything I own into a small backpack, and when I shut my locker door, a sense of nostalgia overcomes me. I was so naïve when I first started here. So much has happened since that day. But you live and you learn, and this is me doing both.

Taking one last look at the dressing room, I have no regrets when I turn my back and walk out the door. My cell chimes and not looking where I'm going as I hunt through my bag for it, I bump straight into a wall. However, the wall smells like juniper and sin.

Peering up, I curse whatever gods are looking down at me, as they are clearly laughing at my expense. Memories of when I saw him last, of when he had his fingers on me, *in me*, assault me, and I kick my ass, yet again, for actually wasting my time on him.

I thought beneath Bull's layers, there was a man misunderstood. But it seems I was the one who misunderstood because what you see is what you get, and what I got was clearly an asshole. But I was the bigger asshole for not seeing this sooner.

I attempt to push past him, but he steps to the left, blocking my path. Squashing down my rage, I arch a brow, silently asking what the fuck he's doing. He doesn't speak, which infuriates me all the more. The last time we were together, it seems he couldn't stop talking.

The memory of him telling me what a desperate, unlovable loser I am still cuts deep. But I refuse to show him I'm hurt.

His astute eyes scan the contents of my open bag. If I didn't know better, I'd say he actually gave a fuck about me. "Where are you going?"

"None of your business. Move." Once again, I try to shove past him, but he stands his ground.

"So it's okay for you to spy on me?" he says, drawing attention to the light bruising on his face. "But I can't ask you a question?"

Deadpanning him, I reply, "I gave you all the answers, and in return, you threw them in my face. Besides, I think I made myself pretty clear the last time I saw you. In case you need a reminder, however, don't speak to me ever again."

I push past him, but he snares my bicep, which infuriates me. Ripping from his hold, I shove at his chest, setting him off balance. "Don't you *ever* put your hands on me again." He must be able to read my rage because he slowly raises his hands in surrender. A sight I've not seen before. But it's too little, too late.

"You're pathetic. You act all big and tough, but deep down, you're afraid. You think *I'm* unlovable, but you're the one who can't even love yourself. You're a fucking coward."

I'm waiting for some smart-ass reply, but I get nothing.

"And for the record, I don't want to fuck you." I curl my lip, repulsed. "All I wanted was to be your friend."

His Adam's apple bobs as he swallows deeply. I hope he fucking chokes.

"Goodbye, Bull. I'd say it was fun, but that's a total lie. Your clumsy groping is already forgotten."

I don't give him time to get a word in edgewise because when I push past him, he moves this time. Walking from the club with my head held high, I don't look back. And it feels good.

"There she is. My beauty." Carlos opens his arms, laying on the charm, while I roll my eyes.

"Stop it with that shit." I smack his arms away from me, not interested in hugging my new boss.

He laughs in response. "Let me show you to your dressing room and then you can sign your contract."

The thought of a contract scares me, but it was the only way Carlos would agree to what I wanted.

Blue Bloods is like being upgraded from coach to first class. I can see why the place is notorious among the pervs of Detroit and abroad. The Pink Oyster was more your stereotypical dark and seedy strip club, but Blue Bloods is anything but that.

This place looks like a country club where they've just added a stage with a stripper pole. There are tables scattered throughout the club with stripper poles attached in the center. This means more than one dancer is on the floor at a time.

Elegant paintings adorn the walls, and a chandelier hangs above the main stage. The stylish décor gives off a prestigious, upper-class vibe. I can imagine this allows the clientele justification for coming here.

There is no stigma associated with this place because it's not a strip club—it's a 'gentlemen's club.' But I doubt any of the patrons are that.

Following Carlos down the red carpeted hallway, I see quite a few private rooms. I don't know how many girls work here, but judging by the size, I dare say a lot. I really should have done my homework, but the truth is, it wouldn't have made a difference.

I'm here for a reason, and that reason is to make cash fast.

"This is your room." When he opens a door and I see a room decked out in the finest furniture and my own private bathroom, I laugh because surely, he's joking. But when he gestures for me to enter, I realize he's not.

"This is my dressing room? Like no one else's but mine?" I ask, stepping past him and peering around the room in awe.

"Yes, of course it is. I told you, nothing but the best for you."

Holy shit.

Gaping at the small chandelier and plush velvet couch, I see that he wasn't joking. The vanity makeup table has a large mirror attached. There are light bulbs around the edge. It's fit for any performer.

There is an alcove in the wall where I can hang my clothes. As well as shelving. The bathroom door is open, and when I see it's fitted with a shower, I can't help but yelp in excitement.

"This is incredible. Thank you," I say, unable to believe this is my room.

I've only dreamed of something like this. Yes, the room was in a theater where I would perform ballet, but this is an impressive runner-up.

Carlos comes up behind me and grasps my biceps. I allow him to touch me because I can't sense any seediness for now. "You're welcome. I'll let you get settled. You sure you're okay to work tonight?"

"Yes." There isn't a moment to waste.

Jordy is spending the night at Patrick's. I wanted to make sure he was okay with staying at Erika's again. When he practically shoved me out the door, I realized it was more than okay. I explained I would be working extra shifts for the next couple of months, but promised it was only temporary, and it is.

When I get enough money together, I am done with this life. Buying the academy is not only for Avery, it's for me as well. I didn't realize how much I wanted it until I was presented with the opportunity.

It's a career I don't have to lie about. For the first time in a long time, I have hope.

I will ensure Avery is well looked after and won't endure her illness alone. She doesn't have much time, which means I will work around the clock to make every single moment she has left precious.

Carlos turns me, so I'm facing the mirror, and we both look at my reflection. "Do you know what I see?"

I shake my head slowly.

"A star," he reveals. "Welcome home."

Smiling, I appreciate the welcoming committee but subtly shrug from his hold. For this to work, he needs to keep his hands to himself because nothing will ever happen between us.

He reads my retreat, but something about his demeanor is almost cocky. Maybe he thinks he's won? But there are no winners here. Only people trying to survive.

He leaves me alone, allowing me to take this all in. I have my outfits in my bag, but when I walk over to the rack of clothes, I realize my outfits look like rags compared to the ones Carlos wants me to wear. They are slutty but still classy enough to keep the patrons guessing what I look like underneath them.

I made it clear to Carlos that I won't go full nude, and he agreed—for now. I really don't know why he's been so accommodating, but I suppose there's only one way to find out. Moving the coat hangers along the rail, I choose an outfit, ready to shine.

I called Jordy to make sure he was all right. He was fine. I was the one who wasn't fine. I can't help but feel like a bad mom. Working all these extra hours takes time away from him. But I remind myself it's only temporary.

A knock on the door interrupts my pity party, and I quickly wipe the tears from my eyes. "Come in."

The door opens, and a young woman pokes her head in. "Hi. I'm Kath, but my stage name is Dallas."

"Hi, Kath," I say, coming to a stand.

When she sees the outfit I've opted for, she whistles. "Holy crap. I can see why Carlos has been bragging about you."

I smile, adjusting the small black dress that looks like it was designed by Freddy Kruger. There are slashes all over it, revealing a lot of skin, but the magic of double-sided tape ensures no mishaps. "Let's hope he doesn't change his mind when he sees me dance. What's it like out there?"

Kath closes the door, which leads me to believe she wants privacy. "The place may look fancy, but believe me, the moment any man steps into a place where half-naked women are, he turns into a fraternity pledge."

I can't help but laugh.

"Carlos has put you on table three to learn the ropes. I'm dancing across from you. If you have any trouble, just let me know. You'll be dancing the main stage in no time." I instantly like Kath. She seems genuine, and in this industry, that's hard to find.

"Are you ready?"

Nodding, I spray myself one final time with my favorite perfume and slip into my monster heels.

"We've got a couple of minutes to spare. But Bossman doesn't like anyone to be late."

"Tell Carlos to take a chill pill," I tease, but when Kath shakes her head, I realize there is a lot more to the story.

"Carlos is the manager, the face of the club, but he isn't the boss or the money behind this place."

This is news to me.

Kath fans her blushing cheeks dramatically. "No one knows his name, but Bossman suits him perfectly."

I think of another man whose name suited him perfectly too. Bull...Bull was full of bullshit. But I refuse to taint my new future with thoughts of him.

I wonder why Carlos never mentioned this to me.

"He's barely around, preferring to be behind the scenes, which is a shame because he is damn *fine*." She bites her knuckle playfully.

"Well, I'm steering clear of men, so whether he's here or not makes no difference to me."

The bitterness in my tone hints of a reason for my distaste toward the opposite sex, but Kath doesn't press for now. We exit my dressing room and walk down the corridor. The lights have dimmed, and the dance music pounding from the main room indicates that business is in full swing.

My heart is beating wildly; I'm nervous to be performing in a new club. The reality of what I'm doing hits home, and I suddenly question my decision. Have I done the right thing?

Now isn't the time to second-guess myself because when Kath parts the red velvet curtain and takes my hand, we are no longer Lily and Kath—we're Tigerlily and Dallas. The place is packed, which is surprising since it's still relatively early. But I feed off the energy in the air because, ironically, these assholes are my ticket out of here.

Dallas escorts me to my table and smirks. It seems my company for the evening is a group of men celebrating a bachelor party. It's no secret men out celebrating the end of an era for their friend results in great tips. So when one of them stands and offers me his hand to help me onto the table, I accept with a sultry smile.

Even though I loathe dancing to pop music, I find the beat and let loose, instantly luring the men in. They sit tall, watching me closely as I use my body to entice them. With the alcohol and good times flowing freely, so does the money. The men reach into their pockets, and I mask my surprise at seeing their large wads of cash secured with gold money clips. Instead of dollar bills, they toss tens and twenties at my feet. It seems everyone here is a George.

The sight has me forgetting why I'm here, and when I look into the hungry eyes of the men around me, they soon replace the blue green kiss from hell. Bull is part of the reason I'm here, and in some ways, I should thank him.

If he wasn't such a jerk, I wouldn't have left, but when I see the stack of twenties on the table, I'm glad I met him because he's made me realize my true worth.

For the next twenty minutes, I give my audience a show they'll never forget. To them, I'm untouchable. A goddess who is perfect. And at this moment, I am. I forget my troubles and the fact I have feelings, yes feelings, for someone who sees me as nothing. But no more. I'm done being runner-up.

When the song is over, the men stand and clap loudly as wolf whistles fill my ears. Compared to the surrounding tables, mine is covered with a large amount of money, hinting I was a hit. I give the men a sassy wave goodbye as Carlos said I wasn't to gather my tips like some common whore. And I like that.

But when someone offers me their hand to help me down from the table, and I lock eyes with him, my newfound confidence takes a nosedive. It's Andre. And it appears he works here too.

Not wanting to ruin the façade, I smile and accept his hand. He doesn't say anything to me, but he doesn't need to. The fact he has fading bruising on his face and his nose looks like it was recently broken does all the talking.

Once my feet hit the floor, I yank my hand from Andre's and make my way through the club. Every part of me is trembling because I suddenly remember when I've looked into those eyes before. I part the red velvet curtain and mask my hysteria until I dive into the safety of my dressing room.

Slamming the door shut, I lean against it, panting loudly and pressing a hand over my racing heart. I'm transported back to the time when my heart was beating just as wildly as it is now…and that was the night I was attacked.

At the time, my attacker's eyes looked familiar. I brushed it off as nothing, but now, I realize I should have listened to my gut. My attacker *was* known to me. I just didn't know it until now.

My masked assailant finally has a name, and that name is Andre. So now, the question I'm faced with is…why?

CHAPTER TWELVE

Bull

My plan was supposed to be simple—find the men who killed my brother and make them pay. One has paid with his life, and another is on the way to suffering the same fate because it turns out I can be quite charming when I want to be.

It didn't take long for me to win Kong over.

We both wanted something from the other—he wanted me to make him rich, and me, I wanted him dead. We both needed the other to fulfill our wants. It's just too bad for him that he won't live long enough to see his dreams come true.

Having a drink with my brother's killer is as stupid as it sounds. But to get what I want, I need to be a chameleon, which is why I'm sitting in some shady ass bar downtown, waiting for Kong. It's been two weeks since I won my first fight, and since then, I've won four more.

My opponents have been pathetic competition, or maybe they haven't been because whenever I see Kong, a rage overtakes me, and it's like I become possessed. I need to destroy anything in my path. And when he enters the bar, those murderous feelings overthrow me, but I reach for my beer, needing something to do other than strangling him with my hands.

He flags the pretty waitress down, hinting he wants his usual, whatever the fuck that may be. "Hercules," he playfully teases as he takes a seat across from me in the booth.

This nickname is one he's dubbed for me as though we're friends. Every time he uses it, I want to rip out his tongue and feed it to him, but I suck it up and smirk.

"Sup, brother." It kills me to refer to him this way, but its double meaning is done with intent. It's because of my brother that I'm here.

"Sorry I'm late. You're lucky you ain't married anymore." He turns over his shoulder, keeping an eye out for the waitress.

"Fucking A," I reply, keeping to my story of leaving my family behind in Seattle. "Bitches are only good for one thing."

Kong bursts into husky laughter while bile rises. "Amen."

The waitress places a bottle of beer onto the table, smiling when Kong tips her a twenty. "Keep them comin', sweetheart."

She nods shyly while Kong checks out her ass as she walks away. "What I would do with a piece of cherry pie like that," he hums, licking his thick lips.

I chuckle in response, but I'm far from laughing on the inside.

"Thanks for meeting me. I wanted to talk to you."

I nod, hinting for him to continue.

"Boss is impressed with you. And so am I. He wants you on his team, full time."

"What's that mean?" I ask, leaning casually back into the booth.

Kong looks around, ensuring no one is listening. "The next fight, it's scheduled in some shithole strip club. The Pink Oyster." I keep my cool. "You know of it?"

"No," I reply calmly.

Kong takes a long sip of beer before leaning over the table. "I know of it real well. The boss is in financial trouble, and he's offered to help her out."

Keeping my poker face in check, I ask, "What does that mean?"

"The stupid bitch has no idea." He snickers while I clench my bottle of beer. "Boss has plans for that place. He is going to invest and help her out of debt, but in reality, he's doing so because he needs a business to help keep his books legal."

That motherfucking asshole.

"It will look like he's running a legitimate business, but in reality, it's the perfect ruse for his dirty money. No one will know. He will keep her as his partner because she won't rouse any suspicions with the Feds. The fight is just an excuse for him to proposition her."

"If the cops find out about the money laundering, she will go down too." My voice is even, but I'm barely holding on.

"Actually, only she will. He will be a silent partner, and if anything happens, he'll make sure it'll all fall back on her."

The leather creaks beneath me as my body hums with utter rage.

"What's wrong?" Kong asks suspiciously, mid sip of his beer.

I need to pull my shit together. If I don't, Lotus will pay. "Nothing. Was just wondering if this owner was single?"

Kong's face relaxes, and he smirks. That was way too close. I need to get my head, not my heart, in the game.

"Anyway," he continues, wiping the beer from his lips with the back of his hand. "Boss is going to come watch you fight. He wants to check out the club as well. He can make you a very rich man. All the money and pussy you could ever want is within reach. Trust me. Whatever he offers you, you'd be stupid to say no."

He looks at me with those dull eyes, expecting me to thank him.

I have a role to play, so I nod. "Thanks for telling me all this. I don't want to be caught with my dick in my hand when I meet him."

"No problem, bro. Besides, it'll be fun to tag team with you. The strippers who work there have major daddy issues and will do *anything* for a tip." When he wiggles his eyebrows and slurs, "One chick there, Tigerlily, holy shit, she is a mouthy little bitch who needs some manners fucked into her," I slam both my fists onto the table, which tips my bottle and spills beer all over the surface.

Kong recoils back so as not to get any on him, but I remain perfectly still.

I can't do this anymore. I can't pretend. I need to kill this varmint like now. But I focus, reminding myself of the bigger picture. Prison rule number two is what gets me by.

"The fuck, man?" he cusses, wiping down his white shirt because a few stray drops have sprayed him.

The couple across from us discreetly give me a sideways glance. I need to calm down. But I can't. Kong has no right to speak her name. Yes, all I've done is hurt her since the moment we met, but she is mine to do with what I please.

Mine? Holy fuck, I have a problem.

But it's too late. I've tried to deny it, and I can't. I know she hates my fucking guts, yet her hatred only has me wanting her more. I haven't seen her since she left The Pink Oyster, but that doesn't mean I haven't thought about her every single *fucking* day.

I knew she was dangerous, but this is bordering on being hazardous to my health.

With Kong still looking at me, I clench my jaw and think on my feet. "My ex was a stripper, that's all. It's a touchy fucking topic for me."

"Sorry, I didn't know," Kong says, appearing to believe my lie.

The waitress quickly wipes up the mess I've made and sets down two more beers.

"It's fine. She fucked all my friends. She said the kid is mine, but who knows." Shrugging, I reach for my beer and take a much-needed sip. My mouth is suddenly dry, and I realize I'm parched and only one taste will quench my thirst.

"That's tough. Fucking women," Kong says with a shake of his head.

This is the *in* I needed. "I almost fucking...killed one of my friends who was screwing her. I just lost control."

Kong shrugs. "It happens, man."

"Has it ever happened to you?" I ask softly, leaning across the table so he can hear me.

He takes his time, but whether savoring the beer or the question, I can't be too sure. "Yes," he confesses, so I continue to probe.

"Some chick fucking your friends too?"

Something comes over Kong, as if he's reliving a memory, and I know which one. "No, not that. Some asshole thought he was better than us."

"Us?" I question, leveling him with narrowed eyes.

"Yeah. But we taught him a lesson."

"What did you do?"

This is it; everything comes down to this.

"We fucking killed him," Kong declares with a snigger. His laughter is at the expense of my brother. This cunt is going to pay.

"Holy shit." I whistle, leaning back in my seat before I act on instinct and headbutt him. "Why aren't they fighting for your boss? I'm little league compared to them."

Kong chuckles as though I've just said something funny. "We aren't the punk ass kids we used to be. My friends are in high places now. They have other people do their dirty work for them."

"Do you still see them?" I try not to sound too desperate, but this is my shot at finding out who they are.

Kong shakes his head. "No. We're all busy," he says

promptly, raising red flags. "But that one incident will forever bond us together."

Hell to the fuck yes, it will.

"Jaws, Hero, Scrooge, and me grew up together. Fucking dirt poor. But we showed all those preppy assholes. We're the ones laughing now. Well, all but one."

I clench my fists under the table, not daring to interrupt his trip down memory lane. I need a name. Give me a fucking name. I know who Jaws is. Who is the fucker I killed? I soon find out who.

"Hero is fucking dead. Poor motherfucker. Got shot dead working at 7-Eleven. He was caught up in some gang war. That's what the word on the street was. But that's what he gets for turning his back on his brothers."

Adrenaline is pumping through me, and I am so riled up, I feel like I'm going to explode. Just as I'm about to ask where his friends are now, Kong shakes his head, returning to the present. "Listen to me, holy shit. Talking like a fucking woman. I'll get us some vodka. I feel like getting fucked up."

I don't press because I don't want to stir any suspicion.

He stands, reaching into his pocket for his wallet. His hand wavers, hinting his story still affects him to this day. It's the one and only thing we will ever have in common. The falter has his wallet opening, revealing something, which suddenly sets me off balance.

I watch Kong walk to the bar, wallet in hand, the wallet that contains a photo of two small kids who I'm guessing are his. I wonder what their names are and if they're good kids. Their smiles suggest they're happy.

Something swarms around me, a gentle buzzing, which will eventually drive me insane if I don't kill the source. Gripping my thighs, I squeeze hard, refusing to allow this foreign feeling, which one could say was guilt, stand in the way of justice. But that's ridiculous. I don't feel guilt. I don't feel—period.

My vengeance is sure to ruin their lives forever, and bile rises at the thought. But I can't, I *won't* let anyone stand in my way. No matter their happy grins, or the fact I know they exist, the inevitable will happen—I will kill their father.

And no one is going to stop me.

I shouldn't be here. I also shouldn't have gotten drunk with the man I'm going to kill in two weeks. But the alcohol helped loosen Kong up, and he spilled the details on when I'll be fighting at The Pink Oyster. Two weeks, which means he has two weeks to live. And I have two weeks to find out where Jaws and Scrooge are hiding.

This cocksucker has taken one too many breaths. It's time he meets his fate. I could have ended him tonight, but when he clammed up on his storytelling, I knew I had to press harder when he wasn't blind drunk.

I cannot allow Kong and Stevie to fuck Lotus over that way. The night of the fight, I will win, and when everyone has cleared, I will kill Kong. I needed a kill site. And now I've found one. The place will be bloody anyway because of the fights, so Lotus won't ask questions when I bleach the place once I'm done.

I know the layout of the club, and I'll convince Lotus to let me handle everything on fight night, ensuring she makes herself scarce, and then I'll have the place to myself.

As for Stevie, I'm still not sure what to do about him. My beef isn't with him, but I can't stand back and let him do this to Lotus. The Pink Oyster is her livelihood. But I'll deal with one drama at a time because when I stagger into the one place I shouldn't be, it's obvious I'm in no frame of mind to be making decisions.

The bouncers are a bunch of pussies as I'm clearly wasted, but money talks. I place a couple of hundred-dollar bills in their shirt pockets and am given the VIP treatment as some chick in a red vinyl dress escorts me inside the dark club.

The pop music playing over the speakers adds to the pounding against my temples, so I take a detour to the bar, losing my chaperone midway. The place is packed, and I wait behind some jock assholes who keep nudging one another in excitement like they're five years old.

My patience is already shot, and just as I'm moments away from leaving because this is a…bad…fucking…idea, I feel it before I even know what the fuck is happening. The war inside me calms, and the noise becomes a gentle hum— something which only happens when…

The lights dim, and the crowd explodes in catcalls and applause. The jocks in front of me turn around, hinting the show is about to commence. I don't need to turn around. I know what I will see. But I'm a masochist and being here proves that.

The iconic introduction drowns out the horrible pop song, making way for "Pour Some Sugar on Me" by Def Leppard. Swiveling slowly, I brace myself for her entrance, but when she splits open the red velvet curtains and marches confidently onto the stage, I realize I haven't braced for jack shit because holy fuck, Tiger is the fucking queen.

Instantly, my hunger stirs, and the need to touch her winds me. But I remain hidden in the shadows as I watch her own that stage with a newfound confidence. She is wearing a skimpy neon bodysuit which dips into a V at the waist. The straps cover her tits, but that's about all. Her bottoms are a tiny pair of shorts which accentuate her slender waist. She looks a lot thinner than when I saw her last.

Her long hair is curled, and her makeup is harsh: thick fake lashes and big red lips, and just as it did the first time we met, I have the urge to smudge her lipstick. But unlike that first time, something is different about her. She seems... harder almost, like the woman who showed me compassion is long gone.

She's different, and when she wraps her body around the pole, I see what it is. When she danced at The Pink Oyster, she did it because she loved dancing. But now, she's doing it for another reason.

Money.

I still can't take my eyes off her, but her passion, her love for dance is gone, and she's just a gimmicky stripper who wants to make a quick buck. She looks completely zoned.

The men eat it up, however, throwing their entire savings

at the stage as she gyrates against the pole.

Her movements are no longer graceful; they're angry. Her eyes are dull and lack the fire, lack the passion that made Tiger who she was. She is fucking pissed off, and this is reflective when she sinks onto her back and slithers along the stage. One chump thinks he's in for the time of his life, but Tiger is soon to shit on his wet dreams when she coaxes him forward with a curl of her finger.

So help me god, if she gives him a mini-lap, a Stevie, or whatever the fuck you want to call it because it all means one thing—him motorboating her when on stage—I will motorboat him with my fists.

He falls for the ploy, leaning toward her, only for her to press her heel against his chest to stop him. His mouth parts, unsure what to do, but this is Tiger's show; it always has been. She shoves at his chest so hard that he tumbles backward into his chair.

The crowd goes wild, and she encourages the noise as she opens her legs and pumps her hips into the air. Some asshole has the balls to lean across the stage and place some clam food into the waistband of her shorts. It looks to be a few hundred-dollar bills.

The song ends with Tiger on her back and the men out of their seats, whistling loudly, while I stare wide-eyed.

What the fuck did I just watch?

She quickly springs up and exits through the curtain at the back of the stage. A woman in a gold bikini collects Tiger's tips before she scampers offstage too.

"Excuse me?" My gawking is interrupted when a pretty

young woman approaches me. She is wearing a short green dress that doesn't leave much to the imagination.

"Sup." I nod, wondering what she wants.

When she steps forward and whispers into my ear what she does want, which is to blow me, I realize I'm not drunk enough for this shit.

"No thanks, darlin'. Go find yourself a pretty college boy."

Smiling, she does just that when she taps the shoulder of the jock in front of me.

I push past him and his group of friends and order myself three shots of vodka which I throw back in quick succession, before ordering a scotch. The vodka does nothing to settle the itch within. Nothing will do that, bar one thing.

"A grand for a one-on-one with Tigerlily." The moment I hear her name, I have the urge to slam the guy's, who is next to me, head against the bar.

His asshole friend, who looks like he enjoys glory holes, shrugs. "That's a lot of cash. You'd want her pussy to be lined with gold for that sort of money."

"It isn't just her pussy I'm interested in."

Lotus's warning comes to mind, and I about lose my shit where I stand.

"They gaslight as a gentlemen's club, but it's no secret if you wanted your dick sucked or wanted to rough one of the girls up, the management would happily turn a blind eye."

Gulping down my scotch, I flag down the bartender that I want another. "Too bad, boys," I calmly state to the guys next to me.

They have no idea what I'm talking about until I make

myself very clear.

"Tigerlily is off the clock for the rest of the night. Maybe even for the rest of the fucking year."

The fucker, who dared speak about Tiger like nothing but a whore opens his mouth, but I soon close it.

"If you go anywhere near her, I'll find out where you live, and I will slit your fucking throat in your sleep." And I mean every single word.

He and his friend exchange worried looks before they run away with their tails between their legs.

"Tell all your friends!" I shout, cupping my hands around my mouth.

The bartender looks at me and smiles. "She a friend of yours?" she asks, placing my drink down in front of me.

Pulling out a twenty, I shake my head. "No."

She frowns, clearly confused, but doesn't press.

With my scotch in hand, I shove aside anyone who stands in my way, on a mission to find her. I shouldn't be here, we've established this, but now that I am, I can't leave without answers. I need to know why the fuck she sold herself out.

This place is like a maze, so I decide to venture down the long hallway and try my luck. The dickhead said there was a possibility of one-on-one time with Tiger. I figure any of the doors leading from the corridor may be the jackpot.

Drunk men are slumped against the walls, groping women who giggle lightly, when, in reality, they should be kneeing these sleazy assholes in the balls. Sipping my scotch, I tune into my surroundings because even though I'm drunk, I can still sense her.

Her presence calls to me, just as it did from the very beginning, but unlike then, I can no longer ignore it. I'm not sure what I'm walking into, but when I stroll down the classy hallway, I welcome everything she's about to give.

Yanking open the second to last door on the right, I give my eyes a moment to adjust to the dark, but when they do, a smirk floats across my lips. "Sorry, man, wrong door." I chuckle when I see a businessman with his pants around his ankles as he is getting his ass flogged by some chick in leather.

He yelps, horrified, while I give her an applauding wink.

Closing the door, I inhale, taking a moment to focus on Tiger and only her. Cherry blossoms bloom a second later. Walking across the hallway, I know I'm right as every part of me is throbbing in hunger. Without hesitation, I coolly turn the door handle and venture inside.

The hallway light allows me to see a sight which only stokes this out of control fire burning within. Tiger is dancing for some whale who is about to lose a hand if he doesn't remove it from her ass. She is gyrating on his lap, but suddenly stops when she focuses on the doorway or, more specifically, me. And when she does, it's clear things are about to get messy.

Our exchange isn't filled with happiness of two long lost friends reuniting. It's filled with wanting to rip the other apart because we were never friends.

The whale huffs and looks over his shoulder to scold me. "Wait your turn, buddy."

In response, I drink my scotch, savoring the burn. Once I'm done, with eyes still locked on Tiger, I snarl, "Get out."

"What?" he questions, annoyed I've just cockblocked

him. But like he had a chance.

"Get out," I repeat low, grinning when Tiger slowly rises from his lap. She is wearing a sheer black dress decorated with a path of diamonds acting as a roadmap to her tits and pussy.

She never breaks eye contact with me. It's game on.

"You can't just come in here." He abruptly stands, revealing a semi, which is like waving a red flag in front of an angry bull. Sweet mother of fuck, if she gave him a RJ, I will happily rip off his cock and feed it to him.

But I remain calm. For now.

"I just did," I counter coolly.

The pipsqueak opens, but soon closes his mouth. He must be able to read he's no match for me. "Fuck this. I want my money back."

He grabs his jacket from the red leather sofa and attempts to push past me. I stand solid, snaring his wafer arm. "No refunds. Now leave."

He doesn't argue and yanks from my grip before making a dramatic exit. When he slams the door shut, the thick air wraps its hands around my neck and refuses to let go.

A pop song that sounds like Britney Spears singing about everything toxic sums up this moment perfectly, which is why Tiger doesn't turn it off. She uses it as her anthem as she strolls toward me, her gaze never wavering from mine.

She stops inches away.

My heart begins to quicken, and I don't know why. I've never felt this before. However, when she narrows her fierce eyes and looks at me like I'm nothing, I finally understand why I'm here.

I need to focus on my end game, and there is only one way I can do that. I need to fuck her out of my system. And I'm pretty sure she feels the same way.

"The only thing real about your performance tonight was the music," I state, relishing in her anger blossoming before me.

She blinks once, the red to her cheeks stroking the monster within me.

"How dare you come here and insult me?" she snarls, shaking her head slowly.

"You insulted yourself. How long has the whale been here? He looks like he has a loyalty card." A whale is someone who spends big and practically lives in the VIP rooms.

She doesn't answer my question. "I thought I made myself clear. What part of never speak to me again don't you get?"

"You're better than that." I point toward the direction of the stage, ignoring her. "You're better than this." I flick one of her curls with my finger.

In response, she slaps my hand away. "Better than what?"

"Better than the zoned sellout I saw on stage," I reply, without pause, because I mean every single word. This isn't who she is, and I need to know why that is.

Placing her hands on her hips, she grins, but it's the type of smile that will steal your soul. "Here, I can be whatever they need me to be and get rich doing it."

"This isn't you." Being this close to her is like a sucker punch to the guts. She looks and smells delicious, and I want to take a big bite.

"How do you know?" she challenges, arching a brow. "I

was me and look where that got me."

Touché.

"I danced because I loved it, and you know where it left me? Broke and barely covering costs. Why bother trying when this is easy? They don't want talent; they want to see me naked. They treat me like a toy…just like everyone else does."

This is an intentional stab because what she once said to me, *about* me, no longer applies.

"You're the first person who has treated me like a human being and not a thing." I wonder what she thinks of me now?

"This is what they want, and it's easy for me to pretend because I don't have to feel."

"So you'd rather be treated like a whore? Is that it?" I question, finishing my scotch and tossing the glass over my shoulder.

"I am *not* a whore," she grits out between clenched teeth. But I've pushed her buttons, and there is no turning back now.

"Aren't you?" I question, folding my arms across my chest. "You say you're not, but what I saw tonight proves that Carlos has bought you."

She gasps, touching over the diamond stud in her ear.

"And you call me a coward," I conclude with distaste. "Takes one to know one…Tiger."

It's the calm before the storm for roughly five seconds before she slaps my cheek. I move my jaw from side to side because she can pack a punch.

"Isn't this what you wanted? What I've always been to you? A whore?" she cries, arms out wide.

"Don't use me as an excuse. This is all on you. Own your

decisions, just as I have done mine."

The throbbing pulse at the side of her neck betrays her anger and…arousal because just when I think she's about to slap me again, she launches forward and grips my hair. It's grown a little longer, and she's able to use it as reins as she yanks my head backward.

I don't move. I let her manhandle me because I deserve it. This is payback. "Okay, fine. You want me to own my decisions, then this is me owning them."

She plants her lips on mine and kisses the ever-living fuck out of me. She devours my mouth, but I don't kiss her back. No matter how badly I want to, I don't. The lack of effort of my behalf infuriates her.

A throaty gasp leaves her when she breaks the kiss, only to shove me toward the chair. I go willingly. I won't fight her…for now. She pushes me down, and I sit, watching as she straddles my lap. Her frenzied fingers fumble with the buckle of my belt, but she eventually gets it undone.

When she flicks the top button of my jeans open and unfastens my zipper, I stare her deep in the eyes. "Take it," I challenge steadily, locking my arms behind my back. "Is this what will make you feel better?"

She wants to use me, treat me like nothing, just as I have done to her.

The quiver of her red lips has my cock twitching—the traitorous bastard.

"Will this make you stop fooling yourself?" Just as I did when we first met, I rub my thumb across her mouth and smudge her lipstick. A whimper leaves her. "Go on then, own those decisions…but trust me, you won't like the consequences."

My warning provokes her all the more. "I'll be the judge of that because this decision"—she thrusts her hand down my pants and grips my cock—"is one I think I'm going to like. A lot."

Gritting my teeth together, I refuse to buckle and never break eye contact with her as she begins to stroke my flaccid dick. No matter how badly I want to reciprocate, I don't. I want her so worked up and blinded by rage that she drops this guise and allows her true self to shine.

She tells me she is doing this for the money, but I don't believe her. There's a reason she left The Pink Oyster. And when I turn my cheek with a sigh, appearing unmoved in her ploys to use me, I get closer to the truth.

"Fuck you," she snarls, pumping my cock faster.

If not for the emotion betraying her, I would give in. But I keep my cool, refusing to look at her because if I do, I won't be able to control myself. She reads my actions as disinterest in her.

"You don't know me. You know nothing," she cries, working my shaft quickly. "All you've done since we met is make me feel like shit."

"Then why the fuck are you on my cock like you can't get enough?" I question because god*damn*, her hands are like a shot of the world's most potent drug.

"Because I want you to know what it feels like to be treated like nothing! I opened up to you because I thought you were different. I shared personal stuff about myself, stuff I've never told anyone before because I, I liked you."

I instantly freeze up. I still don't understand why.

"Pathetic, right?" Her voice cracks, giving way to the Tiger who I know is buried beneath the layers of bogus shit.

"I like someone who doesn't even like me. Someone who thought my apple pie was...nasty," she says, making me feel like an utter bastard because her delicious taste still haunts me at night.

"I never promised you anything," I state, but it's getting harder and harder to keep my desire under wraps.

"I know!" Her small hand fumbles, but she never breaks her rhythm, and each stroke drives me closer and closer to hell. "But I thought that maybe once you got to know me, things would change. That maybe someone would see me for me."

The tremble to her voice, her sadness is a punch to my wickedness, because her pain, her misery makes her real. My cock begins to harden, and for once in my life, I don't fight it.

Tiger is too lost in her sorrow to realize I'm responding to her and continues. "But you're just like everyone else. You play games. Well, I'm done playing. Someone I love, someone who has supported me my entire life needs me, and now it's my turn to support her.

"I will shake my ass and be the bimbo these assholes want because it brings me closer to getting the fuck out of here. I just need enough money to buy the ballet academy so Avery can focus on getting better. Because she will..." When she sniffs, it's the end of me, and I do something I haven't done in a very long time—I surrender. "She will get better. She has to."

Turning my cheek slowly, I meet her eyes, drowning in her tears. "Who's Avery?"

My voice seems to snap her back into the now, and when she realizes what's happening, that sinful mouth parts in complete surprise. Her fat tears trickle onto her lips, and unable to help myself, I lean forward and leisurely lick them from the seam of her mouth.

She whimpers softly, a shudder rocking her on my lap.

"Who's Avery?" I repeat, biting her bottom lip.

She moans, her strokes slowing down. "Sh-she's everything to me. My teacher, in every sense of the word." My cock pulses in her hand because I am barely holding on. "She taught me how to dance. She taught me how to love. She's the closest thing I have to a mother, and she's sick."

Her confession only fuels this moment between us. I don't know what is happening, but it feels so fucking good.

"I left The Pink Oyster because I needed the money, but I also needed—" She trembles when she strokes me from base to tip. "I needed to get away from…you."

Gripping the chair beneath me, I squeeze it so hard, it whines under the pressure. But her admission is music to my sullied soul. It's what I've wanted to hear since I met her.

"Why?" I press, barely holding it together as I pump my hips, encouraging her to grip me harder and stroke me faster.

She does.

"You scare me…" she confesses, working me into a frenzy. "But not in the way you think." Before I have a chance to question her, she begins to rub herself against my cock. I have her hand, her pussy on me, and I don't think I'll ever be able to let go.

"You scare me because of the way you make me feel," she reveals while I arch my head backward, seconds away from coming in her hand. "I haven't felt *this* in so long. I know you're hiding something, something that has consumed you and made you the person that you are. And even though you make me doubt everything I thought I knew, I can't stop thinking about you. And when, for a second, I don't, you just turn up, throwing everything into disorder. I thought staying away from you would help, but it hasn't. I only want you… more."

"Why?" I ask again, not understanding any of this.

She shrugs, her innocence feeding me. "Why does the sun rise? Why is the sky blue? I don't know…I just do. Even though I know I shouldn't…I do," she concludes sadly.

I can't take it any longer. I came here for answers, and I got them. I also came here for something else. I didn't know what it was, but now I do. And I want it. So…fucking…bad.

Seizing her wrist, I stop her from jerking me off because when I come, it won't be in her hand. "You're about to get in bed with the devil. Can you deal?"

I need her to be the smart one. I need her to stop this because I can't. But when she nods, she seals both our fates.

"I am going to break you," I promise, and I don't mean that in the physical sense only.

But Tiger doesn't falter.

"I"—she licks her lips—"I want you to." And that's all the permission I need.

She gets off on being afraid. My fierce, wicked Tiger.

I want to savor her, but I can't. If I don't bury myself inside her in the next five fucking seconds, I will explode. Standing, I take Tiger with me, lifting her from my lap and coaxing her to wrap her legs around my waist.

She watches with wide, aroused eyes as I walk us toward the sofa. Without warning, I toss her onto the leather and stand before her. My zipper is halfway down, and now that I'm standing, she can see my cock clearly.

She quickly shuffles backward on her elbows, trying to escape, but it's too fucking late. There is no going back now. "I haven't done this in a very long time," she confesses, a flush spreading across her creamy skin.

Her admission pleases me more than it should.

Looking up at me with those big, innocent eyes, I crumple. "Neither have I," I declare, which results in her eyebrows shooting up into her hairline.

I want to enjoy her, I really do, but I can't. The damaged voices inside my head won't let me. I don't know how to "make love" because what the fuck is love? I can fuck, but love…I cannot.

"On all fours," I command, stepping out of my boots and socks.

She watches me like a scared little rabbit, but when I stand unmoving, waiting, she does as she's told.

Slowly, she turns around and faces the pillows with her ass high in the air. Her heavy breathing indicates she's nervous, and she should be. Coming up behind her, I run a hand down her spine. A whimper escapes her when I cup her beautiful ass.

Her dress rides up, exposing her small black underwear. It's in the way. With a sharp tug, I rip them from her, but what I see…holy fuck. I take a step backward, needing a second or two.

Her pink pussy is bare, and her ass is firm and round. I want to take a bite. My cock throbs, desperate to be lost in this perfection, desperate to silence the monster within. Dropping my jeans, I step closer and slip two of my fingers into her mouth.

She suckles them, knowing what I want. Her tongue works circles around them, and when she bites down softly, I hiss because it's exactly what I want. Once I'm lathered, I reach around her hip and sink my fingers into a warmth I never want to leave.

Her pussy welcomes me deep, sucking me into the abyss. She groans, shuddering around my fingers. I'm surprised to find her already wet. In and out, I begin to pump, then circle her clit with my thumb. She bounces against me, whimpering when I show no mercy and stretch her wide.

I can't fucking stand it. I need in. "Condoms are in th-there," she stutters, pointing at a bowl on the table. It sickens me this is within reach, but I'm too worked up to ask her if she's utilized the contents of this bowl before.

With fingers still buried deep, I reach out with my other hand and flip open the lid, retrieving a gold packet. Bringing it to my mouth, I tear open the wrapper, and without pause, I roll it onto my cock. Pulling my fingers out of her pussy, I grip her hips and slowly drag her backward onto my shaft.

Inch by inch, she takes me inside her, and inch by inch, I

die a small death. She is so tight, so impossibly tight, and I feel her muscles stretching, adjusting to my size.

"Oh, god," she whimpers, clawing at the top of the sofa with one hand while she braces the other against the wall for support.

Her pleas feed my corruption, and I slam into her, a guttural grunt escaping me. The force pushes her forward.

I am so fucking deep inside her; I need a moment to process this surreal reality. I haven't been with a woman in so long. I've forgotten how they feel, forgotten how they have the ability to turn a man into a savage. This is fucking ecstasy.

Gripping her hips, I begin fucking her hard. She bounces against me, moaning and writhing. Each time I pull out, her body shudders, welcoming me back as I slam into her. Her pussy sucks me in, the warmth, the softness a drug to me. I can't get enough. I place my foot on the sofa to enter her at a deeper angle.

"Fuck!" she screams, still ripping the couch to shreds.

From the sounds spilling from her, she seems to be enjoying herself, but something comes over me, and I wonder if I'm doing it right. I doubt the act of fucking has changed since I've been inside, but I wonder if it feels good. It sure as shit feels good for me.

I can't help myself. The kinks in life feed my depravity because I like to inflict pain. It gets me off. I was never a saint, always a sinner. And my Tiger is the same.

She matches me stroke for stroke, bouncing back on me as I sink into her. I can't get enough and wind her long hair around my fist, yanking back her head. She grunts, growing lax as I dig my fingers into her waist and continue to fuck her senseless.

I'm possessing her, owning her, and she lets me. Transfixed by the sight of my cock sinking into her pussy, I slow my tempo, watching the way we unite as one. She is beautiful, everywhere. And I can't help but feel as though I'm polluting that beauty.

Gripping her ass, I spread her open and hiss when she sinks onto my shaft, moaning in utter ecstasy. "Oh, Bull," she cries, desperate for me to pay attention to her clit, but I don't. I never want this to end.

She collapses onto her elbows and lifts her ass higher in the air. I almost come right then and there because I am so deep inside her, I don't know where I end and she begins. She is so flexible, her dancer body lithe and strong.

I continue slamming into her, each thrust sucking me in deep. By this stage, Tiger is limp, surrendering everything she is over to me. I am wound up so tightly by her submission, and I smack her ass—hard. The red handprint I leave behind is just another step closer to my demise. She reaches between her legs and begins rubbing over her clit. I slap it away, drawing out her gratification.

"Please," she whimpers. "Let me c-come."

"Not until you tell me you're coming back to The Pink Oyster." My voice is riddled with craving, and it surprises me. It's been so long since I've given a fuck about anything.

"No."

Her refusal has me taking it out on her ass as I spank her again. She jars forward with the pressure, but she still doesn't buckle.

"Tiger, don't make me hurt you."

"You w-won't," she challenges, which has my demons roaring to the surface, ready to prove her wrong. But I'm coming to learn my threats only spur her on. She likes the danger, the fear—it turns her on.

Linking my arms through hers, I yank her upward. Keeping her hands locked behind her, I brutalize her in the most delicious of ways. She's trapped, the dip of her spine accentuating her beautiful supple ass. Images of defiling it smash into me, and I'm possessed as I fuck her without apology.

Our bodies are slick, and the noises are primal. Tiger is taking over my mind, body, and soul. I am fucked—in every literal way there is.

"You're leaving here. Tonight."

"Fuck...you." Before I have a chance to reprimand her again, she arches her back and circles her hips, before slamming onto me and showing me who the fuck is running this show. "The only thing I'm doing tonight is...coming."

She throws back her head, the smell of cherry blossoms enveloping me, before Tiger screams and a tremor I feel all the way to my balls rocks her body. She milks my cock, pleasured sounds spilling from her lips.

It's suddenly too much because the knowledge of her coming because of me—of me causing pleasure, not pain—tips me over the edge, and with two quick pumps, I come in waves of utter carnality. It doesn't stop, and my body vibrates so hard, I leave indents in Tiger's skin as I grip her before I fade away.

I'm breathless, sticky, and my body is a live wire, but when Tiger brushes her hair to the side and looks at me over her shoulder, it's like an electrical surge straight to my heart. Her flushed cheeks and the sated look in her eyes have me quickly pulling out. She looks…happy, happy because of me.

As the walls begin to close in on me, I know I need to split.

Taking off the condom, I drop it into the trash can and step into my jeans. I can't get out of here fast enough. I can feel Tiger's eyes on me, but she doesn't say a word. This is a total dick move, but I can't breathe. I need air. I don't know what's wrong with me.

"Thanks," I manage to spit out as I grab my boots, not even bothering to put them on before I'm out the door.

I sprint down the hallway, ignoring the looks of everyone because I'm seconds away from freaking the fuck out. I round the corner, and when I bump into the one person I never expected to see, the clusterfuck of what I just did hits home.

Fucking Andre is here, and he's clearly working at the club. I usually wouldn't care, but something about him being here rubs me the wrong way. However, I can deal with that tomorrow. Now, I need to bounce.

Shoving past him, I jump down the front steps, and the moment my feet touch the pavement is the moment I breathe again.

CHAPTER THIRTEEN

Lily

I wasn't expecting a bouquet. Or chocolates. But I was expecting something...more.

It's been one week since Bull came into work, pissed me off beyond words, yet again, and then gave me the best orgasm of my life. I know it was wrong. I mean, I was angry with him. I always am. But something so wrong felt so right, and I can't explain why that is.

He ran from the room because he was afraid. I should have been mad, but I wasn't. By leaving that way, he showed me he feels whatever this is, too. He has pushed me away this entire time, and I need to know why.

I believed giving in to what I've wanted since I first laid eyes on him would have allowed me to move on, but it hasn't.

I'm left with more questions. I thought he'd at least check in, but he hasn't, which is why I'm sitting in my truck in the parking lot of Hudson's Motel.

I've been parked outside his room for ten minutes, and although every part of me is screaming to just leave, I open the door and take a deep breath. It's freezing out, but my palms begin to sweat as I walk toward his room.

A woman, regardless of the cold, in a tight cheetah print dress comes out of the room next to his, plunger in hand. When she sees me, I instantly freeze, feeling as though I've been caught doing something wrong. "Can I help you?" she asks, arching a suspicious brow.

"I, I'm here to see a friend," I manage to spit out.

"Bull?" she asks, closing the door.

I nod quickly.

"Isn't he the popular boy this morning."

"What do you mean?"

"Some woman is in there with him now." She points at his room with a grin. "She had handcuffs, so ya know…he might be a while."

My cheeks flush for many different reasons.

"Not that I can blame her." She fans her face dramatically. "Nothing but trouble follows men like him."

"Don't I know it," I mumble under my breath.

She bursts into laughter. "Be careful, sweetie. He is toxic… but in the best possible way. I'm Venus. I run this place." She offers her hand, solving the mystery of who she is.

Bull mentioned her when he offered to call her and see if she had any spare rooms for me to stay in. At the time, I thought he was being rude. But now I see he was in his weird, socially awkward way, trying to be nice.

"It's nice to meet you, Venus. I'm Lily."

"Well, Miss Lily, we girls have got to stick together when it comes to men like that." She hooks her thumb toward room fourteen. "Good luck."

I can't help but smile because I instantly like Venus. She is no bullshit, and in this world, that is a refreshing change. My good mood doesn't last because who the fuck is in Bull's room?

With only one way to find out, I walk up to his door and pound on it loudly. When it doesn't open, I continue thumping my fist against the wood. At least one of them isn't handcuffed, so someone can open this goddamn door.

Just as I contemplate kicking it in, the door is yanked open and before me stands a pissed off Bull. I need a moment to process what I see because his resting bitch face is on point; however, while on most days he appears aloof, making him the master of RBF, this morning, he is actually annoyed.

For someone who is supposed to be in the middle of kinky play, he doesn't look to be enjoying himself. The fact pleases me beyond words.

"What are you doing here?" he snaps, running a hand over his head. His hair has grown since I first met him, and the dark color only emphasizes the brilliance to his unique eyes.

"Hello to you, too," I reply, attempting to push past him, but he slams his hand against the doorway, preventing me from entering his room.

"Now isn't a good time. You need to go."

"Rude much?" I, once again, attempt to slip past him, but he stands solid, and I bump straight into a wall of muscle.

My accelerated breathing betrays what being this close to him is doing to me. Images of him behind me, gripping my waist as he took what I freely gave have me wetting my lips nervously.

"Can we talk later? I'm kind of in the middle of something," Bull says, interrupting my trip down memory lane.

I'm sure he is, which is the reason I shove against his chest and barge into his room, preparing myself for whips and chains. I don't get any of that. What I see is a well-dressed woman leaning against the dresser, far from the dominatrix I was imagining.

I freeze, not sure what I just walked into.

A frustrated sigh leaves Bull before he closes the door.

The woman wastes no time as she extends her hand. "Hi, I'm Franca Brown. And you are?"

Walking toward her, I shake it. "Lily." Her grip is firm, no-nonsense, and I wonder who she is. She is beautiful—in a terrifying way.

"Lily who?"

"Lillian Hope," I reply, suddenly feeling the need to give my full name.

"How do you know Bull?"

Franca doesn't believe in small talk it appears. "We work, worked together," I correct.

Bull stands by me, arms folded. Franca isn't here because he asked her to be.

"Worked? You worked at The Pink Oyster?"

I nod, suddenly feeling like I'm under inquisition.

"You stripped?" she asks, cocking her head to the side.

Anger overtakes me because her question is filled with judgment. "No, I danced," I reply, not at all intimidated by her.

"So you're a stripper?" Is she doing this to piss me off?

"No," I state firmly, placing my hands on my hips. "I'm a dancer."

From the corner of my eye, I notice Bull subtly shielding a grin behind his palm.

Franca purses her lips, not appreciating my attitude. "When did you stop working at The Pink Oyster?"

Now I really am under investigation it seems. "Why is this any of your business?"

Franca doesn't like when the shoe is on the other foot. "Because everything involving Bull is my business."

Bull clenches his jaw, the only sign he is unsettled.

"Why? What are you? His mom?"

It's supposed to be a joke, but the joke is on me when Franca replies without pause, "No, his parole officer actually."

My confidence takes a nosedive as I feel like she's just drenched me with a bucket of ice-cold water.

Parole officer...that would mean Bull is on parole, meaning he was in...jail.

What the fuck?

Franca doesn't give me a chance to recover from the bombshell she just dropped. "It's my job to ensure he keeps his nose clean, and I am awfully good at my job, Ms. Hope."

I nod uselessly, still attempting to pick my jaw up from the floor.

"Word on the street is that there is an illegal fighting syndicate operating right under my nose. I wanted to make sure Bull doesn't know anything about it because if he does, things could end very badly for him."

"I told you I didn't," he says, not bothering to hide his irritation. But he's lying. He sure as shit knows because he was fighting in it.

This explains why he hid his face behind that mask. He couldn't expose his identity because his ass is on the line if he gets caught. It's so dangerous, which has me guessing he's doing it for the money. I've seen him fight. He's good. It's easy money for him.

But it seems so risky. I can't shake the feeling he's doing it for another reason. I can theorize later, however.

"And I told you I will get out of your hair when you tell me where you were on the night of the second of last month. I know you called in sick. So, where were you?" Franca pins him with a challenging stare.

She doesn't believe him.

Bull's breathing doesn't waver, and he is perfectly still, but what I know now explains so much. At times, it felt like he was from another planet because he was clueless to everyday things. He is socially awkward for a reason, and that's because he's been in jail, where I can only imagine being too social meant getting yourself killed.

And he will go back there if someone doesn't provide him with an alibi, because on the second, he was fighting.

"He was with me," I state confidently.

Franca blinks once, unable to hide her surprise. "Are you sure?"

Nodding casually, I don't want to appear too eager as I reply, "Yes, positive. He was with me all night." Not a lie because I *was* with him.

Franca digs into her inner jacket pocket, producing a small notepad and pen. "And what did you do?"

"My son had a sleepover with a friend, so I invited Bull over. We watched some movies, went to bed. Nothing too exciting."

Franca writes everything down, but the hard press of her lips indicates she's not happy with what I've shared. "So that's all you did?"

I don't know why I have this instinct to protect him, but when I remember all the times he's protected me, I realize it's because he's been there for me. And it's now time I returned the favor. "A lady never tells."

Franca arches an arrogant brow, seeing me as nothing but a whore, it seems, because my occupation warrants such judgment. It's time I acted like one then.

"But if you really need to know...he, quote, fucked me all night long. End quote. Feel free to write that down." I point at her little notepad with a sarcastic smile.

Bull snickers when Franca flips her notepad closed, infuriated. "That's all for now. I'll be in touch, Ms. Hope."

"No worries. I'll be taking off my clothes on most days, so if you need me, best you call first." I fold my arms across my chest. She is nothing to me, and I will not stand by and allow someone to make me feel like shit for what I do for a living.

Franca doesn't appreciate my attitude. "I'll see you soon," she says to Bull, who nods. "I'll see myself out."

I dare not move, and only when the door slams shut, do I breathe again.

The room crackles with unspoken tension. I suddenly have jelly legs and slump onto the end of the bed. Fluffball curls up next to me. I pat him, needing a moment to gather my thoughts before I can look Bull in the eyes.

"Why did you do that?" His question is filled with complete confusion.

Taking a deep breath, I peer up at him from under my lashes. "The technicalities may be off a little, but I *was* with you."

"Those technicalities you speak of"—he slowly folds his arms across his broad chest—"can get you into a lot of trouble."

Shrugging, I lean back on my hands, desperate to discuss something a lot more important. "You didn't tell me you were in prison."

His jaw is clenched tight. But he must be able to read my resolve. "It's not exactly a conversation starter."

"I suppose not, but it explains a lot."

"It does?" he asks suspiciously.

Nodding, I reply, "Most of the time, it seems like you're from a different planet. I now know why. How long were you in prison?"

I know it's a personal question, but we did have sex, so I suppose I can ask this without feeling like a snoop.

Bull clenches his biceps, then unfolds his arms. "Twelve years."

He doesn't want to elaborate, but I continue to press.

"What did you do?"

He stares me straight in the eye, and without pause, he blankly reveals, "I killed someone."

My face suddenly feels hot, my entire body burning from head to toe. It's slow at first, but when I process what Bull just shared, I envision my flesh going up in flames.

There is no way for me to conceal my horror over what I've just heard. Bull told me he was bad, but I didn't think that sin involved taking another person's life.

"Still want to play twenty questions?" he mocks, but beneath his sarcasm, I can hear the disgust in his voice. There is more to the story, but there always is with Bull.

"Did they deserve it?" I ask softly, not knowing why this makes a difference. He fucking *killed* someone. That should be my cue to leave and not look back. But I don't, and that's because I think of all the times he's saved me.

Yes, this is something *huge*, but does this define who he is? I don't think it does. He's never judged me, and I will give him the same respect.

Bull narrows his eyes, and I wonder what he sees. "Yes, he did. And if I could go back, I would kill him again."

I wanted honesty, and Bull just delivered it to me.

I don't know how to feel. I know I should be scared, disgusted, but I'm not. What does that say about me? "Why did you kill him?"

Bull shakes his head, tonguing his cheek. Was he expecting me to run and hide? He's mistaken if he was. "Why does anyone do anything?"

Unsure what he means, I watch with bated breath as he

walks toward me slowly. "Self-fulfillment." He stops just feet away, scouring over every inch of me. "Revenge." He leans forward, so impossibly close, only to pat Fluffball before turning to look me dead in the eye. We're almost cheek to cheek. "Love," he finally concludes.

"What did he do to you?" I whisper, my lower lip trembling.

Bull's eyes drop to my mouth, and with a smirk, he replies, "It's not what he did to me. It's what he did to someone I loved."

His reasoning now makes sense. I don't pretend to understand because I don't know the full story, but in this case—do two wrongs make a right? Murder is *never* the answer. However, why aren't I looking at Bull like a murderer because that's what he is?

"Why are you fighting?" I ask, unable to shake the feeling this is all connected. "It's a violation of your parole."

Bull surprises me as he grips my chin firmly. He isn't rough. He's aroused. "You're too fucking smart for your own good."

I stand my ground, refusing to be intimidated. I know his secrets, well some of them. I don't know what could be worse than what he just told me. "So you may as well tell me the truth because I'll find out what you're up to."

Bull inhales deeply, as if taking a calming breath. "Maybe another day." He runs his thumb along my chin, then lets me go.

Sitting on my hands to stop them from trembling, I whisper, "Do you feel any remorse for killing that man?"

"No," he replies, coming to a stand.

"Would you...will you...kill again?" I amend, needing to know all sides to this complex story.

He weighs over his response, but I know his answer before he even replies. "Yes."

Exhaling heavily, I don't know what to say or think. This is a game changer; this is reason for me to leave and never come back. I asked for honesty, and Bull has given it to me. It's now my choice what to do with this information.

When my gaze drifts to the clock on the bedside dresser, I suddenly realize there is only one choice to make. "Shit! I have to go."

Jumping up, I pat down my body, wondering where I put my keys. Bull sighs but moves aside, clearing a path to the door. When I notice his glum expression, I quickly backtrack. "I'm running late for work," I clarify as I don't want my exit to appear like I'm running for the hills. "I have a ballet class."

He nods but doesn't seem to believe me.

"Did you want to come watch?" I have no idea what possessed me to ask him this, but it's too late to rescind the invite.

I expect him to say no, but when he mulls over the offer and eventually nods, I can't keep the surprise from my face. "It's for preschoolers. Just so you know."

Bull doesn't seem bothered that he'll be bored to tears as he grabs his leather jacket off the back of a chair. "Let's bounce then."

My insides do a tiny flip flop because no one has ever shown any interest in my dancing before. The few guys I dated briefly tuned out whenever I talked shop. This is new territory for both Bull and me.

Finding my keys in the most obvious place—my bag—I make my way out the door, not wanting my happiness to show. This isn't a big deal. He's coming because I asked him to. It's not a date. He just told me he'd murder again, for god's sake. I need to stop with the fantasy of happily ever after.

Venus is pushing a cart down the walkway. When she sees Bull and me, she gives me a sassy wave. If she only knew what was really going on in his room.

Once we're in the truck, I pump the gas pedal a few times because my truck needs a little TLC in the cold weather. She starts after three tries, and I'm pulling onto the highway. The rock music sounds softly over the radio, seeming to amplify the silence within the truck.

"How long has Andre worked at your club?" Not exactly the conversation starter I was expecting, but it is something I want to discuss with him.

"He was there when I started," I reveal, keeping my eyes on the road.

"What's wrong?"

Bull can read me like a book.

Clenching the wheel, I exhale deeply, hoping it'll give me enough air to confess my truths. "I think...I think he was the one who attacked me that night."

There is dead silence.

I risk a quick glance his way to ensure he's still alive.

"Why?" is his simple question.

"I remember thinking my attacker's eyes looked... familiar. When I saw Andre at Blue Bloods, I recognized where I'd seen them before."

"Motherfucker," Bull curses under his breath, his fist clenching on his thigh. "I should have taken off his ski mask."

I don't fail to pick up on his regret. "What do you think it means? Why would he do that? I didn't do anything that would make him want to kill me." I soon seal my lips when I realize what I just said.

After what Bull disclosed, I decide to keep the murder talk to a minimum.

"It means Carlos will do anything to have you working at his club."

"What?" I question in disbelief.

When he doesn't reply, I cluck my tongue. "You can't be serious?" But it's more than obvious that he is. "That doesn't make any sense. Yes, Carlos has been chasing after me. But to go to those extremes to recruit me is ridiculous."

"It worked, didn't it?"

I'm about to argue, but he's right.

Even though the attack wasn't the deciding factor, it did play a part in my decision to leave.

"Andre almost killed me," I say, shaking the image from my mind. "You saw it."

"Carlos clearly wants you scared."

Turning to look at him briefly, I can see he isn't telling me something. He's not the only one who can read body language.

"What do you know about Carlos?" he asks.

The earrings burn my flesh because I never got a chance to give them back to Carlos. I decided to wear them because at Blue Bloods, when you dress the part of upper-class dancer, you get treated that way.

"He's just another rich asshole who likes to think he owns people. Why?"

"Be careful around him. Something is off about this entire situation. I just don't know what it is. Yet."

"Yet?" I glance at him and shake my head. "Please don't. I need the money. It's just for a few months," I add when he doesn't seem swayed. I omit the fact I signed a one-year contract.

"And you're not curious to know why Carlos would go to the measures he has?"

Pondering over his question, I keep my eyes forward, frightened of what I will see in his. "Of course, I am. But sometimes…you have to think about how your actions will affect another."

I'm expecting Bull to fight me, but I get the complete opposite.

He doesn't say a word.

My students are distracted on a good day. Whether it be a fly on the wall or the ribbons on their ballet slippers, teaching preschoolers is hard. Throw in a tattooed bad boy, and I may as well be teaching myself.

"Mandy." I clap my hands lightly, trying to get her attention. But her big blue eyes are focused on Bull, who is sitting in the corner of the room.

I was going to leave him outside to wait with the moms and dads, but when they set their sights on him, I decided to save him from the judgmental looks and allowed him inside. He sat quietly, but I felt his eyes on me. Every movement, every breath—he collected them all.

Looking at the clock on the wall, I decide to end class a few minutes early because today has been a waste of time. The kids couldn't stop looking at Bull. I bet they've never seen someone like him before. Their parents wouldn't associate with someone like him. Nor would they with someone like me if they knew what I did apart from teaching ballet to their kids.

"Everyone did so well today. See you next week." Turning off the music, I open the door and brace for the stampede of parents.

As I'm packing up the room, Pamela, one of the moms, walks over to me. I already know what she's going to say before she opens her mouth. "Lily, can I speak to you real fast?"

"Sure," I reply, collecting the rainbow ribbon sticks from the floor.

"I don't mean to sound rude, but who is that man?" She tries to be discreet as she gestures with her head toward Bull. She fails miserably.

"That's my friend," I say, flippantly.

"Oh. Well, some of the parents and I were wondering if maybe he shouldn't be in the room when you're teaching."

Collecting the last ribbon stick, I look her straight in the eye. "Why not?"

Her eyes widen as she's taken aback by my bluntness. "He

was, um, distracting to the kids." She doesn't even have the balls to tell me the truth.

"Pamela, they're distracted by air. They're kids. They live their lives distracted."

She nervously tugs at her pearls. "He looks like a criminal," she whispers from behind her hand, finally revealing her true feelings. Technically, he is, but I decide not to share that fact.

Peering over her head, I lock eyes with Bull who sits calmly, but he's aware of what's going on. "You shouldn't judge a book by its cover." Although I am, and that cover is setting me on fire.

Returning my attention to her, I smile sweetly. "I mean, what does your cover say about you?" I don't hide my appraisal of her tight, Botox-filled face and inflatable lips.

She reads the clear fuck you and turns with a huff.

I don't care. When I take over from Avery, this place is going to change. It'll be an elite school for anyone. Everyone will be welcome.

The room soon clears, but not before Kylie, one of my favorite pupils, walks up to Bull and speaks to him. I have to mute my chuckles behind my palm because he appears so out of sorts that she's speaking to him. When he says something to her in return, she skips off, clutching her father's hand. He smiles at me on the way out the door.

Once we're alone, I close the door and pull down the blinds on it. "Sorry if that bore the shit out of you," I lightly say, suddenly needing to fill the silence.

"It didn't," Bull replies, leaning back and crossing an ankle over his knee. He seems to be telling me the truth. Could it be he's a closet ballet fan?

"What did Kylie say to you?" I ask, coming to a stop in the middle of the room.

Something is going on behind those hypnotic eyes. "She asked if my pictures rub off." When I purse my lips in confusion, Bull peers down at his tattooed arm. He took off the leather jacket, so his arms are showing as he's wearing a white T-shirt.

Kylie was referring to his tattoos. "And what did you say?" I ask, laughing.

Bull shrugs. "I told her it was invisible ink, and only she could see it because she was the best dancer in class."

My laughter soon fades because I wasn't expecting him to say something so...nice.

It's now his turn for questions. "What did the plastic soccer mom say to you?"

My exchange wasn't as pleasant as his. "Oh, nothing." I attempt to play it off, but Bull can guess.

"She's right. I shouldn't be here."

"How'd you know?" I ask in awe. It wasn't like he could read her lips because Pamela's back was turned to him. Yes, what he told me today changes things, but I wasn't putting my kids at risk. He would never hurt them. His comment to Kylie only confirms this.

"'Cause someone like her sees someone like me as nothing but trash."

"Well, she can fuck off," I counter, jumping to his defense. "This is why this place is barely standing. Ballet shouldn't only be for those who think they are entitled to it. It should be for everyone. And it will be when I take over."

Bull's poker face is in play, so he catches me by surprise when he says, "Dance for me."

Mine isn't because he's caught me completely off guard. "Dance for you?"

Bull nods once, running his fingers over his thick stubble.

"You've seen me dance," I state, my cheeks heating.

But that's not what Bull is asking. "Dance because you want to, not because you have to." He leans back in his chair, indicating the floor is mine.

I'm suddenly nervous, but I don't know why. Ballet is my happy place. But with Bull sitting just a few feet away, his lips twisted into a devilish slant, I'm fearful my happy place is about to be tainted by the devil. But nonetheless, I walk over to the iPod and choose a song that seems suited for Bull and me.

Standing in front of him, I wait for the intro to kick in, and when it does, I dance like a monster is at my heels. I choose "Animals" by Maroon 5, not your traditional piece to perform a ballet routine to, but all I need is a beat to get lost in.

I incorporate all the ballet steps I've learned over the years but shake up the steps with some contemporary moves. When I dance, I am the drums, the guitars, and the bass, using every sound and rhythm as an extension of my body.

Raising my arms high, I push off into a pirouette, turning on my toes as I'm wearing my pointe shoes. Every part of me aches, but it hurts so good—mirroring how I feel about Bull. Dancing for him is like dancing in front of an audience of thousands.

The adrenaline pumps through me, animating my body as though I'm possessed. And in some ways, I suppose I am. When it comes to Bull, something overtakes me, and I don't know what it is. A foreign entity enters me, throwing good sense to the wind.

I can feel his eyes all over me, watching me closely as I perform a ballet solely for him. Dancing for him gives me an inexplicable surge of confidence. He's seen me dance before, but this is different. This is who I truly am. I can't hide behind my ballet because every confusing emotion bursts out of me.

I end the routine with my arms raised in the fifth position. My breaths are labored, and I am covered in sweat, which only fuels this pulsating energy within. Meeting Bull's eyes, I wait for him to say something, but instead, he stands slowly.

He walks toward me in a confident, slow strut, and I quash down my desire and wait for what comes next. When he's within reach, he stops, tilting his head to the side, eating over every inch of me. He exhales as he unfastens the elastic around my bun. My hair tumbles free, falling around my flushed face as my breathing doesn't slow.

Threading his fingers through my hair, he yanks my head backward, exposing the length of my neck to him. I suddenly feel like his next meal. And that's exactly what I am.

He walks us toward the barre and violently spins me around. I don't have to think or breathe when he bends me over the bar and drops to his knees behind me. His fingers work deftly as he lifts my sheer skirt, pushes aside my leotard, and buries his face between my legs.

Yelping, I attempt to escape because I'm all sweaty, but

Bull holds me prisoner when he licks my sex in one hot swipe. Groaning, I forget about my bashfulness and lose myself in the feel of him devouring my slick flesh.

His mouth and tongue work in unison, eating me out with feral possession. He drives his tongue deep, humming when I rock back onto his face, not in control of my body because it's been so long since someone has gone down on me. Gripping my legs, he parts them wide, opening me up farther.

My leotard is in the way, but the barrier only makes what we're doing all the hotter. Bending forward, my spine bows, granting Bull full access to my body. The coarseness of his beard adds to the sensation of being consumed from the inside out.

I buck onto his face, my body trembling with every flick of his tongue. His mouth is soft and hard as he moves from side to side and up and down, rubbing my scent all over him. The barre creaks under my weight as I desperately chase my release.

Bull reaches around me and begins to rub my clit through the thin material of my leotard. The heightened sensation causes me to gasp. Without direct contact, he winds my body even tighter than it already is. He continues fucking me with his mouth while circling my clit.

I've never come this way before. Sure, I've had guys go down on me, but this is something else. I didn't know I liked this…wickedness until I was with Bull.

He is everywhere, but it's still not enough. I want more. "Oh my god," I pant, not recognizing my own voice.

His tongue and fingers are ruthless, brutalizing me

until I'm begging him to make me come. I can't take it any longer and clench my muscles, whimpering as I stare at my reflection in the mirror. My cheeks are flushed, and my eyes are animated with a light I've not seen before.

Bull suddenly pulls away, and I collapse over the barre with a frustrated grunt. Before I can question what he's doing, he comes to a stand behind me. His face is slick with my arousal, and I instantly remember what he said to me the last time he tasted me.

He reads my retreat and licks his lips with a low, sated growl, proving to me he enjoys my taste after all. "Do you still want me to break you?" he dares, referring to his admission last night.

I nod wickedly in response, meeting his eyes in the mirror. If last night was a taste of what he's capable of, then I want more...more...more. This wickedness helps me expel the ghosts of my past and allows me to be...free.

He grins, a sight I don't see too often, which is a damn shame because it's wrapped in pure sin. "You like it when I hurt you, don't you? The pain, the fear, it gets you off."

Coming to a shaky stand, I ignore his question, ashamed of what my response will be because he's right. When he hurts me, threatens me, it makes me feel alive.

I watch his every move as he picks up a ribbon stick. The red silk ribbon is like a flashing warning, hinting this is the point of no return. He tugs once, the wand detaching from the ribbon with ease. He slowly unravels the length, stretching it tightly in his hands.

"Strip," he commands, and there is nothing negotiable

about his demand.

Even though he's seen me almost naked and been inside me, this is something else. It's a lot more personal and confronting. One-on-one, with no glitter or costumes to hide behind. With my back turned, I fumble with the clip on my skirt, eventually getting it undone, and it lands at my feet.

Never breaking eye contact with him, I slowly pull down the straps of my pink leotard. The material bunches above my breasts as I quickly get cold feet and don't want to go any further. Bull doesn't move. He simply stands still, slowly wrapping the ribbon around his fist.

A part of me knows that if I take this final step, I will be lost to these feelings forever. I haven't felt this exposed since Michael. He took my virginity with softness and love, and even though I am no longer a virgin, this suddenly feels like my first time. And in some ways, it is.

I haven't been with someone I...care about since him, and when I get lost in the heaven and hell only Bull can offer me, I realize that I care about Bull. More than I should. He has been up front, not promising me anything. But this, now, this is enough. No matter what he says, no matter how hard he tries to scare me away, he comes to me, time and time again, proving he feels whatever this is too.

I have inexplicable feelings toward someone who took another's life. No, that doesn't define Bull, but it does stitch together who he is. So, the question is, what will I do?

Letting go of what's right or wrong, I hook my fingers into the material of my leotard and peel it from my body, exposing my breasts. Bull's ravenous expression gives me the courage to roll the leotard down the rest of the way.

Kicking it aside, I stand in nothing but my pointe shoes.

Standing with my back to him makes this a little easier, but Bull can clearly see my front reflected in the mirror. His eyes scour over every inch of me, and when he rubs two fingers across his bottom lip, my nipples instantly harden.

Tilting his head slightly, he drops his gaze lower and lower until it lands on the junction between my thighs. Yes, he's felt what lays hidden there, but he's never seen me like this before. I instantly notice a bulge straining against his zipper.

As I press my lips together, the flush to my skin betrays my response to him. Needing to do something to conceal my blushing, I attempt to bend discreetly to take off my slippers, but Bull shakes his head, a sinful grin tugging at his lips, stopping me.

"Leave them on."

He steps forward, ribbon in hand, eyes alight. I grab onto the barre, needing to anchor myself before I fade away. Bull stops inches from my back, towering over me as he eats me up from head to toe. I can't stop trembling as I await his next move.

I so desperately want him to touch me.

He trails his fingers down my arms, spreading goose bumps evenly across my skin. I lick my dry lips, unable to silence my heavy breathing. However, when he comes to a stop at my wrists, I hold my breath.

Bull doesn't say a word as he guides my arms behind me before looping the ribbon around my wrists. I'm being bound, tighter and tighter, and when he reinforces my imprisonment with a tight bow, my heart begins a deafening tempo.

Watching him in the mirror for any sign of what comes next, I brace myself for utter wickedness when a slanted smirk spreads from cheek to cheek. His longer canine teeth emphasize his predatory actions as he grips my bicep and spins me around.

Face to face, hands bound, I am imprisoned in every way possible, and when Bull's gaze dips toward my sex, I am his willing captive. I want to kiss him so badly, so using what God gifted me with, I rise onto my toes, which makes me level with those bowed lips.

His arrogance is suffocating, robbing me of breath, so I decide it's only fair to steal his. Pressing my lips to his, I savor him with a newfound taste because this kiss is something new. I don't fail to realize every kiss we've shared are ones I've instigated, but with this one, under the hunger, under the need to devour one another whole, there is a longing, a calling to each other's souls.

The fact only has me kissing him harder.

He threads his fingers through my hair, tugging wildly, but the pressure is just right. We kiss without apology, attempting to triumph over the other, but in the end, Bull wins. He guides me through the room, our lips and tongues never missing a beat as he finds the chair in the corner.

Crashing into it, he draws me onto his lap, where his impressive erection brushes me down low as I straddle him. I want to touch him, run my hands all over him, but I can't. A frustrated grunt leaves me. He bites my bottom lip, sucking it deliriously slow before it pops free.

I attempt to kiss him again, but he turns his cheek. He is so frustratingly beautiful.

He reaches down and grips my ankle, drawing it back to rest on his thigh. He repeats the same action on the other side. My legs are now spread wide open over his lap. I'm limber, thanks to my ballet training, and Bull seems to take pleasure in my flexibility as his gaze drops to between my thighs.

He slips two fingers into my mouth, encouraging me to twirl my tongue around them. Once they're slick, they pop free before he sinks them into my sex. I cry out, the intrusion almost too much. I'm sore from last night but push past the pain and focus on Bull's fingers as they slip in and out of me.

I watch with anticipation as he fingers me leisurely, his tattooed hands owning my body as I surrender. He takes his time, thriving on my whimpers because as I arch into his touch, he slows down.

"Bull..." I whimper, desperate for him to go faster and stop skimming around my needy center. I tug at the ribbon around my wrists, but it's done up tightly.

Surrendering...handing over control, after being the one in charge all these years, is utterly intoxicating.

He continues to torture me, taking pleasure in seeing me beg. But he doesn't remain unaffected. I can see the way his eyes drift to my breasts, and I bow my back, hopeful he'll put us both out of our misery and take one into his mouth.

But he doesn't, and I don't understand why.

"I can't touch you," I gasp, rolling my hips as he unhurriedly sinks into me. "But you can touch me. All over."

I don't know why, but I feel like he's asking permission.

He's never had any issues taking before, but now, he almost seems cautious.

"No," he grits out, jaw clenched. He increases the tempo of his fingers.

"Why not?" I press, my breathing arduous.

When he doesn't reply, his silence pisses me off.

"I'm always the first to initiate a kiss. Do you realize that? If it wasn't for your hard-on pressing against me, I would say I was the only one affected by you touching me."

In and out. In and out, he pumps his fingers, punishing me…which is exactly what I want.

"I don't even know your name," I voice my thoughts aloud. Does going by an alias help him deal with whatever demons plague him?

"Why does knowing my name make a difference? You know what this is."

"No, actually, I don't. Tell me. You can talk to my body, but you can't talk to me. Why not?" In response, he rubs his thumb over my clit, evoking a moan.

But I need to focus.

"So what do you want from me? A fuck buddy? Is that it?" My guess seems to enrage him, and he takes it out on my sex.

Rocking against his hand, I continue the inquisition because his punishment feels oh, so good.

"The thing about a fuck buddy is that you actually have to fuck them. All you've done is piss me, oh—" I gasp when he pinches my clit. "Off," I conclude, refusing to let this go.

A feral snarl spills from Bull's lips, as he doesn't allow me a moment of reprieve, before sinking his fingers into me deeply. "Believe me, the feeling is mutual," he heatedly states, narrowing his eyes.

"Good, I'm glad we're on the same page." His touch is electrifying, and I want to come so badly. No matter how frustrated he makes me, I can't help but feel there is a reason he won't let me get close.

"Once I get what I want from you, this is done. Over."

"Couldn't agree more," he replies, punishing me further with his fingers.

"Good. Maybe I'll take Carlos up on his offer after all." Yes, I fucking said that. No, I don't mean it, but it has the desired effect.

Bull vibrates under me, reminding me of a volcano just before it blows. And blow he does.

A feral snarl rips free as he yanks his fingers out of me. I don't have a moment to protest because within seconds, he's unfastening the button and then the zipper on his jeans. "Okay then. You just want me to fuck you? Fine."

I expected this. Hell, I started it, so I raise my hips, awaiting my punishment, and when it comes, I'm regretful I didn't do it sooner. Bull digs his fingers into my waist, dangling me over his cock. "Is this what you want?"

He rubs himself over my entrance, teasing me. "I want you to grow a pair and stop running away. You're either in, or you're out. I won't accept you straddling the line with a foot on either side. I know you feel this too," I say, squashing down my desire.

He's angry with me, livid actually, which is good. This means he cares. This means I'm right.

"Why me? Why do you keep coming back when you can't even kiss me? Tell me!" I cry, desperate to finally unearth the truth.

And it works.

Bull clenches his jaw, nostrils flared as though he's about to tear me to shreds. "Because I'm fucking messed up in the head!" he screams, leaving indents in my flesh as he grips my hips. "I break everything I touch, and the worst thing is…I don't even care. I need to hurt you to feel normal. How fucked up is that?"

I dare not move.

"I have to tie you up and fuck you from behind because it's what gets me off. I feed off your innocence. I want to corrupt it, and I want you to let me because it might erase this darkness within me. I don't want to touch you because I don't want to…pollute you with my sickness, Tiger."

I don't know what I was expecting, but it certainly wasn't that.

"Bull, you're not sick." But he won't allow me to make excuses for him.

"Stop it! This isn't a story where the heroine changes the villain into a hero. I will never be that. It's too late for that. I'm dead inside. What I've done…what I *have* to do to silence the voices inside my head has determined my fate. And I'm okay with that."

Regardless of his dismal outlook, I can sense his pain and the confusion hidden under the layers of hate. Bull told me he has an end game, and what he's just revealed is that end game is literally just that—ending another life.

But why?

"How is that going to make things better?" I press, suspended over him.

With a deliberate touch, he cups my throat, squeezing softly. "I never said I wanted better...I just want to see them all dead."

His admission is what I wanted, confirming what I knew to be true. The confirmation should be my ticket out of here, but it's not. It just makes me want him all the more.

Without hesitation, without overthinking the fact he's not wearing any protection, I shift my hips and sink down onto his cock. Bull frantically attempts to pull out, but I don't let him. I clench my muscles tight and begin rocking my hips.

He moans, still clutching my throat as I move against him.

Using my core strength, I lift myself, then slam back down onto him. Backward and forward, side to side, round and round, I work my body into a frenzy, milking my pleasure from Bull. He allows me to take what I want, meeting me thrust for thrust.

Tilting back my head, I relish in the way his fingers grip me tightly, holding on, anchoring him to me. His pleasured moans fuel my longing, and I pick up the pace. Without my hands, I use my body, desperate to show Bull this is more than just a fling for me.

"Oh, fuck," he groans when I roll my hips, taking him deeper.

Something so sinful shouldn't feel this way, so right. I don't know why the universe has brought Bull into my life, but I can't deny this undeniable pull I feel for him. No matter what he says, it doesn't change how I feel, and feel, I do.

"If you're messed up in the head, needing to hurt me to feel normal, then what does it say about me that I…" I bow my back, arching backward as far as I can go because the angle is ecstasy. "That I allow it? I have all these…feelings because of you. And I don't know what to do about it."

There, I said it.

Bull hisses, clutching my bound wrists and driving into me with impassioned grunts. Our movements are crazed, filled with untamed desire. He said he doesn't feel, but I don't believe him. I know he feels this. And I will continue to force him to feel because I won't give this up.

"And what happens when you break too?" he grunts, hands around my throat and wrists. He bends forward and takes a nipple into his mouth.

Bouncing against him, I squeeze my eyes shut and give in. "I don't…break easily," I cry, shuddering as I explode into a million pieces. "You're right…the pain…the fear…I like it. It makes me feel…alive."

My orgasm is so fierce that I can't gulp in air fast enough. But who needs air when Bull slams his lips to my open mouth, kissing me roughly and catching me by complete surprise. I cry into his mouth, my body convulsing because it's too much. He continues to plunge into me, devouring my sex and mouth.

He is so incredibly warm, and when a sated groan escapes him, I know he's finally let go too. He pulls out, spilling his seed onto my stomach.

We're both breathless, the heat from our bodies setting

the other alight. But when I finally come down from my high, I realize what he did. And so does he.

"There," he pants, freeing my throat and wrists. "I fucking kissed you first."

Yes, he did, and now, I am in so much trouble.

CHAPTER FOURTEEN

Bull

I never expected this to be easy, but I had a plan. It was all I could think about when I was locked up. But sitting in the dark, in a place I shouldn't be, reveals my plans have diverted to something else. Yes, I still intend to beat what I need out of Kong before ending his miserable existence next week. That hasn't changed. But what has changed is this... thing I...feel for Tiger.

It's why I'm sitting in Andre's apartment, waiting for him to come home, so he can tell me what game Carlos is playing. There is more to this. I know it. I doubt he would go to the extremes he has just because he's after a piece of ass...no matter how fucking perfect that ass is.

If Tiger is in danger, then I intend to find out why. And

when the door opens, opportunity comes knocking. Andre flicks on the light, scanning through his mail, oblivious to my presence. I'm lounging in a leather recliner which I have shifted so it sits in the middle of the room. A baseball bat lays across my lap.

I can't believe this guy is muscle for hire. He is so fucking stupid. It takes him a full twenty seconds to realize something is amiss. He stops dead in his tracks when he sees me. I wave my fingers in response.

"I think it's time we have a little chat."

Andre frantically peers around the room for a weapon. Another rookie move.

"I know you were the one who attacked Lily." Saying her name feels all kinds of wrong. When he opens his mouth, I raise my hand to stop him. "I'm not here to argue that fact. I'm here because I want to know why. What does Carlos want from her?"

Andre snickers. "You've got some nerve, breaking into my home and accusing me of attacking a colleague."

"I'm not accusing you of anything because I know you did it. So, the question now is, why?" The wood whines under my palm as I grip the baseball bat, deadpanning him. "This time, I don't just have my fists. This will be a lot easier on you if you just answer my question."

"Fuck you. I'm calling the cops," he threatens, phone in hand. But I call his bluff.

"Go ahead." I rise slowly. "I'm sure they'll be interested to know you attacked a woman, almost killing her in the process. So be my guest."

Andre weighs over my response. He's not going to call the cops. He's just as guilty as I am. There is only one thing he can do.

Spinning quickly, he attempts to run—so fucking predictable. He doesn't make it two feet before he falls flat on his stomach with a winded *oof*, thanks to the baseball bat I used as a javelin. His fat head was the target, and I got a fucking bull's-eye. I don't miss, remember?

He scrambles frantically, but his hands and legs are completely useless because I am on him before he has a chance to scream. Gripping his ponytail, I yank his head backward. When he squirms, I stomp my boot into the small of his back. "You're just making things harder on yourself."

"Fuck you!" he spits, his attempts to break free futile. He is really embarrassing himself.

"Tell me why you attacked her," I press, in case he's forgotten why I'm here.

"I ain't telling you shit, freak." It seems he hasn't. He just wants to provoke me.

Sighing, I reach for the baseball bat. "Suit yourself."

Unlike Andre, I don't fuck around. And he learns that the hard way when I swing the baseball bat down behind me, shattering his ankle.

A moment of silence, then a pained scream leaves him while a pleased smile spreads across my face. "So, ready to talk?"

"You fucker! Motherfucker!" he bellows, twisting, trying to escape. I only press my boot down harder.

"Wrong answer." I'm about to break his other ankle,

foiling any dreams he might have which require the use of both feet, but he finally decides to play by my rules.

"Okay, okay!" he yells, raising his hands in surrender. "Carlos paid me f-five thousand dollars to scare her."

"Scare her? Motherfucker, you almost killed her!" I exclaim, pressing down on his vertebrae.

He wheezes, unable to breathe. "I didn't think she'd fight back. Things got out of hand."

"Bullshit!" I holler, not believing a word. "Lily is a fucking spitfire. You know that."

When he replies with silence, I decide to keep him talking. I break his other ankle.

Hearing the bones crunch feeds my soul, and I tip my face toward the heavens, exhaling.

"All right!" he cries, deciding *now* he wants to talk. "I was supposed to rough her up so she'd be scared and take Carlos up on his offer. But that fucking bitch had it coming! I couldn't resist."

Oh, my fuck...this cunt has a death wish. I can deal with that later. He's no good to me dead—for now.

"Why did Carlos pay you that money?"

"He has big plans for her," he reveals, turning my blood cold.

"What does that mean?"

"It means, there is more going on at that club than you think. Someone wants her. Carlos is just the messenger."

"Who? Give me a name," I snarl between clenched teeth.

"I don't know!" he screams, thrashing wildly when I slam the baseball bat onto the floor inches from his face. "That's all

I know. I swear! Carlos told me to do this for him, and he'd give me a job."

Mulling over his confession, I sadly believe him. Carlos isn't going to confide in a bottom feeder like Andre. He hired him because Andre wouldn't look out of place, knowing Tiger's schedule. Money speaks to lowlifes like Andre.

So done with this filth, I release him, watching him sigh in relief. However, if he thinks this is it, then he's sorely mistaken. Dragging the bat behind me, I come to a stop in front of him. He peers up at me, eyes wide.

"You won't tell anyone what happened. When they ask, you tell them you fell down the stairs. We clear?"

He nods shakily.

"I'll know if you're lying, and if harm comes to Lily, I swear to god"—I drop to one knee in front of him with a sinister smile—"I will break every other bone in your body."

"I won't tell, man. All right. Just give me my phone so I can call someone." He makes grabby hands at his cell, which is halfway across the room.

But that's not happening.

Coming to a stand, I walk over to his phone, pick it up, and as he sighs in relief, I then open the window and toss it outside.

"Hey!" he yells, thumping his fist on the floor. "You can't just leave me here."

"Yes, I can," I reply, walking toward the door.

"Please, I can't walk," he pleads, expecting sympathy. All he gets in response is a snicker.

"I'm aware of that. That was the point of breaking your

ankles," I counter, opening the door. "Now you can slide on your belly like the fucking snake that you are."

Slamming the door shut, I relish his screams that follow me out of the building. I get into my truck, tossing my bat onto the floorboard. I need a minute to process everything Andre just spilled. Tiger is in danger. That much I know. I just don't know why. Who wants her? And what do they want with her?

She can't go near that place until I find out what the fuck is going on. It's too dangerous. If she needs money, I will fucking give it to her. I don't have much, but if I keep fighting…

A thought suddenly crashes into me. I only started fighting to get close to Kong. It was never about the money. Sure, that sweetened the inevitable, but it wasn't the decider. I need to get my head out of my ass.

Gripping the wheel, I take a few deep breaths, desperate to settle this storm within. "This isn't part of the plan," I mumble to myself, but saying it aloud doesn't change how I feel. This is the reason I pushed her away.

"Goddammit." The truck roars to life as I make my way toward her apartment.

On the drive there, I reason with myself that I'll just give her a heads-up and not demand she never return to that place ever again. But who am I kidding? This is going to turn into a screaming match, which will result in sex. It's what we know.

My cell chimes. Glancing at it, I see it's a text from Lotus, asking me to come in early. I know what this is about. Stevie has penciled in the fight for next week. The adrenaline courses through me because the clock is ticking for Kong. He's a dead man walking.

Something Tiger said to me plays on my mind. It has since she first said it to me in her truck.

"Sometimes…you have to think about how your actions will affect another."

The action of me killing Kong will affect his kids because they'll be without their dad. Ending his life has been a long time coming, but it doesn't seem fair that the choices of their asshole father affect them in such a way.

"Motherfucker, focus." I slam my hand against the steering wheel, needing to never forget why I'm here.

Thankfully, Tiger's apartment complex comes into view, and although I haven't called, I decide to visit her real quick. When she put her number into my phone, she also added her address, so I figure that was an invitation to visit.

Parking the truck, I make my way into her building and catch the elevator to her floor. So many doors branch off the long hallway, causing my claustrophobia to spike. I couldn't live this way, having neighbors who know my business.

It reminds me of prison.

The closer I get to Tiger's door only confirms my thoughts because it's obvious from the raised voices inside her apartment that she's arguing with someone. I stop outside her door, listening closely to what's going on.

"You can't just keep skipping school because you don't feel like going! Do you know how much money it costs to send you there?"

"Fine, I won't go. Problem solved." The younger voice hints at who she's arguing with. I should definitely not be here.

I go to turn, but when her door is thrown open, it's too late.

"Who the fuck are you, creeper?" asks someone who I'm pretty sure is Tiger's son.

This is not going to go down well.

"Bull?" With my back still turned, I close my eyes and curse under my breath.

Sighing, I spin around to face Tiger and nod. "Sup."

The boy who stands in front of her is older than I thought he'd be. Maybe ten or eleven, he's decked out in baggy jeans and a graffiti print T-shirt. His blue eyes instantly ascertain me as a threat.

"Who's this?" he asks Tiger, who pales. I shouldn't be here.

She clears her throat. "Jordy, he's just someone I work with."

I'm instantly on his shit list. Smart kid. Too bad his mom doesn't feel the same way. "Oh, so you're her pimp?"

It takes a lot to shock me, but this little punk just succeeded.

Tiger's mouth drops open while Jordy glares at me.

"I beg your pardon! How dare you speak to me that way?" Tiger exclaims, her cheeks turning a blistering red.

"What do I need school for?" Jordy asks. "You went to school, and it didn't do you any good. You take off your clothes for a job. I don't think you went to school for that."

"Th-that's not true." But Tiger's falter betrays her lies.

"Whatever, Mom. I know you don't work at Walmart. I'm not a kid, so stop treating me like one. No wonder Dad and Uncle Chris left you." She reaches for him, but it's too late.

"I'm going to play video games at Clark's."

"You are not going anywhere. You're grounded for life." Just as she's about to chase after him, he shoves past me, and I step back with my hands raised because I don't know what to do. This isn't my place to intervene, but every part of me is demanding I grab this little smart-ass by the back of the neck and make him apologize to his mom.

Running down the hallway with his skateboard under his arm, he disappears into the elevator seconds later.

"I'll bounce." I hook my thumb behind me, but Tiger rushes forward and throws herself into my arms, defeated.

She nuzzles into my chest, crying, while I stand rigid with my arms by my side. I know I should console her, but I just can't. I feel like I'm responsible for this entire shitshow. The best thing I can do is leave, but she won't let me.

"Come inside." It isn't a question. So I follow her into the apartment after she untangles herself from my body.

The place is homey and furnished nicely. There are abstract paintings on the walls and photos of Jordy on the mantel. There is also a photo of a young ballerina who I'm assuming is Tiger with a lady who looks at her with love. Could this be Avery?

Tiger walks into the kitchen and pours herself a cup of coffee. Once her mug is full, she walks over to the freezer and pulls out a bottle of vodka. Instead of pouring it into her coffee, she unscrews the lid and takes a swig from the bottle.

I take a seat at the kitchen table and wait for her to speak.

"I don't know what to do with him anymore," she says, wiping her lips with the back of her hand. "I've tried my best.

I really have. He just hates me." She takes another drink.

"Can I ask you something?"

She nods.

"Do you think your son acts this way because he doesn't have a dad?" There is no judgment in my tone. I am honestly interested in what she has to say.

"It's been tough on him. It's been tough on us both," she shares, nervously peeling the label from the bottle. "Jordy doesn't know much about his dad. Although he's stopped asking about him."

"Will you ever tell him the whole story?"

When she shakes her head, I can't hide my surprise.

"That won't accomplish anything. I…loved his father. So much."

Her saying those words does something to my insides. I feel like she fucking punched me in the gut.

"Life was different for me when he was around. Our love affair may have been behind closed doors, but no one has ever made me feel how he did."

I suddenly wish I kept my damn mouth shut.

"He was my hero. My Prince Charming. I don't want Jordy thinking badly of him because he got scared."

"Scared? He bailed on you when you were pregnant. That's called being a coward," I correct, wanting to find this asshole and beat him senseless.

"I don't want someone who will give me half his heart." Drawing the bottle to her lips, she concludes, "I want it all," before her slender throat swallows down the vodka she throws back.

The sight, her words, leave me unsettled.

Even though I'd rather be having any other conversation than this one, I can't stop thinking about what my actions will do to Kong's kids. Will they turn into troubled youths too? Soon, they will be growing up without a dad, thanks to me.

Needing to change the subject, I ask, "Why does he think you're a hooker?"

Tiger shakes her head. "I don't know. There is no way he could find out. His school is pretty much run by nuns, so none of them have stumbled into my work. I work in Cleveland because it's far away enough that no one I know would come to a strip club in Detroit. Except for Derrick. You don't think?" she says as an afterthought.

"Has anyone at ballet treated you differently?"

She ponders my question, before replying, "No."

"Then it's not him."

"Then who?" she questions, resting her hip against the counter as she continues to nurse the bottle of vodka.

Thinking of where I was before I came here, I sigh, wishing I didn't have to tell her when she's already feeling like shit. "I went to see Andre."

She chokes on her mouthful of vodka, thumping her chest to help it go down. "What?" she wheezes, eyes watering.

"I went to his house, not your work, so calm down."

"What part of 'please don't' don't you get?" she exclaims with a sigh.

"Please and don't are words I'm unfamiliar with," I reply, leaning back in my seat.

She widens her eyes. "Oh, god. What did you do?"

"Nothing. Much," I add with a casual shrug. "I just asked him why he attacked you. He told me what I already knew. Carlos was behind it. He wanted you running scared. And it worked."

"This makes no sense." She shakes her head in confusion.

"He said Carlos is just the messenger and that someone else wants you. Does that make any sense to you?"

"No," she replies, screwing up her nose. "Who is this someone else?"

"No clue. Andre didn't say."

She sighs, appearing to mull over what I just revealed. I decide to give her more food for thought.

"Which is why I broke his ankles."

Her sigh turns into a wheeze as she sucks in a big breath of air. "What do you mean? That's some slang I don't know about, right?"

I firmly shake my head and bluntly reply, "Nope. It means I broke both his ankles with my baseball bat."

"Oh, dear god." Her hand trembles as she draws the bottle to her lips.

I don't know what the big deal is. "He's lucky that's the only thing I broke."

"Bull, you can't go around breaking people's ankles."

"Why not?" I question, genuinely curious. "He had no issues almost killing you."

She opens, but soon closes her mouth. "This is so messed up. I don't know what's going on anymore."

Fucked if I know, so I shrug.

"Why did you break Andre's ankles?" she asks in a small voice.

"Because he deserved it," I counter without thought.

"You are going to get into so much trouble if you don't stop coming to my rescue. Your parole officer made that clear." She licks her lips, before adding, "But thank you. No one has ever broken someone's ankles for me before."

Is that what I did? *Did* I do this for *her*?

My hatred for that cockhead Andre *is* personal. But I couldn't give a fuck about myself. However, when I found out he was the one who hurt Tiger, he became public enemy number one and hurting him was inevitable.

Breaking his bones was just punishment for putting his hands on Tiger.

Heat creeps up my neck, and I don't like it. "I'd better split. Lotus asked me to come in early."

"Oh, of course," she says, but seems disappointed I'm leaving.

Standing quickly, I go to turn, but she reaches out and grips my arm. Peering down at her fingers, I don't flinch. I'm getting used to her touching me. More reason to leave.

"Why did you come here? Not that I'm unhappy you came, but was there a reason?" I can see the hope in her eyes. She's optimistic this is more than it should be…and it is.

But I can't deal with this right now.

"You need to stay away from that club," I reply, dodging her question. Her disappointment feeds me. "But it's your call. You know the risks."

My nonchalant attitude is far from what I'm feeling inside. If she goes into work, I will be forced to stalk her from the shadows.

She lets me go, stubbornly pulling back her shoulders. "Thanks for letting me know, but you're right, it is my call, so I better get ready. I don't want to be late. Now if you'll excuse me, I need to go drag my son back home."

Goddamn her. Why doesn't she listen? What will it take for her to submit? I don't know what this is between us. I just know that whenever she disobeys me, she provokes the evil within.

I slowly walk forward, forcing her to stagger backward until she clumsily bumps into the counter. She peers up at me from under those long lashes, a mixture of excitement and fear pulsating through her.

Slowly reaching behind her, I snare the vodka off the counter and bring the bottle to my lips. The burn is exactly what I need, so I savor every drop. Tiger watches me, chest rising and falling, gripping the counter behind her.

Once I've drunk the bottle dry, I place it back onto the counter. Wiping my lips with the back of my hand, I nod. "Thanks for the drink."

"No worries," she replies, clearing her throat.

The unspoken tension hanging between us leaves me restless as shit. I don't know whether to fight her or fuck her. "Be careful. Or not," I quickly backtrack with a shrug. "Or whatever. Do what you want."

Tiger's lips lift into a slanted smile, surprising me. Standing tall, she replies, "You better be careful...you wouldn't want anyone to think you actually care."

Her and that smart mouth.

Gripping her chin between my thumb and finger, I tip her

face toward me and glower. In response, she giggles. Fucking giggles. "Why do you constantly challenge me?"

"Because it's too easy not to." I don't have a chance to reply because she presses her lips to mine, swallowing my words.

Threading my fingers through her soft hair, I kiss the smartness from her lips, hating how much I need this. How much I need *her*. She wraps her arms around my nape, moaning into my mouth when our tongues fight to be alpha. However, it's not a fucking competition. She knows this. I know this. But she challenges me nonetheless because apparently, it's too easy not to.

"Maybe I should make it hard for you then," I say from around her lips. "Maybe I should tie you up? Teach you a lesson by punishing that hot ass of yours? Does that sound easy?"

In response, a tremor rocks her body, spurring me on.

"Make you beg on your knees?" I bite her bottom lip... *hard*. "Blinded. And bound. Don't ever mistake me for anything but the depraved animal that I am." When I taste the sharp metallic sting, I hum in pleasure.

And so does Tiger.

"Never forget...nothing is ever easy with me." Cupping her ass, I lift her and slam her onto the counter. Kissing her fiercely, she finally surrenders, whimpering into my touch.

She opens her legs, welcoming me close, and I take what she offers because I want it so bad. We kiss without apology, the softness and warmth of her mouth making me forget everything but this. Gripping the top of her thighs, I drag her forward, so she is pressed against my chest.

Giving into sudden temptation, I slowly cup her cheek with an untrained touch, angling her into a position where I can dominate her, but something is almost...intimate about this. Kissing Tiger has always been hot, but this kiss is filled with something else.

The feral hunger is heavy with possession, and the need to claim her suffocates me. I've never felt this way about anyone before, and something happens...my heart, the deadened mass, begins to beat faster. It beats with a passion it hasn't beat with before.

Severing our kiss, Tiger slowly opens her fevered eyes. The flush to her skin hints what I always knew was true—we're in so much fucking trouble. This was inevitable. Now the problem I face is, what the fuck am I supposed to do?

"Don't let your guard down. Ever."

She nods quickly. "I won't."

She seems to weigh over something and reveals what when she reservedly asks, "What was prison like?"

"Easy, compared to being out here." And it's the god honest truth.

With nothing else to say, I run my thumb across her pouty bottom lip before placing it into my mouth. Her bubblegum kisses will be the death of me.

"I spoke to Stevie. Next Saturday, it's happening." Lotus rocks back and forth in her seat, making me nauseous with all her jerky movements.

Nodding casually, I fold my arms across my chest. "I'll take care of it."

She stops rocking—thank fuck—and looks at me as if I've just spoken to her in Swahili. "What do you mean? You can't be here because—"

But I cut her off. "Let me worry about it. You take the night off. Actually, even better. Go away for the weekend. Just don't tell your friend that I'm here." If she lets on that I work here, it will fuck everything up.

"Bull, I can't let you do that. It's too big of a risk for you." There is nothing but gratitude in her tone, which cements what I have to do. There is no way I'm letting that asshole, Stevie, fuck her over. We do this my way.

"You took a chance on me when you shouldn't have. Way I see it, I owe you."

"You owe me nothing," she amends, shaking her head. "You're a good person. I knew that from the moment I met you."

I really wish people would stop saying that to me. If she knew what I intended to do once the place cleared, she wouldn't be so quick to shower me with compliments.

"I have it, all right? Just don't worry about the place. Once you come back, it'll be like nothing happened." And I mean it. It'll be like Kong never existed.

She runs a hand down her exhausted face and nods. "Okay. As long as you're sure. It does give me peace of mind knowing you're here."

"Don't sweat it." I go to leave, but she stops me.

"Bull…don't be like me. Forty and living with regret. I never married or had a baby because I always thought there was time. But trust me, there will never be enough time. Whatever you're thinking…don't hesitate. Do it."

If she realized what she was giving me permission to do, I don't think she'd be so quick with the pep talk. But I appreciate the thought, nonetheless.

"Don't let anyone stand in the way of what you want, Lotus," I say, before walking out of her office, giving her my own pep talk.

It's still early, but I decide to start my shift and go over my plans. I need to make sure I incapacitate Kong quickly, so he can't make a run for it. I'm going to lure him in with free booze and women. There will be neither.

Once he lets his guard down, I will strike and be one step closer to avenging my brother.

I spend the next few hours scoping out any possible escape routes as I need to make sure my plan is airtight. Kong looks like a screamer, so I'll have to gag him right away.

Ricky announces a new dancer, interrupting my murderous thoughts. I haven't seen her before. Looking at the clock behind the bar, I see that Tawny is supposed to be up. I make eye contact with Ricky, who shrugs.

Last I saw, she was with some old creeper who wanted a lap dance. But that was over an hour ago.

Making my way through the club, I walk down the corridor, going straight for the room Tawny likes to use for her private dances. I don't bother knocking and barge through the door, and what I see has me seeing red—literally.

Tawny lies in the middle of the floor, covered in blood. She is groaning, her broken body trembling with winded whimpers. She's alive. Sprinting to where she is, I drop to my knees and look at the damage inflicted on her. Her face is swollen, beaten without mercy.

"Tawny!" I exclaim, gently shaking her shoulder. Her body is limp.

She is lying on her side, so I slowly sit her up, supporting her against my chest. "Who did this to you?"

She begins to sob, collapsing into me.

"If you don't tell me who did this, I can't help you," I press, looking down at her dress. It's still intact. Whoever did this wasn't after sex. He was after something else.

"You," she pushes out between pained breaths.

"Me what?" I ask, holding her tightly as her head lolls to the side.

"He was after...you," she finally reveals. "He a-asked if I knew y-you. I said ye-yes. He said he ha-had a message for you. And t-then he started...hi-hitting me."

My jaw clenches, and something savage overcomes me. "What message?"

Tawny is crying uncontrollably and rightfully so. But she needs to tell me what this fucker wants. "Tawny," I implore, shaking her lightly.

Leaning into me, she sniffles, "He said...they're watching you."

I have no idea who, but what I do know is that anyone associated with me is in danger. My blood runs cold when I think of Tiger.

I want to ask her so many other questions but getting her to a hospital is more important. "C'mon, Tawny. I'm taking you to the hospital."

She's passed out, so I lift her, cradling her to my chest. Taking the back door, I avoid any attention, not wanting word to get out as Lotus doesn't need any more problems. As I lay Tawny across the back seat of my truck, I wonder how much blood I'll have to spill to get my revenge.

This was supposed to be simple. But I should know by now, nothing ever is.

CHAPTER FIFTEEN

Bull

I t's time.

Everything comes down to this.

I haven't slept. I'm too high-strung. But I don't need sleep. I just need my brother's murderer's dead.

The red roses I laid by Damian's grave are a peace token. I know if he were alive, he would be begging me not to do this. But he's not. "I'm sorry, bro." I don't even know what I'm seeking absolution for anymore.

Tiger has texted me throughout the week, but I haven't replied. I can't. Not after what happened to Tawny. Her messages are enough for me to know she's okay. For now.

I should have been stronger and remained hidden. Now she's a fucking target. Anyone who knows me is. Which is why there is no room for error tonight. Once the fight is done, I will torture Kong and get everything I need out of him. He won't spill easily; therefore, I have to ensure my methods of making him talk are effective.

Once I know where Jaws and Scrooge are, I will keep to the shadows. I've decided to quit The Pink Oyster because it's too dangerous for Lotus if I stay. I'll send her an anonymous letter, letting her know what Stevie has planned. I don't want to snitch, but I won't allow that asshole to use her that way.

As for Tiger…I'm doing what I should have done from the very beginning. I'm leaving her the fuck alone.

The wind howls around me, setting an ominous mood for things to come. But I'm not nervous. I'm calm. Gripping the medallion around my neck, I bid farewell to my brother, ignoring the pang I feel, knowing how disappointed he would be with my decisions.

The drive to The Pink Oyster gives me time to think about the plan I've devised. There are three exits in the club, and all will be locked tight. Getting Kong wasted would be the easiest way to subdue him, but I need him clearheaded, so that means I will just have to rough him up…a lot. He can fight, but I'm not a kid anymore.

Clenching the wheel, I peer at myself in the rearview mirror, my matching eyes, eyes so much like my brother's, staring back at me. It's go time.

Parking the truck around back, I ensure no one is watching when I thread a thick steel chain around the side and back door handles and padlock them shut. Extra reinforcements are in place. The place is like a fucking ghost town it's so quiet.

Lotus is staying with her sister in Chicago for the night. I told her not to worry about anything, but I'll check in to ensure everything is okay. I don't want her dropping in unannounced.

There's a sign on the front door indicating that tonight is a private function, so I text Kong that I'm here. He appears a moment later. "Brother," he says, gripping my hand and pulling me to bump shoulders with him like we're friends.

"Sup," I reply, going along with the façade. Not long now. He ushers me inside, before locking the door behind me.

I see that they've moved the tables and chairs, clearing the floor. "So this is the shithole," Kong says, spreading his arms out wide.

I nod, suppressing the urge to rip out his tongue.

"Now, that's not nice," says a voice to my left. "You're insulting my investment."

Looking over my shoulder, I see Stevie with a smug smile. He walks over to us, offering me his hand. "Tommy. I've heard so much about you. I'm Stevie."

Shaking his hand firmly, I nod, keeping talking to a minimum.

"Kong has vouched for you, which doesn't happen often. I need another man on my team. Interested?"

"Maybe," I reply. Folding my arms across my chest, I humor him. "What's in it for me?"

"I like you," Stevie says between snickering. "A man who knows what he wants. You're the best damn fighter I've seen in a long time. I want you on my payroll permanently. You fight for me, winning me money, and I reward you with all the money, pussy, and drugs you could ever want."

All but one interests me.

"What sort of drugs?"

"Whatever you want, but my specialty is pure Colombian cocaine. If fighting doesn't interest you, well, there are plenty of other opportunities for you."

Stevie's smirk hints he believes I'm quiet because I'm impressed with him whipping out his dick. I'm not.

"Sure, I'm down." This will hopefully get Stevie off my case.

"Good choice," he commends, but the joke's on him. "This place will be our cover for all the fucking money we're about to make."

Stevie is a businessman who is involved in many dealings, it seems. Drugs, illegal fighting, and who the fuck knows what else. He's the big bad in the underworld. So is Jaws. There must be a connection here. I just don't know what that is—yet.

"Can't wait," I reply. "Where can I warm up?"

"Come on, I'll show you." Kong gestures with his head, leading the way toward the dressing room.

Following him, I can't help but feel like this is a walk on death row. Does he deserve a special request? A last wish before he's put to death? When memories of what he did to me, to Damian flash before my eyes, I realize this motherfucker's last wish was living for the past fourteen years.

It's now that time comes to an end.

When we walk into the dressing room, I dump my bag onto the floor and pretend to examine my surroundings. Kong's cell chimes, and he answers it. He quickly turns his back and begins speaking softly to whoever is on the other end.

He doesn't speak softly enough, though.

"Listen to your mommy, Yasmin. Daddy is working late." Pause. "Yes, I promise I'll tuck you in tomorrow."

But no, he won't 'cause come tomorrow…he'll be fucking dead.

Something shifts inside me and wraps its hand around my throat. I shove that feeling way, way down because it's got no right to be here. This was decided by *him*.

I leave Kong alone, giving him time to talk to his daughter because it'll be the last time he does. I've just granted him his final wish…he just doesn't know it.

The roar of the crowd fuels this darkness within me.

Violence.

Blood.

It's what I need to survive.

When I hear the shatter of bone, I tip my face toward the ceiling and inhale in triumph. There is no sound like it. My opponent drops to the floor, screaming in pain as he cups his broken arm. At least he's not crying like the other two men I fought tonight.

It's done. Finally.

The masses try to congratulate me, but I shove them aside. I'm not here for praise. Once I enter the dressing room,

I interlace my hands behind my neck and exhale deeply. I can feel the blood pumping throughout my entire body. Ironically, I don't ever remember feeling this alive.

"What the fuck did you take tonight? Holy shit! You destroyed them all." Not yet, I haven't.

Turning to face Kong, I give him a half smile. "I just want to get fucking wasted and score some pussy. These cockheads are standing in my way. Have a drink with me once everyone leaves?"

No isn't an option.

"I may or may not have some lady company coming soon," I say, hoping to sweeten the deal.

Kong rubs his hands together. "You had me at pussy."

"Clear the club out. I'll get changed." Turning around, I unzip my bag, not wanting my excitement to show.

Once he leaves, I exhale slowly because it's finally happening. Taking off my bloody, sweaty clothes, I put on my uniform—white shirt, black trousers, black tie, black suspenders, and Converse. This is a cause for celebration, so I wanted to dress accordingly.

Reaching for my chain, I run my finger over the medallion, refusing to feel guilty about my decision. Slipping it on, I notice my cell light up from inside my bag. It's a text from Tiger. I don't bother reading it because I need to keep my head in the game.

I have everything I need in my bag, so I toss it over my shoulder, check the side and back exits to ensure they're still locked, and then make my way out into the empty club.

Once the fights are done, no one sticks around. This isn't

about socializing. This is about money. And once there is no more money to win, there is no need for people to stay. Stevie left halfway through the fight. He saw enough.

As far as he believes, he's added another minion to his crew. He's sorely mistaken because he's about to lose two. Kong is behind the bar, helping himself to some scotch.

"Going to wait for the girls. They just texted. They aren't far away."

Kong raises his glass in salute. It'll be the last drink he ever has.

My hands shake with exhilaration as I lock the front door. Fourteen years have all come down to this one moment. After taking out my contact, I slip the serrated knife under my waistband at the small of my back. It's all I need. This is going to get bloody.

Whistling, I take my time and stroll back into the club. In my head, I envisioned this moment going down with guns blazing, and once this asshole took his last breath, a piece of me would return. But in reality, I could kill him over and over again, and it still wouldn't be enough.

Kong's back is to me as he looks over the liquor on the shelves. "This place may be a shithole," he says, while I set my sights on him, "but it sure has some good booze. What do you feel like? Whiskey? Vodka?"

Stopping behind him, I savor the silence. It's on. "Your head."

Kong turns to face me, and I give him a second, one fucking second, to process just who I am, and when he looks into my mismatched eyes, he knows…the grim reaper is here.

He instantly reaches for the gun in his holster, but I strike out and punch him square in the nose. He stumbles back two steps, cupping his bleeding face. I don't give him time to regain his footing as I punch him in the ribs and then the stomach.

He's wheezing for breath, and when he tries to stand, I kick down on his kneecap, breaking it. A pained scream rips free as he tumbles to the floor. Without hesitation, I grip the back of his collar and commence dragging him through the club.

He tries to claw at anything he can reach for, but his hands are slippery, thanks to the blood coating them. The trail of bright red feeds my debauchery as I haul him up the stage stairs.

"Why?" he screams, spittle coating his chin. "What the fuck did I ever do to you?"

We can play twenty questions later. Right now, I need to tie this motherfucker to this pole. Tossing him against it, he attempts to stand, but he's not going anywhere, and I make that clear when I press my boot onto his broken kneecap.

He howls in pain and is already on the cusp of passing out.

I toss my bag onto the floor and hunt for the cable ties. Yanking his arms behind him, I fasten his wrists so he's secured tightly around the pole. He tries to stand, but his broken knee won't support his weight. He stays seated.

Crouching down in front of him, I grin at what I see. He's broken, bound, and bleeding. This has only just begun.

"This is only going to end one way for you," I reveal

grimly. "So I suggest you answer my questions, and I won't make it hurt—much."

"Fuck you." Glaring, he spits out a mouthful of blood.

Sighing, I come to a slow stand and allow him to see who I really am. "Wrong answer."

I'm tempted to break every bone in his body, but I need him coherent. I need answers.

"I've been looking for you for fourteen years. So you can imagine my surprise when you all but fell into my lap. Some may say it was fate?" I shake my head. "But I don't believe in that because why the fuck was I fated to meet you the night you..." Inhaling, I steady myself. "The night you killed my... brother."

Kong's eyes widen, and recognition flashes before him.

"I know I look a lot different. Not the scrawny fucker you held back so easily when your friends beat, humiliated, and killed my brother," I state, cracking my knuckles because I want to slam my fists into him so badly.

"What was it you said to me? Can you remember?" I ask, tapping my chin.

"I don't remember shit. You've got the wrong man!" Kong yells, yanking at his restraints.

"Kong," I tsk, shaking my head. "Or should I call you Ethan Da Silva? That's your name, isn't it?" I silently thank Tawny for letting that piece of information slip.

His jaw tightens. "That's not me, man. I promise!" His lies will get him nowhere.

Rolling up the sleeve of my shirt, I show him my tattoo. The spread of four aces. "You see this?" I say, pointing at the blindfolded woman. "This is you. Justice will be rightfully given without fear. That night, you held me back, but instead of blindfolding me…you forced me to watch…forced me to watch your *friends* destroy my brother."

Kong swallows, stuck in the past.

"Each of these are for your friends." I point at the green diamond, which was the stone in Damian's championship ring. "This is for the asshole who stole from my brother. Breaking his wrist wasn't enough. He had to steal from him as well." I move onto the lion. "This is for the fucking coward who had the chance to save my brother, but he didn't. A lion is brave, loyal, something this asshole wasn't."

Kong realizes I've spoken about him in the past tense.

"Which is why"—I smile—"I ended his pathetic life. Hero, or should I say Lachlan, didn't die a hero. He died crying, begging for his life as he pissed his pants."

"*You* killed Hero?" he asks, eyes wide. One of the terms of my plea agreement was that my identity was never released.

"Yes," I reply without pause. "You see this cross here?" I point at the small black cross where the suit should be. "I got this after he dropped to his knees and then I shot him straight through the fucking heart."

Kong shakes his head wildly. "You motherfucker! No! You played me!"

Thriving on his pain, I continue. "I found him, just as I found you. I didn't show him any mercy when he begged. Why should I? He didn't show any to my brother. And that leaves the last member of your little gang."

The blue shark has been a permanent reminder of what

was always destined.

"This is self-explanatory. Jaws was the fucker who took that rock and split my brother's head open. Yes, you all played a part in his death, but Jaws was the one who delivered the final blow," I spit with nothing but hatred.

"So now, you're going to tell me where he and Scrooge are."

Kong hasn't uttered a single word. His surprise is clear. Did he think we were actual friends? "I'm not telling you jack shit," he snarls. "You're going to kill me anyway, so why would I tell you anything?"

Sighing, I don't know whether I'm happy or annoyed he's decided to be difficult because now I'll be forced—and I use that word lightly—to hurt him.

Ambling forward, I stand just out of reach, glaring down at Kong. "Tell me why," I demand. When he remains tightlipped, I stomp down on his knee. "Tell me why us?"

His howls feed the demons, and I reach for my knife. Without hesitation, I lunge forward and stab him in the flank. It's just a scratch, but I know it hurts like a bitch. His white shirt begins to stain a bright red.

"When I shot your friend, I went to prison, and during that time, I learned from the best," I reveal, watching him flail madly, trying to break free. "I know how to torture you for hours. I know where to cut, where to hurt you to keep you alive. I can do this all night."

Just as I lunge forward, once again, he shakes his head frantically. "Okay, okay, fine!" he cries, yanking at his restraints. "I'll tell you what I know!"

A part of me is sad he submitted so easily.

"Jaws is he-here. In Detroit. He owns the fucking city, man! Stevie and he are rivals."

His admission has me arching a brow. "Then why the fuck are you working with Stevie?"

He licks his bloody lips. "Because Jaws didn't need me anymore. He and Scrooge are big league now and won't let anyone stand in their way. When I couldn't do a job they wanted me to do, I was tossed out like trash. It didn't matter that we've been friends since we were kids. I offered to work for Stevie because I needed his protection.

"Jaws wouldn't start shit with him because he wants to fly under the radar. As long as Stevie doesn't interfere with his business, there isn't a problem."

I curl my lip, disgusted. I thought he was the muscle. It seems I was mistaken because he's a fucking pussy.

"That's all I know. I swear! I'm not in their inner circle anymore."

"What job did they want you to do?"

"Jaws wanted me to kill his nephew," he reveals, which has me wondering why. "He has this weird...fascination with his sister."

"What the fuck does that mean?"

"It means what you think it means!" he exclaims. "Jaws is one sick motherfucker. He doesn't care who the fuck you are...if he wants you, he takes you."

"And what about Scrooge? What's his deal?"

"He's the money. He's untouchable. Jaws is the brains. Together, they're an unstoppable, deadly force. Forget this vendetta. You won't win," he says, flinching when he tries to move.

"Give me names." I ignore his advice.

He shakes his head. "That's all I'm telling you! They may have dogged me, but I'm not about to rat them out."

Usually, I would applaud his loyalty. No one likes a snitch. But now, his silence is pissing me off. Violence hasn't seemed to work, so I decide to try another method. "You'll protect those assholes after the way they treated you? No wonder they had no use for you. You're weak. But I know what'll make you talk."

Dropping to one knee, I level him with nothing but pure hatred. "What will your son and daughter think when I do to them what you should have done to Jaws's nephew?"

This is the only time I get a response from Kong. "You motherfucker! Don't you touch them!" He violently tries to break free.

"Give me their names, and I won't be forced to." I point the knife in his direction, indicating the choice is his.

"I can't." He begins to cry. The sight unnerves me.

"Can't is going to determine the fate of your kids." I go to stand, giving Kong credit as he tries to kick me. "All I want is their names. I will take care of the rest."

"Man, please. I was good to you," he has the audacity to say.

Laughing sinisterly, I begin to pace in front of him. "Good to me? I was of use to you. That's all this was. A business transaction on both ends."

"No, it wasn't for me! I thought we were friends."

"Friends?" I snicker, still pacing. "I don't want to be your friend. The friends you kept are the reason you're here, begging for your life. Why did they do it?"

"I don't know!" he screams. The air begins to blister. A storm is coming. "There is no reason. It just happened! We were bored kids."

His response is like spitting on Damian's grave. Storming over, I punch him in the jaw. His head snaps back, connecting with the pole.

"Bored?" I exclaim, kicking him in the stomach. "If you were bored, you could have done a million other things! But instead, you chose to kill someone who didn't deserve to die!"

Kong is wheezing for air as I'm pretty sure a rib has ruptured his lung. But we're not done.

"You said to me…"

But Kong doesn't allow me to finish. He fills in the blanks, sealing his fate for good. "It's time you became a man," he pants, repeating the words he said to me fourteen years ago. "That's what I said. And it looks like you did. Their names are…"

His head lolls to the side. He's on the cusp of passing out. "No, you don't!" I grip him around the neck, forcing him to stay awake. "Tell me!"

A gargle spills from his lips. "Benjamin Solomon and…"

"And who?" I scream, tightening my grip around his throat.

"Jaws is…"

He has three fucking seconds to talk before I slit his fucking throat. "Motherfucker! Jaws is who? Give me a name!"

"I can't, man," he pants, tears spilling from the corner

of his eyes. "Just don't hurt my family. They're just kids." He won't talk. His loyalty would be admirable, but it's just sped up his death.

I wanted to be patient and torture him until he spilled, but I can't do this any longer.

Reaching for my knife, I look him dead in the eye and growl, "So was my brother. And so was I." And with that, I drive the blade straight through his heart. I have what I came here for.

Our gazes never waver as I watch the life drain from him slowly. I wish with each gurgled breath he takes he could breathe life into Damian, but it doesn't work that way. Sometimes, things happen. There isn't a reason for what happened to Damian. He was in the wrong place, at the wrong time, which just makes this so much worse. His death was in vain.

But I have a reason to kill the remaining two players. I know who they are. They're fucking dead.

It takes Kong about two minutes before he takes his final breath. With each second, I breathe with him, growing stronger as his weakness feeds my strength. One may feel remorse, but I don't. My only regret is I couldn't inflict more pain.

Once he's still, I yank the blade out from his chest and wipe it across his shirt, leaving a slash of red in its wake. Inhaling, I tip my face to the heavens as a sense of peace washes over me. I felt this way only one time before.

However, when a strangled gasp sounds behind me, my heaven soon becomes hell. Turning to look over my shoulder, I stare into gentle green eyes, shattering my high.

CHAPTER SIXTEEN

Lily

"B-B-Bull?" My voice is foreign because, at this moment, life as I know it has been shattered beyond repair.

Even though what I'm seeing is clear as day, I don't, I *can't* accept it as truth. There has to be another reason Bull is standing before me with a bloody knife in his hand and a dead man at his feet. But there isn't. The man is dead because of Bull.

Covering my mouth, I swallow down my vomit. My hysteria can wait. I need to get the fuck out of here. Turning too quickly, I lose my footing and almost fall onto my ass. When I see what I slipped on, a hollowed cry leaves me.

Blood.

"Fuck!" Bull storms forward, but I place a shaky hand out in front of me, begging him to stop.

"Pl-please do-don't hurt me. I won't tell a-anyone."

He halts, overcome by melancholy. "I would never hurt you." When I don't reply, he sincerely adds, "You know that, right?"

But I don't. I don't know anything at all. "Please let me go."

"You're not my prisoner. You're free to go," he says, slowly lowering the knife onto the stage and raising his bloody hands in surrender.

The vision will be burned into my memory forever.

I want to ask him why, but does it even matter anymore? He just killed a man...another man. I need to get away from him. For good.

"Tiger, you believe me, don't you?" He interlaces his hands behind his neck, pleading I believe him. But I can't.

Spinning around, I run through the club, images of Bull taking me down like a gazelle in the wild, prompting me to run for my life. I shove open the front door and sprint toward my truck. The moment I'm inside, I slam down the lock and wait for Bull to emerge.

He doesn't.

My hands are shaking so badly that I can't get the key into the ignition. I take a steadying breath. Once they stop trembling, I start my truck and pull onto the highway. I drive on autopilot, barely blinking, too afraid to relive what I just witnessed.

I went to The Pink Oyster because I wanted to know why Bull was giving me the cold shoulder. When I saw the place was closed for a private function, I let myself in with the key I still had. Now I know why he's been MIA. He was too busy planning someone's murder. I don't know who it was. His chin was downturned. But the trickle of blood seeping from his lifeless lips was a sure sign he was dead.

As I clench the wheel, tears stream down my cheeks because I don't know what to do. A normal person would go to the police, but even still, after everything I just saw, I can't do that to him. Something is seriously wrong with me.

I believed him when he said he wouldn't hurt me. How fucking tragic is that?

Pulling into the parking lot at Blue Bloods, I barely have enough time to put my truck into park because I'm going to be violently ill. Yanking open the door, I dry heave outside, wanting to dispel this feeling within, but I can't.

The sickness I feel isn't something I can purge. It will fester inside me for as long as I keep his secret.

The fresh air soothes me somewhat, so I kill the engine and make my way inside. I'm not working tonight, but I can't go home. I don't want Jordy to see me like this. I don't want Jordy to know his mom has... feelings for a murderer.

Keeping my head low, I quickly make a dash for my dressing room. Once inside, I lean against the door and brace my head against it. I need to gather my thoughts.

I just saw a dead person, killed by the man I've allowed to touch me over and over again. Reaching into my back pocket with trembling fingers, I grab my cell. There is only one thing to do.

"911, what's your emergency?" The operator is waiting,

waiting for me to finally do the right thing. I need to tell her there is a dead body at The Pink Oyster and his murderer is Bull. I open my mouth, but I suddenly can't speak.

"I would never hurt you."

Bull's words play on a loop, haunting my decision because I just can't. If I call the police, Franca will have his ass thrown back into prison, where he will remain for the rest of his life. The thought of never seeing him again, never feeling *this* ever again has me quickly ending the call.

It's selfish and morally wrong, so wrong, but I would rather deal with this eternal guilt than be the one to rat Bull out. I knew he was dangerous, hell, he even told me he was. But I never really believed it…until now.

Sliding down the door, I crumple into a heap and draw my knees toward me, hugging them to my chest. Although my mind is racing, I know one thing for certain—I can never see Bull again. No matter how badly I want to fight it, I won't.

My cell chirps endlessly. But I ignore it. I know who it is.

I don't know how long I sit on the floor, staring into thin air. Each minute, each second all morphs into one colossal clusterfuck, and all I'm left with is my utter stupidity staring me in the face. I think about all the times I allowed him to touch me, how I liked it, and how I wanted more.

Those hands brought me to the pinnacle of pleasure and pain, and even when the line began to blur, it was never enough. His hands brought me back to life, but to someone else…he choked the life right out of them. How can someone be so wicked—in every sense of the word?

Running a hand down my face, I wipe away my tears and

decide to freshen up before I go home. Coming to a stand, I make my way into the bathroom and avoid the mirror. I don't need it to know I look like shit.

Splashing some water on my face, I rinse out my mouth, wishing I could wash away the feel of Bull's lips on mine. But I can't. He's imprinted on every part of me.

Sighing, I reach for the towel, needing to get the fuck out of here. But when the door bursts open, fleeing is no longer an option. I lunge for the only weapon within reach—a small silver nail file. Bull is across the room in three long strides, coming to a stop in the bathroom doorway as I shakily extend the nail file out in front of me.

He peers down at the weapon with a deep frown.

I can't control the tremble that wracks my body, but I steady my hand. "Get o-out of here. I've called the po-police."

My warning falls on deaf ears. He storms forward, and I instantly back up until my ass hits the wall. I expect him to disarm me, but he doesn't. He stops inches away and slowly raises both hands in surrender. "Please, please let me explain."

I'm caught completely off guard because his request holds only sincerity. I should shout out for help because nothing he can say will ever excuse what I saw. But my heart, the traitorous bitch, begs I listen to what he has to say.

He takes my silence as submission. "That man I…killed." His pause has my lower lip quivering. "He deserved it. He, and three of his friends, changed my life when I was fifteen years old. They are the reason I am the way I am. Or maybe they triggered who I was always going to become."

The nail file trembles in my hand.

"They took away the only person who really understood me. They killed someone who didn't deserve to die," he reveals, lowering his chin as his chest begins to rise and fall dangerously slow. "Fourteen years ago, they ambushed me and my brother. The asshole I killed; he was the muscle. He held me back as I watched his three friends beat, humiliate, and eventually, kill my seventeen-year-old brother by splitting his head open with a fucking rock."

Tears stick to my lashes. I try to blink them away.

"I went to prison because I found one of them two years later and shot him dead. A perfect fucking bull's-eye straight through his heart."

A stunned gasp leaves me; the mystery behind his nickname has been revealed.

"I went to prison for twelve years for killing one of my brother's murderers. But prison didn't reform me. I didn't repent," he states, slowly lifting his chin to meet my wide eyes. "It just gave me time to plan my revenge. I envisioned all the ways I was going to make those who hurt my brother pay.

"Two down, two to go," he utters, nodding once. "Before I ended his pathetic life tonight, he told me who the remaining two are. Now, I just have to find them and make sure they receive the same punishment as their other two friends. This is about revenge. It always has been."

He yanks down the collar of his T-shirt, exposing the inked flesh over his heart, before reaching for my hand. When his hand locks over mine, a surge of fear and excitement swarms me. He draws the nail file to his chest and forces me to dig the point into his flesh.

I try to recoil, but he holds me tightly.

"You can do whatever you want to me, but all I ask is that you let me finish this. When I kill those responsible for hurting Damian, then I will have no reason left to live."

"Bull, no!" I frantically attempt to pull away, but he continues to coerce my hand until, eventually, a trickle of blood seeps from the wound he forced me to create.

His gaze never leaves mine. "I deserve to die. Tonight, I robbed two kids of their father, and even though I was well aware of the fact, it didn't change my mind. I have no heart, Tiger," he says, revealing why he asked the question in my kitchen about Jordy growing up without a dad.

But his question contradicts his claim. If he didn't have a heart...he wouldn't care. But he does. He may not realize it, but I do. It's why I didn't call the police. It's why I allow my tears to fall.

"I'm sorry for making you cry," he says with regret.

But I shake my head, confusing him. "These tears aren't for me...these tears are for you."

His lips part, and his grip on me slackens, allowing me to release the nail file, which tumbles to the floor.

"I'm the one who's sorry. I can't even imagine what you went through. You were just a kid. You and...Damian"—he squeezes his eyes shut—"both were. I'm not excusing what you did...but I understand."

God strike me down, but I do. There is no right or wrong in this situation. I don't condone taking a life, but the circumstances aren't black and white.

And before me, an amber-blue kiss flickers to life as he

opens his eyes. "Understand?" he asks, shaking his head slowly.

With a hesitant touch, I place my hand on his cheek. "Yes. If anyone hurt someone I loved, I would want revenge too. And the way your brother suffered...oh, god, Bull, I'm so sorry you went through that. Who are the other men?"

He hisses, turning his cheek to sever our touch. But I won't let him escape, not this time. Gripping his chin, I force him to look at me. "Tell me. The thing about secrets is that they're not secrets if you tell someone. Let me be that someone."

"Why?" he questions, the desperation heavy in that single word. "Why would you want to get messed up in my shit? After everything I just told—"

But I don't let him finish. "It's because of what you told me that I want to know. You're not a cold-blooded murderer."

"Then what am I?" he questions, begging me to shed light on this.

"You're human," I conclude, using his words back at him.

Bull sees himself as nothing but a monster. He's not. He is acting on the one emotion that proves he is anything but a villain—love. His love for Damian has driven him to do some awful things. But he has happily sacrificed his life to ensure his brother's death doesn't go unpunished.

Do two wrongs make a right? Maybe this is the exception to the rule? I honestly don't know.

"I hurt everything I touch. I hurt you," he adds, recoiling from my grip angrily.

"Yes, you did, but you also made me feel good. Not just physically, but emotionally as well. From the first moment we met, you've protected me. You didn't have to. But you did. If that doesn't prove you're a good person...then let me show you what I see."

Bull stands rigid, his fists balled by his sides. Undeterred, I wrap my fingers around his wrist and draw his hand to my chest, placing it over my hammering heart. "Every time you're near me, I can't take in enough air fast enough. You leave me breathless with your brutality because you live life unapologetically." His jaw hardens as he slowly unfurls his fist and lays his hand on my chest over my heart. "You're here with a purpose. While most are stumbling through life, you know what you want. Yes, it's not conventional, but it shows your loyalty, your strength to those you love.

"You tell me you're dead inside, but how can you be? You're doing all of this to ensure your brother is never forgotten. You have sacrificed your life to pay homage to his memory. Those men took something away from you."

Interlacing our fingers, I lock eyes with him, realizing my feelings for him are deeper than I thought. "I could only wish for that sort of loyalty. That love."

My cheeks heat because a part of me wishes Bull would show me that sort of dedication.

"Where do we go from here?" he asks, tightening his grip.

Sighing, I pray for my soul for what I'm about to say. "I won't stop you. You do what you have to."

His steady breaths reveal he's weighing over what I just declared. "And you're okay with having that on your conscience?"

"My conscience was stained long ago," I reveal, thinking

of what I did to Christopher. If I didn't follow my heart, things would have turned out so differently. At the time, I thought my love was unbreakable, but how naïve I was.

"I need to stay away from you," Bull confesses, cupping my throat and running his thumb over my racing pulse.

"I know," I reply, hating how this must end. Just because I won't stand in the way of his justice doesn't mean I can stand by and happily watch him hunt down two men—no matter how badly they deserve it.

"I never expected to feel…"

"Feel what?" I whisper, licking my lips.

He inhales, releasing his hand over my heart. "Feel… anything," he clarifies sincerely, which touches me in ways it shouldn't. "Thank you."

"For what?" I question, my skin coming to life as he continues to stroke my neck.

"For seeing something in me that I never will." And this is our closure. Bull is putting an end to something that could have been something wonderful. But it never will be because of what he has to do.

"Who are the other men?" I press. I don't know why it matters. It just does. Maybe this is what I need for my own closure.

Bull slides his fingers behind the nape of my neck and draws me toward him. Our lips are inches apart. "Like me, we all go by aliases. Tonight, I killed Kong," he reveals, while my heart constricts and the world tilts, sending me off balance. "Tomorrow, I kill Scrooge and…" But his words all morph into a spiral of destruction because it can't be.

The walls begin closing in on me, and my skin is suddenly alight. I can't breathe. There has to be some mistake.

But there isn't, and Bull confirms this when he brings this entire shitshow full circle. "Jaws," he concludes, while I gasp, desperate for air.

"Tiger?"

I attempt to pull from his hold, but he grasps me tightly. In a way, I'm thankful because the room begins to spin violently, and nausea rises. But I quash it down. I have one more question. One question which is the reason I felt so connected to Bull this entire time. I just didn't know it... until now. "That's th-three," I whisper, begging there is some mistake. "Who was the fourth?"

Bull arches a brow, but I slap my hand over his, squeezing his fingers. "Who was the other m-man you killed? The man you went to prison for?"

Everything comes down to this. Please, god, let there be some mistake. Please, don't let it be him. But deep down, I always knew he would never leave me. He would never leave us by choice. His choices were taken away from him. And now, I know why...

"His name was Lachlan...Hero was his nickname," Bull confesses, cementing the fact the universe is a cruel, sadistic bitch who was just biding her time, waiting for me to pay my dues.

A single tear trickles down my cheek. What have I done? I've slept with the enemy, the man who destroyed my life... and I liked it...a lot.

"Tiger? What's wrong? Talk to me." But I can't. It's too late for talking. The damage has already been done.

Or so I thought, as it seems this is merely the beginning… of the end.

Bull looks over my head, his eyes sparking with fire. "*You*," he manages to grit out between clenched teeth.

I don't need to turn around to know who stands behind me. But this is my punishment for all that I've done.

Bull loosens his hold on me, and I slowly look over my shoulder, stitching together the lies. Before me stands the man who left, left because I betrayed him.

Before me stands my brother…Christopher…or, as most know him…Jaws.

CHAPTER SEVENTEEN

Bull

I t's too much, too fast, and I need a moment, one fucking moment, because standing just a few feet away from me is the man who ruined my life. He looks a lot different from when I saw him last. Gone are the gangster threads. He's now decked in an expensive suit and gold. He always reeked of power, but now, he is on top of the fucking food chain.

I can't do anything but stare him down, envisioning the ways I'm going to kill him...and kill him slowly.

But my murderous thoughts come to a screeching halt when Tiger sways, reaching for the top of a chair to stop herself from falling on her ass.

What the fuck is going on?

"I missed you," the motherfucker sweetly says. He sure as

shit isn't speaking to me, which means…he knows Tiger. But how? "I'm glad you like the earrings I bought you."

Her fingers flutter to her ears in surprise.

I launch forward, ready to rip out his spleen and ask questions later, but Tiger snares my bicep, stopping me. Inhaling, I peer down at her vise-like grip. She has three seconds to let me go. But when I look into her heartbroken eyes, I realize I'm going to need a lot longer than three seconds.

"Don't," she whispers, shaking her head.

I don't understand what's going on. She soon brings me up to speed.

"He's my…m-my…"

"Brother," the asshole fills in the blanks with a grin.

Although I've heard them both loud and clear, it's like they've spoken to me in another language. This motherfucker, the man who took everything away from me, is her own flesh and blood? Surely, life isn't this cruel?

But I shouldn't have expected anything less.

"He's your *brother*?" I ask her, unable to accept this as truth. When she doesn't reply, I grip her wrist. "Answer me!"

Lowering her chin, she slowly nods, hiding behind her hair.

My heart does something I've only felt once before—it was when Damian died in my arms. It breaks. Breaks because, once again, someone I care for is taken away from me.

"Your brother? Your motherfucking *brother*!" I cry, suddenly needing to put as much distance between us as possible. I recoil from her hold because it's burning me alive.

She rubs her arms, tiny shivers wracking her. She appears

to have shut down. I want to console her, but I can't. How can I?

"Tiger, goddammit! Talk to me!"

"Please," she whimpers, shaking her head, unable to look at me. I'm scaring her, which is what I've always wanted. I don't want that now, but it's too late. Too fucking late.

"Lillian, go to my office," Jaws softly says, reaching into his pocket and producing a set of keys. I watch with wide eyes as he slowly walks toward her and unwraps her arms from around herself before placing the keys into her palm.

"It's upstairs. Tell security to take you."

A ferocious possessiveness comes over me. I want her to tell him to go to hell. To fight like the strong woman I know that she is. But she doesn't. She sniffs with a nod, and on autopilot, she walks out the door.

Jaws waits a few moments, then closes the door, sealing us in a cage. I want to kill him, choke him with my bare hands, but he's packing heat. I wouldn't get within three feet before he put a bullet in me...just as I did to his friend.

"You've grown, kid."

Suddenly, death is a price I'm willing to pay. The last time he called me kid was when his hands were stained with my brother's blood.

"Yes, I have," I reply, barely holding on. "Your friend, Kong, saw just how much. That was the last thing he saw before I stabbed him through the heart."

Jaws's lips twitch before he breaks out into a husky laugh. "I should thank you for taking out my trash," he states calmly.

I'm not surprised he doesn't shed a tear for his once friend.

"You can thank me by telling me where your other friend is."

Jaws coolly places his hands into his pockets. "You found me, or should I say, we found one another. You clearly don't need my help."

He's right. The element of surprise is gone, thanks to the fact I'm sleeping with his sister. Of all the women, why her?

"What do you want?" I'm done with pretenses. This asshole is here for a reason. I'm of value to him. If I wasn't, I'd already be dead.

"No foreplay?" he quips, his straight white teeth gleaming with a sarcastic smirk.

"Your sister already scratched that itch," I counter quickly, relishing in his sudden change of demeanor.

He wanted his nephew dead because he has some sick obsession with Tiger, but why did he wait so long to come back into her life?

"Careful," he warns, clenching his jaw. I can't believe I didn't see the similarities between Tiger and him. I was off my A game because I was too busy…feeling.

Goddammit. This can't happen again.

"Regardless of the fact she can't seem to keep her legs closed, she's still my sister."

"The sister you abandoned," I spit, jumping to her defense.

"She had that coming," he counters without feeling. "That's her punishment for fucking my best friend."

So it appears he knows.

Tiger thought he was oblivious to her sneaking around, but he wasn't. He was always two steps ahead. "You knew?"

"Of course, I knew," he mocks angrily. "I also know what happened to her Prince Charming."

There is so much more to this complex story. And I'm about to find out just how much.

"Lillian's problem is that she's a hopeless romantic. She is also naïve. But it seems you've been doing my dirty work for quite some time now."

"What the fuck does that mean?" I should end this asshole. Now. But I can't. What does Tiger have to do with this?

"It means," Jaws says, tonguing his cheek. "The man you shot...that was my best friend. The best friend who was fucking my little sister and didn't have the sense to wrap his shit up and got her pregnant with that little bastard."

The blood drains from my body. I can't speak.

"You didn't put two and two together?" he mocks with a smirk. "You killed her *soul mate*." A phrase has never sounded so dirty. "You did me a favor. I would have killed him myself the moment I found out she was pregnant. But you beat me to the punch."

"He was my hero. My Prince Charming." I now realize Tiger meant that in the literal sense because the man I shot was Hero...Jordy's father and the love of her life.

I am the reason her life turned to shit. Oh, my fucking god. And she knows. She knows I was the one who shot and killed the man she loved. I robbed Jordy of his father. She also knows I have no remorse for my actions. Our paths crossed long ago. We just didn't know it. Until now.

I need to explain. But what do I say? She knows the truth. Where do we go from here?

"I told her he split because that traitor didn't deserve a hero's farewell. I wanted her to think he was the lying, cheating scumbag that he, in fact, was.

"I knew she was fucking Hero. I just didn't want to believe either would betray me that way. But the gig was up when she grew big with his child." He hums, steadying himself. "How dare he put his hands, his cock in what's mine!"

"Motherfucker, if you cared so much about her, why the fuck did you leave her?" I yell, prepared to kill him over and over again for all that he's done.

"That's her punishment for loving him, loving *them*, more than me. She wanted to be an adult, so I treated her like one. She clearly didn't need me when she was sleeping around behind my back," he cruelly replies, while I hold back my vomit. He is sick. "But I want her back. She's paid her dues. I want her by my side, where she belongs."

Over my dead fucking body...

"That comes a little too late. She's fucking stripping to support herself and her son, your nephew, who you wanted dead," I reveal, because he's not the only one with an ace up his sleeve.

"Ah, it seems Kong remained a little pussy right until the very end." Jaws isn't bothered by what I know.

"Let's wrap this up, shall we?" I spit, not interested in small talk. I need to find Tiger and explain. It bothers me that she is my main priority right now; however, I can question my motives later.

"We both want something," Jaws says evenly. "We can benefit from the other."

I highly doubt that. But I'm listening.

"Word on the street is that you're tight with Stevie, so it's simple. You're going to work for me now. This is the *in* I've been waiting for."

Scoffing, I shake my head incredulously. "I've heard some bullshit in my time, but this is fucking rich. Why the fuck would I work for you? I want you dead, asshole. And I plan on delivering as soon as you stop boring me with your riddles."

Jaws has the audacity to laugh. This is just a game to him. "You can try, but I have something you want."

"Oh, yeah, and what's that?"

"My sister's love."

Clenching my fists, I inhale slowly. "I'm listening." This is why I didn't want to get involved with anyone. Emotional ties mean collateral, and Jaws has a shitload of it. I've hurt Tiger once before, how can I do it again?

"Stevie trusts you, and now that Kong is dead, he'll need someone to fill his shoes. That someone will be you."

It's like my equilibrium is off balance. Every time Jaws speaks, it drifts further and further away from the natural order of the world.

"You will get close to him and learn everything there is to know about his business. This town only has room for one alpha, and that's me. I want his drugs, his fighting ring, and the club. The Pink Oyster is competition, lousy competition, seeing as my club is a 7-Up Factory, but competition nonetheless, with my investment. Not to mention, it's in prime real estate. I've been looking at that place for a while now. I think it's time for Blue Bloods to expand.

"Drugs, strippers, it's all easy money for me. The more I have, the more I get paid. This is smart business."

Jaws owns Blue Bloods? This means he would have known where Tiger was the entire time. And he's only now coming out of hiding. Carlos wasn't behind her attack—it was fucking Jaws. He wants his sister to work here, not because he wants to rekindle their relationship, but because she'll make him money.

This is a new low. He could have helped her financially as well as emotionally, but instead, he continued to punish her for something she did when she was a teenager. He has always been lurking in the shadows, but he's now emerged because he wants something from us both.

Tiger said she felt as if someone had been watching her. I now know who.

"I want it all," he states without pause. "And when I get it all…I want his head on a fucking platter."

"I work for no one, especially not you," I spit, charging forward, not caring when he draws his gun. "I'm no snitch, so better you kill me now."

"Who said anything about being a snitch? It's simple. Just earn their trust and infiltrate their operation. That's all."

I grip the barrel and press the muzzle over my heart. But I'm calling his bluff. He needs me. He wants to get rid of the competition, and seeing as Kong wasn't man enough to do it, he's now recruiting.

"I would, but at the moment, you're of more value to me alive than dead. Besides, you don't leave empty-handed."

"You have nothing, nothing I want!" I scream, blinded by

my rage.

"I actually do," he contradicts, slowly removing the gun from my chest.

Is this supposed to be a sign of...trust?

Hell. To. The. Fuck. No. This ends now.

I strike out and punch him square in the jaw. The sickening crack fuels my inner fury, and I elbow him in the nose. He stumbles backward, which is all I need. I dive on top of him, pinning him to the ground. Over and over, my fists connect with his face, but no matter how much I hit him, it's still not enough.

If I end him now, what will that do to Tiger? I already ruined her life by killing the man she loved. My need for revenge is the reason she's stripping, the reason her life didn't turn out the way she wanted, the way she deserved.

And Jaws knows it.

His gargled snickers ridicule me. "What's so funny, motherfucker?" I yank him up by the collar of his bloody dress shirt, pressing us nose to nose.

"You think you're big game, but you're still the scared little kid I knew."

I raise my fist, ready to end this once and for all, but stop when Jaws puts something I want more than revenge on the line.

Tiger.

"You work for me. Otherwise, I think it's time I got to know my nephew."

My fist trembles midair.

"He's already halfway to becoming a delinquent, so all

he needs is a little guidance by his beloved uncle. It won't take much. He believed me when I told him his mom was a hooker. There is no loyalty there. He resents her."

The mystery of who told Jordy Tiger was a hooker has been revealed. Jaws has been a lot closer than we knew.

"I told him not to tell his mom I was back, and he didn't. It wouldn't take much for me to take him away from her for good."

"You wouldn't dare," I challenge, but it's apparent he would and has.

"Do you really think I want a snot nose kid who is the spitting image of his two-timing father around me? No. But he's a means to an end."

Unable to stand the sight of him, I throw him to the floor and stand abruptly. He snickers, wiping his bloody lip with the back of his hand.

"What did she ever do to you?" I question, unbelieving this tangled web I'm caught in. "She fucked your best friend? Get over it."

And there it is, I see it. A tic beneath his right eye. It appears Tiger is both our weaknesses.

"I won't allow you to blackmail me with her. I'll tell her everything. I'm sure she'll be interested to know you've lied to her this entire time. How long have you been watching her?"

He's not bothered by my threat. "At first, I couldn't give a fuck what she did. She made her choices. It was time she lived with them. But when she started stripping, she interfered with my business. And I can't allow that to happen.

"She was hot shit, but when I saw her...let's just say,

nostalgia struck. I missed my little sister. But she wasn't so"—he licks his lips—"little anymore."

I clench my fists.

"So tell her what you want, but we both know she won't believe you. You *did* kill her son's father and, in turn, destroyed her life," he states flippantly.

"When she asks why I didn't tell her the truth, I'll tell her what she wants to hear. I was just playing the role of big brother, trying to protect her from the pain of knowing the love of her life was dead."

"She isn't stupid. She'll see through your bullshit." My claim lacks conviction because I can't be too sure.

"Maybe she will, which is why I have a backup plan. Her son." Sitting up, he clutches his side, wincing. "You can either do what I want, or I will make him pay for your lack of cooperation. The cops wouldn't think twice if a punk ass kid went missing. Imagine what that would do to my sister? She'd need the shoulder of her big brother to cry on, no doubt."

This asshole has thought of everything. I either do what he says, or I destroy Tiger's life—again. He has collateral in the way of her and Jordy.

"If I do what you want, what do I get?"

His eyes light up a devious green. "My word that no harm comes to my sister and her bastard."

"That's not enough." I shake my head firmly. I know this makes me a selfish motherfucker, but I need reassurance these cunts will pay. "I want you and Scrooge to pay your dues. Only then will I…" God forgive me, "agree."

Jaws licks the blood from his lips. "Fine."

"What are the terms?" I ask, needing to get my head into the game. The rules have changed.

"You get close to Stevie, ensuring he hires you to be his muscle now that Kong is gone." His voice is dripping with delight at the fact. "I want to know all about the fighting syndicate. That's easy money for me. I can't lose betting on the right horse." He means me. "Find out what you can about his other dealings. Where he gets his shipments from. How much. I want to know everything there is.

"Encourage him to buy The Pink Oyster. I was going to approach Lotus myself, but the bitch won't be so accommodating with me. Stevie can get the club for a steal. Money better in my pocket than hers."

"How do you know all this?" I ask, wondering just how many people he has working for him.

"I make it my business to know the comings and goings of people who are of use to me. I found out about your little *fling* with my sister, now didn't I? I couldn't believe my luck when I did my research and found out just who you were—two birds, one stone. It was like destiny brought us together once again."

It takes all my willpower not to headbutt him out cold.

"I was happy to remain in the shadows and allow Carlos to take care of it, but when you walked into her world and she couldn't stay away, well, it wasn't a coincidence. It was fate. I see the way she looks at you. She likes you. And you like her. Shame on you. Emotions make you weak." There's a bite to his tone. Could he be speaking from experience? "You should know that. It really is poetic justice for you both."

His comment throws me off center. I need to derail this

because I can only deal with one headfuck at a time.

"What's your issue with Stevie?"

He grins, but nothing is pleasant about the gesture.

"That's a story for another day. All you need to know for now is that I want him to think he's on top when I take it *all* from him...just as he did to me."

This is fucking personal. He is looking for a fall guy—and I fit the bill.

He makes his to-do list seem so simple, but what he's asking goes against everything I stand for. A fucking snitch. But I humor him.

"I do all this; you leave Tiger and Jordy alone?"

He nods once. "Yes. Not a hair on their heads will be touched. Oh, and this agreement means you leave her alone. You're dead to her. We clear? You make sure she can't stand the sight of you. If she goes anywhere near you, or vice versa, it'll be the last thing she ever does."

"And you and Scrooge? What about *your* heads?" I question, inhaling and exhaling heavily.

"I promise you a fair fight," he replies, which has me vibrating violently. "When it's all done, we will fight, man to man. No guns. No tricks. May the best man win." He's clearly confident he'll win, but he underestimates my rage and the fact I can smell bullshit from a mile away.

There will never be a fair fight.

"Fair? There is no fair in this situation! How is what you did to my brother fair?"

"I hardly remember him, so I don't know what you want me to say." His carefree comment is further insult to Damian.

I can't do this. I can't make a deal with the devil. How can I work with him, knowing what I do? But if I don't...Tiger will pay. And Damian's death will never be avenged because Jaws will kill me. All of this would have been for nothing.

My hands are tied. Is my revenge worth more to me than her? I could end him here and now. He is injured, and it wouldn't take much for me to pin him down and choke the life out of him. But he came here armed—in every sense of the word.

"I could kill you right now," I caution, meaning every single word.

"You could," he counters, untroubled. "But if my friends don't hear from me, it won't end well for my sister. End being the operative word in the sentence." I don't need a Venn diagram: I either do what he says or he will end her life as easily as I ended her son's father.

"If you're so powerful, do it yourself. Stevie isn't hard to find!" I spit, angered.

"I could"—he purses his lips in thought—"but I don't want any fallback. It's not good for business. Neither does Scrooge. He has a family to think of. Keep your friends close and your enemies closer as they say. Besides, it's more fun this way."

This makes no fucking sense, but I am so done with this asshole. I need time to think. And I need to see Tiger.

Jaws has always been two steps ahead. I need to catch up to speed. But before I go, I want to know one thing that has plagued me for fourteen years.

"Why?" That single word carries so much emotion. He

says he doesn't remember, but he's lying. He knows he can do this because I will do anything for revenge.

He promises me a fair fight because he owes me this. And I will ensure I don't lose.

Jaws smirks, a victor's grin. He knows he's won. I've just sold my soul to the devil. With a casual shrug, he calmly replies, "Why not?"

And that's it. There is no light at the end of the tunnel. No resolution. They killed my brother because they could. And I promise here and now that I will do the same.

This is just the beginning.

"You've got yourself a deal."

He rejoices in victory. "I own you now."

But before he has a chance to celebrate, I knee him under the chin, knocking him out cold. The sight of his lifeless body does nothing to appease my demons. But it'll do—for now.

"I belong to no one."

This "deal" buys me time to devise another plan because once he's got no use for me, he will get rid of me. There will never be a "fair" fight because that would mean he's honorable. And that is something he is not.

Better I be an inside man, gathering enough ammo to bring down an empire, than a dead man.

Calmly opening the door, I find the room flanked by four bodyguards. Of course, he has backup, which is the reason it's not his time—for now.

"Take me to her," I demand, shoving past them. When one of them tries to stop me, I elbow him in the face.

I am a live wire, and no one will stop me.

"Upstairs. Last door on the left," one of them says, clearly not interested in ending up like his friend.

Without a moment to waste, I march up the stairs, taking them two at a time. Upstairs is roped off, but when the two guards see me coming, they quickly remove the rope. My gaze is focused on the last door on the left and nothing else. I don't have a game plan. All I know is that I need to see her.

I burst through the door, frantically scanning the room for Tiger. I don't have to look far. She's sitting behind Jaws's huge wooden desk. When she sees me, her eyes widen, and she comes to a quick stand, using the chair as a barricade between us. "Please don't."

But I can't. If I don't touch her, I'm terrified she'll run away. "Your brother is the asshole who killed Damian," I reveal on a rushed breath, needing to get it out.

She shakes her head frantically.

"It's true," I persist, shoving the chair out of my way. She backs up, hitting the bookshelf behind her. She's trapped like a scared little rabbit. Usually, nothing would please me more. But not now.

Her flighty eyes dart to the door. She's petrified.

Instantly, I stop, raising my hands in surrender. I owe her the entire truth before I crush her. "You once asked me what my name was. It's Cody, Cody Bishop. When I was fifteen, four men killed my brother. One of them was your brother and the other was—" She closes her eyes, tears streaming down her face. But I need her to know it all.

"The other was Lachlan, or Hero. Was he the man you loved? Is he Jordy's dad?"

The air is so thick, I can barely breathe.

"Lily, please, answer me."

It's the first time I've used her name, and it has the desired effect.

With the slowest of movements, she opens her eyes and breaks my fucking heart, a heart I didn't even know could break ever again. "Yes," she whispers, cementing this clusterfuck once and for all.

At the time, I thought running into Kong was a coincidence, and the universe was finally cutting me a break. But now I know he was familiar with The Pink Oyster because he knew one of the dancers personally—he knew Tiger was Jaws's sister. Maybe he encouraged Stevie to go into business with Lotus as a fuck you to Jaws.

But I suppose I'll never know.

"You said his name was Michael? I don't understand."

Tiger sniffs, a look of nostalgia passing over her. "Michael Jordan was his favorite basketball player. That's where I got Jordan's name," she revealed. "When he called, I couldn't call him by his name because I didn't want Christopher knowing who I was speaking with. So I called him Michael. The name just stuck."

Her nostalgia, however, is about to be ruined by the truth.

"The night my brother died... he, your beloved *Michael*, was the one who could have called an ambulance. Your brother gave him the choice, but he chose wrong. He ran away like a fucking coward, leaving Damian to die. Although he wasn't the one who delivered the fatal blow, your brother was the one who did that. He held my brother down like he was nothing but a rabid dog."

"Stop," she pleads, but I won't. She deserves the truth—finally.

"Scrooge broke his wrist and then stole his championship ring. Hero pressed his boot on Damian's spine, while your brother pissed on him. Kong held me back, leaving me helpless as I watched them. When your brother split Damian's head open, he killed me too. They all did.

"So when I found Hero"—I deadpan her—"I had no issues ending his life."

"He changed after that. I knew something had happened. He wasn't like them," she says, enraging me.

"I'm glad it took my brother's death to change him into your Prince Charming!"

She turns her cheek, wounded, but I have no regrets. The only regret I have is letting her in.

"He was going to propose to you," I reveal, without emotion, while a stunned gasp leaves her. "When I shot him, he was reaching into his pocket to show me your engagement ring, to thank me for sparing his life. I wasn't one for sentiments, however. He took that away from me."

"Oh my g-god," she sobs, muting her cries behind her hand.

"So maybe you're right. Maybe he did change. But that change came at the expense of my brother." I can't stop the venom from spewing. I need to hurt her because I am angry, so fucking angry. She is standing in the way of my revenge.

But I'm not angry with her—I'm angry with myself for being so weak. If only I had fought her harder, they'd all be dead. But now, I have to sacrifice everything I've learned to keep her safe.

I already destroyed her once before. I can't do it again.

"Michael was terrified of Jaws. He didn't mean to—"

But I storm forward, gripping her chin hard. "Don't you dare make excuses for him! Scared or not, he should have done the right thing. But he didn't. And he paid with his life. And so will your brother."

"I beg of you, don't hurt him. Christopher is all I have—"

"Then I feel sorry for you, Tiger," I spit, leveling her with nothing but pure disgust as she begs for his life. If only she knew what he thought of her. "You had no issues turning a blind eye before you knew who it was."

Her lower lip trembles as she casts her eyes downward, ashamed. "Everything is different now."

"You're right. It is. Your brother, he's the enemy. And so are you if you side with him."

"He's my flesh and blood," she reasons, sealing this forevermore. This is the last time I will ever feel anything again.

Letting her go, I slam my lips to hers, owning, possessing, and devouring her because she is mine. She always will be. She gasps, then wraps her arms around my neck, violently kissing me back. I thread my fingers through her long hair, committing the smell, the taste of her to memory because this is the last time. Our goodbye kiss.

Our tongues collide in a frenzied union, unable to keep up with what our bodies want to say. She is the only person I am willing to sacrifice everything for—and to do that, I have to hurt her. To keep her safe, I need her to hate me. It's the only way.

Her small whimpers, and the way she twists herself around me, regardless of what she knows, shows me that what she feels for me is more than just a casual fling. And I feel the same way. I wondered if she meant more to me than revenge, and the answer is yes. She does.

"*Let her go.*" That voice. I've missed that voice. But I suppose I can hear it now because finally, for the first time in my life, I'm doing the right thing.

With a final kiss, I do what Damian says…I let her go.

Her eyes flutter open, unsure why I stopped. Kissing the tip of her nose, I cup her cheek, hating myself more than I already do. "I *will* kill your brother. And I'll…kill you too if you stand in my way."

She blinks once, turning a sickly white. "Wh-what?"

There is no emotion in my eyes. It's gone. And I doubt it'll ever return.

I stumble backward when she shoves me off her. I silently praise my fiery girl. I knew she was there. She just needed a little push.

"I remember thinking nothing could be worse than when you told me you killed someone. That someone turned out to be the only man I ever loved. But I was wrong. We are so done. Over. If you come anywhere near me or my son, *I* will fucking kill *you*."

I applaud her slowly. "Try it, darlin'. I dare you."

"You ruined my life, and then you threaten to kill me. I should tell Franca what you've done."

Her threat is empty. She wouldn't do that. No matter how badly she'd like to think she could, she won't. It's the reason she didn't call the police when she found me covered in blood.

"Do what you gotta do, and I'll do the same."

She doesn't flinch as she slaps my cheek. "You don't stand a chance against Christopher."

"We'll see," I challenge with a smirk, moving my jaw from side to side.

Everything good inside me, the good because of her is washed away, leaving behind the blackness I've carried for fourteen years.

"Your brother isn't a good guy," I warn, wishing I could tell her everything I know. But what would be the point? She wouldn't listen. I am the boogeyman, after all. I am the man who destroyed her life.

"Neither are you," she counters, daring me to argue. But I don't.

"I never said I was," I deadpan.

Her expression hardens as she pulls herself together. Every part of me hopes she will fight, fight for me. I need her to be the one. As selfish as that is, I can't be the one who walks away. But Tiger proves just who has the bigger balls. "Shame on me for not listening. It won't happen again."

She shoves past me, a newfound confidence running through her veins. This is her claiming back her life, putting an end to an era of doubt. She saw herself as someone unworthy of love because everyone left her behind. But now that Jaws is back and she knows the truth about Lachlan, she realizes that she *is* worthy.

She always was.

She looks at me like I'm nothing, and I am. What I did to her, to her son, unmasks the monster within me. And I like it. This depravity makes me feel alive.

I've orphaned three children, and if I had the choice…I'd do it again. I may be in bed with the devil, but the finale will be worth the burn.

"If you'll excuse me, it's time I told my son the truth. It's time I told him all about his father who didn't leave us, but instead, died an innocent victim because of you." And there it is…hatred.

Finally.

"He will never be innocent. Never forget that."

"No one is," she counters with fire. "But with Christopher back, we can try to be a family again."

"You can try," I patronize with a smirk.

"Fuck you."

"Been there, done that," I say with a shrug. "It wasn't worth the trouble."

Tears of anger burn her eyes, which is what she leaves me with as she storms out the door. When it slams shut behind her, I inhale deeply, pushing down the urge to run after her.

Once I've calmed somewhat, I round the desk and take a seat behind it. I run my finger along the polished surface, whistling at all this wealth that I will enjoy burning to the ground. Reaching for the phone, I dial a number, ready to kick-start this shitshow right now.

"Hey, Stevie. Bad news," I say when he answers. "Kong split. Something about Jaws gunning for all of your blood. He wants your empire, man."

And watch the web I spin.

Somehow, I thought killing Kong would make me feel better. But all it's done is make things so much worse. I suppose with every action there is a consequence, and this is mine. Killing Kong has changed the course of everything, but I suppose that's the case when you rob someone of their life.

Poetic justice, some may say. I shouldn't have thought it was ever going to be this easy.

"Fuck," he curses, the panic clear in his tone.

This is the moment I swoop in and save the day. "Now that you're a man down, how about you let me show you what real muscle does?"

"You want his job?"

"As I see it, you don't have a choice. You need protection. I need money." Leaning back in the chair, I place my feet on the desk and cross my ankles casually. "So what do you say?"

"Come see me tomorrow. I'll text you the address."

I hang up. The job is as good as mine.

It shouldn't be this easy, but it is.

Gripping the medallion around my neck, I finally feel at home. This is one step closer to getting what I want, because the world is a jungle, and we're all just fucking animals—we're Jaws, Bull, and Tiger, and we're ready to tear one another apart.

BOOK TWO COMING APRIL 30, 2020!

ACKNOWLEDGEMENTS

My author family: Elle Kennedy, Vi Keeland, Lisa Edward, Christina Lauren, Natasha Madison, L.J. Shen, Kylie Scott, SC Stephens, Helena Hunting, Penelope Ward, Mia Sheridan—love you!

My ever-supporting parents. You guys are the best. I am who I am because of you. I love you. RIP Papa. Gone but never forgotten. You're in my heart. Always.

My agent, Kimberly Brower from Brower Literary & Management. Thank you for your patience and thank you for being an amazing human being.

My editor, Jenny Sims. What can I say other than I LOVE YOU! Thank you for everything. You go above and beyond for me.

My proofreaders—Lisa Edward—More Than Words, Copyediting & Proofreading and Rebecca Barney—Fairest Reviews. You're both amazing.

Sommer Stein, you NAILED this cover! Thank you for being so patient and making the process so fun. I'm sorry for annoying you constantly.

My devil, Andrew England, you're exceptional—inside and out. How's the nose ring though?!

James Rupapara—your photography is magic.

My publicist—Danielle Sanchez from Wildfire Marketing Solutions. Thank you for all your help. Your messages brighten my day.

A special shout-out to: Josi Beck, Tijan, Kat T. Masen, Natasha Preston, Cheri Grand Anderman, Amy Halter, Lauren Rosa, Gemma, Louise, Kimberly Whalen, Ryn Hughes, Ben Ellis—Tall Story Designs, Nasha Lama, Natasha Tomic, Heyne, Random House, Kinneret Zmora, Hugo & Cie, Planeta, MxM Bookmark, Art Eternal, Carbaccio, Fischer, Bookouture, Egmont Bulgaria, Brilliance Publishing, Audible, Hope Editions, Buzzfeed, BookBub, PopSugar, Aestas Book Blog, Hugues De Saint Vincent, Paris, New York, Sarah Sentz (you're my fav!) Ria Alexander, Amy Jennings, Jennifer Spinninger, Kristin Dwyer, and Nina Bocci.

To the endless blogs that have supported me since day one—You guys rock my world.

My bookstagrammers—This book has allowed me to meet SO many of you. Your creativity astounds me. The effort you go to is just amazing. Thank you for the posts, the teasers, the support, the messages, the love, the EVERYTHING! I see what you do, and I am so, so thankful.

My reader group and review team—sending you all a big kiss.

My beautiful family—Daniel, Mum, Papa, Fran, Matt, Samantha, Amelia, Gayle, Peter, Luke, Leah, Jimmy, Jack, Shirley, Michael, Rob, Elisa, Evan, Alex, Francesca, and my aunties, uncles, and cousins—I am the luckiest person alive to know each and every one of you. You brighten up my world in ways I honestly cannot express.

Samantha and Amelia— I love you both so very much.

To my family in Holland and Italy, and abroad. Sending you guys much love and kisses.

Papa, Zio Nello, Zio Frank, Zia Rosetta, and Zia Giuseppina—you are in our hearts. Always.

My fur babies— mamma loves you so much! Buckwheat, you are my best buddy. Dacca, I will always protect you from the big bad Bellie. Mitch, refer to Dacca's comment. Jag, you're a wombat in disguise. Bellie, your singing voice is so beautiful. And Ninja, thanks for watching over me.

To anyone I have missed, I'm sorry. It wasn't intentional!

Last but certainly not least, I want to thank YOU! Thank you for welcoming me into your hearts and homes. My readers are the BEST readers in this entire universe! Love you all!

ABOUT THE AUTHOR

Monica James spent her youth devouring the works of Anne Rice, William Shakespeare, and Emily Dickinson.

When she is not writing, Monica is busy running her own business, but she always finds a balance between the two. She enjoys writing honest, heartfelt, and turbulent stories, hoping to leave an imprint on her readers. She draws her inspiration from life.

She is a bestselling author in the U.S.A., Australia, Canada, France, Germany, Israel, and The U.K.

Monica James resides in Melbourne, Australia, with her wonderful family, and menagerie of animals. She is slightly obsessed with cats, chucks, and lip gloss, and secretly wishes she was a ninja on the weekends.

CONNECT WITH MONICA JAMES

Facebook: facebook.com/authormonicajames
Twitter: twitter.com/monicajames81
Goodreads: goodreads.com/MonicaJames
Instagram: instagram.com/authormonicajames
Website: authormonicajames.com
Pinterest: pinterest.com/monicajames81
BookBub: bookbub.com/authors/monica-james
Amazon: amzn.to/2EWZSyS
Join my Reader Group: bit.ly/2nUaRyi

Printed in Great Britain
by Amazon